PENG

Blac

T. R. Bowen spent much of his childhood in India and Egypt.
He was briefly at Winchester Art School. At Cambridge most
of his time was occupied by acting and he became president of
the Marlowe Society. For a number of years he has written
screenplays for TV and has continued to act. *Black Camel* is his
second novel, following *The Death of Amy Parris* (available in
Penguin) which also features Gio Jones and John Bewick.

Black Camel

T. R. BOWEN

PENGUIN BOOKS

PENGUIN BOOKS

Published by the Penguin Group
Penguin Books Ltd, 80 Strand, London WC2R ORL, England
Penguin Putnam Inc., 375 Hudson Street, New York, New York 10014, USA
Penguin Books Australia Ltd, 250 Camberwell Road,
Camberwell, Victoria 3124, Australia
Penguin Books Canada Ltd, 10 Alcorn Avenue, Toronto, Ontario, Canada M4V 3B2
Penguin Books India (P) Ltd, 11 Community Centre,
Panchsheel Park, New Delhi – 110 017, India
Penguin Books (NZ) Ltd, Cnr Rosedale and Airborne Roads,
Albany, Auckland, New Zealand
Penguin Books (South Africa) (Pty) Ltd, 24 Sturdee Avenue,
Rosebank 2196, South Africa

Penguin Books Ltd, Registered Offices: 80 Strand, London WC2R ORL, England

www.penguin.com

First published in Penguin Books 2002
4

Copyright © T. R. Bowen, 2002
All rights reserved

The moral right of the author has been asserted

Set in 11.75 on 14pt Monotype Garamond by Intype London Ltd
Printed in England by Clays Ltd, St Ives plc

For Sara

Death is the black camel that kneels
unbidden at every gate.

Arab proverb

Prologue

The letter had been laid on the window-sill on a sunny afternoon: the third day of perfect late-summer weather, high pressure lazily circulating around the south-east corner of England. The window was barely ajar. Across the small farmyard (where farming hadn't taken place for a generation) the barn door was half open. From the window where the letter lay there was a view of the sea. It was here she knew he would come to look out at the sea some time during the evening, when he returned. He would recognize her writing and read her pained apology, read of her love for him, before looking across to the black timber barn, to the door which stood half open, leading to the threshing floor, where his life would change.

In the warmth of the afternoon there was no hint of the storm to come. There was a continuous hum of bees about their business. The birds were mostly silent. A pair of house martins yickered through the yard for some minutes, scooping insects. The torpor returned. The sun crept. Inside the barn, the body on its rope twisted in the air currents which, despite the stillness of the day, followed the temperature gradient between inside and out.

When it came, the change took barely two hours. The sunlight grew hazy. The sky took on a metallic coppery sheen. Behind the haze, huge mountains of cumulus were building and darkening.

A whisper of colder air stirred the leaves of the old fig tree and let them settle again. Minutes later a wind began, cold and moist. It sucked the dust in the yard into a miniature tornado, then blew it away. The loose weatherboards in the barn's gable end began creaking; the door banged open, swung and swung again.

Single heavy drops fell out of the purple sky. A low roaring began in the trees. The sea disappeared in a dark curtain which hissed towards the small farm. When it hit, the roar turned to a howl.

Through the small gap in the window where the letter lay, the storm screeched, wild, irregular. It lifted and dropped the envelope repeatedly, drifting it towards the edge of the sill. As it tipped, a gust caught it, twisting it. It fell to one side. It landed momentarily on the curved shoulder of an old radiator. Then, like a sinking ship, it slid into the dark space between the radiator and the wall.

In the barn the body swung, awaiting its beloved discoverer.

It was more than seven years later that the radiator, leaking now, was removed from the wall. The envelope, water-stained yellow and grey, lay in the corner of the wall. It was ignored most of the day. A good clear print of the sole of a working boot was added to its discoloration. At three o'clock it was tossed with other debris into a black bin bag. The plumber, sensing that it contained something, retrieved it and held it to the light. Disappointed that the contents were letter-sized rather than bank-note-sized, he returned it to the owner of the house.

Part One

I

It had been unseasonably cold and still all day. In the shadow of the college walls, the grass had kept its skin of frost until late afternoon, when warmer air flowed in from the south-west and turned to fog.

Fog is a regular phenomenon in the Cam valley, but that night it was unusually dense. Even from across the modest width of the river, the weighty Tudor details of St Anne's Old West Court and the Master's Lodge were invisible. The jettied windows of the Lodge inaccurately reflected the light of the college's modern building on the opposite bank, but otherwise only the bulk of the buildings showed, dark against the diffused glow of the street lights beyond. Trees dripped. The grumble of creeping vehicles rose and fell.

A man stood in the grove on the riverbank opposite the Fellows' garden, listening intently. The pub by the Old Jewry Bridge had been closed for more than half an hour now. The youngsters who had been talking and messing about outside it had drifted away. Members of the college moved about occasionally, although none had crossed the Gibbons Bridge for some time now.

He glanced twice at the illuminated dial of his watch. The listening and time-checking continued for a number of minutes before he heard what he had been waiting for – the sound of a door opening at the Porters' Lodge, the crunch of gravel underfoot, and finally the squeak of the door's self-closing spring.

If he followed his normal routine tonight, the man he was waiting for would appear round the wall ahead of him shortly. He would light a cigarette, smoke it, and then head down into the car park under the most modern part of the college, the Raschid Building.

Footsteps.

The man reached down into the briefcase beside him, willing his own steadiness of movement, a steadiness which was unnatural to him – reminding himself of how many times he had rehearsed this.

Heavy footsteps had crossed the gravel and were now moving over paving stones, one of which was unstable. He heard the hollow knock of the stone's disturbance and prepared himself.

Alan Whear grumbled to himself as he left the Lodge. 'Sodding fog . . .'

The college clock began to chime the quarter as he passed the pale shape of the Gibbons Bridge. He'd take God knows how long to get home in this shit. And it'd still be hanging around, wouldn't it, when he set off back tomorrow morning? He paused and lit the cigarette he'd been looking forward to for the past two hours. He thumb-flicked the match towards the river. The fog in the shadows swallowed it. He never fancied walking through the college smoking, so he stepped off the gravel to stand above the steep grass slope of the bank, the river swilling invisible below.

Whear smiled; a moment of self-congratulation as he breathed the smoke in. The way he'd talked himself into this one – college porter! Laugh. Magic. Old Cranesmith had helped; course he had. But it wasn't as if he had any reason to, not really, except he'd known him all those years ago; and then only to speak to. Hardly a connection. No, he'd done it himself. Brilliant, that's what it was. Bleeding brilliant . . .

Whear smiled again. And then there was *her* . . . Every time he thought of her he was dazed with disbelief. For a moment he was entirely still, as he relived what they'd done together last time. It disturbed and excited him. He reminded himself that he could always walk away, always could. No strings, she'd said not. He could walk away. He felt himself harden. He smirked. Wouldn't be walking away just yet. He drew in another lungful of smoke and fog.

Whear sensed rather than saw the man as he stepped out of the shadows. He cupped the fag in his hand as he turned, uncertain as to whether he was allowed to be smoking anywhere at all in the college. He wasn't sure, in fact, if this was one of the dons. Couldn't know them all, could he, in the time? There was something vaguely familiar about him though; what he could see of him, under that hat.

Whear acknowledged the man with a nod and was about to move off when the man spoke. The voice was brittle, classy. It was so old-fashioned polite it was an affront.

'Mr Whear?'

Whear was surprised. Gawd, he probably *was* a don.

'Yeah?'

'Mr Alan Rex Whear?'

'That's right.'

A car started up somewhere in the car park. The man's arm rose as if in accusation, rigid like a mechanical doll. He was holding something. At its end blossomed a tiny eye of flame.

Whear fell instantly, a leg spasm jerking him backwards down the bank. His lifeless body executed a rough somersault, finally thumping down into a moored punt, making the internal fittings clatter, wood on wood. The punt sent some wavelets across the general drift of the stream, then settled.

As if the shot were a signal, a breath of wind began from the north. It whispered up the river, through the shallow canyon of college buildings, and half an hour later a delicate breeze had established itself. By daybreak, when the air was still again, all that was left of the fog was a miasma hanging above the river.

The following morning, in the gardens of the college next to St Anne's, a man and a woman stood talking.

Through the mist which still hung above the placid water, bulbs could be seen flowering on the far bank of the river, blue and violet and white, under bare trees. The sun was still only a brightness in the sky, but it promised to break through.

So, despite the fact that she had much to do, Sally Vernon lingered. She was a senior member of the college, allowed to roam its premises at will, allowed on occasion to dine in hall, but was not part of the fellowship. She lingered, partly for the pleasure of being where she was, but she was also intrigued by her companion's behaviour, despite having tried to avoid him earlier.

Brendan O'Keefe was a big man with slabby cheeks studded with dark moles and he had stiff, brushy hair. He was frowning, agitated, staring down at his feet, where his right shoe toyed with a larger than average piece of gravel. He was telling Sally about an undergraduate production he'd seen of *The Revenger's Tragedy*, but he was clearly distracted by something.

'I liked the farce. They handled the farce quite well.' He spoke jerkily, frowning down at his foot as it pushed the pebble to and fro.

'The *farce*, Brendan? I thought *Revenger's Tragedy* was a blood-and-guts Elizabethan job.'

'More or less. Jacobean, in fact. The farce is unbelievably cruel, in tune with the temper of the age. I'm sure I don't need to remind you what happened to priests of the true religion if they were caught on English soil?'

Sally had been warned by a friend early on that O'Keefe could be a fierce Catholic who, given the feeblest excuse, would try to convert you on the spot.

'You might have to, Brendan, I'm a scientist. I know the punishment for treason was hanging, drawing and quartering. Is that what you mean?'

'Correct,' O'Keefe replied. He sounded disappointed, as if he'd wanted to tell her the grim details. 'Yes . . . And isn't it in *The Revenger's Tragedy* that we get the immortal line "What? Old Dad dead?" Yes,

I'm sure it is. And I'm sure I didn't hear it last night, come to think of it. That wasn't wise of them. Big mistake to cut an iota of the ridiculous. Part of its richness. Part of the popular tradition. Eating your own children in a pie, all that. Carnival grotesque, carnival beauty, all that colour and vigour you'll find in the ceremony of Latin countries, which we've suppressed and lost . . .

> *"Does the silkworm expend her yellow labours for thee?*
> *For thee does she undo herself?"*

He's addressing his murdered mistress's skull . . .'

O'Keefe's voice trailed away to a whisper. The frown deepened and then cleared. There was a tremble in his soft, rich voice. Sally was reminded that he had been a celebrated amateur actor in his youth, something which had served him well in his brief career at the bar, before he gave it up to teach law.

> '"*It were fine, methinks*
> *To have thee seen at revels, forgetful feasts*
> *And unclean brothels; sure, 'twould fright the sinner*
> *And make him a good coward . . .*"'

which I suppose is the point of *that*.'

O'Keefe, without looking, jerked his head towards the river. Sally turned. Moored in mid-stream was a punt with a figure slumped in it.

Was it *that* which had been troubling him?

'I don't know why, but I do hate that sort of thing,'

he said. 'In the theatre, fine. But jamming things under one's nose. Like those bloody buskers who come into your carriage and start singing at you when you're travelling on the Underground.'

'Is it rag week?'

'Hardly, Sally . . . God knows what it's supposed to be.'

O'Keefe sounded depressed.

'Do you have an Artist in Residence at St Anne's at the moment? Do we, for that matter?' Sally asked, doubtful. 'Perhaps it's an installation. It's very realistic, I must say.'

'But it's disgusting, don't you think?' O'Keefe suddenly turned toward the figure in the punt. 'Are you an installation?' he burst out belligerently. '*Art*, are you? Well you can sod off!'

They were both looking towards it now. There was a brief silence. Then they turned to look at each other. A sudden questioning panic was in the air. Sally felt a chill run from her neck up into her scalp. The chill was overtaken by another sensation: of foolishness.

As she realized that what was slumped out there in the river was no stunt, she felt stupid. She, who had attended more post-mortems than she could remember . . . For one chilly moment she thought she saw the figure move. Then she realized it was the punt shifting in the current, light catching the glistening mess at the back of the head.

'Oh Christ. Oh Christ . . . Oh Christ,' O'Keefe mumbled. He was in a state of gawping paralysis.

'I'll go and get one of the porters,' Sally said.

A few minutes later, she returned with Bisley, the senior porter of her college. O'Keefe had fled. Bisley stood on the riverbank, hands on hips, belly jutting.

'That's not our section of the river, Dr Vernon.'

'I dare say not.'

'Definitely not. That belongs to St Anne's. That punt is theirs, at any rate. You see? It has the St Anne's colours across the stern of it.'

'So it does.'

'That's a St Anne's problem, that is. I'll ring Mr Wells, to alert him.'

It was inevitable, Sally supposed. Half an hour after Bisley took over, she found herself shaken by what she'd seen. She left the Scientific Periodicals Library where she had tried to begin work and went to a café to recover herself.

Sally had only been in Cambridge for a matter of months. She'd met Brendan O'Keefe a number of times since her arrival. She'd once spent part of a dinner party explaining to him how and why she had made the move. For years, she had run her own university lab in Norwich. Her work there – an under-funded investigation of DNA sample contamination – had attracted the attention of one of the new venture biotech companies. The offer to set her up with her own lab, with proper funding and a serious salary, in the end had proved irresistible.

She'd soon regretted opening up to O'Keefe. At first she'd taken his big, passive presence to indicate patience. He'd reminded her of a man she'd once loved and wasn't sure she didn't even now. But where John Bewick's sympathetic attention seemed bred in the bone, in O'Keefe it was soon worn out. His patience was quickly exhausted, his supportive noises became perfunctory.

So she had listened to the story of his career. She could recall little of it now, only that she had been made curious by hints in the language he used. She remembered 'The Protestant heresy' and the phrase he had used by the river, 'true religion'.

By the third or fourth time she met him, Sally understood how off the wall he was. Everything they discussed was dragged kicking and screaming back to the issue of his religion, Catholicism; its historical persecutions and martyrdoms. She had begun to avoid him, just as he had begun to seek her out. She would have avoided him that morning if she hadn't been buttonholed.

Outside the café window, King's Chapel towered, its rank of gothic verticals sharp in the sunlight, bland gold. Sally stared into the empty coffee cup in front of her. The milk foam was drying round the rim. O'Keefe's reaction to seeing the body on the river had been very strange, she now thought. She was astonished at how he had gone to pieces over the incident. For someone who believed the death of the body to be a stepping-stone to the afterlife . . . She didn't understand it.

Sally herself had seen many corpses. The circumstances had been ritual, lab routine. Only once, at a distance, had she seen a man die. That death had been at John Bewick's hands. Self-defence, of course, and partly accidental, but his preparedness to go the distance, to take another life had left her frightened. The physical vitality which had at first excited her became oppressive, a threat. She had withdrawn.

Nagging at her too was the extra employment she had recently been offered. When she first considered it, her confidence had been riding high. She had thought it would be amusing to be seconded to the company where Bewick was employed. Cambridge Risk and Security International sounded sexy, interesting, above all unacademic.

Since so many prosecutions nowadays depended on DNA, Sally had been asked by the director of CRSI, Peter Schrager, if she would be willing to go on their books as occasional consultant. She'd almost agreed on the spot. Forensic use of DNA was her forte, after all. It also meant facing up to her past with Bewick, to show herself that she'd moved on.

Now she had her doubts. A course of lectures to CRSI staff and invited police had been mooted by Schrager. She wasn't sure now that she'd even accept the consultancy. She realized that she didn't want to meet Bewick. Then again, she resented the idea of turning it down because of him.

To comfort herself, she thought of Anthony and her new life. Sweet Anthony and his motherless children. She disliked what she was thinking and feeling. She left the café and began walking, deliberately too quickly for comfort.

Sally was brought down further by another cloud:

the oppressive threat of scandal. It was nothing to do with her, but involved one of the nicest and most friendly women she'd met since she came to Cambridge. It sickened her to think of the rumours swirling around about Miranda Griffiths, wife of the Master of St Anne's. She didn't believe them for a moment. They were malicious, she was sure. She hoped they would soon be proved false, although she didn't know how they could be, without worse scandal. Meanwhile, she cursed the people who took such delight in them.

Detective Chief Inspector Giovanni Hywell Owen Jones marched into his paper battlefield of an office. One of his DIs put his head round the door.

'How was the doctor, Guv?'

'Mind your own bloody business, Baynes.'

'Suit yourself.'

'How do you know I was at the doctor, anyway?'

'You told us.'

'Did I? Well, mind your business. You do not ask men of my age and shape how they got on at the doctor's.'

'Sorry, Guv.'

'It was *horrible*, if you want to know.' The Swansea accent gave 'horrible' a dark nasal judder, grim, mysterious. Jones slumped at the desk.

'Sorry, Guv. But you've lost weight an' all. Looking good. You know ...'

Jones grunted and contemplated his desk. 'God, look at this ... Oh God!' He picked up the nearest piece of paper.

The visit to the doctor had, in fact, been quite positive. His weight was down, his blood pressure was down. At least he'd be able to report back to Eilean that things were improving. What made him miserable was the thought of the years ahead. It was, as the doc said (who looked as stressed and unfit as he did) a regime for life.

Gio Jones hated jogging. Even the achievement of being able to keep going for two or three miles irritated him somehow. Stripping to a pair of trunks for the purpose of swimming took every ounce of social courage. He loathed that too. He hadn't touched a ciggy since Christmas. He detested the schoolmarmy virtuousness of it all.

His phone started ringing. He groped for it under a drift of papers. 'Ah . . . Boss . . .' Jones said, wary. It was Superintendent Hutchings, his immediate superior.

Baynes watched as Jones's face fell and his voice flattened. Eventually he put the phone down. There was pulpit-quality outrage in his voice: 'There's a body in the river at St Anne's College. Do I need this? Do I?'

'I dunno. Do you?'

'Have you noticed the way the Academic Species operates? Have you? God!'

'What's the matter?'

'How they seem to respect what you say? Same time, they make you think what you do is slightly less useful than kicking dog turds into the gutter. God all sodding mighty.'

*

DCI Gio Jones leant out of the small rowing boat to examine the freeboard of the punt. Then he heaved himself into a position where he could see into it. He pulled on a pair of thin plastic gloves. There were several smears and splashes of blood. As he found each one, he identified it carefully with a marker. He couldn't connect them into any sort of significant pattern. Maybe the pathologist would do better.

He eased himself back into the rowing boat, which was being handled by a uniformed constable. He was breathing heavily. Still bloody unfit, he thought, but maybe better than a month or two ago. Chrissakes, who cares?

'Did Bob Baynes ring Sandham, by the way?'

'Yes, Sir. He did, Sir. 'Bout an hour, he reckoned. Erm . . . 'bout eleven.'

Jones looked at his watch. It was twenty to eleven.

Arnold Sandham was Professor of Morbid Anatomy and Histology and a fellow of St Margaret's College, which was at the far end of the Backs. He was also the local pathologist of choice when the police at City West were landed with a murder.

Jones glanced over and met the glaucous eyes of the corpse. What sort of man had he been? It was the face of a bully-boy charmer, he decided. The sort of man Jones was normally very wary of. The sort of man who would rapidly become an enemy. Not really clever, but shrewd and good at putting you in the wrong somehow. Dangerously opinionated. No more now. Poor sod.

There was a look of surprise on the face, made

theatrical by its fixity. Centred between and above the eyes a small hole with a puckered blue-purple rim to it. Jones had so far avoided looking behind the head, although his peripheral vision was telling him that the corpse's brains had oozed out like volcanic spillage from the broken skull. Deep breath.

'Round the back, will you? I want to look at that chain.'

The chain which hung down over the stern was identical to the one carelessly piled on the forward platform of the punt: a couple of metres of it terminating in a blunt spike for jamming into the turf of the riverbank. With his gloved hand Jones tested the tension of the chain over the stern. It was taut.

He avoided looking at the blood-black and grey porridge clotted at the back of the corpse's skull.

Instead, Jones looked about him: five-hundred-year-old brick walls, stone-mullioned embrasures, leaded panes in iron frames. Then the small hump-backed bridge built in a paler stone, with the carved panel at its apex, a river god garlanded with flowers, from the chisel of Grinling Gibbons. On the other side of the river, gardens and the college's modern expansion, glass and white reconstituted marble.

A man stood on the bridge watching him. A short, upright, military type; poker-faced. As soon as Jones's eyes met his, he turned away. The light seemed to catch his skin as if it was varnished. He disappeared through the low arch beyond the bridge.

Was there any significance to the punt being placed just here? None that Jones could see. Nevertheless, he noted its position in relation to the buildings. He knew that he should get a diver now, to have a look at the other end of the chain. But he thought of the delay involved in getting one; never mind what it would do to his budget.

In his mind's eye he could see the killer pushing the punt off with his foot, expecting it to drift at least down to the next bridge, perhaps all the way to the weir at Jesus Green. The shoving off could have easily dislodged the chain on the stern.

A devout disciple of the cock-up theory of history, or of anything else come to that, Jones reckoned the punt was stuck here by mistake. The body was probably in it by mistake as well, for heaven's sake. He tugged the chain. It freed itself immediately. It had been lightly snagged on something. Good. He enjoyed his private moment of vindication.

Jones had taken the precaution of declaring the grassy slope above the river a no-go area, part of the crime scene. At the top of it, the police surgeon was now waiting. The punt with its grim cargo was secured. The police surgeon was unfamiliar to him. Looked about fourteen; they seemed to get younger every year. Jones knew he was likely to learn little from him. He wished Sandham would hurry up.

Jones was about to scramble ashore, to hand over his place, when a tiny irregularity caught his eye. He bent down to see better. He pulled on his half-removed glove and reached down beside the corpse's leg. Jammed between two slats of the duckboards was a small plastic animal model, about two centimetres long. It was a camel. Originally a nondescript brown, some bored child had tried crudely to blacken it with a marker pen. Nothing to do with anything but, like a good boy, Jones enveloped it and marked: '*1 toy camel. Black*.' Then he made way for the surgeon.

Peter Schrager, director of CRSI, slashed his signature across the morning's letters. Outside, the pale turquoise glass of the University's new law library shone through the trees like distant water. The phone on his cluttered desk gave a brief warble. He heard it being answered in the outer office.

Mrs Harmon came in herself, which was unusual. She gathered up the signed letters. 'The Senior Tutor, Dr Miller, St Anne's College.' The studied neutrality didn't prevent her sounding impressed by this title. She was a natural snob.

Schrager picked up the phone. 'Dr Miller, good morning.' Schrager's greeting was warm, charming. He didn't like what little he'd seen of Brian Miller, who was gloomy and brittle. They had met twice.

'Erm, tell me, should I call you Major?'

'Not at all, plain Mister. I dropped the title when I left the army. What can I do for you?'

Miller told him about the murder. He explained that there was a general assumption that the victim was one of the porters. But that was only because he was dressed like one. The police hadn't let anyone near them yet.

From the window of his office in St Anne's, Miller looked across the river at the crime scene. The body was still in the punt, shielded from the public gaze, and mostly from his, by white screens. They looked as though they might have been placed there by a lighting designer on a movie set. The bank above was streaked with polythene pathways, shining like water, spilling down the grass slope. Surrounding the area, defining it rather arbitrarily, was a ring of plastic incident tape.

'And they're camped out there like some bloody archaeological dig,' Miller complained. 'How long are they going to be?'

Schrager assumed, correctly, that the question was rhetorical. 'How can we help?'

He wasn't prepared for the surge of frustration from the other end of the line. Miller sounded angry, but it was a desperate appeal as well. 'I just want someone to sort the bloody thing out!'

'Why don't you come over? We're only the other side of Queens' Road. I'm not too happy discussing tactics on an open line.'

'Oh. Right. Yes, very well. Might you have someone who can help?'

'Yes, indeed.'

'You see, we've got royalty coming here next month.'

'To the college?'

'Yes. The person concerned has been persuaded to be our patron, as a matter of fact.'

'Well, good for you.'

'She's opening a new twenty-bed children's unit on the City Hospital site, the Sir Michael Dowling Wing.'

'Sir Michael Dowling, eh?'

'That's right. And then coming here to accept the patronage of the college. Sir Michael is also funding a fellowship in paediatrics here at St Anne's. So it'll be quite a day . . . At least, I hope it will be. This business . . . my God! This could torpedo the whole project.'

'So you need someone to liaise with the police and perhaps talk to the press, if necessary? Yes, I see. A facilitator.'

'That's it, just about. The Master says it should be someone who can make sure the whole thing isn't blown up out of all proportion.'

'Have you thought of a PR firm?'

'Yes. The Master and I discussed it just now. We thought it might be counter-productive. We feel that that course might actually generate its own publicity. At this stage we want to maintain as low a profile as possible. We need someone whose middle name is discretion.'

'I see . . .'

'So, can you help?'

'Ordinarily I could. One of our consultants would be the perfect man. He's an ex-policeman. Also a graduate. He's the best hostage negotiator in the businesss. The degree of sensitivity required for that would stand your cause in good stead. You won't find better. The trouble is, he's on holiday. Leave it with me. With your help, I'll try to locate him.'

'May I know his name?'

'John Bewick.'

'Like the car?'

'Pronounced like that, yes. Spelled B-e-w-i-c-k.'

2

Jones was fed up. He surveyed the crime scene, making sure his young officers were keeping to the polythene walkways he'd established across the area.

'Oi!'

A look of injured innocence: 'Sir?'

'Mind where you're putting those elephantine feet of yours!'

'My what feet, Sir?'

'You heard!'

Also, the crime scene was too public. He noticed his officers getting self-conscious. There was an audience hanging over the nearby bridge, gawping. Where the hell was Sandham?

Jones became aware of someone standing beside him. He turned to find himself confronted by a lean, haunted-looking man, mid-forties, gold-rimmed specs. His face was deeply lined, rough textured; humourless mouth.

'Well . . . ah . . .' the man said in a well-educated drawl, 'that's to say . . . how long do you think you'll be now?'

Jones stared. Not because he wanted to be impolite – wasn't averse to the idea, mind you – but because it was such a dumb question.

'Is that a foolish question?' the man asked. 'I

suppose it must be. How was the poor fellow killed? It is a man, is it?'

'Yes, it is.'

'Do we know who he is?'

'No, we don't.'

'I see. Well, all I want to know is the state of play. This is going to . . . I mean seriously interfere with . . . Anyway, I'm Senior Tutor. Miller. Brian Miller.'

'How do you do, Sir. Detective Chief Inspector Jones. Senior Tutor, eh? Good. Perhaps you'd like to have a look, Sir? You might be the one to tell me who the poor bastard is.'

Miller lifted his bony head and looked away, as if Jones had made an obscene suggestion. After a moment, however, he swallowed and then nodded. 'All right.'

A newish but battered Toyota squirted gravel as it braked clumsily outside St Anne's Porters' Lodge. A tall, awkward figure in a mustard-coloured suit stepped out of it.

One of the younger porters confronted him. 'I'm afraid there's no parking there, Sir . . .'

'Ah, really? Really? You find somewhere for it then, will you?' Professor Sandham said over his shoulder as he retrieved his case from the back seat. 'Keys are in it. I'll pick them up from the Lodge.'

'But –'

'No buts,' said Sandham as if amiably admonishing a child. 'I'm a senior member – St Margaret's. I'm also the pathologist – and there's a corpse to attend to.'

Sandham raised an eyebrow, flung out a long leg and strode into college, humming to himself.

Jones had heard him arrive and was waiting.

'Giovanni!' Sandham marched over the uneven flagstones. His loudness and brutal attempts at charm had once got under Jones's skin, but he'd come to realize that Sandham was an acute witness and was constantly observing. The loudness seemed to be a means of keeping the world at arm's length so that he could focus on what was engaging him.

Sandham pumped Jones's hand in greeting. 'What do you have for me, Giovanni?'

'A shooting.' Jones gestured to the punt.

'Male?'

'Yes. He's just been identified. Name of Alan Whear. College porter.'

'Really? Really? Been much inclined to shoot the buggers at St Margaret's myself from time to time. Let's have a look, then . . .'

Sandham paused at the polythene track which led down the steep bank. 'This safe?' He began to take his shoes and socks off. 'All right for you poor wretched plods with your rubber-soled monstrosities. Smooth leather, on the other hand . . . I'd be skiing down it.'

Carrying his shoes and socks, Sandham made his way to the punt. Jones left him to it and went to speak to the porters.

'So the victim might have been having a bit on the side, you reckon then?'

Jones thought this was mild enough, but the man clammed up. 'He just talked about women a lot, you know.'

Wells, the head porter of St Anne's, was about Jones's age, early forties. He was locking up a store where spare stacking chairs were kept. Jones was trying to imagine him with the sideburns and flowered shirts he had favoured in his own hilarious teenage years. He couldn't see it. Wells's clipped and closed presence fitted the black suit he was wearing as if he had been groomed from birth for this funereal image.

'You been at the college long, Mr Wells?'

'Man and boy. Ever since. My family've been porters here since Victorian times.'

'God, you must almost feel the place belongs to you.'

'Not really . . .'

'Seen many changes?'

Wells shrugged. 'Not really. Human nature is what it is. The lot now, the undergraduate lot I mean, well, they haven't got any proper manners, but they're nicer. See what I mean? You always get a mixture, don't you? All the senior members got phones now, that's the biggest difference; you're not running around the college all the time . . .'

'So you don't think Whear had a bit on the side, then?'

Caught off guard this time, Wells stared and Jones saw a definite discomfort.

'Told you. He just talked about women all the time.'

Wells knew something.

Jones sighed. 'I've spoken to a couple of your colleagues, the two on duty. They didn't seem to know much about Mr Whear.'

'He hadn't been here very long, as I said.'

'Were you involved with choosing him for the job?'

'Not really. Dr Cranesmith suggested him and I thought he seemed all right.'

'Would this Dr Cranesmith have imposed Whear on you if you hadn't wanted him?'

'Course not. Be no point in that, would there?'

'Then you were involved in choosing him.' Jones took in the hostile look this provoked and went on, 'Did Whear have anything to do with your family?'

'What? What are you talking about? No.'

'Then why did you start stammering and blushing when I asked you if Whear had a bit on the side?'

Wells closed up completely. 'I know nothing about Mr Whear's private life,' he said through pursed lips. 'Nothing.'

Jones looked at him for a long moment, sighed and trundled off. Blown that one, then. 'Nimby pimby fuckhead,' he murmured to the ancient cloisters as he walked away. He decided to talk to the two porters who were about to come on duty. He wouldn't get any more out of Wells. Gloomy bugger.

The picture Whear's colleagues gave of him was remarkably consistent: Whear had been OK, but was acknowledged to be a bit pushy. He'd always been talking about women, but the general feeling was that his wife was the boss. He had a lockerful-plus of dodgy jokes. He hadn't been a heavy exerciser, but thought of himself as a hard man. One of the porters reckoned he might have been in the army.

That much had been easily come by. It told Jones little more than he had already intuitively understood. On his way back, he made his way up on to the Gibbons Bridge. He watched the brown water sluice past for a moment. He felt lost and didn't understand why. He glanced over at the crime scene.

So Whear, it seemed, was just the man he'd imagined him to be on seeing his dead face. A charm that was troubling because you never knew when the switch might be thrown, when the fists might be used. Not clever, but shrewd. Shot dead. What had he been mixed up in? Apart from another woman. What?

Brian Miller had been told that Peter Schrager would see him just before lunch. When he arrived, he was greeted by a pleasant woman, offered coffee and told that the director had been held up, but hoped to be with him in ten minutes. Would he mind waiting?

Miller sat himself in the small but stylish reception area. He watched the water feature for about half a minute, then picked up one of the booklets on the table. It turned out to be a brief history of CICS – Cambridge International Criminology Service – before it became CRSI – Cambridge Risk and Security International.

In the 1930s and 40s, it had been a charitable foundation, loosely attached to the University, known as the Nashe Criminological Research Foundation, after the rich childless judge who had been its principal benefactor. It had also attracted some funding from the Home Office. In 1959, when the University opened its own Criminology Faculty, the Nashe Foundation was detached from the University and was taken under the wing of the Home Office. Reconstituted as a commercial concern, it marketed both the teaching of criminology and the training of investigators in the latest sciences of detection. It was one of the very few Home Office departments which made money.

Then, in the late 1980s, as the brochure coyly put it, 'CICS was given the opportunity to compete in the international marketplace.' In other words, as Miller was later to tell the Master of St Anne's, 'It was another bloody Thatcherite sell-off.'

Miller snorted aloud, unaware of the arrival of Peter Schrager.

'Dr Miller? Hello, let's go into my office.'

'Have you talked to your royal visitor's office?'

'They're aware of the situation. They'll be monitoring the press coverage.'

'Good. Can you tell me Sir Michael Dowling's connection with the college?'

'None, really. He was staying with Lord Beauman and saw a copy of *Cam*, the Alma Mater mag, you know?'

Schrager nodded.

'Well, there's an ad in it asking graduates if they'd like to fund a chair or a fellowship and have it named after them. Dowling made it known to Lord Beauman that he might be interested, if it was open to outsiders. A number of colleges were a bit dubious about Dowling. We welcomed him with open arms. We've always been one of the most democratic colleges. Least snooty, at any rate.'

For 'least snooty' read 'most impoverished', Schrager thought. 'And then you managed to link him into the royal patron idea?'

'Oh, that was the Master, Sir Terence.'

Schrager had been told that Sir Terence Griffiths was a one-man PR machine, whose most significant qualification was a degree in photogenics and charm. 'He'll be an asset in all this, won't he?'

Miller looked troubled. 'Of course. He's immensely busy, as you can imagine. But yes, an asset.'

'You get on well with the Master?'

'Of course. He's a delightful man . . . Have you managed to locate this man Bewick you mentioned?' Miller asked.

'Not yet. I'm working on it. Do you know anyone in the Foreign Office?'

'Why?'

'Because John Bewick is in Majorca, we think. I've checked the Consulate there. The boss is a woman called Audrey Fyldes. There's a fighting chance she's Oxbridge. A lead on her would be helpful.'

'I'll ask around.'

Jones found Sandham kneeling on the bank. Barefoot still, his knees were in the back of his shoes to protect his trousers, which were rolled halfway up his calves.

He had lifted one of the polythene walkways and was poking around underneath it. He stood, tucking a spatula into a plastic bag, which he then sealed.

'Somersault,' said Sandham. He was sombre now.

'Yes?'

'Here . . .' Sandham placed himself at the top of the bank, facing away from the river. 'Receives bullet here. Instant brain death. Breaks open back of the skull. Goes straight over, landing on his shoulders and the back of his head. Skull now caved inwards. Somersaults. Lands almost on his feet at the bottom of the slope and collapses into punt.'

Sandham lifted the polythene halfway down the slope to reveal a smear of flattened and torn grass. 'Where he somersaulted, probably. I think I found some brain tissue there. We'll see.' Sandham smiled; mockery and challenge: 'Question is – did he do it himself?'

'*What?*'

'Weapon could be in the river. I'll test for explosive traces. That'll tell us if he handled the gun at all.'

'You seriously think . . .?' Jones began, in a tone of outrage.

'No. Frankly, Giovanni my friend, I don't. Of course I don't. You've got yourself a good old-fashioned murder.'

'Any idea about the weapon?'

'Not very powerful. The bullet could be anywhere. I doubt if your budget would stand the search.'

'I want it though. Might be the one thing we need.'

'Up to you. You can calculate where it might have

hit the wall the other side. That's quite soft, that Tudor brick, you might even find a chip out of it. Though I doubt it. Most of the bullet's energy would have been used up breaking open that poor devil's skull. May not even have got as far as the wall. Do you really want to search the river-bed mud?'

Sandham looked at Jones's gloomy face and laughed as he pulled on his socks and shoes.

'Stop fretting, Giovanni. We all have budgets. You should take pleasure in not having to do something because your budget won't stand it. A budget is one of the few excuses left to modern man to cultivate idleness, which as we all know is the secret of a long and contented life.' Sandham bellowed his laugh: 'What? Don't you think?'

'What I think is that you're one of the least idle men I've ever met.'

'Am I? Am I? I've always thought my indolence as boundless as ocean. Well, well!'

'So, it's murder?' Jones demanded, although it had never seriously occurred to him that it wasn't.

'Of course it is. But I'll let you know about the test, nevertheless. Negative evidence.'

'OK, ta.'

Jones looked round. A car had been let in through the main gates. It was parked quickly and accurately. A woman emerged, locking it remotely as she walked away over the Gibbons Bridge. She was smart and her walk was graceful, despite the speed and nervous energy.

'Who's that?'

'Ah yes. That's the Master's wife, Miranda, Lady Griffiths. The jewel in St Anne's crown. She's got a title in her own right, never mind being married to Sir Terence. She attracts a lot of envy.'

'Any particular reason?'

'Women are particularly savage. She seems to be good at absolutely everything she does.'

'Well I'm good at everything too. Hardly anybody envies me.'

'Not that I've ever seen you in a skirt, Giovanni, but I suspect the answer might lie in the legs.'

'Ah, yes. That'd be it,' Jones said, although he was secretly rather proud of his legs.

'A lot of charm. People tend to distrust that, I suppose. Including me, really.'

Jones nodded, glum. He found himself wondering what Bewick would make of her. He should be handling this, and probably would have been if he hadn't ratted on the force and got head hunted by CRSI or whatever it was called nowadays and taken that poncey job with them.

Bloody Bewick. Together, he and Bewick would have sorted this bloody college lot, no bother. Without Bewick he could see himself, well, quite possibly floundering. Quite probably, more like. Bloody Bewick.

The sun was rising out of the flat grey sea and driving the mist from the limestone hills above Puerto Pollensa. It promised to be another beautiful day.

The event had started half an hour earlier. The

swimmers coming out of the gloom over towards Alcudia had looked like a herd of amphibians disturbed by a predator. They kept a tight formation, abandoning stragglers in their wake. Then they burst from the water between two marker buoys and sprinted up the beach towards the bike racks. Bemused locals and tourists stumbling home from a night of serious clubbing watched in disbelief.

In the pale, pre-dawn sea, moving in steady rhythm, clawing and fluttering the water, the massed swimmers had been monochrome. Now they were butterflies, incandescent with day-glo, body-hugging colour, their brief lycra costumes striping, swirling, winding around them.

Perfunctorily wiped, bare feet were slid into bike shoes and velcroed. The featherweight, wildly coloured machines, with their ridiculously thin tyres, were straddled on the move. The shoes locked automatically to the pedals and in huddles of two or three, the competitors biked off into the dawn-pink hills. The second stage of the Majorca Triathlon was underway. A mile had been swum, forty kilometres on the bike had begun, then there were ten thousand metres to be run.

Karen hadn't enjoyed the swim at all. She disliked the mass starts to open-water swims, the jostling and implicit aggression. She actually preferred pool swims where you swam against the clock. She thought this was wimpish of her. Everyone agreed that mass open-water swims were the real thing. And Bewick had helped her out, staying close through the worst of the early chaos, before he left her to forge steadily through the pack to near the leaders. He was on his bike before she emerged from the water.

Karen's transition took less than a minute. Still dripping sea water, she carried her bike at the double through to the next timing station, then she straddled it and was away.

After the thrash and tunnel vision of the swim, this was bliss. The sun was beginning to warm her back. Her front was being cooled in the bike-generated wind. Up the lime-pale-powdered roads, past the white holiday villas in their green gardens, the climb steepening, the pressure steadily coming on.

With the first few kilometres behind her, Karen began to notice the other riders, spots of brilliance in the softly coloured landscape, one not far ahead. If Bewick had been there to see, she reckoned, she would have seen him. Amongst the multitude of slender, slow-twitch-muscled athletes, the type which formed the core of such endurance events, Bewick stood out like a rock. Nearly eighteen stone, six foot four, he was better suited to a national rugby squad. Considering the muscle weight he carried, and the fact that he was nearly twenty years older than most of the serious competitors, his results were outrageous.

Suddenly she realized that she was only a few metres from the competitor in front – which was illegal. Using the slipstream of another rider, draughting, was a disqualifiable offence. Either you overtook or you dropped back. She decided to hurt herself a little and pedalled quickly past a super-skinny young bloke. He didn't seem to enjoy pressing the metal much but he'd probably rip her apart on the run.

She still hadn't caught Bewick by the end of the ride. As she came into the transition area, she looked for Bewick's bike amongst all the others hooked over the pole where they'd left their kit.

As she began her run, Karen pushed herself, trying to get rid of the drunk jelly-leg sensation she always get when running after being on a bike – as if her brain was expecting much more forward movement than was happening. She was soon through it and about ten minutes later she had Bewick in her sights.

'Well done,' he said as she came alongside.

She could see he was suffering a lot more than she was, carrying all that weight, despite his smooth running style. They ran in companionable silence for a while. Slowing had allowed her to relax and lengthen her stride. She began to feel full of energy again. Bewick seemed to sense it.

'Off you go. Let's see some naked aggression now.'

'Naked is down to you, Boss. Or should that be up to you?'

'Go on.'

'Laters.'

She set off. She ran with wings. The time alongside him had been like mid-air refuelling. She was pumped with high octane.

Two kilometres later, she hit the wall and everything began to hurt, including her spirit. She felt the chilly ache in her legs where lactic acid had begun to build. An ache had begun in her lower back too, from the pounding. She changed her stride pattern. That helped for a bit.

She knew that she should try to push through this, relaxing every part of herself, but somehow she couldn't. This, it seemed, was reality. As if all the last weeks and months had been leading to this moment of disillusion.

'He doesn't love me,' she said to herself. She'd known this to be true, she realized, ever since. Didn't stop it hurting, though, when she heard it in her head.

Her running grew tighter and slower and more miserable. It was just a question now of getting through the last two k. Other runners began to go past her, including the cyclist she had overtaken.

She looked back as the last kilometre post came up. She didn't want Bewick to overtake her, she realized. She didn't want to be the object of his concern, his protectiveness, which had once been one of the most seductive things about him, and was therefore, now, the most undermining.

'He doesn't love me.'

All the serious moves had come from her.

He came to her for her open optimism and her ability to blow away the depression which sometimes settled over him, dampening everything he did. But that was rare. What she usually encountered was his even temper, his wry self-control, which kept her at a distance of *his* choosing. She didn't want to be there. She hated where she was.

Angry, she pushed her aching legs into another rhythm. The pain was held in suspension.

Suddenly there was clapping, bright faces, colour-zany costumes, a cheering crowd of the kids who'd finished.

The PA system boomed DJ perkiness as she neared the line. 'And Karen Quinney is a, hang on, wow! A Detective Inspector from Cambridge, England! So watch yourselves, lads . . .'

No I'm fucking not, she thought, not any more. Friendly jeering and cheering, wolf whistles. Karen, unsmiling, raising a fist in salute. Chill it, she told herself.

'Well done, Karen. Karen Quinney, competitor number 102.'

'Feel a hundred and two and all,' she said.

Karen walked hands on hips amongst the recent arrivals, every vertebra burning. She had a freebie water bottle thrust into her hand and began drinking from it greedily. She saw Bewick appear and walked back towards the finishing line. Before she got there she was approached by a young guy whose vest told her that he was running for an army team, the Combined Support Corps squad.

'Me and the lads,' he said with an ingratiating sideways look, 'was wondering what you was doing this evening?'

'What I'll be doing this evening,' Karen said, with no trace of a smile, 'is shagging the bloke who's coming in now.'

The soldier looked at her hard. He snorted with surprised laughter. Then he turned. Towering over them both, Bewick was walking towards her with a half-smile of greeting. His chest rose and fell still, but his arms hung loose. The soldier left.

'Well done,' Bewick said, smiling. 'Where will the times be posted?'

'Let's go and ask.'

She took his arm and the insides of their biceps slid over each other, wet with sweat. Karen's stomach flipped and she hated herself. Pushing away the sense of hopelessness that stalked her, she reminded herself that she could be dead tomorrow. Enjoy. Be thankful . . . You don't do thankful, she heard herself say.

Karen went out on to the apartment balcony. She was wearing the kimono Bewick had brought her back from Tokyo. She glanced back. Bewick lay with his eyes closed. His heavily muscled body was half covered by a white sheet.

Out on the balcony she moved a chair into the shade. She did it carefully. She didn't want to disturb him. She wanted to be alone, even if it was only to think about him. On the drive back from the tri finish, he had been tense, despite the gruelling physical expenditure which normally left him relaxed.

She was jumpy, she realized, about what might be causing his tension, without having a clue as to what it might be. It annoyed her. From the glass she was holding, she dabbed mineral water on to her neck, to catch the breeze drifting in from the blue waters of the bay.

It was nearly two years now, since she and Bewick had become an item. Time to get used to it, to get to know him. Well, she wasn't used to it at all, not in the sense of the sex getting to feel routine. As for getting to know him . . . he remained a mystery, more distant, if anything, than when they first met.

She'd tried to make him intimate with details of her own life. Bewick joined in with this. He remembered what she told him and was very attentive. On the other hand, she felt she hardly knew a blind thing about him.

She'd tried. Each line of inquiry came up against his cool grey eyes and a tolerant smile. He wasn't closed. He was friendly. There seemed nothing neurotic in the way he just didn't reply to questions about himself. What she'd found out would hardly cover a postcard.

His father had been in the forces and had been posted abroad during much of Bewick's childhood. An army grant had meant boarding school in England: St Matthew's College in South London. Bewick had been the youngest Chief Superintendent in the force, nationwide. He'd been married to a woman called Nina, had two stepdaughters, Miranda and Sophie, whom he was still in touch with . . . She knew little more than that.

He had very few friends, if any. A lawyer who'd been at school with him . . . Plenty of acquaintances, some of whom thought of themselves as friends. Karen doubted if it was mutual. There was always Gio Jones, of course, but their relationship was more like a running duel. Then, like a shadow, the rumours of his violence . . . She puzzled a lot over what it was that prevented him talking about his past. He wasn't stupid. He must know that it was alienating.

At least she was out of the force, or soon would be. And at least that was still a secret from Bewick. It was pathetic enough, but it felt like some sort of control over her own destiny.

She'd been amazed at how straightforward it had been, once she'd made the decision. She'd declared that she wanted to leave. Her boss, Detective Chief Inspector Jones, had persuaded her not to leave irrevocably. Why not take a year's unpaid sabbatical instead? She might change her mind, after all, and it would be pretty dumb of the force to lose all that training. He'd square it with his Super, he said.

Gio Jones had been a doll. He had a soft spot for her, she knew, but never mind . . .

Men always liked her at first. But men who wanted the conquest of her were rarely kind, like Jones had been. They usually ended by calling her a chilly bitch, as if their dumb behaviour was somehow her fault. She liked men with friendly, pretty wives, like Gio Jones.

Bewick, as always, was the exception. The kindness never failed, the lust never faltered. But he didn't love her.

Karen watched the white sails cutting through the ruffled waters of the bay. She was saddened by the anger she felt. She knew where it would lead. She knew Bewick's response to it wouldn't be what she wanted. Frustrated, she stretched her aching body. The blue and cream silk fell away from her legs. There it was: admirable smooth-skinned muscle running into elegant ankle. Was this all he wanted? Chilly logic told her it must be so: her fine body now, and one day his freedom.

She heard him moving in the bed. She drank off the glass of water. She stood up and went in to him, undoing the kimono as she went. The silk slid from her. She pulled back the sheet and got in with him.

After they'd made love, Karen got up without a word and showered. She came back into the bedroom. She was turned in on herself and irritable. Bewick was lying where she'd left him.

'Going to tell me?' he asked without opening his eyes.

His omniscience infuriated her. She boiled over, amazing herself.

'I'm out of this, John. I've had it up to here. I'm a stupid cow for starting it. For certain I shouldn't've stayed with it. You don't love me. Never could. Not properly. Oh, I know you haven't lied about it. I think you've even tried to protect me from your not loving me. But you don't. And that's it. I *hate* knowing you never will.'

She stopped, gasping for breath, wide-eyed, astounded; as if she'd just been pitched into white water and it was all she could do to keep her head above the surface.

Bewick was now sitting up. He looked at her steadily. He nodded very slowly. He looked desperately sad. So sad that, for a wild moment, she began to hope.

'*Do* you? You bloody don't and you know it! Fuck you!'

He half closed his eyes. Then his whole body moved – a gesture of resignation.

What did he mean? All the paths to discovering what he felt were barred to her. She was lost, drowning in disappointment and anger. She shook with the effort to control her tears. She walked back out on to the balcony. She stood gripping the rail, staring blindly at the blue bay fading into haze.

Her head whirled. She couldn't stay another hour in his company now, not after this. She could kip at the airport if she couldn't get a flight straight away.

She heard him come to the door. Christ! Don't come near me. *Please.*

'I'm sorry.' The familiar deep voice was coloured with something she couldn't identify. Pain? Irritation? He was unreadable; nothing new.

'Yeah. We're all sorry. Sorry's our middle fucking name.' She rounded on him and again surprised herself. 'And I'm out of the force an' all!'

He looked at her, said nothing, but his face was alive with questions.

'I don't know why! I've had it, that's all.' She took in his look of disbelief. 'It's not just the sexist shite we get. The merry lads, the well-if-you-can't-take-a-joke boys. Dumb fuckwits. It's something more. I can't explain it. It's to do with what I am. What I want to be.'

A man was standing in the garden below, looking

up at the apartment block. She turned her back on him. 'I just know I want out.'

She turned away. The man was still in the garden.

'You should . . .' Bewick began.

Karen interrupted, glad not to have to explain herself further, 'There's some git down there . . .' She glanced at Bewick and realized the man down in the garden couldn't see him at that angle.

The man was pink-faced and overweight, young, twentysomething. He was wearing a crumpled linen suit and black lace-up shoes, white shirt, battered panama. He had to be English.

The man moved out of sight towards the entrance. A few moments later the doorbell rang.

Karen picked up the entryphone. 'Hello?'

'I want to speak to Mr Bewick.'

'Who is this, please?'

'Thwaite, British Consulate. Tom Thwaite.'

The accent fitted, as did the young fogey appearance.

'I'll see if there's anyone of that name here,' Karen said. 'Ring again in a couple of minutes.'

She told Bewick and described to him the man calling himself Thwaite.

Bewick pulled on trousers and a T-shirt. He left the apartment. Karen heard him crossing the flat roof overhead as he made his way to the fire-escape on the landward side of the building. She was used now to the extraordinary precautions Bewick took when faced with strangers, especially when away from Cambridge. In Cambridge, she reckoned, the unusual was so much more obvious. She had tried to find out the nature of the threat that he was so careful about, but of course had got nowhere. She had no idea where it originated. The best compliment Bewick ever paid her was what he offered one day instead of an explanation: 'I've been more careful since I met you.'

Minutes later, she heard voices in the stairwell. Bewick came in with Thwaite.

'God, air-conditioning. Brilliant, brilliant. Yah. Right. Good.'

'Drink? Beer? Wine? G and T?'

'Fantastic. Love to. Thanks. Vino Bianco, por favor.'

Karen went to the refrigerator.

'What's all this about, Mr Thwaite?'

'Message. That's all. From Cambridge. St Anne's College?'

'Go on.'

'Someone's been networking their socks off to get an armlock on the boss . . .'

'Who's the boss?'

'Consul. Audrey Fyldes. Probably Cambridge swung it. Audrey is a Newnham woman, so someone got the wife of the Master of St Anne's, Miranda Thingy, Lady Griffiths, to armtwist. Audrey melts. "Yes of course, Lady Miranda, we'll scour the island!" Well, the brillo pad in question is me.' Thwaite gave a grunt of pleasure: 'This is nice!' He took another swill of the wine, rolling it around his mouth like someone who knew what he was doing.

'What's the message?'

'Are you somewhat famous, Mr Bewick?'

'Not at all. What's the message?'

'Only that Audrey seems to have heard of you. And to be impressed. Anyway . . . the message. Right. There's been a murder at St Anne's College. One of the porters, apparently. They need someone to take it over from their end. Your boss chap, Schrager, suggested you might do it.'

'Do what?'

'Talk to the cops? I don't know. Apparently there's some gross little Welshman throwing his weight around, upsetting the ivory tower inmates.'

Bewick and Karen exchanged a glance.

Thwaite took out a slip of paper and handed it over. 'Tickets have been provisionally booked. Those are the reference numbers if you want to make use of them.'

The next evening, Gio Jones was pounding the pavement of Lensfield Road in a pair of new Nike Air Max which a friend had brought back from the States, where they cost half as much. He moved with the slow, self-conscious roll of the inherently unfit. Plod by profession, plod by nature. He knew what he looked like. He also knew that if he tried to make his movements more spacious and elegant he would simply look comic at such a slow pace. So he kept going, roly-poly, clumsy, dogged. He had made such a fuss about coming out that afternoon that his eldest, Joanna, had asked him why on earth he bothered.

'So you get to enjoy a full set of parents for the duration!' he'd snapped. She'd been so upset by the implications that he'd had to spend quarter of an hour trying to allay her fears. So here he was running in near darkness.

Jones lived in an Edwardian terraced house off Mill Road, near the old Anglia Poly now uprated to a University. The sound of student parties in the summer drove him mad and he was constantly threatening to move. But now that the Council had a noise squad he hung on, hoping it would make a difference.

His run took him through the back streets to Trumpington Road, coming back past the Scott Polar Institute and the antique shops by the Catholic church. Sometimes he'd stop to admire objects he'd never be able to afford, then jog round Parker's Piece and home.

He approached the church on the Scott Polar Institute side, intending to give the antique shops a miss, as he was later than usual. A car was making a muddle of backing into the church precinct and the traffic was held up for a moment, as he was himself. Amongst the traffic was a taxi. In the back, clearly lit by headlights and street lamps, sat Karen and Bewick. They were upright, elegant, staring ahead; aristocracy of the fit.

Jones turned his head away and kept moving, following the car unnecessarily into the darkness of the church car park. Anything not to be seen by her. Bewick's wry comments he could just about deal with, but not the humiliation of being seen by Karen. For years she'd been his fantasy. He'd dreamt of her with the intensity of the unathletic schoolboy scoring the winning try, hitting the winning run, diving the perfect score. Even now, when he knew she was out of the force . . . temporarily, he hoped, my God how he hoped it . . . even now she could have this effect.

Jones stood panting by the church gates, staring after the taxi. It had just occurred to him that she and Bewick weren't supposed to be back for another week. Then he remembered his last phone call to Miller. Miller had sounded as if he was trying to distance himself from Jones. He'd informed Jones that the Master of St Anne's had instructed him to employ a security firm to handle their dealings with the police: CRSI. He knew in a flash of certainty why Bewick and Karen were back. The college must have employed Bewick as their fixer.

That was all he needed.

3

Jones got the driver to drop him at one of the cash machines in Trinity Street.

'You go on. I'll walk.' And he'd probably get to St Anne's first, with the anti-car one-way system they had now in the ancient centre.

Jones dawdled up the street. He had once loved walking through Cambridge. Not now: he hated how it had all been tarted up – gift shops where there'd been print shops, high-street names where once there'd been individuals, bookshops turned into banks. Nevertheless, as the street unfolded itself to his interested eye, he couldn't deny his pleasure. The walls of Caius pressing tight against the pavement, then the narrow opening of the street into the cobbled area in front of the Senate House with its stolid black railings and its pale columns. Ahead stretched King's Parade, commercial and domestic one side, then royal, religious and grand on the other. He stood, his mind wandering, reminding himself of Sandham's advice about idleness. He was allowed to stand and stare. He bloody well was.

'So where are the wretched police when you need them?' It was a country-house voice, an echo of family portraits and game dinners. Jones turned. It was Old Foley, white-stubbled, his cheeks red with broken veins, giving an illusion of healthy old age until you saw the bloodshot eyes, the quivering hands, the pathetically fragile wrists. His trousers were too short, exposing naked red and blue ankles above decrepit boots; all his clothes had a sheen of dirt.

'Hello, Foley.'

'Who the hell are you?'

'Police, Foley.'

The man took a step nearer. Jones winced in the blast of alcohol fumes.

'*Really?*'

'Your lucky day, Foley. Ask and it shall be given unto you.'

'Well, I'll be damned . . . Anyway, someone's stolen my coat.' He was wearing a coat.

'You're wearing it.'

Old Foley looked down at his sleeve, mystified for a moment. 'Well, I'll be . . . No, no,' he said fiercely. 'Not this one! Dammit. You doubting me? I turn my back for a moment and whoosh! No coat.'

Jones looked at the five plastic carriers filled to bursting which were lined up against the plinth of the Senate House railings. 'I expect the bastard took it and then put it into one of those bags of yours.'

'Did he? The bastard! But why would he do that?'

'To wind you up, Foley. You know what these fellows are like.'

'I *do*. The swine. Are you really police? You seem a fairly civilized sort . . .'

Jones set off down King's Parade; Foley followed.

' . . . not like the general run. Bastards. Why do they wear those silly bloody helmets, for one thing?'

'I wouldn't leave those bags of yours. You know what these fellows are like.'

'I *do* . . . You sure you'll be all right now?'

'I'll get by.'

He tottered back to his bags. He was harmless, distracted from his rantings as easily as a child. Jones never minded his encounters with him. He enjoyed them, in fact. Foley was like a relic of the old Cambridge he missed: the city with odd, mad, bleak, untidy corners; the Cambridge before corporate investment infiltrated its laboratories.

Jones made his way to St Anne's. He wondered if the Bursar, Cranesmith, had sorted out the room he'd asked for. For a couple of days he'd seen Baynes and the lads struggling with a smaller room allocated to them by Wells, as far from the street as you could get. Wells's revenge, no doubt. It was wasting time.

Jones knew there was always the chance of the quick breakthrough which unravelled many investigations in the first couple of days. It hadn't appeared. He knew he was struggling. In this case, he'd particularly hoped for an early breakthrough. At least it would have left Bewick with fuck-all to do except make congratulatory noises. Mind you, Bewick hadn't appeared the day before, so Jones now reckoned he'd been a bit paranoid about assuming that CRSI would appoint him to the case. That cheered him up considerably.

*

'This do?'

Dr Cranesmith opened the door to a pleasantly bright room. As the light caught his face, Jones realized for the first time that Cranesmith was the man who'd been watching him from the bridge that first day.

They were in a Victorian range of buildings which formed one side of a court. The open side went down to the river. The room was plain and faced south through gothic windows.

'Perfect, ta. Long as it has a phone jack and a plug for the kettle.'

'I doubt you'll be disappointed on that account.' Cranesmith glanced at Jones with a lopsided grin. One side of his face was shiny and immobile from scar tissue. They found the plug sockets under the table in the window.

'Hope we won't need it long. Week?'

'That's fine. The decorators have finished.'

Jones looked round the paint-fresh, barely furnished room – the two tables, the chair and the empty bookshelves – trying to think of anything else he could usefully ask for. 'That handle of yours – is that an academic-type Doc? Or do you actually get people to say "Aaah" and bang their knees with a rubber hammer?'

'It's a PhD.'

'And you're the Bursar?'

'That's right.'

'So what does that mean?'

'It means I'm the general administrator of the college, budgets and employees, that sort of thing.'

'So you don't teach?'

'No.'

'So what's with the PhD?'

'That was in my youth. Before I went into the army.'

'The army, eh?'

'I was a soldier for more than twenty years. It's a recognized career move. The forces, early retirement, college Bursar.'

'So what did you do in the army? Was that admin too?'

'Mostly it was, yes.'

'Right . . . right. And here in the college now, you're the man who hires and fires, are you?'

'As far as the staff go, that's generally true.'

'So it was you who took on Alan Whear, was it?'

'I recommended him. We have a small committee of the fellowship to oversee the appointment of most of the staff.'

'How small?'

'Six of us.'

'Why did you recommend Whear?'

'He seemed keen. He'd been a squaddy himself once. Tough regiment. You don't get in there without a bit of self-discipline.'

'You hadn't come across him in the army at all?'

'I took him on trust. The army obliges you to make judgements about individuals. I think I got him right. He was fine.'

'Fancied himself with the women, so I've heard.'

There was something icy in Cranesmith's reply. 'I'm

not aware of that being an employment handicap, are you?'

'No, no. Just wondered if you'd heard anything. Blind man in the dark, I am . . . at this stage. Any idea why anyone should have a go at him?'

'God knows. Unfinished business from his earlier life?' Cranesmith shrugged. His eyes seemed to cloud. He gestured to the room. 'So this will do, will it?'

'Thanks. Very nice, ta.'

They walked back through the college. The next court was sober, classical stone. Cranesmith told Jones that it had been built just after the Civil War with money given to the college by one of Oliver Cromwell's relations and named after him: Walton Court.

'Is it true, by the way,' Jones asked, 'that the Round-heads used King's College Chapel as a stable?'

'No,' Cranesmith replied, 'you're thinking of Ely Cathedral. And, loathsome as they mostly were, they didn't do it there either. Royalist propaganda. Come through here.'

'Why loathsome?'

'Imagine a bunch of born-again Bible-bashers armed with machine pistols.'

A low arch in an age-blackened brick wall fronted a short, white-washed passageway which led into the cloisters of a further court. They walked down it.

'This is Pelham Court. It's by far the most inter-esting in the college. You can still see medieval England here. St Anne's had hardly any money until after the Second World War to alter its existing build-ings, so they've survived in a very original state.'

Cranesmith stepped out of the cloisters. 'You could be looking here at a small religious foundation from before the suppression of the monasteries. This is how old Catholic England would have been.'

There was an edge in Cranesmith's voice, as if the passing of Catholic England actually mattered to him.

'Amazin' to think,' Jones chipped in, 'that the Prods and the Papists are still at it, isn't it?'

Cranesmith gave him a sharp, evaluating glance. 'I think you'll find,' he said, 'that the struggle for men's souls will continue as long as we remain a recognizable species. Liberal atheism will always crumble in the face of passionate belief.'

'Don't need to convince me, Doc. I've crumbled more often than I care to remember. And I'm Welsh.'

'It was a second-generation Welshman, by the way,' said Cranesmith, 'who suppressed the monasteries. Henry VIII was the son of Henry Tudor. Welsh.'

Jones looked for a glimmer of humour, irony even, but could see none. Jones suddenly had the unnerving feeling that Henry VIII was someone known personally to this bloke. Met him last week. Glass of ale. Bit of a crack . . . Fuckin' 'ell.

'Oh,' said Gio Jones. 'Well, at least I'm half Italian. What's that, by the way?' He pointed to an octagonal tower attached to the old kitchen buildings which rose above the cloisters on the far side of the court.

'Do you really want to know?' Now Cranesmith was being rude.

'Probably not,' Jones replied.

'No, I thought not. It's where Dr Miller has his rooms.'

'Ah yes. Him. I'm supposed to be seeing him soon.'

On Bewick's recommendation, Karen had rung Schrager from Majorca to set up an interview. She'd taken some persuading. Bewick had explained that there would be no need for her to work alongside him at CRSI. He was sure Schrager would want to recruit her.

Bewick's manner towards her was almost unchanged, which was a relief. It was confusing, though. Lover to friend, seamlessly; it wasn't how these things were supposed to happen. He was as generous with his attention as he always had been. She responded in kind.

They were so polite. All that was missing were the public intimacies of glance and touch which had marked them out as lovers. Underneath, for her, gaped the hole, the absence, the bitter knowledge that sex with him had gone. She wondered what it was like for Bewick. Did he ache like she did? She caught herself hoping that he did, but knew, or thought she knew that he didn't.

She sat now in Schrager's office, feeling dazed while he read her CV carefully through. They'd already talked for more than half an hour. Schrager had made it clear that he'd already made preliminary checks on her.

'This is all good stuff.'

'Sorry?'

'Your CV. Very impressive.'

'I was lucky with my senior officers.'

'So when do you want to start? I've got a lot on. I could use you.'

'Straight away, you mean?'

'This afternoon, if you want. There'll have to be a probationary period, by the way.'

'OK.'

'Very good. Do you want to start right away?'

'Why not?'

'All right. How are your IT skills? You could spend the rest of today getting acquainted with the operations room. Frasier'll show you the ropes. See how you get on.'

Miller walked briskly through the cloisters, his clothes flapping around his skinny, hard frame. He stopped and greeted Jones. He smelt of some sort of perfume Jones couldn't place. It reminded him of old women in his childhood. Jones had been looking up at the ancient, grubby brickwork of the tower in which Miller had his rooms. He glanced at it again.

'Paolo Longhi is who it's named after,' said Miller. He grimaced. 'He stayed in it for a couple of years when he was at Cambridge in the late sixteenth century. Would you care for some tea?'

They walked across Pelham Court. Jones stared into the late-sixteenth-century gloom and at the endless late-sixteenth-century steps stretching up the tower into it. He swallowed stoically. They began climbing.

'Longhi was influential for a time. He was selling the idea that all great religions are the same at root. He said that religious wars are the result of misunderstanding those roots. Well, they are. It is often a deliberate misunderstanding, however. If some power-mad psychopath wants to dehumanize his enemies, then religion is usually the best excuse. But he'd find others, if religion didn't serve.'

Jones let him hack on, concentrating on his own leg muscles. Would he suffer the humiliation of a plump man's pause for breath? On Miller went, a relentless sardonic edge to his voice, talking, it seemed, without the need to breathe.

'Cambridge was flattered to have a scholar straight from the Catholic ranks evangelizing revolutionary notions. Longhi was very Renaissance, very hip; heretical just as they were. Became less and less pleasing to the Protestant authorities here, however. So, after a couple of years, Longhi was denounced. He in turn denounced England and left. Returned to Italy. Straight from the frying pan into the fire. Literally, in his case, as he was burnt at the stake in 1598.'

Jones's legs were aching. He saw to his relief that Miller was fiddling with a door ahead of him, and moments later they were standing in a modest, sparsely furnished room, book lined, white panelled, high above Pelham Court.

Jones realized that, despite his legs, he wasn't much out of breath. Getting fitter, perhaps? 'Well,' he said cheerfully, 'at least the poor bugger had a tower named after him.'

The tea came in large porcelain cups. Miller continued cranking on about Paolo Longhi's ideas, including something called Hermetic Neo-Platonism.

'You know, telling me all this is, well, about as much use as trying to teach a donkey how to use the Internet. Sorry.' Jones smiled apologetically. 'Tell me about the evening Whear was killed.'

'What?'

'Tell me about it. What you were doing, where you were.'

Miller went pale, Jones thought, or was it his imagination? 'What on earth do you mean?' he snapped.

From a man who understood Hermetic Neo-Platonism this was a bit rich. Jones tapped his fingers on the mahogany table. Miller lifted his face, defiant.

'All I'm trying to do,' Jones said, 'is establish who was where, what they might have heard. Fair enough? Where were you? Did you hear anything?'

'I was with my mother. In Ely,' said Miller, in the tone of someone who had been attending a sacred ritual. 'So no, I didn't hear very much: apart from her snoring.'

Once Jones had reassured him that he had never been thought of as a murder suspect, Miller climbed down off his high horse. In fact, Jones wasn't discounting him as a suspect at all; nor anyone else on the planet, come to that.

Jones had been friendly and sympathetic. He was beginning to regret it. Miller had been telling him, at life-story-length now, how he was a man who had always courted the quieter path in life. As he talked on in his dry-gravel voice about the excitement he got from the publication of his papers and his books, his election to fellowships, Jones's mind wandered. He tried to think what his own most exciting moment in life had been. He decided it was when, a year or so before they got married, Eilean had agreed to go to bed with him for the first time.

They'd been walking along the cliffs above Mewslade, the light going. They'd been arguing about a play they'd seen at the Theatre Royal in Swansea the night before. A sea fret, half-rain half-mist, had drifted in. When he kissed her, her face was wet. The woods, the glistening sands far below, the sea beyond, must have all been grey. The colour, the fireworks, must have all been in his head.

'It was in Austin, Texas, last year that I decided things should change,' Miller was saying. 'It was a conference for writers on modern history. There I was, a mature man, and I felt *homesick*. Imagine that! Homesick; at my age! It wasn't as if I'd been exiled. I was returning a few days later. Extraordinary. Extraordinarily unwelcome. I decided then that it should all change. That I should take more control of my life.'

Down in Pelham Court, a small group of Japanese tourists were firing off cameras at the Master's Lodge, five hundred years in one two-hundredth of a second. Jones realized that it was lavender Miller smelt of.

'And that, really, is how I came to be involved in our royal visit. It was an opportunity I felt I should embrace. Everyone was quite surprised. They were happy for me to do it. I'm beginning to see why. The meals, the parking, the security – I mean that alone! Then the flowers, the chapel, where to do the hand-shakes, where to do the photographs, where to accommodate the public. Nightmare. Endless lists and flow charts. Still, we were just about doing it, until . . .'

Jones was staring at him, eyes popping.

'Are you trying to tell me that you've got royalty coming *here*?'

'Yes. We're to have a new patron. Hasn't anyone told you?'

'No, they bleeding haven't. Soddin' hell!'

'Sorry?'

'When are they coming, for Christ's sake?'

'Next month.'

'God all bleeding mighty!'

'Well, I don't really see how it affects you,' said Miller.

'Don't you just? Well I shouldn't spend too long thinking about it.'

Miller looked at his watch. 'As I told you on the phone, we've employed a chap to handle things from our end over this – I mean because of the royal connection. And, well, I'm supposed to be meeting him about now. I'd rather hoped it might be yesterday, but no matter. Would you mind?' Miller waved his hand vaguely as he finished up his tea.

Jones defied him, settling deeper into his chair. 'This chap, who'll be "handling things from your end" – his name wouldn't happen to be Bewick, would it? John Bewick?'

'Good God. Do you know him?'

'Know the bugger?' Jones tried miserably to think of the appropriate hyperbole, but couldn't. 'Yeah. I know him.'

Miller met Bewick at the main gate. Jones had returned to the crime scene to check on his team's progress, or lack of it, as they wound up their investigation of the riverbank.

If Miller had had any fears about Bewick's suitability as a representative of St Anne's and its affairs, they couldn't have been allayed by the sight of an outsize individual swinging in through the college gates on a bicycle – not the sensible, basketed, don's delight still much favoured by senior members, not even the sturdy mountain bike which all the kids were riding, but a racing skimp of a thing on pencil-thin tyres which looked as if it would buckle under the man's enormous frame.

'Are you Dr Miller?' Bewick towered over him. He was wearing a dark suit which sat uneasily on him, as it might on a heavyweight boxer. A scar ran up into his short hair.

Miller tried his best. 'Come to the SCR. We'll have a coffee and I'll try to, ahm, get you up to speed.' He looked worried.

'I had a fairly comprehensive briefing yesterday from Peter Schrager. I decided to spend the rest of the afternoon clearing my desk so that I could have a clear run at your problem.'

'Thank you, yes. Mr Schrager did explain.'

*

'What're you doing, Boss?'

'Hiding. What the hell does it look like?' Jones had stuck himself behind a tree so as not to be seen by Bewick.

'That's John Bewick, isn't it?'

'Well it isn't Mike Tyson.'

'What's he doing here?'

'The college have brought him in to make sure we keep our little noses clean. Sod the lot of them.'

Miller sat with Bewick in the otherwise deserted senior common room in the Raschid Building. Outside the day was still fine. Punts occasionally slid past the old buildings along the river. Through the faultless glass of the SCR's big windows, the scene was like a dream of the ideal academy.

'When our vainglorious press discover the royal connection,' said Miller, 'that's when we'll need you most. What's your experience of handling the press?'

'Sufficient,' said Bewick. 'I suggest you talk to her office immediately and ask to speak to her publicist. I think the best course would be to tell the press before they find out. Certainly I'd be making contingency plans for a postponement of your event.'

'But the whole ghastly thing might be forgotten by the time she comes.'

'It won't. It'll depend on how it's viewed.'

'Yes, I see.' Miller looked depressed.

'So you'll be in touch with her office?'

Miller nodded. 'What will your first move be?'

'Find out who killed your porter.'

'Isn't that the job of the police?'
'Yes.'

Jones hid again, busying himself behind the screens, when he saw Bewick coming out of the modern part of the college.

The next thing he saw, ten minutes later, was a back view of Bewick walking along the footpath beside the river in the company of one of the porters – the youngster about whom Sandham had laughingly complained. Knowing Sandham's talent for confusing parking with vehicle abandonment, Jones sympathized with the lad.

Jones went to find a lavatory. When he came back he saw that Bewick's bike had gone. Baynes told him that Bewick had in fact come over to the crime scene to ask if Jones was around.

'Why didn't he wait?'

'Said he had to get on.'

'Well, we all got to get on,' Jones grumped. 'Snotty bastard.'

It began to rain.

From the doorway, Schrager watched unobtrusively. Frasier was taking Karen through the basic routines they had developed for CRSI, particularly the protocols for new clients. He returned to his office. The phone rang and was answered by his secretary. She looked up as he came in. 'Sir Michael Dowling?' she asked.

'Sure, I'll go through.'

Schrager remembered Dowling's charitable connection with St Anne's. The chair in paediatrics he was going to fund. Dowling's face immediately came to mind, a buccaneer softened by business lunches. His rise to celebrity had been rocket-powered. His astute funding of political parties and politically correct charities had made him unignorable. He had been knighted young. He was forty-two.

Dowling came on the line: 'Mr Schrager?'

'Yes.'

'You're the Director of CRSI?'

'Correct.'

'Michael Dowling here. I need your advice. I . . . I don't think we should discuss it over the phone . . .' The affable energy of the cockney voice was familiar because famous. His opinion was constantly sought on the state of the economy, partly because he was a practitioner and partly because his public mode of speech was short, precise sentences, which were natural soundbites. But mostly it was his flamboyance, his unpredictability, his reputation as one of life's happy gamblers which made him a media favourite. Given his articulacy, the effect was telling when he hesitated, as he did now. 'What I'd like to do is make an appointment for you to come out here . . .'

'That's near Ely, isn't it?'

'Correct.'

'That's possible, of course . . .'

'I realize it'd be at least half a day of your expensive time.'

'Thank you. Can I ask why you have chosen to ask CRSI?'

'Recommendation,' Dowling said bluntly.

After checking his diary, Schrager agreed to a date.

'I'll say no more now – on the phone,' Dowling said. 'See you on Tuesday.'

Sounds of the traffic – surf sounds, a disjointed parody of waves on a beach – drifted up the narrow back street into the hired room. That at least was normal: modern, unwelcome, its brutality a comfort.

He sat in the room's single armchair. The window beside him juddered occasionally to the tune of a passing HGV. He was sipping Scotch, trying to maintain a level of anaesthesia, of disturbance in his thinking, something to take away the picture of Whear's face which floated in front of him. If he moved his eyes the ghost came too, as if softly etched into his retina.

It seemed to pulse. As the pulse repeated, there was first the face, with its question; then the absence as the gun knocked Whear flat. Again and again he saw it. And as he did so he felt a creep around his bowels, like motion sickness, which he knew to be fear.

Perhaps the girl would rid him of it.

He had thought his reason, his considerable intelligence, would come to his rescue sooner than this. The only crumb it offered was that the experience was like illness. He would get over it. Next time he would be inoculated against it. Next time would be easier. Whenever that was. *If* ever that was, however determined he might be.

Niki Whear watched the big man ease himself out of the old Volvo. He stood beside the car for a moment, looking round. Then, ignoring the rain, he headed for the house.

Niki Whear worked at a building society in Cambridge, but was now on compassionate leave in the aftermath of the tragedy which had overtaken her and her small son. Her mother and sister had come over to support her, which she found burdensome. They were out just now. She'd made up a detailed shopping list to get them out of the house for as long as possible. After all, they liked each other much better than they liked her. She had more money than either of them and much more pzzzazz.

The doorbell rang.

'Yes?'

'Mrs Whear?'

'Are you police?'

'No. I represent the college where Alan worked.'

'What do you want?'

'I need your help.'

'Who are you?'

'John Bewick. My remit is to deal with the police on behalf of the college. I'm also there to try to handle any media attention that may result. I realize that you may not have much interest in that – in how it may affect the college, I mean.'

'Dead right. The college can take a jump.'

'Some of it could impact on you, however, so it's in everyone's interest . . .'

'What're you talking about?'

A warmth of concern for her seemed to colour his expression. As she watched him think before he replied, she realized just how big the man was. She was surprised at how little it intimidated her.

'I don't know what I'm talking about, really,' he said. 'It may be nothing.'

'What?'

'I've just got the feeling that the impact of this . . . Well, I think things could get very messy. I don't know why. Just a feeling I have.'

'Messy. In what way?'

'Don't know. I'll probably need your help to find out.' He smiled briefly, self-disparagingly. 'I'd better come clean about one thing. I used to be a copper. So if I begin to sound like one, you'll know why. I suppose the plods asked you if Alan had any enemies, that sort of thing?'

She snorted with contempt. 'Like I told them – he had one bleeding enemy, didn't he? If you're asking me do I know who it is; then no, I don't.' She stared at him, defiant. 'You want to come in and talk, don't you? Get me on your side.'

Towering over her, he put a hand on the door jamb and pushed at it gently, amused. 'That's the game . . .' His fingers were long, square ended. They took her attention, distracting her.' I'd also like to know something about Alan,' he went on. 'I know so little at the moment.'

'What do you want to know?'

'I need facts, facts, facts . . . and a cuppa.'

'You've got a nerve.'

'I'll go easy on the cuppa initiative if you like.' He smiled.

Without thinking it through, she knew she wanted this man in her debt. She sensed that his goodwill was going to be a reliable investment. Blue chip; ten times better than her sister's or even her bloody mother's, come to that.

'I do tea,' she said. 'I'm not sure I do facts. You'd better come in.'

On the night her husband was shot, Niki Whear had cooked for a couple who lived in the same street. They had a young baby, still transportable by carrycot. They stayed at her house until late. She was telling Bewick about it when she checked herself. They were sitting just inside some glass doors which gave on to a small patio at the back of the house.

'You know, I've just realized something,' she said. 'Why didn't I think of it before?'

'What's that?'

'When they told me about Alan . . . I don't think I was really surprised. Isn't that *bizarre*?'

'Any idea why you weren't surprised?'

'I think . . . I was thinking, I reckon, that it was the sort of thing that might happen to him.'

'Do you know why?'

She shook her head. 'Just a feeling I had.'

'How much did you care for him?'

'What sort of question is that?'

'Is it too personal?'

'Why do you want to know?'

'Because I know so little. You've told me a lot, I know. Bits of the jigsaw. But at this stage I don't know how to start making the picture. Your telling me you weren't surprised – that's like a glimpse of the whole picture.'

'And what I felt about him – that's part of the big picture?'

'Yes.'

She looked down at her hands for a moment. Then she laughed humourlessly. 'I thought he was a rotten bastard, if you want to know. He was the usual shit.' She said it defiantly. Speaking like this of the dead, of her dead husband, she expected a reaction. There was none. The grey, watchful eyes moved over her. The face with its friendly-seeming creases stayed calm; just the slightest nod of the head.

'I loved him,' she said. 'He'd had a rough time. He needed love. He'd been out in the Falklands. I gave it all – myself, you know, everything, solid love – and I got nothing back. He didn't know how to love. He wasn't just selfish. He was stupid selfish. He'd lost me even before William was born. William made a difference for a bit. But he thought a baby was just for Christmas. He'd cleared off in his head before he started this latest thing.'

She paused, tears welling. She wiped at them angrily with the back of her hand.

Bewick waited, as if the tears were normal, acceptable. Then: 'Why didn't Alan clear off, in fact?'

'I earned more than him. The house was mine. Where would he go?'

'His latest thing was an affair, was it?'

'Yeah.'

'Do you know who with?'

'Yeah.' She lowered her eyes, looking away, uncertain. 'I reckon . . . I reckon I do. At the college . . . One of the women there.'

'Who?'

'If it's who I think it is, then I just don't get it. Why would she bother with him? What would she see in him?'

'What you saw in him, perhaps?'

'No, but I'm just Miss Averagely Attractive. She . . .'

Bewick waited again. The silence stretched, then she said, 'It was the Master's wife. Miranda Griffiths. Lady Miranda.'

4

The Jones household was in ferment when the door-bell rang. Gio's twelve-year-old-son, Barry, was screaming top-lung abuse at the TV – Chelsea *vs* West Ham, bad decision from the ref.

'God's sake, Barry!'

'Waste him! Shoot, destroy!'

Jones looked round. His youngest, Megan, sat on the stairs laughing at him. Mind you, she always was. Nine years old and always laughing, and not just at him, but at life it seemed, and herself. Her face was covered in chocolate.

''Ow's my little currant bun, then?'

Megan pealed again. A door slammed and Joanna marched past him without acknowledgement. By some quirk of the teenage brain he was still being punished for snapping at her days ago about jogging.

The doorbell rang again.

Jones sighed. He'd be interested, mind, to watch the complete turnaround in Joanna if it was one of the half-dozen lads who were hanging round her these days.

It was Bewick, wet from the rain.

'What the hell?'

'Why were you hiding from me, Gio?'

'What're you talking about. Go *away*!'

Eilean appeared behind him, dark haired, sweet expressioned, tired. 'Hello, John. Come in. Want some food? We'll be feeding the herd in a minute.'

'There won't be enough,' Jones said. 'Look at the size of the bugger. I'm not letting him in.'

'You're looking good, Gio.' There was a warmth in Bewick's voice, which conjured up their long rivalry and friendship. 'You've lost weight.'

'Don't you patronize me, you exercise junkie, you jog freak. Look at you. Two ounces of fat on you and you'd go into terminal depression. What you doin' here?'

'Can you explain it, Eilean?' Bewick asked. 'He was hiding from me; thinking I wouldn't notice . . .'

'Oh, sod off!' Jones was blushing.

'Hiding behind trees like a sad flasher.'

'Hello, John. What's a flasher?' Soccer done, Barry was on the prowl. 'What's for supper, Mum?'

'Food,' Jones said. 'And a flasher, as you well know, you provocative little lout, is someone who hides in bushes, then jumps out waving his plonker at passers-by.'

'Sad,' Barry said, smiling at Bewick. 'You coming to supper?'

'Are you? Please stay.' Joanna, her spirits miraculously restored, appeared on the staircase behind them, now playing the ideal daughter. 'Dad would really like that.'

'This comes from the Land of my Mothers! The next

village . . .' Gio Jones held the bottle high above his head. 'It's true.'

He knew he was drinking too much. Eilean came back from seeing to the children and gave him a wry look as he opened the second bottle of Chianti. Jones saw the look, but he was defiant. He was going to have to face Bewick's analysis of the Whear case soon and he wasn't looking forward to it.

'How was Majorca?' Eilean asked.

'Good. We had a really good apartment. Belongs to friends of Karen's parents.'

'How is Karen?'

Bewick didn't immediately reply. 'Last time I saw her, she was fine.'

Eilean looked surprised, said nothing. Jones wondered what the hell he meant. He'd only come back with her a couple of days ago.

'What you being so coy about? Chucked her out, have you?' Jones asked, Chianti-fuelled, belligerent.

'No. She's decided to move on. She's leaving the force too, as you know. Which I guess must be a part of it.'

Jones took a moment to absorb this. 'And who put her up to that, then, eh?' he demanded, accusatory.

Bewick's expression didn't flicker. 'Leaving me was probably to do with living with me. As to the force . . . it isn't overwhelmed with sensitive New Men, is it?'

'Oh, unlike stockbroking, you mean?' Jones's down-the-nose sarcasm was savage. 'Or medicine?'

Bewick smiled. 'You know what I mean, Gio. This is lovely wine. Did your mother's family really come from Tuscany?'

'Stop trying to change the subject, you bastard.'

'Karen said you were very constructive, very nice about it.' Bewick turned to Eilean. 'Do you think the force suited her, Eilean?'

'I don't know her well enough, John. I couldn't say.'

'I asked, because she doesn't seem to know herself why she's getting out of it.'

'Might only be temporary, anyway.' Jones was glad he was hot from the wine, because the chat about Karen actually made him feel tearful. He knew in a chilly flash that he would miss the agony of his constant contact with Karen; mourn it like a death.

'You're being very calm, John,' Eilean said. 'She's very beautiful. Don't you miss her?'

'Yes, I do.'

Bewick's reply hadn't been a shut-out. It had been a confidence, friendly, forthcoming, but utterly opaque. Jones poured the wine. Bewick's inner life was hidden metres deep, untouchable.

'Didn't Barry have some maths he wanted help with?' Bewick asked.

'No, no, John. That's beyond the call of duty. It really is. He's doing it now. It's his problem if he watches soccer for nearly two hours. I'll just have this glass then I'll go and sort him out. You and Gio have got a lot to discuss.'

'What makes you think that?' Jones was peering at the label. 'Next village but one, matter of fact.'

Eilean ignored him. 'How is the Whear case?' she asked Bewick.

'It's getting interesting, I think.'

'In what way?'

'Tell me, Eilean, what do you think about crimes of passion? Can it be just sexual jealousy that makes people kill?'

'I don't know. What do *you* think?'

'I've bought a theory . . . I mean I've saddled myself with a theory . . .'

'What?'

'That people will only kill when killing seems to be the only way out of their private nightmare. For the hopelessly weak it's the ultimate power trip, for the completely dispossessed it's the ultimate ownership, and so on.'

'Well, ownership would come into a crime of passion, wouldn't it? Don't the French let you off if you kill your wife's lover? Or is it just your unfaithful wife? Man's ownership of his wife's body, that sort of thing. Reputation. Status. How can I ever hold up my head again with my unfaithful wife walking around for all to see? Ditch the bitch.'

'So it could be about the reassertion of power, the reclaiming of possession?'

'I'd say so.'

Jones wondered what the hell Bewick was playing at. Bewick had thought through all that stuff Eilean was coming at him with. He and Bewick had discussed it often. Why was he pretending that this was new territory for him? Then he realized: Bewick had discovered something.

A few minutes later, when Eilean had finished up her wine and left, Bewick told him what it was.

'*Who?*'

'That's what Niki Whear said. Miranda, Lady Griffiths. That's what she believes.'

'Well, Arnold Sandham . . .'

'The pathologist?'

'That's him. He was saying that this Griffiths woman is good at just about everything she does — envied by all.'

'So?'

'And she's a looker.'

'So?'

'So why would she mess around with a no-hoper like Whear? Rough trade? On her own doorstep? Chrissakes, I don't see it. You sure you got this right?'

'Niki Whear said she didn't believe it either, at first. She believes it now.'

'How did she find out?'

'She was at some reception at the college and Lady Miranda went out of her way to befriend her, which she thought was bloody odd. Then she caught a look between Whear and Lady Miranda which she thought was well out of order. Then she got an anonymous phone call telling her what was going on.'

'Male or female?'

'Male.'

Jones pondered a moment. 'You believe it?'

'Niki Whear didn't, as I say. So she followed him

after work one night. She saw them together. I think she's telling the truth. So yes, I believe it.'

'You realize this puts Sir Terence bleeding Griffiths right in the frame? Gawd, what a pig's arse.'

Bewick said nothing.

Jones's voice took on a tone of mock hysterical outrage. 'I'm going to have to interview the man as a *suspect*. Adviser to the government! Gawd . . .' He took another swig of Chianti. 'If somebody offered me early retirement . . .' Jones lapsed into silence and stared at the floor for some time. Then he looked up. 'Karen really left you?'

'Yes.'

'Why?'

'She knew I didn't really love her as she wanted.'

'And how's that?'

'Wanting her to have my children would be a fair test, I suppose.'

'I see. You know that scientist woman is around? Whatsername? Vernon. Sally Vernon. I seen her a couple of times.' Jones watched for a reaction.

Bewick just nodded. 'I know,' he said. 'She might be co-opted by CRSI. Occasional DNA expert.'

'You know it was her who found the body?'

'No, I didn't know that. You've interviewed her, then?'

'We only spoke on the phone. Pity she doesn't know more. She'd be a brilliant witness. No, she and this other bloke, one of the St Anne's dons, saw it sitting in a punt in the river. Apparently this chap who was with her, O'Keefe, went to pieces when he saw it.'

Jones saw a quickening of Bewick's interest.

'Have you talked to this O'Keefe?'

'No, not yet.'

'I should, if Sally mentioned it. She wouldn't have mentioned it unless she –'

'I realize that,' Jones interrupted, pissed off. 'He's on the list. Of course he is. As I said, she's a quality witness. Anyway, you've decided to avoid her, have you?'

'No.'

'You know what? People think I'm a bit provocative. I've just realized why. It's knowing you. Chip away at most people and sooner or later *something* happens. You get a reaction. With you, nuclear artillery wouldn't do the job.'

Bewick smiled. 'It's up to her,' he said. 'She knows where to find me.'

Miller walked along the platform at Cambridge Station, staring at its chewing-gum-dotted surface, his head so bowed that he nearly cannoned into one of his colleagues from St Anne's.

'Ah, Nicholas. Hello. Yes, sorry. Off to London?'

'That's it.' Cranesmith briefly gave him his lopsided grin. 'Been to see your mother?'

This was known to Miller's colleagues to be a weekly ritual. His mother lived a normal, comfortable life, but, according to Miller, complained about it endlessly. Asked why he kept the visits up, Miller's reply was that it was a matter of duty. Others suspected that he took some self-flagellatory pleasure in the visits, that his mother's approval meant more to him than perhaps it should.

'Yes.'

The two men began strolling to the south end of the platform, where the London departures took place.

'So,' asked Miller, 'it's the Imperial War Museum, is it?'

'That's the idea.'

'Did you tell me you were working on the campaign in Burma?'

'That's the idea. Fourteenth Army in Burma. The squaddy's experience.'

'I envy you, I must say.'

Cranesmith had a reputation for having led an odd and interesting life. He had come up to Cambridge on a placement from the army. All through his subsequent military service, he had kept up the habits of scholarship. In 1979 he had published a defining account of British-led imperial native armies, *Joining the White Tribe*. When he retired from the army, shortly after the conclusion of the Falklands campaign, he was invited to apply for the post of Bursar at his old college, St Anne's. He had accepted on the understanding that there would still be time for research.

'Oh, I like to be envied,' Cranesmith said. 'Details please.'

'Well . . . a life of action, followed by one of scholarly retirement. What better?' Miller explained, mournful.

'Sounds good, put like that. Curious how we can't seem to view our own lives from the outside. We view them through the interior muddle. "Scholarly retirement" is crap, I'm afraid, old man. I'm married, for a start. Don't therefore live in college. So . . .'

Cranesmith was reckoned to be unfortunate in his marriage. His wife suffered from depression and was seldom seen at college gatherings.

Miller and Cranesmith were standing now outside the stationary Liverpool Street train, when a brisk, bright-eyed man with an armful of newspapers marched around the corner: Peter Schrager.

Miller seemed put out. 'Mr Schrager . . . What are you doing here?'

'John Bewick working out well, is he?'

'Yes, yes. He is, as a matter of fact. He's been very helpful.'

'Interesting chap, don't you think?'

'Oh yes. I'm very grateful. I should have contacted you. I see that. I'm sorry. It was very good of you.' Miller was shrinking away from the other two men in an agony of resentful embarrassment.

'For God's sake, man! I'm not looking for gratitude. Your college is paying what it's paying. I was just interested. Here, you can look at these now.' Schrager dumped the newspapers on Miller.

'What?'

'I haven't checked them all, but the ones I've looked at . . .' Schrager lowered his voice, 'are all running some sort of royal story. None of 'em has mentioned St Anne's. They haven't made any connection between royalty and the college.'

'I see.'

'So far so good, then, eh?'

'Yes, yes indeed. Thank you. I'll look at them. Thank you.'

Clutching the newspapers like a man holding a baby for the first time, seeming to offer his own clumsiness as an appeal for indulgence, Miller made his way out of the station.

Schrager and Cranesmith didn't know each other, but now introduced themselves and boarded the train together. Schrager felt a rapport with Cranesmith as soon as he discovered they shared a military background. They explored this as they waited for the train to move. They sat opposite each other during the journey. Delicate probing by Schrager revealed that Cranesmith had a similar opinion of Brian Miller as he had.

'A bit of a complicated old baggage,' was how Cranesmith put it. 'Not surprising really, considering the amount of time he spends with his mother, who sounds like a megaton ache in the anus.'

Schrager nodded. Mrs Miller's foibles, her blithe egotism, had been recounted to him, too.

The drinks trolley came up the train and Schrager bought them a coffee each. He asked Cranesmith about Bewick, and the college's attitude to him. Cranesmith too seemed to think Bewick was a success.

'Although that Welsh policeman . . . pushy fellow.'

As Cranesmith was talking, a couple of lads, buried deep in the beat leaking from their headphones, struggled up the aisle with huge backpacks. The second one knocked the paper cup of coffee in Cranesmith's hand, which spilt, some of it on to his trousers.

Cranesmith was furious. 'Stupid fucking yobs!' he hissed, his face suddenly red.

The two lads lumbered on impervious, but Cranesmith must have been aware, Schrager thought, of the attention he was attracting elsewhere, as he vented his barely controlled fury.

'At least the brain-dead morons'll be deaf as well as dumb before they're twenty-five. Jesus!'

Cranesmith rummaged in his briefcase. For a wild moment, Schrager wondered if he was looking for a gun. Schrager had already handed him the paper napkin which had come with the coffee, to soak up the worst of it. There wasn't much, anyway. Cranesmith now found a handkerchief in his case, and set off for the lavatory.

Schrager was relieved he'd gone. He'd never witnessed an outburst of anger so intense over something so trivial.

It was the moment Sally Vernon had been dreading for months now, since the day she'd moved to Cambridge. She'd walked around the corner from the Arts Theatre box office, where she'd been buying tickets. At the far end of St Edward's Passage she saw him. He was silhouetted against the stonework of King's, golden in the morning sun. Bewick was looking in the side window of a clothes shop, which specialized in college colours. She stopped. She saw him take a deep breath, as if resigning himself to something, then begin to move towards her.

She turned away. She hurried past the east end of St Edward's church, which stood in the centre of what had once been a very small medieval square. She turned again into the Passage, on the north side, where David's Bookshop stood. She waited behind the foliage of a fig tree which grew in the churchyard, spilling a branch over the low wall. Normally she would have smiled at herself for hiding behind a fig leaf; not now.

Bewick didn't appear in that part of the Passage. So she walked the few yards to the outside shelves of David's shop and browsed the titles there. A few minutes and he would be well on his way to wherever he was going.

She was conscious that her heart was thumping. She wondered if what she had just done was sensible. It was, she realized, only the equivalent of what she had been doing mentally for more than a year now: avoiding all thought of him. Was it a mistake? Should she have exchanged some pleasantries and gone on her way? There was nothing to be embarrassed about, was there? They hadn't even made love. They nearly had; just once. It was she who had ended their relationship – if there'd been one, for God's sake! What was all this hiding in corners about?

She stood quite still. Tall, creamy complexioned, her brown hair lifted by a breeze, her broad forehead, her darkly brilliant eyes . . . a passer-by would at that moment have thought her beautiful. It wasn't exactly sadness she felt, more an acceptance of the endless discontent of human arrangements. Not really unhappy, not cast down; her positive vitality was intact.

As she put a book back on the shelf, she realized for the first time that it was in Spanish, which she didn't speak. She would have laughed if she hadn't been so cross with herself.

Sally wondered if Bewick had been consulted about the St Anne's murder. The thought clouded for a while her disappointment with herself at avoiding him. She resented him for what he made her feel, was furious with herself for allowing him to affect her like this. It was an insult to Anthony. It really was. She reminded herself of Anthony's claims on her as lover, as friend.

Anthony was shy, sombre, beautiful. His infrequent, coaxed smiles were radiant, heartbreaking. His childhood had been a blank of neglect which he had somehow survived, scarred but intact, his moral imagination still functioning. Unbelievably to Sally, Anthony's wife had walked out on him and the children two years before. Sally was necessary to him, valued.

Five minutes later, she was in a payphone outside the library. 'Mr Schrager? Sally Vernon. About the possibility of joining you as a consultant?'

'Sure.'

'You were interested in the odd seminar on forensic DNA and the PCR problem?'

'Yes, indeed. So what do you think?'

'I think we should try to sort something out, don't you? May I come in and see you?'

Schrager sounded pleased.

There, thought Sally, no avoiding Bewick now.

'Murder, my dear Giovanni!' At the other end of the line, Sandham was at his most irritating: ebullient and self-satisfied.

'Get away,' Jones said, dry as dust.

'No need to be so dour, Giovanni. You know it doesn't suit you. Anyway, no explosive traces on victim's hands. Traces on face and upper-body clothes suggest a shot from not many feet away. How're you getting on with it all?'

'Oh, just lovely, ta.'

'Any discernible motive?'

'Oh yes.'

'What?'

'Really juicy.'

'*What?*'

'Torrid college doings. Adultery in Academe.'

'*Really?*' Sandham's enthusiasm was grubby schoolboy. 'Who? Tell me. Go on, you bugger, tell me!'

'No.'

'I think you're a frightful spoilsport. I hate you. I shall ask around. I'll get there. I'll sniff it out, y'know. This is Cambridge – from whose high tables nothing is hid.'

'Cheers, Sandy.' Jones put the phone down.

*

Peter Schrager sat in his office reading the papers. In the first couple of days, the broadsheets' reporting of the murder at St Anne's college had been restrained, by current standards. And even the tabloids, with their inverse snobbery, had implied that this was the sort of thing Oxbridge deserved and had mostly ignored it.

His secretary came in.

'Not a single follow-up today,' he said, referring to the papers.

'But when they discover who the new patron of St Anne's is to be . . .'

'God forbid.'

'They're bound to, sooner or later.'

'You can just see it, can't you? PUNT MURDER PATRON! CLUEDO COLLEGE! I hope Bewick gets this one sorted out sharpish.'

5

Jones was asleep. He dozed in the corner of the small office until discomfort woke him. He blinked, staring, not knowing where he was. The place wasn't his – too bloody tidy, for a kick-off. Ah, yes: St Anne's. The Master's secretary was supposed to be getting him tea. He looked at his watch: bloody hell!

Footsteps clacked outside and the secretary came in, without any tea. She looked about fourteen: flat, pale hair, specs, unsmiling. 'The Master will see you now.'

Jones followed her up stone steps, clumsy with resentment: not a dicky bird about how his time had been wasted.

The secretary opened an oak door studded with iron nails. 'Make yourself comfortable.' The door closed.

Jones looked at the room stretching in front of him, refusing to be impressed. The gallery of St Anne's Master's Lodge was celebrated, not particularly for its beauty but for the completeness of its survival. Fifty-eight feet long, the light from its ten grand windows spilling across its pale floor, the centuries-old box was unremarkable except that every plank, all the glass and plaster, every nail almost, dated back to Henry the Seventh.

Still waiting, Jones wrinkled his nose and frowned. He was trying to pinpoint his dislike of all this wobbly glass and beaminess. Something tugged at his memory, but he couldn't catch it.

'Yes, it is rather lovely, isn't it?' said a good-looking man, who seemed to materialize at the far end of the room. 'So sorry to have kept you so long.' Professor Sir Terence Griffiths, Master of St Anne's, extended his hand to be shaken.

''S all right,' Jones mumbled, hating himself.

'You'll want to talk to me about the horrible business of this poor porter of ours. Of course.' Sir Terence's voice, light and sinuous, fell into a hushed sympathy. 'Of course.' It was an odd voice, blending light, musical Welsh with Oxford drawl to produce an accent both amiable and snootily highbrow.

'I can tell you very little about it, I'm afraid,' Griffiths was saying. 'I came home from a feast at Trinity, which is my old college, at about twelve. I read some papers in here for about an hour as I had a meeting yesterday – the Educational Strategy Committee – at Number Ten. Then I went to bed.'

Jones knew he was being told not to trade on any connection between them on account of nationality. They may both have come some distance from the same part of Wales, but the distance between them, on the socially vertical scale, was even bigger.

'Ah,' said Jones, as if he was sceptical of Griffiths's statement. Griffiths shifted in his chair, perhaps irritated. Jones deliberately deepened his accent. 'But wasn't there some big dinner here in college, to do with this here new Professor being appointed?'

'I'm sorry, you've lost me.'

'Some chap called Dowling giving you some money?'

'Oh, *that* . . . Yes, Sir Michael was entertained by the committee to discuss his funding of a fellowship, possibly a chair, in paediatrics. My presence wasn't essential.'

'An' which gate did you come in by, would you say?'

'Gate?'

Jones could see the cogs whirring before Griffiths replied, 'Bishop Lunn's gate on St Anne's Lane. What's the relevance?'

Settling into the role of the village bobby, Dai-notebook-and-pencil, Jones made a little show of consulting his notes, although he knew what he was going to say. 'Which is locked at twelve, it says 'ere. So you come back before twelve? Or do you perhaps have your own key?'

'No, I don't.'

'So you come in before twelve?'

'That would seem to be the implication.'

'That would,' Jones agreed, as if confirming the existence of God. 'How soon before twelve?'

'I don't know. A minute or two.'

Jones knew from his conversations with the porters that Griffiths had, in fact, come in at least fifteen minutes earlier.

'And you settled to your reading then, did you, straight away, like?'

'Yes,' said Griffiths, impatient. 'Why is this relevant?'

'Because, Sir,' said Jones, still playing Dai Plod, 'you might've heard the shot which killed Whear.' Or done him in yourself, you slimy git.

'Well, if that's what you're after, then I'm afraid I didn't hear it,' smoothed Sir Terence, smiling.

Jones looked as confused as he dared. 'And you were reading in here, were you, Sir?'

Griffiths gestured to the magnificent triple pedestal dining table in the centre of the room. 'Yes, I was. I was sitting at the table.'

'Well, that's odd.' Jones gestured to the river end of the gallery. 'He was shot just out there. General agreement seems to be just after quarter past midnight. Well, that is odd.'

'If I heard it, I wasn't conscious of hearing it. It may be that one doesn't hear such things because one is not expecting or thinking in terms of such things.'

Jones stared, as if he only just followed this.

'I wasn't conscious of it,' Griffiths said patiently, apparently convinced by the Dai-notebook impersonation.

'And you went to bed about one o'clock?'

'That's right. My wife was already asleep.'

'Ah yes, your wife.'

Jones looked down at his notes. Christ! Could he really tell this Teflon-coated, Number-Ten-visiting smoothie that he suspected him of murdering his wife's lover?

'Your wife . . .' he said again, frowning at his notes to give himself time to think.

'What about her?'

Jones looked up; a quick reflex. He caught Griffiths's fixed glare of concentration on him, utterly cold and hostile. In a moment it was gone. My God, Jones thought, maybe . . . but Griffiths now smiled, amiable, sociable.

'I asked her just now if she'd order up some coffee, in fact,' he said. 'I'll see where it's got to.' Griffiths propelled himself out of his chair. His movements were elegant, quick and fluid. He had an exceptional face, Jones thought: a handsome beak of a nose, clear skin, bright eyes and a determined, sensual mouth. 'Miranda?'

Griffiths had opened the door. Jones caught another glimpse of the stylish woman he'd seen crossing the bridge on his first day at St Anne's.

'Yes, it's just been brought through,' she said. 'I'll get it.' She disappeared.

'Anyway, your wife . . .'

Jones tried to ask Griffiths if he knew that his wife had a lover. He realized to his disgust that he wasn't going to do it. He lapsed into embarrassed silence. He'd always wondered what it must feel like to be impotent. He knew now. He hated himself. What was it? Was it the government connection? Normally he'd have relished wading in. Was it because of the woman herself? He didn't know.

'What about my wife?'

'Your wife was asleep, you say?'

'Yes.'

'I'd like to speak to her, nevertheless, as the shot may have disturbed her.'

He noticed the flicker of hesitation from Griffiths before he said, 'Of course.'

'Do you know anything about the victim – Mr Whear?'

'I'm not involved in the college's employment process at that level. The Bursar is, so he'll know something about Whear's background, I'm sure. Dr Cranesmith is the Bursar.'

'Right.'

'I'm reasonably confident, by the way, that this has nothing to do with the college itself. Whear had only been with us a few weeks.'

'Sure,' said Jones as neutrally as possible, hoping to irritate.

The door opened at the far end of the gallery and Jones saw that it was being pushed ajar by Lady Griffiths's hip. She walked briskly across the shining oak floor carrying a tray of coffee and biscuits.

'Here we are then,' she said, smiling at him.

Griffiths looked at his watch and stood. 'You wanted a word with my wife,' he said charmlessly, 'and I'm a bit late, so why don't you two have this coffee?' Without looking at his wife, he set his face in a placid smile and walked off.

Lady Griffiths put the tray down slowly. Jones could see how antagonized she was. Good manners came to her rescue. 'How do you like your coffee, Chief Inspector?'

'Oh . . . erm, white. One sugar. Ta.'

'You're Welsh, I imagine?'

'Swansea, yes.'

'My husband comes from Carmarthen.'

'Uh-huh.'

'You knew?'

'Well, south-west Welsh, you know. His accent . . .'

'He'd be quite surprised you could tell, I think,' she said. Did he detect some malicious pleasure in her voice? 'I'm Miranda, by the way.'

She really was gorgeous. As far as he could tell, she was at least ten or twelve years younger than her husband; turning forty soon, he guessed. A testing time, when the indulgences of thirty-something come home to roost – mostly around the waist and liver. He should know. But then he'd always been a short-arsed number. He remembered once reading a typically irresponsible piece of journalism which said that the best way of avoiding a heart attack was not to be short. Oh well, he'd thought, that's that then. Death sentence. Make merry.

Lady Griffiths had done something about it. She was keeping herself sexy fit. For that fish-eyed git who attended Education Committees at Number Ten? She couldn't be, could she? He was beginning to become convinced by Niki Whear's story. But why Whear?

She handed him his cup of coffee. He noticed that she hadn't poured one for herself. 'Look, I really can't speak to you now, I'm afraid,' she said. 'I'm a by-fellow at Newnham and I'm supposed to be there in ten minutes to talk to one of my groups. When would suit you?'

They agreed to meet soon. As she walked from the room, she impulsively speeded up as she neared the door. Jones reminded himself that she'd said she was late. But she'd left him alone in the place, which was odd, however public a space it was. It looked as if she'd been hit by an emotion she didn't want him to witness.

It took him a moment to realize he was free to sniff around. He wandered over to a semi-circular embrasure midway down the gallery. It was windowed all round and jutted over the court – a panoramic view through whorled and rippled glass, further distorted by rain dribbling down it.

Jones opened the window. The rain was heavy. Beyond the cloisters stood the Longhi tower, where the Senior Tutor, Dr Miller, had his rooms. Jones was invisible from below. He could hear voices and leant forward to listen.

'Is Dowling affected?' he heard Cranesmith say below him.

'In what way?' The voice was Miller's.

They were standing in the cloisters, Jones realized, out of the rain.

'Is he backing off funding the fellowship again?'

'Because of the Whear business? We've heard nothing. He'll follow where royalty leads. That's my belief. According to the Health Trust people, that was what swung it. Once he knew it might be opened by royalty, then he was suddenly on for funding an entire new wing.'

'I see. Doesn't sound very mature. But we know that, anyway . . . He may do anything.'

'We'll find out at the next committee meeting, presumably.'

'If he comes.'

'He said he would. Why shouldn't he?'

'No reason.'

'He's invited us to his house, by the way.'

'Us?'

'The committee.'

'Oh.'

'It's an interesting place. Designed by Alfred "Gothick" Warrington.'

'He was a Trinity man, wasn't he?'

'Yes. And his archive was willed to Trinity. He was a great constructor of follies and secret passages, that sort of thing. His forte was Tudor revival.'

Jones eased himself into a position where the two men became visible. Cranesmith, lean, upright from his military days, making the most of his modest height. Brian Miller, on the other hand, bowed over, round-shouldered, as if trying to disguise his tallness. Of the two, he reckoned he preferred the world-weary Cranesmith. Brian Miller's harshness combined with an unattractive naivety; he was charmless. Twenty years ago, his awkwardness might well have been appealing. But now – it was as if his life had continuously disappointed him and taught him little.

Cranesmith was a sexy old bastard in his reptilian

way. There was sensual knowledge written on him, clear to see. Jones had been told that there was something of a mystery surrounding his wife, whom hardly anyone in college had met. The explanation was that she suffered from depression.

There was a knock at the door and Baynes came in. 'Hello Boss. You on your own?'

'Yeah.' Jones stared down into the court below, the grass brilliant in the emerging sunshine. He heard Miller and Cranesmith move away.

Baynes wandered over, looking around the room. 'Nice.'

Jones grunted. As if to himself, he said, 'I mean, he had plenty of time!'

'Boss?'

'God, I'd really like it if Griffiths turned out to be the one. Supercilious prat.'

They made their way out of the medieval room.

'What did you want, by the way?'

'I interviewed that Dr O'Keefe.'

'Yes?'

'He went to the theatre that night. I've logged the notes for you. Used to be an actor himself when he was a student. Showed me some of his reviews. Not bad. Anyway, he said he went straight back from the theatre to St Anne's.'

'And?'

'I had a word with some of the students in the play. General feeling was that he was well pissed. One of the lasses in the play left the theatre with him and he insisted on walking her back to her college – Clare – the court across the river.'

'And?'

'And, well, he didn't walk off in the direction of St Anne's. Anyway, later, this lass was rung on her mobile by a friend in Trinity who persuaded her to go over for a drink. On the way, she went across the Garret Hostel Bridge and there was this row going on in the alley near the law schools. She glanced up the alley on her way past and there was this fellow having a right old barney with a tramp, well, a down-and-out of some sort. She reckons it was O'Keefe.'

'Good lad. Well done.'

'May mean nothing, of course. Only that he didn't go straight back like he said. Oh yeah, and another thing – Frank Dalmeny says do you want him to book time on Holmes to check the victim?' Holmes was the National Crime Database.

'Why not? Let him go geek mad.'

Melancholy possessed Karen. She was jogging south out of the city. Trees towered over this stretch of road. It was a haunted landscape. From his house, then over the fields to Grantchester, then back through Trumpington and across College Fen, at dawn, at dusk, at night, at noon: rain, shine, fog, snow. How many times had she run the length of this road beside him, or, running alone, dreamt of him?

She was up to speed now. She could feel the sweat creeping out from under her running top and slipping down the muscle grooves of her spine, cooling the naked part of her back.

Karen's recent past had been divided into life before him and life with him. Here was the new one: life after him. She felt beaten, assaulted by the sullen ache, the tears, the misery. She ran harder. She hated herself for ending it, even as she knew she was proud of herself for doing so.

Half an hour later she had completed the four remaining miles of her circuit. She steadied to a jog and then walked the last hundred yards or so to where she'd parked. Across the road a car boot was open and a woman was unpacking carrier bags from it. Karen looked again. She strolled over. 'Sally? Sally Vernon?'

Sally's frown of concentration disappeared, surprise took its place. It was the openness Karen remembered about her, the willingness to come out and meet. And that nice skin.

'My God,' said Sally, 'the blonde.'

A wry smile. 'Yeah, that'll do. 'Bout sums it up.'

Sally took in Karen's enviable athleticism, her muscle glossy with exercise, her poise. There was something else, though. 'Are you all right?' she heard herself ask.

'Course I am.'

'You were very kind to me once,' Sally insisted. 'And –'

Karen nodded, as if impatient. 'I've just left that bloke you fancied so much,' she blurted out. Suddenly she looked fragile.

Sally heard, but didn't hear. She stared.

'John Bewick. I've just left him . . . again. I got out of your way once before, remember? Well, I'm doing it again. He doesn't –'

Sally saw the jaunty, sexy mouth tense in an effort to stop tears.

'Oh, fuck this,' Karen murmured.

The front door opened and a man came out. 'I really will have to go, my angel, I'm sorry . . . Oh . . .'

'Anthony, this is Karen Quinney. Anthony Richards.'

Karen and Anthony greeted each other and then he was on his way. He was an elegant, slim man with a nervous smile that came and went quickly. His apparent boyishness was accentuated by his blond, curly hair.

Sally offered Karen a drink.

Karen checked her watch. 'Kick me out by quarter to, won't you?'

'Police work?'

'No, that's going to change an' all.'

They went into the house. Karen liked it. It was less of a bachelor pad than her own place; more sexy-comfy.

They stood in the kitchen while Sally poured them fruit juice.

'Why have you left him?' Sally wondered if she'd been too blunt. In fact, she'd been trying to adapt to what she took to be Karen's style.

'I wasn't getting anywhere. I reckon I knew as much about him two years ago as I do now. And I want to think about babies some time soon. I know he doesn't want them. Not mine, anyway.'

'Did he say that?'

'No. He didn't need to.'

'But did you ask?'

'He didn't need to say it,' Karen insisted. 'I knew.' She looked at Sally searchingly. 'Did he ever talk to you about it? Having kids, I mean.'

Sally shook her head.

'No. Course he didn't,' Karen went on, 'and even if he did talk about it, you wouldn't be able to tell what he felt about it. Would you? If anything, you think, well, he must've been through all sorts of pain and stuff, mustn't he? But ... At least that's what I thought ... That's what pissed me off – all those closed doors.' Karen frowned and shook her head again. 'But he's not ... I mean it's not even closed doors really, is it? It's like he's saying, "Yeah, course you can come in," but he's managed to clear the room out before you get in there. Did he tell you *anything*?'

'I wasn't with him long enough.'

Karen thought for a moment. 'No, I guess not. Was that what you meant by me being kind to you? Me moving over to make room for you?'

'I thought it was the kindest thing anyone had ever done for me.'

'I reckoned he loved you, or might have loved you. What went wrong?'

'I'm not sure I know.'

'Try, eh?'

Sally tried; she also tried not to hold anything back.

For a moment, she was back in the cabin of a small boat being thrown around, even on her mooring, by a storm. Bewick was kissing her – for the first time. Then they heard the unmistakable sound of a gunshot above the shrieking wind . . .

She told Karen how she had been attracted to Bewick by the very things that in the end so disturbed her that she had withdrawn from him: his physical power combined with his intelligence. 'Our affair might have begun that night. But then –'

'"Might have"?'

'I saw him kill a man. It – put me off. Oh, it was an accident. Technically, it was an accident. As I'm sure you know. But I knew he was prepared to take a life.'

Sally told Karen how she had been sensitized to the possibility of violence. Shortly after she met Bewick, she had broken her long engagement – to a man from whom she had begun to fear cruel things. She knew Bewick had been acting that night in self-defence. She knew that hers was an unjust judgement; but his fierce determination to win and his cool head as he went about it had frightened her off.

'But you don't think he meant to kill that bloke, do you? If he hadn't been killed by accident first, I mean?' Karen protested. She couldn't sympathize with this sensitivity of Sally's; didn't understand it.

'No, of course not.'

'Then I don't see –'

'I can't explain it. It's what I felt. It seemed to change everything.'

'OK.'

Well, there was the difference between them, Karen thought. Perhaps Bewick wanted someone like Sally, who was wary of him in this way, although she couldn't see why. For Karen, his capacity to fight was something which gave him stature. Her father had been a fighter. If Bewick didn't turn it on her, and there'd been no hint of that, then it wasn't an issue.

'So,' Karen eventually said, 'not much happened.'

Sally shook her head. 'We didn't even sleep with each other.'

'I see.'

'I feel rather defensive telling you that.' Sally laughed. 'Inadequate, somehow. I mean, you must know him so well. You must think – well, I don't know what you must think.'

'I thought when you came on the scene last time that he'd met someone who really got through to him. I knew *I* didn't.'

Sally laughed again, but without much humour. 'I know him as little as you – Well, less, I suppose. There's one thing I did find out, which surprised me. He had a child, you know.'

'*What?*' Karen was transfixed.

'I know. But he did.'

'But . . . why haven't I heard about this? His own kid?'

'Yes. Something happened to her. I don't know what. I was told about it a couple of months ago.'

'Who told you?'

'Someone who was working with the police here in the early eighties. He knew John Bewick.'

Karen was still looking shocked. She put down her glass of juice and shivered. Sally picked up one of her knitted cotton sweaters and put it around Karen's shoulders. 'Here.'

'Ta.'

'This man told me that the child's mother, who was American, suffered severe post-natal depression. Really bad. She was hospitalized, sectioned, the lot. John Bewick brought the child up for three years with the help of his sister and a nanny. When the mother was rehabbed she kidnapped the child and took her to the States. John went out to try to find them, but couldn't.'

'Well, if *he* couldn't find them . . .'

'That's exactly what I thought. If Bewick couldn't find them, then . . . they probably *can't* be found. God knows what might've happened to them.'

There was silence.

'Why didn't he tell me?'

Sally watched the honey-blonde skin pucker as Karen frowned. Her mouth turned briefly down with an impulse to cry, but then she breathed deeply and seemed to calm herself. 'When was all this?'

'Nearly twenty years ago. They were married young. Nina and her children came on the scene a lot later.'

'I see.' Karen snuggled the sweater closer around her. 'Poor bugger.'

'Yes. I never imagined feeling sorry for John Bewick. But I did when I heard that.'

'Sure.' Karen looked Sally in the eye. 'So what're you going to do about it then, eh?'

'What can I . . .? Sorry, I don't know what you mean.'

'About John Bewick. I've cleared off. It's an open event now.'

'What should I do? What d'you mean?'

'Don't go all pink and fluffy on me, Dr Vernon. You know what I mean.'

'I'm not sure I do.'

'Why did you move to Cambridge?'

'Work,' Sally protested. 'A job.'

'Yeah?' Karen was cynical.

'It's true.' Even as she said it, Sally knew it wasn't the whole truth. When she and Bewick had parted, there'd been the dregs of a hope that, somewhere in herself, she'd find the strength to address what had kept her from him. But she still felt that fear, which spoiled the little which had happened between them.

Involving herself with Anthony and his children had sorted out many of her confusions. She knew it satisfied much. It was only occasionally now that she dreamt of meeting Bewick on perfect terms, with a light heart, with a courageous eye that could see him whole, the violent capability included, and not turn away.

She knew it was fantasy. His life had moved on. She felt protective towards Anthony. The fantasy wasn't reasonable on any level. She realized Karen was asking something. 'Sorry?'

'So what's with this place? This Anthony bloke?'

'It's nice. It's all right. I live here. He lives with his children. His wife walked out, you see, left the children. Sometimes he comes over, and vice versa. I'm very fond of them. It's good.'

'"Nice ... good ... all right"? What's this, Dr Vernon? How do you spell "nice" in red roses, eh?'

'It's not passion. I know that. But I know what it is and I like it.'

'OK.' Karen jumped to her feet. 'Fuck! I'm going to be late!'

They walked quickly to the door.

'Can we talk more?' Karen asked.

'I'd like that.' Sally took out her wallet and gave Karen a card. 'Give me a ring. It's all on there.'

Karen handed back the sweater. She hugged Sally, who was surprised by it. Surprised too at the strength of the body holding hers for a moment. Karen felt stronger and firmer than Anthony.

'Thank you,' said Karen. 'I wasn't asking for help, but you've helped.'

It had begun raining again. Karen ran to her car and drove away. On the radio, they were talking about flood warnings and the distribution of sand bags.

When Karen arrived at CRSI the next morning, Schrager asked her to go through to his office. Her immediate thought was that she was going to be told that it wouldn't work out, that she was out of a job again. Not a bit of it.

'I need a personal-security audit done.'

'OK.'

Of course she wasn't going to get kicked out. What was wrong with her?

'There are a number of problems, as I see them. I want us to check them out. Mainly you'll be there to see if the client gets on with you. You may not be team leader, but I'm planning for you to do most of the liaising with the client.'

'Who is it?'

'Sir Michael Dowling. Know him? Who he is, I mean?'

'As seen on TV.'

'Yes.'

'So what does he need us for?'

'God knows. Probably his partner is fucking someone else. Maybe someone is blackmailing him. Just a chance that someone has kidnapped his favourite cocker spaniel.'

'Can't wait.'

'He was fairly low key, I don't think it's anything urgent.'

He tried not to believe it, because it seemed too good to be true, but he knew that over the past days there had been an alteration. Away from the lurid butcher's shop of his dreams, working some dark coil, the worm of vanity had gnawed its way towards consciousness.

His brain had been numbed by its obsessive repeat of the shooting. Something – whether bored familiarity or even some sort of acceptance – had diluted the nausea. He was functioning almost normally. He could make his way through an evening of ordinary social activity without being frozen into stony panic by the thought of what he had done.

That night, was it just the drink? He felt a unique rawness of vitality. It was inexplicable to him, until the worm of vanity finally had its say. It whispered to him how he had achieved the extraordinary . . . He had avenged. After all the self-punishment, the racking of his spirit, all the self-questioning in the light of his beliefs, he had arrived here. He felt a quiver of joy at his own sacrifice. Despite all, despite the moral chains of education and liberal culture, how far he had come! Despite everything, he had managed to make himself into a man who could avenge. He began to overcome despair. He began to discover the will to go on. He could prepare.

6

'You look great. Stop fretting. The tie is perfect. You could be a don yourself.'

'Do us a favour.'

'It's true, love.' Eilean smiled at Jones, who was in his best suit. He was wearing the tie Jo and Barry had given him for his birthday. He'd been saving it for a worthy occasion.

'God, I'm dreading this.'

'Why? John will be with you.'

'I won't find out a bloody thing. I shouldn't have agreed to it.'

'Of course you should. You'll be fine. Just don't drink too much.'

As he came down into the hall, Joanna was there. Without modifying her look of filial contempt, she said, 'You look brilliant, Dad. Wicked.'

Led by the Master, resplendent in gowns and gaudy hoods, the senior members of the college and their guests filed into the ancient dining hall of St Anne's.

Jones followed Bewick up to High Table, trying not to look around him like a tourist. He leant forward and muttered to Bewick, 'What do we think of it so far, eh?'

Bewick ignored him.

'Benedictus, benedicat. Per Jesum Christum Dominum nostrum. Amen.'

Grace said, a deafening racket exploded as the undergraduates dragged benches across the medieval tiled floor, and then sat themselves at the long oak tables.

High Table, where the senior members of the college sat, was raised on a dais. The woodwork here was more elaborate than in the body of the hall, a pair of doubled columns supporting a broken pediment. To either side of it hung gilt-framed portraits of two of the college's more significant benefactors, Sir Thomas More and, earlier still, a Lord Vaux, later Abbot Edmond of Blythburgh. Above the panelling, plain creamy walls stretched upwards towards the permanent dusk below the formidable hammer-beam roof.

To his intense relief, Jones found himself sitting next to Bewick. On his other side was a woman academic. Opposite him was a large, jowly man with an odd, jokey glare and a grand voice who introduced himself as Brendan O'Keefe. Jones remembered the statement Baynes had got from him about finding the body: a model of sweet reason, quite a contrast to his reported behaviour. Next to him was Cranesmith. O'Keefe gestured to the woman beside Jones: 'Petra Svenson. This is Chief Inspector Jones. Brian Miller suggested we invite him.'

'Really?'

'The establishment continually tries to nobble its critics by giving them knighthoods and so on, so Brian thinks that Chief Inspector Jones might be nicer to us if we invited him to dinner.'

'I'm sure the Chief Inspector won't fall for that one. In what way has he not been nice to you?'

'He's been treating us all like suspects.'

'Well, presumably we are.'

A plate arrived in front of Jones with a little pink blob on it. A couple of green leaves were arranged alongside. They didn't look like lettuce. He studied the menu, printed and set in a little silver holder. *'Mousse au Saumon, feuilles d'ail sauvage.'*

Jones supposed that meant salmon and these two green leaves. He glanced at Bewick, but he was turned away, talking to the man on the far side of him. He surveyed the table. At one end sat the elegant Sir Terence Griffiths with his guest, who looked like an Arab businessman. At the other, nearer end sat Brian Miller. On Miller's right was Lady Miranda. Miller's attention on her was intense, although he looked as if he was trying to disguise it.

Was he in love with her? Jones wondered. Miller was drinking in her presence like an addict. She was being merely polite. He couldn't hear what they were talking about. Hermetic Neo-Platonism, no doubt.

Well, he asked himself, what would Mr – sorry Dr – Miller think about this honey pot of a quick-minded female passing over a man like him for a yob with a lockerful of grubby jokes? He might be extremely pissed off. Extremely. Given Miller's shyness and his capacity to panic, which Jones had seen, the discovery that the secret love of his life was betraying his devotion with someone like Whear . . . could be . . . Could be. He smiled. He'd just arrested Miller, broken his alibi, extracted a confession and sent him for trial. Wham, bam!

'May we share it?'

Jones became aware that the Svenson woman was talking to him, her pale-blue eyes wide open.

'You were smiling, Chief Inspector.'

'Was I? Miles away, sorry.'

'You must have a lot on your mind. How extensively have you spread your net?'

'Sorry?'

'For *suspects*.' She said it as if having jolly fun playing *Cluedo*.

'Suspects? Oh God, just about everyone in the United Kingdom could be a suspect.'

'No clues, then?'

'Clueless, completely.'

There was half a laugh from O'Keefe and Svenson. Jones considered again the tempting role of Dai Plod, but decided he wouldn't be able to sustain it all evening. 'We know a few things,' he said briskly. 'The murder weapon, for example, is unusual. The crime scene was highly organized, which implies someone whose life is organized, too; someone who plans. Also, someone who moved around the college invisibly; that's to say, he's either part of the college or looked as if he should be. There's been no report so far of any stranger . . .'

'So Petra was right. Members of college are all suspects,' O'Keefe chipped in, smiling uncomfortably.

'You said it, not me.'

Both Cranesmith and O'Keefe were poker-faced. Jones glanced towards the head of the table, where the Master was being served – the signal that they all should eat.

'But why,' asked Petra Svenson, picking up her napkin and wiping a smear of salmon mousse from her mouth, 'why would anyone in college want to murder Mr Whear? He'd only been here a brief while. Hardly time to get to know him, never mind long enough to get to hate him.'

Jones sensed a frisson of discomfort in those around him. Also, there was a coaxing, false-innocent tone in the way Svenson said this. Did everyone know about the relationship between Miranda Griffiths and Whear, or at least the rumour of it? He watched Svenson as she ate. For a moment he saw, behind the greying, scraped-back hair, the gawky schoolgirl with big hands who had used her cleverness to elude the world and make a place for herself here.

'What do you think, Chief Inspector?' O'Keefe asked in his rich, authoritative voice, as if Jones were an unpromising student.

'No idea,' said Jones. 'We're looking into Alan Whear's history, his background. The more light you throw on the victim, the more likely you are to see the shadow of the killer.'

'My dear Chief Inspector, what a compelling image,' said Svenson. 'Positively Platonic.' She chortled girl-ishly.

'What tonic?' Jones was getting fed up with being

patronized by this lot. There was silence. Embarrassment, Jones hoped.

'Plato,' Svenson said bluntly, sounding apologetic.

'Oh, him again.'

A waiter came to his rescue, filling his glass. He
took a gulp. Then he remembered what Eilean had
said about drinking too much. He knew she was right.
He told himself to remember it. He wished he was at
home. He must have been looking fed up because
Svenson turned to him now with a smile.

'We're all very disturbed and fascinated by this
dreadful event; you must forgive us our impertinence.'

Jones mumbled something conciliatory. The conversation turned.

'In what sense did you mean Platonic, Petra?'
Cranesmith asked. 'As in cave, I suppose?'

Jones ate, deliberately not listening.

After the main course, the occupants of the High
Table left for the gallery of the Master's Lodge. There
desserts, sweet wine, cheese, port and coffee waited
for them.

Jones found himself sitting beside Petra Svenson
again. For some reason she seemed to have taken to
him, or maybe she felt sorry for him.

Bewick was now a few places away and was being
questioned by O'Keefe about his work at CRSI. Those
around him were listening intently. Jones knew that a
focus of attention like that would put him off his
stride completely. He marvelled at Bewick's ease.

'We run security audits –'

'What does that mean? Making sure people aren't going to be broken into?'

'There's that. We also check they aren't being bugged; check their IT security; check their IT's not being abused – downloading inappropriate material, that sort of thing. Then there's the personnel audit.'

'What does that mean?' O'Keefe insisted, his big voice edged with aggression. '"Personnel audit"? It sounds fairly murky.'

'It is murky,' Bewick replied mildly. 'Most secrets are murky. Information is information. It's the use to which it's put . . . What we find is very straightforward, usually: theft, abuse of trust, fake credentials, fake CVs, that sort of thing.'

Bewick went on to talk about some of CRSI's other activities: checking chains of evidence, hostage-taking management, providing personal security, acting like an old-fashioned private eye.

'We also have a number of experts we can call on, in fields such as fingerprinting, DNA analysis, forensic archaeology and so on . . .'

'Sounds as if you're in the right town,' said O'Keefe.

'We are.'

Cranesmith leaned forward. His eyes seemed to glitter. For a moment, Jones thought, he looked fanatic. 'Your basic approach is scientific, then, is it?' Cranesmith asked. It sounded as if this was a preliminary to his setting some sort of trap for Bewick.

'Three hundred years ago, Science was one of the Arts,' Bewick said, 'and I aim to keep it that way.'

His audience laughed. Cranesmith settled back and looked away.

Petra Svenson had just finished her careful peeling and slicing of an apple. She gave one of her chortles and said, 'I like this room, don't you?'

Jones wrinkled his nose. 'I'm prejudiced,' he said.

Svenson looked at him hard. 'Prejudiced? Against what? Can one be prejudiced against Tudor architecture?'

'Can you remember a time when you couldn't buy fresh cream?' Jones asked.

'I think so. But —'

'Well, I'd been sent to live with an aunt in Aberystwyth at the time . . .'

They were interrupted by the arrival of Miranda Griffiths. She leaned over Jones. He could smell her perfume.

'Chief Inspector! How nice to see you again! I'm sorry we haven't been able to talk yet.'

Jones was immediately aware of the coldness that settled over Svenson, who stood up. 'Will you excuse me, Miranda? I must have a word with Brendan.'

'Of course.'

'Perhaps later, Chief Inspector?' Petra Svenson smiled and moved off.

Miranda Griffiths moved a chair closer to Jones and sat down. 'Petra hates my guts,' she murmured as if still pleased by the discovery. 'Completely polite. Always polite. Can't stand me. Interesting.' She looked over at Bewick. 'How well do you know Mr Bewick?'

'Ever since. He's a bit of a chum.'

'That sounds more "how long" than "how well".'

'Nobody knows him well. Don't think anyone ever has. There's a chap, a silk, called Dundas, who was at school with him, and even he –'

'Alec Dundas? I know him.'

'Well, he'll tell you.'

'*You* tell me. What's he like?'

Jones had been here before; a woman befriending him to find out about Bewick. None had been quite in this one's class, mind. He flicked a glance at her and found himself hoping that Niki Whear was wrong. Her vitality, the light in her eye, her quick-wittedness – if all that had been given to the sort of man he'd guessed Whear to have been – bloody grim.

Then he remembered that he didn't want Miranda Griffiths to be mixed up with her own husband, even. And Bewick? Would he mind her being mixed up with Bewick? God knows. Sod it all. He knew one thing: he minded being used. He knew that. He minded that.

He realized she was smiling at him.

'No?' she asked. 'Don't want to talk about him?'

'It's not that.'

'Did you ever work together?'

'Yes, sure. He was the youngest Superintendent ever, before he got poached by this CRSI lot. He's clever. He may look like a second row forward but he'd hold his own with you lot, I reckon.'

'No doubt.'

'We got on well, as a matter of fact. They were good times.'

'And now?'

'Now I don't see so much of him,' Jones grumbled, letting his resentment show. 'Is there a toilet I can use?'

On his way back to the Master's gallery, charged up with the virtuous vow to drink water or coffee only for the rest of the evening, he met Petra Svenson again.

'Hello. How was the beautiful Lady Miranda?'

'You tell me.'

'Why did you come to this do? I mean, if you are obliged to interview her, having dined here puts you in rather a difficult position, doesn't it?'

'Listen,' Jones grumbled, 'don't think I'm not an expert in self-contempt. I'm a black belt. I beat myself up on a regular basis.'

'Sorry.'

'Do you think I might need to interview her, then?'

'I was being hypothetical.'

'Were you?' Jones asked, disbelieving.

She looked at him steadily for a moment. 'You've heard the rumours about her, haven't you? Yes, I can see you have. Well, they're true.'

Jones stopped, rooted by the conviction in Svenson's voice.

She walked on, then realized he'd stopped. She turned. 'If you ask me how I know, I won't tell you. But I'm a scientist; I deal with evidence all the time.'

'Is Dr Miller an admirer of Lady Miranda?'

They had arrived at the ancient, wide staircase that

would take them back up to the gallery. From above came the murmuring of the company, occasional laughter.

Svenson's smile was evaluating, humourless. She said nothing. She began to climb the stairs. After a few steps she turned. 'You were staying with an aunt in Aberystwyth . . .'

'Oh yes. Well, for a treat, she took me out to lunch. But she was a bit of a Stalin when it came to food, Auntie Marge. She took me to a café which was all this olde-worlde-beamery-Tudory stuff and for pudding they served prunes and cream, so-called. The prunes were tinned brown sludge with stones, and the cream . . . Well, you wouldn't want to shave with it. Never seen a cow. Anyway, she sat over me with her brolly at the ready while I consumed my treat. Took hours. Finally, the all-chemical cream made me throw up, not entirely missing her feet, I'm pleased to say. So you see, the glories of Tudor England only remind me of vomiting along with Auntie Marge.'

Petra Svenson laughed, probably dutifully. They were near the top of the staircase now, with its heavy vine-and-rabbits carved newell post. A portrait in a massive gold frame, an apopleptic Augustan divine with eyebrows like caterpillars – Joshua Broade, DD, Master 1723–33 – stared disapprovingly down.

When they reached the top, Petra Svenson stopped. The big oak door to the gallery was open a crack. Through it they could see Miranda Griffiths. She stood out from all the surrounding people. Her silky hair reflected the candlelight brilliantly. She looked as if she were spotlit on a stage. Her eyes glistened as she talked.

In the shadows, Miller stared at her, a grim set to his mouth. Near him was Cranesmith, with a small, fixed, lopsided smile on his scarred face.

'Did Miranda talk about me?' Svenson asked.

'Yes. She said you were very polite.'

'I wonder if she realizes how much people hate her.'

'Who? Why?'

'I can't tell you that. It would be hearsay,' Svenson said severely.

'But –'

'No,' she barked and then turned away. She entered the gallery all smiles. Jones followed. He was at a loss, feeling patronized again.

No one paid him any attention. He hoped it was the amount they'd drunk. One of the fellows he hadn't been introduced to was doing one of his party pieces: an imagined meeting between the Queen and Andrea Dworkin.

Svenson didn't rejoin Jones, but went to the chair on the near side of Sir Terence Griffiths, which had been vacated. Jones noted that none of the dons who had been sitting next to Bewick had moved. For a few minutes, no one talked to Jones. He watched Miranda Griffiths leave the table – loowards, he assumed.

He sat with his cup of lukewarm coffee, wondering how the hell Bewick could be so casual about losing Karen. He remembered the last time he'd been in a car with her. She'd been driving. He'd watched the only part of her body that he could, without being tackily obvious, which was her forearm as she changed gear – light tan, left over from her last holiday; blonde hairs; elegant muscle; elegant wrist; strong, intelligent hand. Never had he felt so physically unworthy.

Jones moaned quietly to himself. Self-conscious, he cut it out. No one, thankfully, had noticed. He compared it with the focus of attention on Bewick. Christ, how he resented the bugger. To distract himself, he began listening to the conversation nearest to him. Something about some bastard who went around smashing up the stained glass in the college chapels during the Cromwellian era. They'd be on to Plato in no time.

As he listened, he began to notice an odd encounter taking place just beyond the circle of light from the room's many candles. Behind Griffiths's back, Brendan O'Keefe was confronting Miranda Griffiths on her return. Some sort of pleading seemed to be going on, although heavily masked.

Miranda Griffiths was, Jones thought, refusing some request of O'Keefe's. He looked desperate. Eventually, she shook her head and walked past him, her face tense. As she approached, she scanned the room and caught Jones's attention on her. She smiled conspiratorially, but Jones could see it was a reflex cover-up, a pretence that the incident had meant nothing. Instinctively, he glanced at Miller. Tight-faced, alert, Miller, he reckoned, had missed nothing.

Was it out of order, Jones asked himself, his pure and simple-minded lust for Karen? Of course it was.

Even though he knew he'd never do anything about it. He supposed that in some people's book that'd make him even more contemptible, a complete wanker. A vision of Eilean popped up. Was she less desirable? Matter of fact, no. In the end, no, she wasn't. A neat figure, a bit on the plump side these days ... her true virtues were laughter, a kindly eye and a forgiving nature. These were riches. Jones told himself to grow up ... whatever that meant.

He saw Cranesmith get up and move over to the fireplace. Jones wandered over. Cranesmith was building up the fire, pushing a smouldering log with his foot.

'Hello, Chief Inspector. How is your investigation?'

'Absolute apple pie.'

'Uh-huh.'

Was it just a dry irony he'd developed, or was he taking the patronizing piss as well?

'Tell me something, will you?' Jones asked. 'Why does Dr Svenson dislike the Master's wife so much?'

Cranesmith straightened up, candlelight reflecting off the shiny skin on his scarred face. 'I thought you might have worked that out by now.'

'Well, I bloody haven't, have I? So throw a dog a bone, eh?'

He must have sounded very pissed off, because Cranesmith wagged a mocking finger at him. 'Now, now ...'

'C'mon: why does she?'

'Well, it may be because Petra's not exactly indifferent to Brian Miller. They played opposite each other a lot on stage when they were undergraduates. They and Brendan O'Keefe were all near contemporaries.'

'Yeah?'

'Yes.'

'And Dr Miller —?'

'Well, quite.' Cranesmith was looking beady, as if Jones was being ridiculously pedantic.

'And Dr Miller isn't exactly indifferent to the Master's wife.'

Cranesmith shrugged.

'Hello, Nicholas.' Miller had joined them at the fire. 'Brendan is going on,' Miller said, holding his glass of port close against his chest, blinking at Jones but talking to Cranesmith. 'Usual stuff, about how England is a naturally Catholic country. You know the form.'

'Brendan O'Keefe has a bee in his bonnet,' Cranesmith explained to Jones. 'One of his theories is that it's because of the lack of proper ritual in our Protestant-run churches that England is so good at things like trooping the colour, royal jamborees and so forth. Our loss of sacred ritual has to be expressed somehow, according to him, so we've attached it to Queen and Country.'

'Hmm . . .' Jones mumbled, doubtful.

'But that is pretty much your position too, Nicholas, isn't it? Your being a Catholic?' Miller asked.

'What?' Cranesmith was curt.

'Well, that England is naturally, well, Catholic.

Would have been better off Catholic. What a devastating thing the Reformation was, and so on.'

Cranesmith shrugged, his mouth working occasional tight little smiles. 'His theory about ritual doesn't follow necessarily, though, does it?' he asked. 'The only interesting thing about it is that Brendan thinks it.'

'So you're a Catholic?' said Jones. 'Real and practising, I mean.'

Cranesmith didn't reply. He looked away, as if the question were an impertinence.

Jones was curious at first, then irritated. 'What's wrong with that? Or is it like asking someone how they vote? Bit more public than that, I'd have thought. For God's sake, we were discussing that sort of thing the other day.'

'Yes. Dr Cranesmith is a practising Catholic. There is a strong recusant tradition in the college. I, personally, am an agnostic,' Miller said primly. He rocked pointlessly on his heels, then turned away.

Jones glanced at Cranesmith, who was looking at him steadily; an utterly unfriendly stare. A junior fellow appeared and offered Jones a glass of port. He glimpsed the label and saw that it was twenty years old. Oh, what the hell . . . Miller wandered off.

Another silence. Jones wondered why Cranesmith had been so touchy about his Catholicism. Cranesmith pushed at the fire again, then went down on his haunches, picked up the poker and rearranged the logs. He seemed unaware of Jones, completely ignoring him. He looked as if he were sunk suddenly in an all-embracing depression.

Jones took a swig of port: fruit and woody perfumes, nice. Eventually, being ignored got to him. 'I was told the other day,' he said, 'that you can tell a real practising Catholic by how they say "mass". They make it rhyme with arse.'

As he'd hoped, this got a reaction out of Cranesmith. He stood up, fixing Jones with a positively hostile stare this time.

Before he could speak, Jones asked, 'So what's your view on the Ulster thing? Some poor bastard got it from the UDA last night. Four kids.'

'What on earth are you talking about?'

'What would a Papist's view of the Prods be?'

'*What?*'

'Technically. I mean, if I came to you and said, Hello sweetheart, I'm a Protestant. Not an orange-bollocked Paisleyite, you understand, just a normal-sized Prod. What'd be wrong with that, in your book? What would the Pope say?'

'I realize you're trying to be provocative,' Cranesmith said, 'but you're also being offensive.'

'No, no. I'm trying to be offensive, matter of fact.'

'You're out of your depth a bit here, aren't you?'

'Stop patronizing me and answer the question. I'm a Prod; what's the man in white's response to that?'

'He'd say that, unfortunately for you, you're a heretic,' Cranesmith said, icy calm.

'I see. And you believe that too, do you?'

'Of course.'

'So, when you were in the army, did you do a tour of Ulster?'

'Yes.'

'Wasn't that difficult for you?' Jones asked.

'Why?'

'There you are, policing a divided community. You share the beliefs of the minority. The police you're supposed to be cooperating with belong, almost exclusively, to the other side. I'd call that difficult.'

Cranesmith was barely containing his anger. 'Listen, I have the same attitude to the IRA as the average law-abiding Catholic did to the gunpowder plotters four hundred years ago. Exactly the same: utter disapproval. On two counts. Both because of the collateral murder of innocents and because of the retribution from the majority that it invited. And indeed received.'

'Yeah. I see.'

'I'm glad you do.'

'This business of being a heretic. What does that mean?' Jones asked.

A bulky figure appeared beside Jones. O'Keefe had joined them. 'It means that you are damned,' he said.

'Damned?'

'Yes.'

'So what does it mean, practically speaking? Being barbecued at the stake, that sort of thing?'

'It has been known, under some regimes,' replied O'Keefe. 'The view would have been that burning at the stake was a mere pin-prick compared to the fires of hell. Probably considered a homely introduction to the heretic's ultimate fate.'

'Gordon Bennet. And what about nowadays?'

'Hell is conceived of in more humane terms.'

'Like being forced to watch daytime TV?'

Cranesmith gave him a scathing look, but O'Keefe seemed not to hear him. He was away in some gruesome world of his own.

'You know, of course, about the punishment of Catholics in the Golden Days of Good Queen Bess?' O'Keefe said, his voice loaded with clumsy irony.

'Yeah, I think so,' Jones replied. 'A bit of a Sam Peckinpah moment, wonnit?'

O'Keefe ignored him again. 'You were tied to a hurdle and dragged head down through the streets to the place of execution. There was a fire burning there, a table and a gallows. Your hanging was designed to half-strangle you, not kill you. They wanted you alive enough to witness what then happened to you. You were brought down from the scaffold, your throat crushed. You were fully conscious. You were laid on a table, stripped naked. There, the executioner cut off your genitals, as unworthy of generation, and threw them into the fire.'

O'Keefe's voice was rising. He seemed unaware of it. 'Then your body was opened. The executioner shoved his hand into you, searching for your heart. He wrenched it out and severed the blood vessels. Then he held it up to the holiday crowd and cried, "Behold the heart of a traitor!" That, too, was then thrown into the fire.' O'Keefe was now loud and furious. 'During all this, it's presumed that you died, but when and what of, God knows. The rest was a human abattoir. The arms and legs were chopped off and burnt. Your head was severed and jammed on a pike –'

Suddenly, O'Keefe was conscious that his large, actorish voice had silenced all those within earshot, which was half the room. He broke off, swallowed, and said, 'And all this was for merely harbouring a Catholic priest.' He frowned and stared into the fire.

Jones looked at the big, bleary eyes with their heavy lids. He was amazed – not by the details of the hanging, drawing and quartering, whose outline every schoolboy knew. It was the violence of O'Keefe's outrage, the extreme identification with something that had happened so long ago.

Jones looked across at Bewick. Should have known better – Bewick's unreasonable calm betrayed nothing. The Master was plainly aware of some sort of commotion, but had successfully kept his Arab guest's attention focussed on himself.

'And what if you just gave the chap a cup of tea?' Jones asked. 'Your Catholic priest. I mean, didn't actually put him up for the night? What would be the punishment for standing the fella a pint, sort of thing?'

Cranesmith flicked a concerned glance at O'Keefe, as if he feared some sort of violent reaction. 'For God's sake!' he hissed and then turned away.

Jones didn't know if it was an actual shove or an unintentional shoulder barge, but O'Keefe marched off and Jones found himself sitting on the floor, his suit dripping with twenty-year-old port.

Cranesmith took his time moving to help. Miller

was there before him, but both were forestalled by Bewick, who lifted Jones on to his feet as if he was a child.

'OK?'

'Yeah, yeah.' Then in an undertone, 'Get *off* . . .'

'Good.' A quick glimmer of a smile, conspiratorial, and Bewick left.

'Are you all right?' Miller was frowning.

'Sure.'

Jones looked at his suit. White-linen napkins appeared. One was wielded by Petra Svenson, who dabbed at his lapels in an unpractical way.

'What did you say to him?'

'I was sending him up about Catholic martyrdom.'

'Aah . . . unwise. Still, he really ought to behave himself. He's been very peculiar recently.'

Miller hovered. 'I must apologize on behalf of the fellowship,' he began coldly.

'He didn't mean to knock me over,' Jones interrupted. 'I caught my foot on the thingy.'

Miller looked relieved and left. One of the junior fellows came up to him. 'Let me get you some more port.'

He phoned from the public box on Chesterton Lane, across the road from the steep riverbank. When Simmonds answered, he wasn't surprised. He knew that the place would still be cut off. The water level in the river was worse than last night, when he'd seen the workshop lights burning after midnight. There was also a fatality about the fact that Simmonds was there. It meant he must go on.

He went to the pedestrian crossing. Dawdling, he wandered across it, getting in the way of a couple of men pushing their bikes, who were in a hurry. The men openly expressed their hostility to the dirty, hunched figure in its smelly overcoat and broad-rimmed fedora, who moved so slowly. He mumbled as he moved.

The couple who lived on the furthest of the three narrowboats below him usually stayed in the pub until well after closing time. From the stern of their narrowboat he would be able to gain his objective.

He made his way down the slope, willing himself not to hurry. Not altering his pace, he passed the two upstream narrowboats, hearing a snatch of dialogue from the TV playing in the second.

The traffic droned.

He stepped aboard the third narrowboat as soon as he came level with it. He walked to the stern. His goal was a small, derelict landing stage about four or five feet off the end of the barge. It stood within the garden of a boarded-up house and wasn't accessible from the bank itself. With barely a hesitation he jumped. The stage held.

He stood, hardly daring to move or breathe, as if this were the most difficult and dangerous part of what he had to do. The house was squeezed in between the pub and the public riverbank, from which it was separated by a thick hedge. Out on the dark river, a mallard racketed. He looked around: everything normal. From the hedge he removed the length of wood he had pushed into it two nights before. Inside the overcoat was another piece, flatter, three screws in place. With the screwdriver he had brought he made the join.

The garden was overgrown with brambles and ash saplings: a decade and more of free growth. He put on the thick gloves he had brought. He went to a bank of nettles on the far side of the garden. In it, black and green with lichen, was the upturned hull of a small, abandoned glass-fibre boat.

The gloves protecting his hands and the brim of the fedora covering his face, he tugged the boat free of years of nettle growth. He watched the opposite bank. No one was on the bench over there – the few people using the river path were on the move. Upstream, the footbridge was still busy with people crossing. He tipped the boat into the water: a small splash; ripples; the duck again.

The boat's painter, synthetic rope, was still attached and whole. He secured it and stepped back into the shadows. He watched the pattern of people passing across the river and along the bank. Eventually, he picked up the crude oar he had made and stepped into the boat.

It felt peculiar to him, stern sculling again after all these years; peculiar because so easy. The figure-of-eight movement of hand and wrist, which translated into a propeller-like motion of the oar blade astern, was part of his brain's permanent wiring, it seemed.

He sculled with the current, past flooded gardens, laid-up punts only just clear of the water, under the bridge. On the Chesterton bank now were the college boathouses, the water halfway up their concrete hards. On the Midsummer Common bank, their trunks inundated, willow succeeded willow, gliding past. Beyond them, the Common was a lake. The Fort St George was dark, only accessible by boat. From somewhere he heard laughter, a sparkle of jazz. Nothing moved on the river. Near the Victoria Avenue bridge, a pair of swans slept on the concrete steps to the permanent growl of traffic overhead. The houses began to peter out. He fingered the gun in the disgusting coat pocket. Not long now.

Bewick and Jones walked into King's Parade. A three-quarter moon was moving in and out of the clouds.

After the incident with the port, the dinner guests had begun to disperse. Cranesmith, O'Keefe and Miller had all made their excuses to the Master and gone. Miranda Griffiths left shortly after. Petra Svenson had stayed, as if to make amends to Jones. Bewick had been introduced to the Master, Griffiths, who'd chatted to him for about half an hour, unable to bring the conversation round usefully to the subject of the killing of Whear because of his Arab guest. Then, by one of those silent understandings, the feast was at an end.

'If I were you, I'd want to talk to Lady Miranda at this stage. Quite a lot,' Bewick said as they passed Oddbins.

Jones told Bewick about his interview with Sir

Terence. 'But Lady Miranda made an excuse,' he added. 'Still is making one, as far as I can tell.'

'Not surprised.'

'What the hell does that mean?'

'If Niki Whear is right . . . You must see how pivotal she is.'

'Pivotal, eh? There's lovely. One for the notebook, that. Pivotal.'

'You can see the effect she has on people. Stop being a jerk, Gio. It's the only motive you've got so far.'

'But the crime scene was clean as a clinic. Personally, I don't connect that with sexual rage, do you?'

Bewick thought for a moment. 'I guess not. No, maybe not. I wonder what a crime scene motivated by religious or political rage looks like?'

'Eh?'

'If it wasn't sexual. You're right. This could be a quite different passion. There are religious converts and political idealists as well.'

'And they're like *lovers*?'

'They all have one thing in common – the moment of commitment, the moment their lives change. And that moment is the great excuse. The excuse for everything they do afterwards – any sort of deadly behaviour, which may have nothing at all to do with what they feel at the moment they fall in love, or give themselves over to some creed, or whatever.'

Jones told Bewick about O'Keefe's outburst.

They passed the massive columns of the Senate House and turned into Senate House Passage, with its few old lamps. A bike rattled past, then another. Excited chat from the two round-faced girls riding them: 'Karl Popper thought Plato was a fascist.'

'Yeah? *Right . . .*'

'Well, a totalitarian at least.'

'Yeah . . .?'

The young enthusiastic voices faded.

'I think I'm going back,' Bewick said as they turned into Garret Hostel Lane. 'It's not that late.'

'What?'

'To St Anne's. But we might as well do the circuit.'

So they continued on. As they crossed the Garret Hostel Bridge, the river was a muddy swirl below them, threatening its banks.

'Glad I don't live by the river,' Jones said. 'Streets are a foot deep below Barnwell.'

They reached the crown of the bridge and looked down into the turbulence.

'Why on earth are you going back to St Anne's?' Jones asked.

'To talk to Miranda Griffiths.'

'Oh yeah? And what d'you think the delightful Sir Terence will think of that?'

Bewick didn't answer.

'Well?'

'I'm not ringing doorbells, Gio. You said she asked about me.'

'So?'

'Have you ever tried focussing on your mental image of someone instead of knocking on their door?'

'What!'

'You heard.'

'No. I haven't.'

'You should try it. It sometimes works.'

'What d'you mean, *works*?'

'They get restless and come to the door, or a window.'

'I don't believe this. How much've you drunk?'

'You can wake people up, too.'

'You realize, don't you, that I tell people that you're a hero – Captain Rational, the Man with the Pitiless Intellect. Robological. Then you come on like some dippy spoon-bender from Llasa. How d'you think that makes me feel? Where's my cred gone, you bastard?'

'Anyway, worth a try,' said Bewick, smiling.

'And another thing,' Jones complained, as they walked past the floodlit piers of Clare College West Gate. 'This is *my* investigation, *my* witness. I'll thank you to . . . to remember it,' he finished lamely.

'All right, Gio. If she tells me anything relevant, I'll hand it on.'

'She won't, though, will she? She'll be in bed – reading Plato, no doubt, they all do – and she'll stay there, never mind you standing outside curdling your brain cells, trying to be telepathic, or maybe just pathetic.'

'I dare say you're right, Gio.'

'I am.'

'Still, worth a try.'

'Aw, pivotal off, why don't you?'

*

Miranda Griffiths sat in bed reading. She'd heard her husband go to his room about twenty minutes before. She put the bookmark into her book. She discarded a couple of pillows, arranged the remaining one and turned out the light. She noticed there was moonlight on the curtains, so she slipped out of bed and drew the curtains. She was struck by the brightness of the light on her white silk pyjamas. She took a step backwards into shadow, as if she was aware of a presence that might be watching.

Spread out below her was the garden of the Master's Lodge. It was shaded from the light of Walton Court by its high walls. Its formal shapes were defined by moonlight only. Almost immediately, she became aware of the man standing in the court beyond, standing where she was bound to notice him. She knew at once who it was.

Bewick walked through the empty court, its windows mostly darkened. The single lamp filtering through the leaves of a Japanese maple was no match for the silver brilliance of the moonlight. Ahead of Bewick, a narrow wedge of dim, yellow light spilled across the stone. As he passed the staircase entrance immediately before it, one of the names painted on the reveal caught his eye: Dr P. B. O'Keefe.

Through the cleft between the curtains, a man as tall as Bewick could, if he stretched, just see in. Two candles burned on a chest of drawers. The crucifix that stood between them was as agonized a version of a dying man as Bewick had seen. It took a moment

before he noticed that this domestic altar had a suppli-
cant. Bowed in the shadows, his head almost on the
floor, knelt a big, fleshy man, naked apart from boxer
shorts. Across the random scatter of moles on his
back were more regular lateral marks – weals raised
by a whip, or a cane. Faintly, Bewick could hear what
he took to be mumbled prayers. Even muted, the
actorish voice was unmistakable. O'Keefe's right arm
reached out and bent. The knotted whip cord struck
his own back. Bewick heard a grating sound. O'Keefe
was kneeling in a tray of gravel.

Once dressed, Miranda made her way down the old
service stairs to the scullery. She took the garden key
from the shelf and slipped out of the door by the iron
pump. Across the small knot garden, the door into
Walton Court was hidden in the shadow thrown by
the deep brickwork of its arch.

When she stepped out into Walton Court, Bewick
had gone. She walked across the court towards the
library passage. Above and to either side were ancient
windows. Through the muzz of the glass she could
see the silhouetted bookcases. There was no one in
the passage. She turned. As she did so, she glanced
across to another arched passage which led through
into Pelham Court, where a light burned all night.
There, against the whitewashed interior of the arch,
she noticed, as she was sure she was meant to, the
shadow of a man. After a hesitation, she moved
towards it. As soon as she crunched the gravel near
it, the shadow moved away.

She found him waiting in the cloisters of Pelham Court.

'Mr Bewick?'

'Lady Miranda.'

'No please, just Miranda.'

'Sure.'

She knew the acoustic qualities of the cloisters and had kept her voice low, a quiet whisper. 'May we talk?' she asked now.

'Of course.'

'Where do you live? Is it far?'

'Not at all. Ten minutes' walk. Five on a bike – less.'

Bewick gave his address in Baccata Lane, Homerton. Miranda returned the way she had come. Bewick continued on his way to the Gibbons Bridge and the main gate. The door of the lodge clicked quietly shut.

The small boat nudged the tide line of twigs and rubbish brought across the fields by the flood water. He stepped out of it, moving now like an automaton. He secured the painter to a damaged scaffold pole which he jammed into the corner of the concrete-block wall. Twenty metres away, the lights still burned in the workshop. He watched for a moment and then began moving towards it.

'How d'you get here, mate? I reckon there are at least a couple of hours to wait, the rate water's dropping at the moment. What can I do for you?'

'Is your name Simmonds?'

Who was this git? He looked like some fucking hobo and talked like the House of Lords.

'Yeah it is. What do you want?'

'Robert Gordon Simmonds?'

7

Bewick answered his doorbell. Miranda Griffiths stepped into his organized, unluxurious house. Her intelligent eyes were troubled. She looked around at its sparseness, the odd fine piece of furniture, the bright, abstract paintings, the book titles.

'Drink?' Bewick asked.

'That would be good. Thank you.'

'Red? White? Scotch? Coffee?'

She glanced at his glass of white wine. 'That?'

'Of course.'

Bewick went to fetch the bottle. On the low table in front of her was a copy of the local evening paper. There'd been a sectarian killing in Ulster that morning, despite the official ceasefire. A young father of four shot on his way to work. Bewick returned and saw that she was reading the headline. She realized that he had noticed. 'Don't start me on it,' she said. She took the glass from him. 'Thanks. What were you waiting for when I came to the window?'

'You.'

'But I might have been asleep.'

'It was worth a try. I knew you might want to talk to me. It wasn't purely chance.'

She frowned briefly, as if she didn't know what he meant.

'Do you know what I wanted to talk about?'

'Possibly.'

Bewick said nothing more. He took a glass from the fruitwood corner cupboard and filled it. He handed it to her, looking straight at her. There was something illusionless, a benign acceptance, in his expression. He still said nothing.

'You know, don't you? What people are saying,' she said.

'I've heard rumours.'

'Do you believe them?'

'I don't believe much, without corroborative evidence.'

'But you work on instinct, too. You said as much at dinner.'

'Of course. But then I start looking for evidence. I'll believe things on a provisional basis . . .'

'So how do your instincts rate the rumours about me?'

He looked at her calmly as he replied, 'As true.' He smiled briefly before adding, '– Provisionally.'

She nodded. She was relieved, if anything. 'How sure were you that I wanted to talk to you?'

'Reasonably. Gio Jones told me you'd had a word with him.'

'That's all you had to go on?' She looked at him hard, but he said nothing. His expression remained friendly, interested.

'I sensed you might want to talk without the whole world knowing. I thought you might guess I'd make myself available. That's all. It was worth a try.'

'So it seems. How very interesting. What a curious man you are.' She looked away as if embarrassed by what she'd said. 'May I sit down?'

'Of course.'

There were two sofas facing each other on either side of the fireplace. She sat down. She looked at him, looked away, thought for a moment and then said, 'I'm an adulteress.'

Bewick's expression didn't change.

'When I heard that word – adultery – as a child, I thought it was to do with growing up, becoming adult. Perhaps it is.'

'Perhaps.'

'You're not embarrassed by this at all, are you? No, I can see you're not. I can feel myself being drawn into a confession . . . Is that a good idea?'

'The whole truth would be helpful.'

She laughed; he smiled.

'Oh God – I'm sure there's no need to tell you how it happened. There are a hundred reasons. I'm sure you've heard them all before. It's just the usual human mess.' She was silent for a moment. 'I should never have married,' she added.

She drank a mouthful of the wine, which was good. She glanced at the bottle and saw that it was Jasnière, which she'd never heard of.

Bewick said, 'Tell me about Alan Whear.'

'I didn't like him much. Poor Alan . . .' She was silent for a while. 'Why do I feel tearful? I really didn't like him much. I disliked him, in fact. The tears are for myself, I suppose.'

'In what way didn't you like him?' Bewick asked.

'He was . . . like my husband. He shared my husband's attitude to women. He thought women should know their place and was likely to get confused if they didn't. I can't believe some of us are still fighting this battle.'

'I would have thought your husband was clever enough not to show that he thinks that.'

'Oh, he disguises it, all right. But it's there. And it's worse the more distinguished he gets.' She frowned, was silent, and then began again. 'Terry was a rich kid, but he chose a field where only brains counted. Double first. Doctorate. Fellowship. Every step was a battle won, a triumph. He was like a young Napoleon. Now he's a monster of the establishment: Mastership, Knighthood. He's a First Consul now. Would like to be Emperor.'

Her voice trailed away, full of a tired disgust, disappointment. Then she threw back her head and let out a bright 'Ha!' of laughter. 'Do you know that wild portrait of Napoleon crossing the Alps by David?'

Bewick shook his head.

'No, indeed, why should you? Well, as hero worship it's magnificent, because it's painted by a natural hero-worshipper who happens to be a genius. It's also a pack of lies. Napoleon crossed the Alps in bright sunshine, riding a mule. David has done him on a rearing white horse against storm clouds and snow. It's pure propaganda.'

'And you think Sir Terence, too, would like to be viewed in that way?'

'Exactly.'

'And Alan Whear?'

'He had two things in common with Sir Terence: his gross vanity and his contempt for women. Of course, I didn't get that properly until I saw him with his wife. It was unbelievable. She's cleverer, she earns more, she's much more stylish, and he treated her like shit. It made me angry.' Her face darkened. The curve of her mouth was now set in a hard line. 'It was about anger, all this.' She spat out the words. 'Anger at the way men behave. I meant to use him the way women are used. I wanted him vulnerable, then I wanted to tell him to fuck off. And if he'd made a fuss, then so much the better. Let it rip.'

'To punish your husband?'

'Of course. Also to give Niki Whear the excuse to kick the bastard out. But mostly I wanted to embarrass the hell out of Terry and what he's become. I had to push it to the point where he couldn't pretend any more. I had to do something extreme to get through his slobby self-satisfaction. I was angry, yes.'

'With yourself?'

'Of course. I was furious with myself. I'd let myself down. I couldn't believe I was the object of a man's contempt. What I vowed I'd never be. I couldn't believe it. You act for the best. You adapt. Then one day you wake up and you find you're living in a prison of lies, of half truths. How could I not have seen it happening? How could I have been so blind? I was very ashamed.'

There was a silence. She complimented him on the wine. He thanked her and lapsed into thought.

'Yes. It was meant as punishment for all three of us,' she said to herself. She looked up at Bewick. She watched him for a few seconds. Then suddenly she was caught in the full beam of his attention, sober and searching.

'Do you have any theories about what happened to Alan Whear?' he asked.

'No.'

'None at all?' He seemed mystified that she should know nothing.

'I've thought about it, of course. Because his being killed doesn't make sense to me. I think it must have come out of something in his past life which I didn't know about. He didn't seem to be aware of any threat.'

'Who knew about your involvement with him?'

'Sir Terence would be more interested in avoiding scandal than murdering a lover of mine, if that's what you mean.'

'You sound very sure.'

'Accuse Sir Terence of a *crime passionnel* and he'd think you were talking about Häagen-Dazs. Did you speak to him tonight?'

'Only in a general way. Gio Jones has interviewed him.'

'Ah, yes. How well do you know Inspector Jones?'

'Known him for years.'

'What do you think of him?'

'He's very clever, very astute. He disguises it as well

as he can, but of all the cops I've met, he's the one I'd choose.'

'To be in your team?'

'Yes.'

'I'm glad we got on, then. Will you apologize to him for me – for avoiding talking to him properly, I mean. I wanted to speak to you first.'

'Sure. And who do you think might have guessed about your involvement with Whear?'

'What difference would it make to know that?'

Bewick looked at her for a moment. Then: 'Hasn't it occurred to you there might be someone – not your husband – who is in love with you? Who loathed the idea of your being involved with Whear?'

She looked at him in wide-eyed surprise. 'As a matter of fact it hasn't occurred to me. I suppose it's possible.'

'Maybe someone within the college, who believed in the collegiate thing, was fierce about the reputation of the community . . . someone who had a dread of scandal, someone obsessed. He could have convinced himself that the destruction of Whear was the only way of averting a disastrous scandal and of saving you, as he thought, from yourself.'

She didn't reply. He waited a few moments and then asked her, 'Does that make sense to you?'

'Yes. Unfortunately, it does.'

'Do you have anybody in mind whom it might apply to?'

'No. It makes sense because I could see it happening. I know how obsessive life in college can make emotionally stunted people. You know Alan was in the army?'

'Yes.'

'I thought it was something to do with those days. I hate the idea of it being to do with me. Do you really think it might be?'

'It's one of the possibilities. Should be thought about. Can you think of anyone?' She didn't reply. 'I've been told that Dr Miller –'

'No, no. Brian's just a dreamer. He wrote me a sonnet sequence once. Ten really quite good poems. We were very much younger then. They were a sort of warning against marrying. Wiser than he knew. He thought they were anonymous, poor man. No, he's an idealist, a fantasist. He's vain, too; couldn't bear the idea of a refusal.'

'A description that might fit any number of violent men.'

'I can't believe that he –' She stopped.

'What?'

'Since, I suppose, the beginning of last year, I'd always thought of him as a lightweight. He has a sort of gravitas now. Perhaps something happened to him. My God, I'm beginning to doubt him myself . . . What do you think?'

'I don't know enough to have an opinion.'

She looked at him, her head to one side, as if she didn't believe this. The electric light on her hair shone like a source of light itself.

'Really, I don't,' Bewick insisted. 'And then there's

Professor O'Keefe. How much do you know about him?'

'You do have a habit of scoring bull's-eyes, don't you?'

'Chief Inspector Jones is very observant.'

'Yes, I suspected he was. Well, Brendan is certainly one of the obsessives I was talking about. He has a loopy belief that he can convert me, make me see the light of God. I'm sick of it. The man is guilt-driven, eaten away by it. And as far as I can tell, his religion is of the most miserable kind, all pain and weepy redemption. Horrible. And –' She broke off, frowning. Bewick waited. She glanced up at him and realized he was waiting for her to go on. 'And,' she began again, 'I'm not sure how much he's aware of it, but this whole conversion thing is like trying to enforce an intimacy . . .' She laughed. 'Spiritual harassment. It ought to be an indictable offence.'

Bewick nodded. 'Gio Jones was telling me how obsessed O'Keefe seemed to be with martyrdom and methods of execution.'

'I've heard it all, I sometimes think that it's a symptom of something deeply sick and that his religion is just a fig leaf for some grim and disgusting perversion.' She was quiet for a moment. Then she looked up at Bewick and said with no conviction, 'I should go.'

'Of course. There was one more thing . . .'

'Yes?'

'Gio Jones told me about another of the fellows he was talking to, who was in the army, about his being

Catholic . . . I mean fiercely partisan. It's unusual in my experience and I wondered if Gio had got it right.'

'The Bursar, you mean? Oh, Nicholas Cranesmith is fierce enough. He's had some bad things happen to him, despite his good career.'

Bewick described to her what Schrager had told him about his journey in Cranesmith's company, when coffee was spilt on him. 'Peter Schrager thinks Cranesmith is more than a little crazy; very neurotic.'

'Well, a loveless marriage can do all sorts of damage. I've never understood why people turn to God in such circumstances, but they seem to. Faith touches the oddest people.'

'Are you a believer yourself?' Bewick asked.

'No. The origin of matter is a mystery. That's as far as I go. Even if the physicists come up with their theory of everything, they're not going to get over that one.'

She finished her wine. 'Do you still think that Alan's death was something to do with me?' she asked.

'It's possible. I have to keep thinking about it.'

'Why were you asking about Nick Cranesmith in terms of his religion?'

'I don't know. It's another passion. We're dealing with a very strange case, very self-contradictory.'

'You really think Alan might have been killed for religious reasons?' she asked in disbelief.

Bewick indicated the copy of the *Cambridge Evening News*, with its murderous main story. 'Well,' he said, 'the killings in Ulster aren't about the Pizza Hut franchise.'

*

The road passed under a long march of pylons, diminishing to the wide horizon of the fens. A couple of miles later, Karen found herself driving past a verge fronting a hundred metres of high wall. Ahead, stone blocks curved out across the verge to mark the entrance. She slowed and turned in. Two notices: one asking drivers to announce their business to the answerphone set into the gate column; the second giving the name of the house – Ealand Priory.

After saying she had an appointment with Sir Michael Dowling and that she was with CRSI, Karen was told she must move through the gates as soon as they opened. Two CCTV cameras high on the columns watched her. Moments later, she saw vertical and horizontal bolts slide open. The tall, wrought-iron gates parted slowly to let her through.

Although she didn't know what to expect, the house was a surprise. After driving through the gates, Karen entered a shallow belt of woodland, which blocked her view of the house. As she emerged from it, the road, which was raised on a low causeway, swept off to the right. It took the eye to a small bridge over the river and then to what appeared to be a grand Victorian school with a large chapel attached.

Dowling's secretary led the way through the big house. To Karen it looked like an old film set. The secretary stopped at a pair of carved doors, knocked and entered. Another woman looked up from a computer and shook her head.

'No? Any idea . . .?'

The woman shook her head again.

'OK.' The secretary withdrew.

Karen had been looking out of the window. 'Is that really a church, or chapel or whatever?'

'No, just a hall. It's called the great hall. Sir Michael uses it for entertaining, really. There's a chapel off it, which is quite small. I'll try to find him, if you wouldn't mind waiting.' She led Karen back through the house, along the corridor connecting the main reception rooms. She showed her into a drawing room. 'I'll try to organize some tea.'

'No need. I'm fine.'

'Won't be long.'

The secretary left. Karen hadn't liked her company. She had had the feeling that everything about her was constantly being judged, from her car to her accent.

Schrager was returning from London by train, which was late. He got off at Ely.

'Mr Schrager?' A good-looking man in his thirties sat in an open sports car outside the modest ticket office.

'Yes?'

'Welcome to the fens. I'm here to fetch you. I think Sir Michael meant to come himself, but I couldn't find him . . .'

'Good of you. Sorry to have kept you.'

The man reached a hand out of the car to be shaken. 'I'm Robin Coleridge. I'm writing the great man's biography, but that's not the half of it,' he said, with a self-mocking laugh.

They drove out of Ely and north-east into the fens.

They passed a prosperous-looking farm in an island of trees, surrounded by black fields. Schrager kept his eyes on it as they passed.

Coleridge chuckled. 'You'd think, wouldn't you, that places like that were only made possible because they drained the fens. Not true. The fens were always one of the richest parts of England. You only have to look at the churches.' He drove on in silence for some minutes, humming to himself.

'This may seem a dumb question to ask his biographer,' Schrager said eventually, 'but do you know Sir Michael well?'

Coleridge laughed. 'Not particularly. I'm working on it. Shall I tell you the story so far?'

Coleridge told him of Dowling's rough-end-of-Kentish-Town childhood, of his strong mother and feckless father, his wheeling and dealing as a truant teenager, his attempts at proper jobs, his eventual reversion to what he knew best – dealing – from which had come fortune, fame and honour.

'Why has he ended up out here?' Schrager asked.

'It's not like other parts of England. That's to say, socially speaking. It's more egalitarian, a bit tougher, a bit more Australian, if you know what I mean. I think Michael likes that. He likes being Lord of the Manor, but he likes being it somewhere where most people don't value the fact that you are. He'd feel very uncomfortable in your average home-counties grand house.'

'How grand is his house here?'

'It's meant to be a small, late-Tudor palace with its own chapel. In fact, it yells fake at you. It was built for the Honourable James Charles Macey, just before the First World War. He was a fantasist. If you were to give him the benefit of the doubt, you could, I suppose, call him a Romantic. That's to say, a late-eighteenth-century hippie who wanted to live in a haunted abbey, who dabbled in the occult, who would like to have believed in the powers of darkness, who went walking in the mountains to experience the sublime, who ate opium and so on. Except he built the thing in 1912. It's full of completely unnecessary hiding places, secret doors and so on.'

Schrager was bored by now and only took in the last few words of this. Dutifully he asked, 'What sort of hiding places?'

'Oh, you know the sort of thing. There's a window seat. You release a hidden catch and the seat lifts up. There's a ladder down into a secret room. That sort of stuff. Priests' holes. I mean, what the hell do you *do* with them, apart from show them to your dinner guests?'

'Well, quite.'

'The whole place is sort of Hollywood baronial. It annoys me, actually. I mean, imagine having the money to build something like that, and then building something like that. But I suppose I don't have to love it, do I?'

'Does Sir Michael love it?'

'Sure. But it suits him. He isn't a purist. He doesn't have any historical education to burden him. As far as he's concerned, it's fun and it's romantic. Jolly good luck to him. The cedars of Lebanon are nice.'

Karen looked about her. It was a large, white-panelled room, with a carved fireplace and tall, glazed doors leading to a corridor, which had matching doors opposite opening out on to a terrace. Below the terrace was a lawn with a big, old tree in the middle of it. There was water lying in the fields beyond.

The room looked as if it had been sorted by an interior designer. It had none of the muddle of a family home. Everything went together. It occurred to Karen that she didn't know whether Dowling was married or not, whether there was a wife involved in all this domestic smartness. There were coffee-table books on the coffee table, on art and the countryside. None of them really interested her. Next to the books was a pile of magazines. She found a copy of the *New Yorker* and began to look at it. Some minutes later, the secretary came in.

'Sorry about this. I can't locate him.'

''s cool. I'm fine.'

'You don't mind waiting?'

'No, I'm fine.'

'I'll look outside.'

A few minutes later, Karen saw her, walking across the lawn away from the house. She looked at her watch. The waiting was beginning to irritate. Something in the panelling in the corner beyond the fireplace caught her eye – part of it was in fact a door. She went over and pushed it open.

Beyond was a surprise. A big, stone-floored gallery with a vaulted ceiling led through to a stable yard beyond. Tables stood along each side of the gallery, and behind them were rows of hooks. Above the hooks, echoing the patient heads of the horses in the stables, the preserved masks of foxes and small deer stared glass-eyed across at one another. On tables and hooks, the riding kit – hard hats, silks, lunge whips, toppers, boots, crops, gloves, jackets, Barbours, capes – all immaculately cleaned, folded, gleaming. It smelt of leather. And money.

Karen returned to the drawing-room. The secretary had disappeared from the empty gardens. The carriage clock on the mantelpiece uttered an impossibly delicate chime.

Karen went back into the gallery, leaving the door open behind her. She walked to the far end. The stable yard was startlingly clean. The only mess she could see were the few wisps of hay that had fallen from the horses' mouths. As she walked into the yard, she was the centre of attention: big, brown, equine eyes rolled, necks craned, ears twitched; one sniffed and snorted.

When she heard the other sound, she first thought it was a digestive rumble from a horse further up the yard. Then she realized it was a human grumble: an angry man.

'Jesus, Jesus, Jesus!' Then more inarticulate grunts of disgust and anger. She could also hear straw being shifted around. She moved quietly closer, but the noise stopped, as if the man sensed her presence. She walked normally to the stable where the noise had come from.

Her head appearing in the doorway cut the light and he turned.

'What?'

'I'm looking for Sir Michael Dowling.'

'Who the hell are you?' He was very aggressive. 'What're you creeping around for?'

'I'm with CRSI. We have an appointment with him. So I'll fuck off, shall I?'

He looked at her silently. He stood stock still in the mess of the kicked-around straw bed, wearing a suit and tie, glistening with sweat. She recognized him as Dowling from photos and his TV appearances. He was smaller than she expected, a bit overweight but clearly energetic and, at this moment, looking frightened. What was all this about? A new therapy – straw kicking? Keep your spiritual balance – get shit on your shoes. Weeurrd.

'Who are you?'

'Karen Quinney.'

Silence. Then, 'OK. So why did you come out here?'

'Nobody could find you. I got fed up with waiting. I saw the horses. So –'

'Wasn't the stable yard locked?'

'I came through that place where you keep all the kit.'

'From the drawing-room?'

'If that's what you call it. My mum'd call it the lounge.'

'Fair enough. Would you mind going back there? I'll join you in a couple of minutes.'

When Karen returned to the drawing-room, Schrager had arrived. Robin Coleridge had joined the search for Dowling. Karen told Schrager about her encounter with him. She would have said more, but the woman Karen had seen earlier at the computer opened the door and another, older woman brought in a tray of tea with scones, cream and jam.

A minute later, Dowling came in. He was transformed. He'd taken his jacket off and was now wearing a sweater and an open-necked shirt. He was at ease, looking like a more authoritative version of Gio Jones, minus an inch or three on the waistline.

He smiled at Karen. 'Listen. I'm sorry we kicked off like that . . .'

'Forget it. It's fine. Honest.'

Karen introduced Peter Schrager.

'The director of CRSI?' asked Dowling.

'That's right.'

'Good. And you . . .?' he asked, turning to Karen.

'She's one of my best officers,' said Schrager.

'Right.'

'She's ex-police and has run a number of witness-protection programmes.'

'And would the witnesses be able to recommend you?' Dowling asked.

'They were alive and healthy when I left them.'

Schrager shot Karen a glance. Had she sounded

stroppy? He didn't like the way Dowling was looking at her.

'How about pouring the tea?' Dowling said.

Schrager picked up the milk. 'I'll do it.'

'Do you ride, Sir?' Karen asked very formally, trying to widen the distance between herself and Dowling.

'Yeah. Time to time. Why do you ask? Do you?'

'I was thinking about the security implications, that's all.'

'Yeah, right.'

'Can you tell us what sort of threat we should be considering?' Schrager asked. 'Or are we talking more generally than that? Just a security audit?'

'Someone wants to kill me,' Dowling said, as if it was obvious.

'I see. You've been receiving hate mail?'

'No. Not exactly.'

'Are we talking about a person or an organization?'

A short hesitation, then Dowling said, 'A person, an individual.'

'So it's personal, it's somebody we might be able to identify?'

'We might.' Dowling sounded very dubious.

'Good. Well . . .' Schrager waited. Dowling put some jam on a scone. It looked like displacement activity to Karen. 'Obviously,' Schrager went on, 'we need all the information we can get; we need to gauge the scale of the threat.'

'It's real, believe me.'

'Sure, but . . . If you're concerned, about it, Sir, I can guarantee watertight discretion.'

'Listen, there's someone out there who wants to blow my head off. I want you to stop them.'

'Without knowing who they are.'

'You got it. Protect me. Blanket protection. I want blanket protection,' Dowling repeated, as if he was pleased by having thought of the term.

Schrager took a deep breath. 'I see. Do we have a time limit on this?'

For some reason, Dowling found this very funny. He laughed. 'You mean how long do I want to live? Is that what you mean?'

Schrager barely smiled. 'I meant how long would you be prepared to afford us, Sir?'

'What sort of figures are we talking?'

'Well, it's front-end loaded. There are set-up costs. Then there's vehicle hire. Chopper hire. Surveillance kit. But the core expense is the team. You'll need an eight-person team. That's three hundred K plus per annum.'

'For a moment there, I thought you were going to frighten me.'

'You can live with that?'

'Can I live without it? Yes, I can live with that. For as long as it takes. Good excuse to get rid of those sodding horses, for a start. One of 'em cost a hundred thousand guineas. Would you believe? Dunno what got into me.'

'So can you tell us how the threat's been communicated?'

'It hasn't. I just know it's there. Right?'

'You put us in the position of driving in fog, Sir.'

'Just assume. It'll be someone with a gun. That's what I reckon.'

'And how far back does the threat go, Sir? Why are you talking to us now, particularly? Has something happened?'

'Just assume. Do you want the job?'

Watching Dowling, Karen was looking for some sign of paranoia, of neurosis. Some betrayal of the inner state which could convince this well-fed success-story suit that some psycho wanted to deconstruct his skull. She could see none. He didn't look scared, either.

'If we agreed to take it on, when would you want us to start?'

'Now.'

'I'd need two or three days to assemble the team.'

'All right.'

'What sort of security equipment do you already have, Sir?'

'The usual. You want me to show you?'

'Be helpful.'

'I'm serious about two things,' Dowling said as they walked through the house. 'Staying alive and making money.'

The grounds outside sloped gently. Ealand Priory and its estate occupied a low fen island of clay and gravel in a curve of the river. Nearby were the drainage channels of Picton's Eau and the newer lode, which had been engineered by Sir Charles Ortham a hundred and fifty years ago to protect the previous house on the site.

Trees began several hundred metres away, beyond the park.

'Do you own those woods?' Schrager asked.

'Of course.'

While Dowling was showing Schrager the alarm systems already in place, and introducing him to the resident staff, Karen went out to fetch her car. Coleridge met her in the hallway and introduced himself. He told Karen about the biography he was writing, his place in the household. Karen could see he was flirting but didn't discourage him; at least he was the right age.

Coleridge escorted her to the car. 'Who found Sir Michael?' he asked.

'I did. He was talking to his horses.'

'He does that. They're Janine's, not his.'

'His wife's?'

'No. Live-in lover – ex. She walked out about six months ago and left him with her horses. Fair enough – he bought the valuable ones. Are you guys going to take the job?'

'We might. I don't know. Do you know what it is?'

Coleridge chuckled. 'Yes, of course.'

'Do you like him?'

The boyish charm flickered then returned. 'What sort of question is that? I'm employed to write about him. He gives me an office and about forty minutes a day or less. It's not a normal relationship.'

'You don't, do you?'

Coleridge looked at her, seriousness ghosting across his face for a moment, then he laughed again. 'Of course I do.'

Karen shrugged and got into her car. He closed the door for her. As she eased the car through the yard and round to the front of the house, in the mirror she saw him looking drained and miserable.

Schrager and Karen finally drove away from Dowling's house.

'What is it about the rich? I've noticed it before. How they make their houses like posh hotels, sort of dead.'

'Yeah.' Schrager wasn't interested.

'He didn't sound very fazed by it, did he? The threat, I mean. Whatever it is. Reckon he's telling the truth?'

'I don't know.'

Karen told him about Dowling kicking straw. 'Weird or what?'

'Weird.'

'Could be to do with the horses. They're his ex-girlfriend's. She walked out on him not long ago.'

'Makes sense. Maybe you saw him deciding to sell them off.'

'Yeah. Figures.'

'So are you going to be all right with this?'

'I'll be OK.'

'He'll be a trophy client. He's got more connections than the cerebral cortex. It'll do the company good.

Frasier will organize the team. You'll have to take your shifts, but mostly you'll be there to nurse the client. You know, if you hadn't turned up on our doorstep, I think I'd've had to have invented you.'

8

Bewick and Jones sat outside the pub, talking in undertones, drinking Adnams.

'So what did Miranda Griffiths tell you?' Jones asked.

Bewick squinted against the light. He shifted his chair to let the young barmaid squeeze past.

'Ta,' she said, pert. She couldn't be more than eighteen, cheeky little wench. For a moment, Jones felt like asking her if she was in fact old enough to be doing bar work. Then he realized he was just jealous of her flirtatiousness towards Bewick. He was annoyed with himself. And he was hungover. He'd not drunk that much at the college dinner, but had put away too many glasses of supermarket Scotch telling Eilean all about it when he got home. That morning he'd tried an early morning jog, but it had made his headache worse. He realized Bewick hadn't answered.

'Well?'

'Sorry?'

'Lady Miranda Griffiths. What did she tell you?'

'She confirmed what Niki Whear said.'

'*Really?* What on earth did she do it for?'

'Self-punishment, she said.'

'That's it, is it? Self-punishment.'

'Yes. She didn't like him. She also wanted to give Niki Whear an excuse to give him the elbow.'

'Get off. Loadabollocks.'

'It's what she said.'

'And you believe her, do you?'

'It's what she said. She's complex. I don't think she's just a rough trade merchant. I don't disbelieve her.'

'Hmm.' Jones was cynical, non-committal. He was confused. As far as what Lady Miranda had told Bewick, well, he couldn't see it, but he was experienced enough not to write off what he didn't understand. He took a deep breath and looked around. The Ibuprofen had at last got rid of his headache.

They were overlooking the quay and the weir, built at the head of the navigation in the days when Cambridge was one of the most important ports in eastern England. Now, young men in boaters competed to punt tourists down the river and back, Anglo-Saxon gondoliers.

'So where are we?'

'Moving towards the centre. Slowly.'

'You think so?' Jones was cynical.

'I think so.'

'You were going on to Eilean the other evening about a crime of passion. Were you just showing off or did that actually mean something?'

'I find crimes of passion difficult to get on terms with.'

'I'm not surprised. You're a seventeen-stone

refrigerated fitness-freak. Should think they scare you shitless.'

'I have to keep telling myself that they're about control, then they make sense. Like most violence, they're about despair and control . . .'

Jones was surprised. Bewick was absorbed, self-involved, down. It was as if he was talking about himself. The ugly shadow that lay over Bewick's reputation was the rumour of his capacity for violence. Jones had never associated Bewick with despair, though. His appeal lay in his apparently steady-going nature, his consistent cheerfulness, which could settle into an odd placidity when he was concentrating on his own thoughts. But then he had always been a mystery. Jones had long ago given up trying to predict anything he did.

'Well, I thought the lot of them were sitting on their hands.'

'How do you mean, Gio? Who?'

'The lot I was talking to: that woman Svenson, and O'Keefe and Cranesmith. Oh, and Miller.'

'What do you mean, sitting on their hands?'

'Controlling themselves. They should get out more. Seriously they should. Bunch of neurotic gits.'

'Yes . . .' Bewick was off in his own thoughts again.

Jones made a face. 'D'you really believe this, though? That one of these ivory-tower inmates is out of control?'

Bewick looked at Jones as if he'd just woken up. 'What was Miller doing the night Whear was killed?'

'He was staying with his mother, he said. Something about her snoring.'

'I see.' Bewick nodded, thoughtful again.

The rain had stopped. Sally paused on the Old Jewry Bridge. Beyond was the pool which divided the upper river from the lower. A couple of punts were being mishandled round each other, near the frothing outfall of the upper river – much shrieking and laughter. She didn't at first notice what the big teenager on the far bank was doing. With two younger ones giggling beside him, he was searching for stones and, when he found one, he was throwing it with considerable accuracy at a duck he had already injured.

Sally rejected shouting, as her voice would be lost in the general mayhem from the punts. Then she saw Bewick sitting outside the pub with Chief Inspector Jones. As soon as she saw him, she realized he had noticed the boy, too.

'Oi!'

Bewick's roar cut across the forty metres or so, silencing nearby conversations. The boy turned. He saw Bewick. He seemed to calculate that, what with Bewick having to get to the bridge before crossing the upper river, he was safe enough. He deliberately picked up another stone and threw it hard at the injured bird. It missed. Then he turned to give Bewick a hard stare. But Bewick wasn't there. He was vaulting the gate of the weir. One step on the narrow brickwork beyond and he was across. A moment of disbelief, then the boy began running.

Jones shouted at Bewick to leave it. Then he started after him. He was terrified. If Bewick caught the boy – Christ! At first there seemed no hope of it. Bewick was running at no more than three-quarters of the boy's speed. But his pace was even. The boy was sprinting and quickly exhausted himself. They were barely visible in the distance when Jones saw Bewick catch the boy, turn his shoulder and throw him to the ground. The boy lay there for a moment, then suddenly scrambled to his feet and ran back towards Jones.

It took Jones a moment to realize that the boy was now charging towards him. God! I don't want any part of this, he thought. He now *wanted* Bewick to catch the little bastard.

Bewick did, about fifty metres from him. Jones shouted at Bewick again to forget it.

Bewick was holding the boy, who was tall, about fifteen, muscular. 'Empty your pockets.'

'Who d'you think you are?'

Without appearing to hurry, Bewick turned the boy around and forced his arm up his back to a point just short of pain.

'John – Leave it out!' Jones was panting as he came up to them.

'You're getting quite fit, Gio.'

Bewick's voice, Jones heard with relief, was in neutral. If he was angry it was under control.

'Empty your pockets.' Nothing happened. 'Tell him to empty his pockets, Gio, will you?'

'Do it, lad. Please.'

Jones's real fear of what Bewick might do was written all over him. The boy emptied his pockets. They yielded the ID Bewick was looking for. Firmly and slowly he pushed the boy back against the nearest tree. Then he returned the money and bits and pieces to him. The boy pocketed them. He licked his lips. His eyes were flicking. Jones could see he was now frightened.

'John . . .' Jones was ignored. He felt sick.

Bewick was looking at a plastic card – membership of a video club with the boy's name and address on it. He studied it for a few seconds as if to memorize it. Then Jones saw him raise his eyes to the boy's. The boy couldn't hold his gaze. Bewick said nothing, but continued to look. He was about two feet from the boy, taller but not overwhelmingly so. As he watched, it seemed to Jones that the boy shrank in size. Bewick didn't move. He just stared. Once the boy tried to meet the stare, but immediately switched away. His face taughtened. He began to sweat.

Jones noticed the smell as the boy's bottom jaw began to quiver. Jones looked down. The pale jeans were stained. A mixture of piss and shit was running down the inside of the boy's leg. Bewick handed back the card. He had to press it into the boy's hand.

Bewick walked away and Jones followed.

*

Sally, still on the bridge, was transfixed by what she'd seen. She told herself not to be sentimental. She imagined what might have happened if the boy had tried to defend himself against Bewick. It was all very fine, thinking of Bewick as a defender of the defenceless. She reminded herself of what she had once seen him do.

She looked at her watch. She was late. She hurried away. Despite her scepticism, she knew she was glad to have seen what she had.

Back at the pub, a small crowd had gathered. The injured duck, a female mallard, had been captured by one of the punt gondoliers. A debate was going on about what to do with it. Bewick appeared. He went to the woman who was holding it and took it from her with a firmness that silenced any possible protest. He handed it to Jones.

'The Chief Inspector will look after it,' he said, and headed for his car.

Jones caught up with him a moment or two later. 'You bastard. You bastard. I'm not looking after it. You sort it out.'

'We'll find a vet, Gio.'

The vet said the wing was badly bruised but not broken. Given proper care, it would soon be usable. He bound the wing to the duck's body. He gave Bewick and Jones the name of an animal sanctuary which might accept the bird.

Jones sat with the duck nestled in a cardboard box on his knees, as Bewick drove him back to City West.

'By the way, meant to tell you – I was talking to Cranesmith, the Bursar fellow – army type.'

'I know.'

'He was telling me that he knew Whear before he gave him the job at St Anne's.'

Bewick shot a glance at him. 'Knew him? How?'

'From when Whear was in the army. Cranesmith came across him in Ulster. Whear was in one of these hard-man outfits, difficult to get into, so that was recommendation enough for Cranesmith.'

'I see.'

The first person they saw as they turned into City West's car park was lanky DS Frank Dalmeny, anorak ultra-cyber nut. Unusually, he looked quite pleased with himself.

'Hello, Boss. What you got in there?'

'A gorilla suit. What does it look like?'

'Looks like a duck.'

'So why ask?'

'What you doin' with a duck?'

'Ex-Chief Super Bewick has adopted it as his charity of the month. Ask him about it and he'll probably beat you to a liquid pulp.'

Dalmeny laughed. It sounded like someone coughing in church. 'Hallo, Mr Bewick. Good to see you.' He turned to Jones again. 'Have I got news for you!'

'What?'

'I've been on Holmes. Whear – the victim – he had a record. Robbery an' all the trimmings.'

'Did he, by God!'

'Do you love me?'

'I think we might be obliged to.'

'Yeah.' Frankie walked off. Even in his moment of triumph he looked as if the mortgage rate had just doubled.

'Well?' Jones looked at Bewick. 'That changes things, dunnit?'

In his messy office, Gio Jones looked at the notes that Frank Dalmeny had made. With the duck in its box tucked under his arm, Bewick looked over his shoulder. Whear's crime had been robbery, as Dalmeny had said.

Not a competent one: Whear and his accomplice, Simmonds, had been picked up on video as they robbed a country house. The man who had supplied the number plates on the car they'd used had come forward. The antiques they'd taken were invisibly marked. The police found most of them in a lock-up shared by Whear and Simmonds. They were on remand for three months before the case came up. Agreeing to plead guilty from the outset gave them maximum discount and served them well. Previous good character, good army service record, character witnessing and time already served led to a modest sentence.

Jones looked round at Dalmeny. 'Anything else on either of them?'

'No, Boss. Not a snivel.'

'Do we have a last known address for this Simmonds?'

Dalmeny frowned and crossed the room towards them. He pointed a long, bony finger at the paper. In the middle of a complicated doodle, Jones managed to decipher 17 Eden Row. And then, woven into the doodle itself, the name of a fen-edge village, Monkswell.

'Thanks, Frank. Run everything you can on this Simmonds, eh?'

'OK.'

Once Dalmeny had gone, Jones shut the door of his office and turned to Bewick. 'Well? What d'you reckon? Reckon they came away with something on that robbery? A painting or something?'

'And negotiated with the insurers, you mean?'

'That's it. Perhaps all that incompetence was deliberate. "Look at us. Poor little amateurs. Never do it again, Your Honour." Perhaps they didn't need to do it again.'

'And when it came to pay day, Whear got naughty?'

'So Simmonds banged him. What d'you reckon?'

'Why in the college?'

Jones was silent. Like Bewick, he knew that people usually commit crimes at a location where they feel relatively safe. He shrugged. 'It's possible though, isn't it? Using the college might have been to divert attention.'

'It's possible that Sir Terence Griffiths is so stuffed with pride that he couldn't bear to be cuckolded by a common porter.'

'In my dreams. God, the man's such a *twlch*!'

'But does it feel right?'

'Well . . . doesn't feel wrong. I don't know. Bloody hell.' Jones rubbed his face again. He yawned and apologized. 'I've been burning the candle a bit. Tell you what – that effing Griffiths could grease his way through a clapboard fence.'

Bewick laughed. He looked down at the duck in its box. 'So when are you going to get this poor creature sorted out?'

'I'm not. You do it. You've got the address.'

Bewick looked at him for a moment, then nodded. He made his way out. 'Keep me up to date on Simmonds, won't you?'

'I might.'

About twenty minutes later, there was a knock at Jones's door. Dalmeny reappeared. 'Something else I meant to tell you, Boss.'

'Yes?'

'Bloke who offered to put up the bail for Whear and Simmonds which was refused – yeah?'

'Yeah?'

'Bloke called Dowling. Michael Dowling. Wondered if it was the same Michael Dowling who goes on telly – who got the royal tap on the shoulder?'

Bewick's phone switched to the answering machine after four rings.

'Hi. Gio here. Just to tell you we're still getting no joy from Simmonds's number. We'll send a car over to Monkswell. Tomorrow morning, probably. We're a bit busy here. If we don't get a result then, I'll be asking for a warrant perhaps. How's the duck?'

*

Bewick arrived at the Wildfowl Sanctuary near Wicken Fen. The young woman volunteer who was on duty, an undergraduate from the University Vet school, smiled as she saw the sombre care with which the big man handled the female mallard, which was clearly as relaxed as any wild creature could be in such circumstances. She was also aware of how relieved he was, once the brief formalities were over, to be rid of the reponsibility he had taken on.

Bewick went back to his car. On the bonnet he spread out one of the Ordnance Survey maps he kept in the glove box. Rain began to spot it. Bewick glanced up at the thick blue-grey cloud. Monkswell was five miles away to the south-east.

Bewick drove across the fens through a storm of rain, which threatened the already half-drowned land with an imminent return to its pre-drained state. The roads were narrow, with occasional passing places. They were dead straight, following lines drawn on the drainage map by Vermuyden and his Dutch engineers more than three hundred years before.

The rain pooled in black fields. Some were completely covered, sky-reflecting sheets. Green crops were bowing under the weight of wind and water. Trees threshed. The road dog-legged, coming straight again, parallel now with a drainage lode which once carried water transport to the distant fen-edge villages.

He could see the fen edge now, a low blur of rising ground, blown rags of cloud moving quickly over it. Bright-green weed narrowed the grey water of the lode. A steel box bridge crossed it, choked with ash and alder, relic of a forgotten railway. As he reached the fen edge, the landscape changed. The straight lines of ditch and road and field gridding the old bed of the sea marsh ended abruptly. The road wound around the curve of the ancient foreshore into the one-time port village of Monkswell.

Simmonds's house had been built by the council between the wars in the vernacular style of the district, on a generous piece of land.

As he was looking for somewhere to park, Bewick noticed a car outside Simmonds's house. He noticed it because it was occupied by two men. He slowed and took his time choosing a parking place. The men seemed to be arguing about something. The car was an old scarlet Sierra, sparkling clean. The men were close-cropped; tough. They looked like squaddies, but then most men did nowadays.

Bewick parked. As he was getting out, the Sierra started up and was moving off quickly before he was able to pick up on the number. It was H something three something. That was all he got. He had an image of the men, but it was a single snapshot. Given a properly conducted ID parade, Bewick might have found himself with a problem. Later, talking to Gio Jones, he found it difficult to explain this initial interest in the two men.

'It's because you're a cop. Or bloody should be,' Jones would impatiently reply. 'It's in your urine, darlin'.'

Bewick moved to the house and rang the bell. He rang it three times before he gave up.

He walked around the back to the garden, which was mostly vegetable plot. Somewhere to sit, somewhere to dry clothes, then the rest was lines of healthy-looking veg. in the healthy-looking soil. Bewick walked down the grass path to the end, where there was a black wooden hut with a corrugated-iron roof painted a blood-red magenta. It was unlocked.

Bewick stepped inside. Neat rows of cuttings and seedlings in pots, nowhere to hide or be hidden. Tools were hung on the wall. A pair of shears was hung between two nails. Bewick took it down. The blades were sharp and oiled. Surveying the rest of the tools, it looked as if they were equally well maintained. Bewick closed the door.

Now shut in, he stood, slowly turning on the spot. It was a well-ordered place. Even the old jacket and the cap hung on the door seemed just right. One more glance around before he went fixed on the only anomaly. Stuffed into the angle of roof and wall was a piece of cloth, some sort of heavy serge. It looked as if it were blocking a hole – gnawed or pecked by a bird or a rat, perhaps. But then it would surely have been patched properly, wouldn't it? All around was evidence of this. The replaced latch of the door was carved from beech. The opening split in a spade haft had been glued and bound. Chipped pots were repaired. There was even a weld to keep the window catch in commission for another few years.

Bewick pulled out the cloth. It kept its shape – it had been there for months, years even. It hadn't been folded, just stuffed into the darkest corner. As he suspected, there was no hole there to explain it. As soon as he began to open it out he realized what it was. It was a sandy-grey beret, its leather rim dry and rotting. He turned it over. The front had once had a badge on it, which had been torn off, leaving holes in the cap. Inside was a label. Bewick offered it to the fading light from the window. It read R. SIM-MONDS. The maker's label was also in place:

Kangol. Suppliers of clothing to HM Forces.

Bewick continued to study the beret. Then he carefully squashed it into its original folds and shoved it back where he had found it.

For his own interest, Bewick walked to the far end of the garden, where the ground beyond the fence fell suddenly away, marking the ancient edge of the fen. The cloud was thinning now and brightening. The wind was backing steadily to north-west. Spreading below him were the flat black fields, their horizon lost in the distant fog of moisture. Bewick turned to get the cold wind in his face. A tiny dot of colour caught his eye. Below him, near where the dark gleam of the road began, ruler straight, to push out across the fens, was the red Sierra. It took Bewick a moment to realize that it would be hidden from the road by a thicket of bramble. Who were they waiting for? If they *were* waiting. What were they doing there?

Bewick walked back down the garden. Without making it obvious, he kept an eye on the upstairs windows. Nothing moved. As he approached his car, he saw the red Sierra again. It drove past the end of Simmonds's road and disappeared.

Bewick drove away from the village along the Devil's Dyke, the huge defensive earthwork thrown up from fen to forest by an unknown Dark Age ruler, an ancient Maginot line. Eventually the road turned and cut through the ramparts.

It was a beautiful evening. The sun, setting in crimson cloud, shone through the huge envelope of a hot-air balloon which was drifting just above tree-top height, looking for somewhere to land. Bewick was nearing Bottisham when he saw the Sierra waiting in a side road. He tried to read its numberplate but got no further than last time. Moments later, it pulled out after him.

Bewick drove steadily back towards Cambridge; if anything, more slowly than usual. The Sierra kept station with him about four cars back until the round-about near the airport. It made to follow then kept going, roaring off back towards the fens.

Bewick parked the old Volvo outside Niki Whear's house.

When she answered the bell after the fourth ring, Niki Whear was poker-faced, defensive. This hardly altered when she saw who it was.

'I'm busy. What d'you want?'

'I'm looking for a mate of your husband's. Hoped you might be able to help.'

It was a simple request – like finding someone for the cricket club reunion; something like that. He was so casual, so easy, she didn't know whether to be pissed off or reassured.

'Who?'

'One of his army buddies, Simmonds.'

Her face darkened in suspicion. 'You been watching me or what?'

'The police want to talk to him. He's not at home. No, I haven't been watching you. I haven't seen you since you made me a cup of tea.'

She was indecisive. After a few moments she said, 'Come in, then.'

Niki Whear led the way into the living-room. A woman was sitting there. She was a similar age to Niki Whear, but fear and anxiety were making her look ten years older. Her face was grey, she was exhausted, defeated. She was clearly agitated by Bewick's intrusion.

'Sorry, Tina, m'love,' said Niki. 'Think we ought to talk to this fellow, though. Mr Bewick, this is Martine Simmonds. She's looking for him an' all.'

'We've had a missing-persons call, Guv.' Like a troubled giraffe, Frank Dalmeny peered round the doorpost into Gio Jones's office.

'Not now, Frankie.'

'You could be interested, Boss . . .'

'At the moment, Frank, I'm not interested in being interested.'

Jones was working his way through the Whear case-file, Crime No. 6491. He'd established in his own mind the complete uselessness of the witness statements.

The forensic report amounted to telling him that the victim was shot at short range with a hand gun. No drugs traceable in the fibres of his clothes. Great. Wow. The pathologist's report gave him little more. The exhibits file contained one small plastic toy. It was hopeless.

'Fair enough,' Dalmeny said. He unwound himself from the doorpost and disappeared.

Jones recognized his own symptoms. He was going over and over the material, praying he'd stumble on the vital connection. It was a substitute for changing the whole direction of the investigation, which he knew he was going to have to do and didn't want to. The matter of Simmonds, Whear's crime partner, was something he couldn't ignore. The fact that they couldn't locate him . . .

Jones sighed. He got up from his desk and stretched. He'd have to go after Dalmeny. He knew how sensitive the bugger could be. He felt different when he stretched. Less flab. He stood in front of the part of the window where he could get a bit of reflection. Chest out, stomach in. Disappointing. Still one of life's little tubs. Ah, well.

Dalmeny was washing a coffee-stained mug in the small utility room, the kettle steaming.

'Caught me at a bad moment, Frank,' Jones said.

'Fair enough.' Dalmeny did his best to stifle any satisfaction he felt at this apology. He seemed to be concentrating on the brown rims inside the mug into which he was now piling sugar. Dalmeny's touchiness was as legendary as his computer skills.

'So what was it, then?' Jones knew he'd have to wait. God Almighty, it was worse than dealing with a teenager. 'Any bearing on the Whear murder?' he asked gently.

'Maybe,' said Dalmeny, secretive, aloof. He poured water into his coffee. The way he did it took Jones back to childhood and posh Mrs Llewellyn ignoring her servants when she met them in the cornershop. Don't get sarcastic, Jones reminded himself.

'So what've you unearthed with that brilliant machine of yours?'

Clink, clink, clink from the stirring spoon. No reply. Gawd, this was going to be a long one. Had he got the patience?

'Missing person, you said?' Jones waited. 'Cross-referencing, was it?'

Dalmeny shrugged. What the hell did that shrug mean?

'This missing person,' Jones said, still very patient, 'has something to do with the Whear case . . .' He suddenly realized who it might be. 'This missing person isn't his mate, Simmonds, is it?'

Another shrug.

Jones knew he was right. He counted to ten. 'Well, when you're in a mood to impart the information,' he said, struggling to keep the sarcasm out of his voice, 'you'll know where to find me.'

'No need to be like that,' said Dalmeny.

'Like what?'

'Like sarcastic like that.'

'Is the missing person Simmonds?'

'Yeah.'

Jones made one last effort to be warm, friendly, paternal. 'Let's hear it then, Frank.'

'Went off to work Friday. Hasn't been seen since.'

'Anything else? Who reported it?'

'His wife. She wasn't that worried. She tried his workshop on the phone – nothing. So she rang the next-door business – some sort of breakers' yard – and they said he wouldn't be there 'cos the place was cut off by the river flooding. So she thought he was on one of his benders. Naughty dog.'

'And that's fairly common, is it?'

'Seems to be. Her statement just said he went off now and again and then he'd come back with his tail between his legs and looking like a dead cod.'

'Anyway, she's worried now?'

'Yeah.'

'OK, Frank. Right. Thanks. Where's this workshop, then?'

The approach road to Simmonds's workshop was a potholed track lined with the debris of illegal tipping, run-down warehousing, a compound full of dogs and the windowless shell of a burnt-out garage.

Baynes stopped the car well short of the track's end. Ahead was a quagmire. He and Jones walked along the verge where the grass had bound in the mud. Across the swamp was a workshop: asbestos roof, bricks were the cheapest commons, the windows peeling steel, thirty, forty years old.

'Bloody hell. I might have known it.'

'What, Guv?'

'There's his bloody bike.'

'Whose bike?'

'Fucking typical.'

Bewick appeared around the corner of the building. He looked sombre.

'Hello, Gio ... Baynesie. Was going to save you the journey. But I'm glad you're here.'

'Oh yes? Why?'

'Come and see. I'd just dealt with a door when I heard you. Come round.'

Nothing'd changed, Jones reflected. Bewick still dishing out the orders, me still trotting along. To assert some independence, he insisted on putting on his wellies.

At the back of the building, Bewick had forced a lock. He stood back to let Jones lead the way into an engine-repair shop which was very warm inside. A big Lister gen-set stood stripped in the middle of it. In the far corner, a plywood and glass partition made a tiny office. As they walked across to it, the seeping smell grew stronger. The flies inside were audible.

'Oh, shit.'

As Jones opened the door to the small, partitioned-off space, the stench hit them like a warm fog. A man was sitting at the desk, head back, mouth open. As they entered, the back of his head exploded in angry buzzing. The flies formed a bizarre black halo around his head for a moment and then returned to their task. In his forehead, off centre, was the entry wound.

Grim and white-faced, Jones turned to Bewick. 'Remind you of anything?'

Bewick nodded. 'You'll find the bullet this time.'

'Yup.'

Part Two

Part Two

9

After stabilizing the crime scene, the first thing Jones thought about was preserving the muddy approach. The heavy rain had left very few prints on it: most of them would be those of Baynes, Bewick and Jones himself. He had a polythene pathway laid and he put a team to work making plaster casts of the very few prints there were. Jones then put in a request for extra officers. He submitted a revised budget, set the police surgeon to work and rang Arnold Sandham. As he left the workshop, Jones found Bewick by his bike, staring out over the sodden meadow which led to the river.

'What is it?'

'I was thinking about the flooding we've been having. Half the fens are under water. Coe Fen was a lake a few days ago.'

'So?'

'Did you see it down here?'

'No.'

'Looks as if the river got pushed up on to this meadow. See that line of debris? I wonder how deep it would have got over the other side?'

'Sure. Listen, have you got time for a pint?'

They headed up the track towards the old village of Chesterton, the big man balancing himself on the ultra-lightweight bike, the short, plump one walking briskly beside.

'You're definitely fitter, Gio. Look at you.'

'Just concentrate on not falling off that pretentious machine, will you? It might stop you patronizing me. I've got a car waiting for me just there. You'd better push on, sonny.'

At their table outside the pub, they could hear rowing coaches abusing their squads. They caught occasional glimpses, between the houses below, of the boats slipping past.

'Well?' Jones said.

Bewick stared at the road, where nothing was now moving. There was an intake of breath, as if he were about to speak, but he didn't. His pale-grey eyes darkened under lowering lids.

Jones waited, then asked, 'I suppose it is the same bastard who did both, isn't it?'

'Yes.' Another silence, then Bewick added, 'Too much in common otherwise.'

'Like losing their criminal virginity together?'

'And the rest.'

'The rest?'

'They share their first crime. They share a stretch inside. They share not re-offending. They share a carbon-copy death.'

'So?'

'Do you know what they also had in common – I mean, before they robbed that house?' Bewick asked.

'Norraclue.'

'I've spoken to Niki Whear again. Simmonds's wife was there. Their men were in the army together. Same regiment.'

Bewick seemed excited by this. Jones couldn't see it.

'Oh, yes . . . the Bursar, Cranesmith – he told me that he gave Whear the job because he'd been in some sort of tough-nut regiment.'

'It was the AOR. Tough nut's about right.' Bewick smiled. 'Psychopaths to a man.'

'One of the special forces lot?'

'Yes. Air Operations Regiment.'

'Who learn how to kill people in several languages? What do you know about them?'

'Not a lot. Nobody does. But it opens a whole new can of worms, doesn't it?'

'Yeah.' Jones sounded depressed. 'I was really looking forward to it being a lust-maddened professor; y'know – Plato in one hand, shooter in the other. Who the hell'd want to knock off a pair of second-rate robbers who haven't even re-offended?'

'Charlie Smew might be able to tell us.'

'Oh, Gawd . . . I suppose he might.'

Smew was that rare thing, a man of violence who could organize and think. He was currently doing twelve years for GBH and taking an Open University degree in Industrial Archaeology.

'I'll arrange it,' Jones complained.

'Might be worthwhile.'

'I hate being condescended to by villains. Smew's one of the worst. I feel like saying, You're the one banged up, mate. You're the one with no women, wine or family life. You're the one who'll be damn near sixty when you get out. How dare you condescend to me? Bastard always does.'

Jones took a sip of beer. He looked up to see concern on Bewick's face. 'What is it?' he asked, chin up, cocky.

'You look wiped out, white as a sheet.'

Jones turned away. 'Tell you the truth, the blood and . . . that stink . . . made me want to puke.'

Bewick nodded as if he understood, as if he shared it. Except he looked solid as oak, healthy, tanned. 'Sure,' he said, a picture of sympathy.

A police car drew up beside them. DS Baynes got out of it.

'What d'you want?' Jones barked.

'Have a pint, Baynesie,' Bewick said.

'Oh ta, Sir, thanks. Adnams, if they got it.'

Bewick went into the bar.

'No need to call him "Sir", the bugger's a deserter. Wha' d'you want?'

''s funny, Boss. Don't know what it's about, really.'

'Well neither will we if you don't let us in on it.'

'Yeah, sorry . . . this bloke, Peters . . . Day before yesterday evening . . . He's got a small paint and body-panel shop off that track as leads to the victim's premises.'

'I know. So,' Jones prompted,' . . . day before yes-terday evening . . .?'

'Yeah. He saw this fellow go down to Simmonds's workshop. Peters noticed him because he looks just like that bloke who's always on the telly, whatsisname, Dowling, who's just been knighted.'

'For services to bent politicians.'

'Maybe.'

'I probably exaggerate. So what's funny about it? Apart from the fact that this knight of the realm may have been the murderer.'

'Well, this is it.'

'What is?' Bewick came out with a pint for Baynes, who repeated what he'd told Jones.

'And now I think it's my turn to tell you something,' Jones said with the air of a man holding a royal flush.

'I'm listening.'

'My favourite computer-nerd at the station came up with a titbit concerning our virgin criminals, Simmonds and Whear. Someone tried to put up bail for them but it was refused. That person was one Michael Dowling.'

'Let's go and find Mr Peters,' said Bewick. He locked his bike. Baynes drove them back.

Peters emerged from his paint shop in protective clothing, which was clouded with fine sprays of colour. Outside his office, Peters took off boots, gloves, hood and mask to reveal bristly red hair, a broad, unsmiling face and a steady, self-confident pair of blue eyes. He gave Jones a long glance and led the way into his modest office.

Peters had a surprising voice, light and squeaky. He told Bewick and Jones that he'd noticed the man because he looked so uneasy. Then he realized how like Sir Michael Dowling the man looked. Peters had seen Dowling on the news just the previous week.

Peters turned to Jones. 'Looks a bit like you, actually, except –'

'Except not so fat?'

'Well –'

'It's been said before,' said Jones with a friendly, tolerant smile – this bloke could be a key witness, for God's sake. 'Sir Michael plus a few kilos of best Welsh blubber, that's me. So, you saw this bloke heading towards the workshop – on foot – yes?'

'Yes. Lots of people don't like bringing their cars down here. The rutting, the mud. You know.'

'Also, cars've got numberplates which can be traced.'

'What I'm saying is I didn't think it was odd, you know, him being on foot. Also, you could still see the flood water. I mean, it was up to Bob Simmonds's workshop. You couldn't have got to it in a car.'

'Right.'

'There was something nervous about him. Don't know what it was. He just –'

'His body language?'

'Yeah. His body language. You couldn't describe it. You just knew the bugger was scared. Anyway, I was looking and – you know, I reckon it *was* him. The more I think about it now, the more I reckon it *was* Dowling that I seen. Smaller'n he looks on TV, but that's sometimes the way, isn't it?'

'Sure.' Bewick nodded encouragement.

'Was there anywhere he could have been going, apart from Simmonds's workshop?' Jones asked.

Peters thought for a moment. 'Not really. There's nothing happening next door. The car breakers would've packed up and gone home. Was getting dark. I could see him all right, though. Marion had the light on in her office upstairs. Like a bloody lighthouse. Then the phone rang, so I didn't see exactly where he went.'

'Did you see him go back the same way later?'

'No. He could've thought better of it and turned round while I was on the phone. Or later. I was finishing off a panel.'

'This is very helpful, as you can imagine,' Bewick said. 'We'd be very grateful if Sergeant Baynes here could take down a statement.'

Peters nodded. 'That's all right.'

'One thing more, Mr Peters.' Bewick looked at his most sombre. 'I'd counsel against talking to anyone else about this. Sir Michael Dowling is a wealthy man, by all accounts. If we were mistaken – or even if he were falsely able to prove that we were – the consequences of his sueing for slander would be formidable. You can be assured that your anonymity will be preserved by us.'

Fuck him, thought Jones. He can even sound like a bleeding brief. He could never've come out with a speech like that himself. He'd have got up Peters' nose, made him suspicious, scared him off. In Bewick's hands, Peters was actually looking grateful, for God's sake.

They left Baynes to take Peters' statement. Later, in the car on the way back, Jones said, 'So! Enjoying taking over my investigation, are you? Talk about a bloody primadonna!'

'Try not to be a jerk, Gio, and I'll tell you something interesting.'

'Fuck off.'

'Suit yourself.'

Jones drove in silence, his head slightly turned away from Bewick, feeling increasingly childish. When he could stand it no longer he said, 'All right. All right. No need to rub it in. What is it?'

'Karen has been offered a job by Schrager.'

'So? We all know that. What sort of job?'

'This guy Dowling thinks someone's trying to knock him off. He's looking for protection. From CRSI.'

'Dowling? Protection? I see. From your lot. Christ, is he?' Jones said nothing for a while. His brain was whirling. Then, 'Too late for poor bloody Simmonds, isn't it?'

'And you say Dowling offered to put up bail for the pair of them?'

'Exactly. Why would he do that? What connection could he possibly have with them?'

'What indeed?' Bewick murmured and lapsed into silence.

Jones waited.

'Well, they didn't grow up together,' Bewick said. 'Simmonds was from the Govan in Glasgow. Whear was Liverpool. Dowling was north London. Talk to

Karen, Gio. See if she can find out any connection. This is getting weird. I like it. Which would you rather do? AOR or Charlie Smew?'

'Slash my wrists or Beachy Head?'

They'd spent the afternoon setting up infra-red towers and their CCTV scanning links around the inner perimeter of Sir Michael Dowling's house. This encompassed all the buildings adjacent to the main house: the great hall garages, guest annexe, stables and workshops. The only building not within the perimeter was the guest cottage. Recently refurbished with a modern alarm system, it was about seventy metres away. It was decided that the cottage should be Karen's. The rest of the team, all men, should use the guest apartment, converted from a couple of the hay lofts, which was bigger. The control room was also located there.

There was a problem with two of the CCTV cameras, so Frasier secured replacements from the factory in Peterborough by phone and sent his techno whizz, Bernard, to check them out and bring them back. Frasier suggested Karen walk the grounds while he sorted out the walkie-talkies.

Apart from the electrical pylons marching over the horizon, the landscape around the house was pleasant enough. Karen was only vaguely aware of it, however. She was looking at it through a distorting lens: the agenda of cover and fields of fire. There was rising ground at the back of the house. The slope was topped with mature trees, which gave an appearance of height to the modest rise, a welcome illusion in the flat world of the fens. On one side, leading off the service wing, was a walled orchard. On the remaining side was a flat field, half drowned. The woods ended two hundred metres from the house and its gardens. Between the wood edge and the gardens were paddocks for the horses, sufficiently high to have escaped being waterlogged, so far. The flat field was fallow, chemically burnt, yellow and brown patchwork amongst the pools.

Frasier had given Karen a telescopic gunsight. She sat at the edge of the woods looking down at the house through it, identifying those parts where the inhabitants might be vulnerable. A sniper, she realized, would have a number of problems. If he remained in the woods, even this modest elevation would make it difficult to identify anyone he might be shooting at. She'd watched Frasier almost complete a crossing of the yard before she'd made out who it was. Also, shooting downward was notoriously difficult to compensate for – it took skill and experience to be accurate. And the high, brick walls around the yards and the vegetable garden were completely protective, provided you didn't stray into the middle of the walled areas. The garden and the big-windowed rooms which faced it were a different matter.

Karen made her final notes. The pleasantest thing about this place, she now thought, was the way the river curved its way around the property. In contrast to it were the ruler-straight drainage channels and the mechanical march of the pylons in the distance, also gleaming in the watery haze. Swallows were crossing and recrossing the paddock in front of her, scooping insects. A small plane hummed its way out of earshot. The sweet farmyard smell of the horses drifted up to her . . .

She heard the footfall and froze. Her heart quickened. Suddenly she was on her feet.

'God, I wish I could have that effect on everyone.'

It was Coleridge, the bloke who was writing a book about Dowling.

'What the hell are you doing?'

'Following you. I heard that you were going to be using the cottage. I thought I might show it to you.'

'No, thanks.'

Coleridge had a slightly blank expression and his cheeks were red. Karen put him down as a lunchtime drinker.

'Go on, it's on your way back.'

'All right then, show me the cottage.'

The cottage was set up for guests of Sir Michael and only used when the house was full. It was luxuriously furnished, pretty and soulless. The nicest thing about it was the view of the main house.

'What d'you think?' Coleridge asked as he opened more cupboards to show her.

'Well, it's not my taste.' Karen was irritated by Coleridge's helpfulness, as if the cottage was some sort of gift he was offering her. She knew how to open a cupboard, for Christ's sake.

'Nor mine,' Coleridge agreed. 'This is actually the best bit of architecture on the estate, this cottage. A late-Regency gem. All these bloody Peter Jones frills and furbelows are the last thing it needs.'

'Yeah, right.' Karen tried to sound as uninterested as possible. 'Did you say Sir Michael won't be back?'

'That's what he said.'

'I don't think my boss knows that.'

'He doesn't want to come back until all the systems are in place.'

'I see.'

'He'll have told your boss, somehow.'

'Sure.'

'He's an exploiter, but he believes in the flow of information. Well, that sort of information, at least.'

'What does that mean?'

Coleridge sat himself on the kitchen table. He looked uncomfortable. He wanted to say something but was panicking, she thought.

'What?' she asked, disgusted with herself for the softness in her voice.

'I'm psyching myself up,' he said with a boyish smile. 'You're a fearsome woman.'

'Crap.'

'I think perhaps I should warn you –' He ran out of courage again. 'You wouldn't have anything to drink, would you? No, of course not. You haven't moved in.' He went to the fridge and opened it. 'Fancy some champagne? You could count as a guest.'

'No.'

'Well, I'm going to have some.'

'Suit yourself. You know the rules.'

He began to open the champagne. 'Yeah, I do.' He

eased the cork out with hardly a noise. He looked pleased. 'A duchess's fart; that's all it should be.' He found a glass and poured himself some. 'Yeah, this place was mine for a bit, when I started on this thing.'

'The book?'

'Yeah. Then I took a guest lectureship in the States for three months. When I got back it had been turned into designer purgatory. They changed just about everything except the locks. I think actually that Sir Michael was punishing me for daring to take time out.'

It was odd how unmagnetic his handsomeness was, Karen thought, how unsexy. 'As I said, you don't like him much, do you?' she asked.

'Do *you*?'

'I don't know him, do I?'

'No . . .' Coleridge looked away. His face seemed to tighten. 'No.'

'What were you going to warn me about?'

'Well, I thought it seemed important, but I expect you'll have seen it anyway. Perhaps it isn't important.'

'What isn't, for Christ's sake?'

'He's a liar, a fantasist. He tells me the story of his life, so I think OK, I'll do a bit of background on this, and then I find out that it's garbage. Trouble is, he'll take a strand of truth and weave it into a mess of lies, so you begin to doubt yourself. And then you begin to think he's the really creative one. I mean, there's about four years that are a complete blank. I reckon he might've been in prison.'

'When was this?'

'Mid–late eighties. He said he worked abroad, was a bit of a beachcomber, was a surfie in California for a bit, bummed around. It doesn't add up. I reckon he was in the nick. You sure you don't want anything to drink?'

'No thanks. So how do you go on with this, day by day?'

'I don't. Not any more. You've just heard my resignation speech.'

'When are you going to give it for real? Tomorrow?'

'He's not here, as I said. He's staying at his club for a couple of nights. Then he's coming down to the Priory for his thrash.'

'What thrash?'

'I found him this place, you know. I just knew it would suit him. I never even took a finder's fee. My God, he should be so bloody lucky. He loved it at first sight. I knew he would. Well, anyway, he's organized some caterers to wine and dine the funding committee from St Anne's as well as one or two business chums.'

'I hope Peter Schrager has been alerted. Are these people vetted?'

'The only serious criminals he mixes with are on the boards of financial institutions. Stripy shirts and Church's shoes – not abbreviated shotguns.'

'What the hell use is it for us to set up a weather-proof system here if he fucks off for the week and then invites a gang of potential assassins to dinner? Christ!'

'You're getting paid.'

'That's not the point and you know it.'

Karen walked out. Coleridge hurried after her. Her pace meant he had to break into a run to do so.

'You realize that Dowling will probably tell you soon that he doesn't need you, after all,' he said, already beginning to breathe hard.

'Fine. It'll cost him.'

'He's not a consistent person. He's a nightmare to be around on a personal level. I think sometimes he does things just to *be* inconsistent. In business he's calm and decisive. The riskier it gets, the tougher it gets, the calmer he is. He's brilliant at it. Personally he's a complete muddle.'

'Why don't you go back to the cottage and finish your champagne?'

'All right, I fucking well will.' He sounded tearful. He turned and started running.

Bewick had cycled off, saying he'd talk to the Bursar of St Anne's, Nicholas Cranesmith. Left alone, Jones tried to work out how Sir Michael bloody Dowling fitted into the equation. Couldn't do it. Never mind try to work out why someone might knock off Alan Whear out of extreme and obsessive jealousy, and at the same time might be overwhelmed by some obscure need to knock off Simmonds as well. Couldn't be done. The case had moved sharply away from St Anne's and its fellowship. His efforts there had been a waste of time. Nothing new in that. His mobile rang.

'Boss . . .'

It was Baynes – to tell him they'd found the bullet.

*

Walking through to Walton Court, Bewick came across Cranesmith removing a notice from the door of the library. 'This is hardly helpful,' Bewick heard him saying to himself. Bewick moved quietly and easily, and Cranesmith hadn't heard him coming. When he saw who it was, Cranesmith looked briefly embarrassed.

'This is hardly helpful,' Cranesmith repeated.

'What's that?'

'Brendan is in one of his anti-reformation moods – again.'

He handed Bewick the piece of paper he'd removed from the door. On it was a computer-printed photograph of an ornate crucifix, and underneath a single word: 'Sacrilegium.'

'Meaning?'

'Meaning that Brendan objects to the conversion of the old chapel to a library.'

'When did that happen?'

'When the new chapel was built, in 1867.'

'I see. Slight time lag . . . Tell me, do you think the opposite of premature is postmature?'

'I'm sure that would do.'

'Dr O'Keefe's point being that the chapel's original foundation was when the college – all England indeed – was Catholic?' Bewick asked.

'That's right. I wish he wouldn't do it. It hardly argues for the sanity of the man. And that's something we could all be tainted by.'

'We?'

'The college.'

'You don't mean the Catholics amongst you?'

'We too; of course.'

Cranesmith closed down completely, cold and polite. By now they were walking across Walton Court towards where Cranesmith had his rooms. Nothing was said for a while, then Bewick asked, 'What do you know about Sir Michael Dowling's provision of a fellowship – or is it a chair – in medicine here? Are you on the funding committee?'

'Yes, I am.' Cranesmith gestured to the staircase in which he had his rooms. 'Why don't you come in?'

Cranesmith offered Bewick a chair by the window and made him a cup of coffee. Bewick sipped it out of politeness from time to time. It wasn't to his taste.

'Dowling approached us about a year before he was knighted for services to charity. He was quite heavily committed by then, but even so he tried to get out of it once he'd achieved his knighthood. If Sir Terence hadn't managed to get a royal on board I think he'd have pulled out.'

'How much is it going to cost him?'

'I couldn't possibly tell you that. All I'll tell you is that a professor is paid forty something a year. So a sum which would be guaranteed to generate that sort of figure plus five per cent to allow for inflation would be about the mark.'

'Less than a million at today's rates then, but not much less.'

'You said it, not me. Less, of course, if it's only a fellowship.'

'And the Dowling Wing at City Hospital?'

'His contribution is public knowledge in that instance. Six million.'

Bewick nodded. 'I can see why he wanted the sick-children endorsement – big build-up of media credit there. I don't associate him with the Dowling Chair in Paediatrics, though. What's in it for him? There are other forms of respectability which come a lot cheaper.'

'I think he was told that the chair in itself isn't the point. It's long-term stuff. Who'd remember Mr Lucas if Newton or indeed Hawking hadn't been Lucasian professors?'

'Do paediatricians change the world?'

Cranesmith laughed, with his lopsided grin. 'You can't have everything.'

In the court below, Bewick could see Brendan O'Keefe walking to a neighbouring staircase, where he had his rooms. He was wearing an odd-looking loose-sleeved top, which made him look like a monk from the waist up. He was talking to himself and plucking at a rosary, half hidden in the sleeves.

Bewick turned to Cranesmith and asked, 'Do you know anything about the AOR?'

Cranesmith glanced quickly at Bewick, then looked out of the window himself. 'It was the regiment young Whear was in. Is that why you're asking?'

'Yes.'

'I know they're a tough bunch. But I imagine everybody knows that.'

'Sure.'

'And they're a secretive lot,' Cranesmith said.

'Were you ever in the same theatre as them?'

'Sure. Ulster, Falklands. But as I say, they make the SAS look like chartered accountants.'

'And the Falklands is where you met Alan Whear?'

'On the boat going out, in fact. Once we were ashore, our units were engaged in different operations.'

'What did you think of him?'

'I hardly exchanged a word with him. He'd won some competition we were organizing on board ship. That's why I remembered him. Our CO had had the foresight to bring aboard some of those all-purpose ghastly medals that they hand out at amateur athletics competitions. He'd even managed to have them engraved. I gave Whear his medal. He also stuck in my mind as being a bit of a greaser. Well, most college fellows don't object to a bit of deference, so I recommended they took him on as porter.'

'So you hardly knew him at all?'

'No, that's right. I happened to remember him, that's all. AOR had their own agenda and it was only tenuously connected to ours. You know their HQ is out at Lotheny Airfield?'

'No, I didn't know that.'

'I should ask Sir Terence to ask one of his chums in Whitehall. It'd take clearance from the MOD to get into the place.'

Remembering the discovery of Simmonds's body, Jones took a deep breath. Clean air, please. Another gulp of it. Nausea threatening even now.

Inside the workshop something lingered, a

dampness, a creamy supuration. Where the light was brightest, the windows crawled with sluggish flies. The prints team were at work, concentrating hard. In their poly gloves, they always reminded Jones of super-fastidious housewives as they dusted and peered and sticky-taped.

The bullet had hit the top of a filing cabinet, glanced upwards and buried itself in the polystyrene tiles on the ceiling. A young DC, Darren Martin, was hovering. He too was wearing poly gloves.

'Took some finding, Guv.'

'Sure.' Jones looked up at the grubby tiles, many of them broken.

Although distorted from its encounter with bone and the metal cabinet, the bullet was still in good enough shape to be used by ballistics. Jones looked around the office. Baynes came back in.

'What's that?' Jones asked. A boot lay on the desk. 'Nobody took it off him, I hope?'

'No, no, Guv. He done it himself. Or someone did. It's all been by the book.'

In fact, Jones had an uncertain memory of the boot, lying beside a couple of telephone directories, as now. He'd hardly given it a glance. Simmonds's fly-blown body had been rather more compelling. Well, there it was. One boot on the deceased's desk. A meaningless oddity? Itchy foot on the part of the victim?

Jones imagined a machine which might measure the brain activity associated with itching: a final flicker of light across a monitor, then . . . He looked down at the self-sealing plastic pouch, the lethal small lump of metal in it.

He knew he was going to dream about this. He thought of his family. The kids had been difficult since Whear'd been found. Eilean and they were caught in a cycle of exhaustion. The kids sensed his attention wasn't on them and became attention-seeking. At the best of times, Eilean had more than enough to deal with . . .

For a moment, he hated his job. What was he doing? There were alternatives, for Christ's sake. Karen was out of it and good luck to her.

'Get it bagged and labelled,' he snapped at young Martin. He sensed the reassuring glance Baynes gave the boy. Annoyed even by this, he turned suddenly to look at the boot, obstructing Martin. It was a beefy Yank walking boot. Stamped into the leather and embroidered on the tongue was the maker's name: Camel Boot. The embroidery was yellow on black, although it was difficult to see because someone had crudely filled in the lettering with a black pen.

Jones turned to the prints team. 'You checked this out?'

'Not yet, Boss.'

'Leave it then,' he said to Martin. 'I'll be on the mobile.' He headed out.

'Boss . . .' Baynes made to follow him.

Jones turned. 'What?' he snapped.

He felt guilty. He realized that he was in a fog. Something about the boot made him feel he should know why it was there, but he couldn't place it. Made him cross.

'What is it?' he asked more gently, pulling himself together.

'Over by the door, Boss. Beside where you come in. I marked it.'

They made their way past the stripped-down generator. Jones wondered if anyone would ever be putting it back together again.

'It's the only one, in fact,' Baynes was saying.

'Only what?'

'Footprint. Reckon he might've stood there for a bit, or something.' An old utility wardrobe stood near the door into the workshop.

'What's in there?'

'Overalls, Boss.'

'Right.'

There was a chalk line round a piece of polythene on the floor beside the wardrobe. Jones glanced back towards the office. Anyone entering by this door would be partly visible as they came in, but would then be hidden if they stepped closer to the wardrobe.

Baynes fumbled in his coat pocket and produced a torch. Then he knelt down, reached into the shadow and lifted the polythene. The impression was faint, but photographable. It looked like the pattern on the sole of a boot, or perhaps some sort of specialist trainer: narrow, wavy lines seemed to cover nearly the entire sole. Where the other foot had been, there was no more than a smear in the dust.

'Not that boot on the desk?' Jones mumbled, then

answered himself. 'No, no. Reminds me of something, though. What is it?'

'Looks a bit like the way they cut the middle of a tyre tread, I reckon. The fellas searching the mud outside've found nothing like it.'

'No?'

'I asked 'em to check. Zero. So maybe it's an old one, but –'

'Doesn't look it, does it? Don't know why.'

'No, Boss.'

'OK. Get it recorded. Reckon you can enhance it?'

'Sure. Frankie's c'mpooter'll make it look like literature.'

'Good. Well done, Baynesie.'

Jones looked over towards the office. 'Christ! Can I still smell it, or is it my imagination?'

'Reckon we'll be smelling it in our dreams for a bit, Boss.'

10

Karen's doorbell rang. Gio Jones was on the door-step.

'Sir?'

'Don't "Sir" me,' he said jauntily. 'First John Bewick and now you. I feel like the last rat on a sinking ship. I know you're leaving 'cos of us boys being horrible to you little girls. Institutional sexism. But I still feel abandoned.'

Karen smiled. 'Come in,' she said. 'I'll make some tea.'

Jones enjoyed a sinful shiver as he crossed the threshold into Karen's flat. He had never been there before. He had often tried to imagine it. Not far wrong: it was bright, clean and fresh. There were one or two surprises: the print of Renoir's meadow with poppies above the mantelpiece in the living-room – a cosier image than he'd expected. Also unexpected was the Sony laptop, whose price he knew, having been told it in awed tones by his son. On one wall was a glass cabinet displaying silver cups. Opposite it hung a pair of boxing gloves, brown leather, glossy with care. The room was an unshared space: this is me, this is what you're negotiating with.

Karen came in with tea, caught him looking around, ignored it.

'You're looking fit, Sir. How much weight've you lost?'

'How dare you? A man with my bodily architecture. Asking him that sort of thing. God Almighty.'

'But you train an' all. I've seen you running.'

'Oh, Gawd.'

Jones laughed. The fact that she'd seen him lumbering around in his over-clean Nikes ought to spell the end of his fantasies about her, oughtn't it? It ought to be a relief.

She was looking concerned. 'No, it's good. I admire it. It's easy for me, I've been jumping around since I was four years old. But I broke my leg once so I know what it's like to get back to fit.'

'It's not getting back to fit, Karen. It's getting from never ever fit to not dropping dead.'

'It takes bottle, that's all I'm saying.'

'Whose are the gloves? Not yours, I hope?'

'My Dad's. He was army boxing champion, eleven stone four. Middleweight.'

'Middle? Christ, sounds light as a feather to me.'

'He was a lovely mover, true. Sugar Ray Leonard of the Service Corps. Ever see the Hagler–Leonard fight? Classic. One of the greats. Fighter versus boxer. Raw power versus speed and subtlety. Massive.'

'Who won?'

'Leonard ... My Dad's principles won. Learn, avoid, strike. No one gave Leonard a hope in hell.'

'That your Dad's silver?'

Karen looked round at the cabinet. 'Yeah. They're his.'

'You got on with him, did you?'

'Only when he was dying. He never really forgave me for not being a boy.'

Jones looked at the athletic elegance, the clear skin, the shining hair. My God, I'd have forgiven you, he thought. He wondered what sort of stupid sod couldn't rejoice in this sort of beauty. 'He must have been mad,' he said, and immediately wondered if he'd overstepped the mark. Then he remembered that Karen was no longer his subordinate. 'Listen, I've heard CRSI are sending you to work for Dowling. That right?'

'Yes,' she said, still dubious about the compliment he'd given her.

'Something you ought to know.'

'Sir?'

Jones told her about the sighting of CRSI's client near the Simmonds murder scene, and that the police surgeon reckoned that Simmonds had been dead for some days.

Karen nodded, lost in thought. 'I think he may have seen the body,' she said eventually.

'Tell me.'

Karen told Jones about the state she'd found Dowling in, swearing to himself, kicking straw in the stable. 'Sort of reaction you might expect, don't you reckon?'

'Maybe.' Jones sounded dubious.

'He's still shit scared of something. Doesn't that mean he thinks he's next?'

'Or that there's someone he still has to eliminate

and he's scared of having to do it. Anyway, thought you ought to know what you're heading into.'

'Yeah . . . Sounds as if you need someone in close.'

'Up to you. We're going to have to talk to him.'

'Guess you are.'

'So it wouldn't be a bad idea if you prepared the ground. Don't fancy tangling with an irate self-made millionaire. A collegeful of potty academics has been quite enough, ta.'

Gio Jones drove west from Cambridge, past Sandy in Bedfordshire, until the HMP sign directed him past an industrial estate and over a low hill. He drove through a plantation of larch. Half a mile ahead of him was the cluster of low buildings which was his destination.

Harnton was a surprise. The perimeter gave it away, of course, but inside the razor wire it might have been a conference centre or an experimental housing development rather than a Cat. B prison.

Jones hated prisons: the overcrowded squalor, the stink, the drugs, the endlessly threatened violence. They were wreckers of already dodgy lives. He knew their utility. In his more disillusioned moments, he knew that the only guaranteed preventers of crime were lousy weather and prisons. He hadn't been to Harnton before as it had only been open a year or so. He was dreading it.

First impressions weren't bad, though. The officer on the gate knew who Jones was and checked his ID politely. Next surprise was the reception, which was like a private hospital. Prisoners and screws were on first-name terms. Most remarkable, he realized as he was accompanied through a light and pleasant communal area, was that the building didn't have the unwashed male stink of prisons he'd known. Perhaps that would come in time, the smell of anger and fear permeating the fabric of the place.

As they moved through the building, there were prisoners in evidence everywhere. That was unusual. In your average prison they were banged up most of the day.

'How long are the lads allowed out of their cells?' he asked the officer with him.

'Eight till twenty-one hundred.'

'Blimey.'

'They're queuing up to get in here.'

'Not surprised.'

Charlie Smew was a good-looking man of fifty-two. He was halfway through a twelve-year sentence. He had cropped, receding hair which gave him a high, intellectual-looking forehead. A straight nose divided a pair of assessing eyes. He had a narrow upper lip above a truculent fuller lower lip; square jaw; muscular neck. He was calm, polite and clinically depressed.

The Governor of Harnton had warned Gio of this. 'You'll find him a changed man.'

'What happened?'

'He lost it. Someone broke him down. Fights. Provocation. More fights. He nearly killed the other bugger, who was a menace. Solitary. I had the other one transferred away. Smew went into serious depression, despite the fact he'd won. Gave up his degree course.'

'It's beginning to sound like any old prison.'

The Governor smiled. 'He's getting what help we can give him.'

'No, really, I'm impressed by this place.'

'Thank you.'

'Will Charlie talk to me, d'you think? Any point trying?'

'He might. He's given up. He's cooperative but he's given up. I feel sorry for him. He was such a cock of the walk. A classic pain in the neck. Now he's –' The Governor searched for the right word but eventually said again, 'He's given up.'

Smew talked to Jones with so little interest that it was impossible to guess whether he was telling the truth or not.

Jones had been beating about the bush, reminiscing about fellow criminals, judges they had both known, fellow officers. Jones deliberately mis-assigned a name to a witness in a murder trial. Smew corrected him. Encouraged, Jones got to the point.

'Then there was that pair of idiots who robbed Wood Ditton Grange. Remember? Somebody filmed them doing it or something; had a video-cam handy.'

'No, it was an early CCTV. Never've got convicted if they both hadn't of sung. Terrible quality, that CCTV. Couldn't tell a pig from a piss-pot on one of 'em cameras. Useless as ID.'

'Right, that was it. And they never got rid of the stuff, did they? All still in his lock-up.'

'Yeah . . .' Smew seemed to be losing interest.

Jones tried to sound as if he wasn't interested himself, only speaking to keep the conversation going. 'Whatever happened to them? I heard one of 'em turned out to be a grass.'

'No. That was that Spanish bloke.'

'Morales?'

'That was it, Pablo. Low Morals, he got called.' For the first time the ghost of a smile drifted over Smew's face. 'Yeah. He died from a kicking he got given at Pentonville. Yeah . . .'

The pleasantness of this memory lingered. Then he turned to Jones. 'What you want to know about these boys for?'

For a moment, Jones thought of denying he wanted to know anything. No point. In the face of Smew's hard stare, he shrugged, acknowledging defeat.

'What can I do for you, Charlie? The Governor seems a reasonable sort.'

'Yeah . . .' Smew lapsed into apparent indifference, although he might have been considering the offer.

'These two lads . . .'

'Amateur dickheads. Complete fuckwits.'

Smew must have decided to trade, Jones thought. 'I was wondering if they'd come away from that robbery with more than we'd reckoned.'

'How d'you mean?'

'Something valuable enough for the insurance company to keep quiet about, so they could negotiate a ransom to get it back later. Something . . . like a painting, maybe.'

Smew thought about this. Then he said, 'Why you so interested?'

'Someone's shot them both.'

'What? Contract?'

'Don't think so. It was single shot, front on. Organized enough, but didn't shout pro at me.'

Smew was looking mystified. 'Single shot, front on?'

'Yeah.'

'Nobody I've ever heard of.'

'And you haven't heard of a painting or anything super valuable coming from that crap job of theirs?'

'Where would that get you?'

'It'd save my time.'

'They was in the army, wasn't they?'

'Yeah.'

'So what else do you want to know?'

'Anything anyone might have heard from when they were doing time. Who might have a grudge. Anything . . .'

Smew seemed to lose interest again. Was he going to make an offer?

'One of my Julie's blokes was a squaddy too. Pathetic little geezer. Half my age and I could've torn him up for arse paper. She's with someone else now.' Smew's face darkened. Jones sensed he was about to hear the trade.

'Your daughter?'

'Sure. This bloke of hers now, Jarrett . . . He – I've heard he slaps her around. I want to know if it's true. Nah . . . I know it's true. I want to know how bad it is. Find out how bad it is. If he's messing her up I'll have his bollocks on my Christmas tree.'

'I'll find out how bad it is, Charlie.'

'I'll do some research.'

'That's great. Thanks.'

Smew shrugged. Thanks meant nothing.

So what was it, if it wasn't fear? He looked around the room and wondered how many hours he could stand being in it. Was it anger – seething silently under the crust, self-directed turbulent anger – which had its jaws in him? Perhaps there was no difference.

His progress had been thrown back. He knew that. He felt shipwrecked; isolated by what he had done. He'd always thought of himself as independent to a fault, so why did he mourn this particular exile from the human race?

He laughed; wondering if it weren't a form of laziness!

He knew he wasn't naturally an active man – he had always had to drive himself into the active life. Research was his talent. Patient detection in the archives. His habitat was libraries, the ghostly corridors of knowledge. He knew that it was in laboratories and in libraries that the world was permanently altered.

He had forced himself many times to forsake those quiet places with their hoarded treasures of the human mind, the dusty silences, the footsteps walking away to another century, the clap of a turned page . . .

What's more, he'd done it. He had triumphed. He was not being eaten away from the inside by the poisons of guilt. So what was this? He had suffered, certainly, but justice and conscience were reconciled. So what was this?

Something had drawn Bewick out to the stretch of the fens where Dowling had his Edwardian palace. As he'd explained to Jones, he had no idea why he wanted to see it, but he knew he did. He found it easily enough, as it was marked clearly on the Ordnance Survey. He observed the strict security at the entrance and drove away without attempting to get in. He parked about half a mile away and walked part of the perimeter of the land, which gave him distant glimpses of the house, until, after an hour or so, it began to rain. The fields had barely recovered from their previous inundation. He returned to his car.

It was about four miles outside Cambridge that he noticed that he had picked up a tail. Keeping three or four cars back was the red Sierra.

Sally Vernon stood at the sink in the kitchen of her tidy house. She was lost in thought. The washing of pans went more slowly. She was examining herself on the subject of John Bewick.

She'd thought once that his physical strength was scary sexually. She had witnessed that strength in violent action and that had been frightening. She knew enough women who had been subject to violence from men, enough to make her imagine what it might be like to be on the receiving end of Bewick's aggression. But violent men imposed control on others because they weren't in control of their own lives. That didn't fit Bewick. He was one of the most relaxed individuals she'd ever met.

How would he use his strength when making love? she wondered guiltily; immediately thinking of Anthony, his kindness and patience. Was it anything to do with that? And if not, what the hell was it? Why was she so unnerved by the thought of meeting him again?

She dried her hands and picked up the phone. Her mother answered almost immediately.

'I was thinking of coming down for a day or two.'

'Well, your father will be pleased. He says he's forgotten what you look like.'

Sally could hear her mother's dry voice echoing in the stone-flagged hallway, in the house she had known all her life.

'What's the matter?' her mother went on. 'Is dear Anthony proving a handful?'

Mrs Vernon always referred to him as 'dear Anthony', not because she liked him much, but because his charm and diffidence annoyed her.

'I'm sorry, would that be very inconvenient?' Sally replied in a voice drier than her mother's. Having provoked an irritated reaction, Mrs Vernon seemed content and proceeded to be charming.

Half an hour later, Sally locked the house and drove to the centre of Cambridge, where she wanted to buy a book before setting off for Norfolk.

*

Denzil Holetown was built on generous lines. He carried many more stone on a frame an inch or so smaller than Bewick's. His beard and hair had turned white over the past few years. Against his black skin, they were bright and arresting, making him seem, if anything, younger than he was.

As Bewick drove into his car-repair yard, Holetown was between buildings. He put down the electric-window motors he was carrying and stepped out in front of the old Volvo, as if daring Bewick to drive into him.

'Still in this old heap? Put it out of its misery, man. I'll give you the name of a nice vet.'

Bewick got out. Bear hugs and back slapping: Holetown liked Bewick and, unlike most men, wasn't intimidated by him.

'What you doin' here?'

Bewick explained. For some time now, Holetown had felt in Bewick's debt. A few years before he'd been harassed by a couple of young CID officers. Warned that he'd be digging a bigger pit for himself by complaining, he had complained nevertheless. After throwing the book at them, Bewick had sent the two officers on a racial-awareness course.

Holetown told him to park up. He then closed the steel and mesh gates to the yard. He took Bewick into his cupboard of an office, which had a view of the road. The red Sierra had already passed once before the gates were closed. It repassed now. Then it parked. Holetown offered Bewick a whisky. They drank.

'What you reckon?'

'I want you to do something very humiliating, Denzil.'

'Uhh?'

'I want you to lend me your car.'

'What do I get home in?'

'That's the humiliating bit.'

Holetown threw a glance in the direction of Bewick's medieval Volvo. 'I get it. People sue each other for loss of reputation, y'know.'

'Thanks, Denzil.'

'Have I said yes?'

'You haven't said no.'

'It's parked at the front.'

'I know.'

They swapped car keys. The entrance to Holetown's yard was on one street. The entrance to the premises to which the yard belonged had its forecourt on the next street. Holetown led Bewick through the alley beside these premises, which he rented out as offices.

Bewick drove Holetown's immaculate Mercedes round the block, and pulled in several cars behind the Sierra.

It was nearly dark before the two men in the Sierra gave up and decided to move on. Bewick, meanwhile, had checked their numberplate and discovered that it supposedly belonged to a shop assistant in Truro. Gio Jones had offered to send a car or three, but Bewick asked him not to.

The Sierra turned into Newmarket Road and headed east. It had one tail light brighter than the other. Bewick was able to keep his distance.

*

Sally approached the chevron-painted roundabout and was carved up from her left by a red car; a Ford, she thought. It annoyed her and she followed the car round more quickly than she usually would. She told herself to calm down and fell back. At the next lights, two of the cars behind her peeled off towards Fen Ditton. She glanced in her mirror, and looked away. Something nagged at her. What was it? She looked back at her mirror. Was she seeing things? Dimly, a trick of street lighting showed her the unmistakable Bewick, now only two cars back from her.

There was a bus-stop lay-by beyond the lights, and when they turned green she pulled over into it and then turned to catch Bewick's attention. He drove straight past her as if he was staring down a tunnel. She hooted briefly then pulled out to follow.

She asked herself what on earth she was doing, but then reasoned that he was going the same route as her. So why not? She knew it wasn't sensible. She didn't care.

It was a decision she would always remember. Until now, she'd thought that ordinary, daily life was unlike science, had different rules; was in fact common-sensical. At that moment, the moment she decided to follow Bewick, she understood that life wasn't like that. Like science, life moved forward in a series of wild insights, which were or were not justified by subsequent events.

Past the airport and Marshall's he tracked them, with four cars between. There should be no hold-ups between them and the A14 now. On the A14, they headed east, beyond Newmarket, then took the A11 towards King's Lynn.

It wasn't until they'd turned off towards Lynn that it occurred to Sally that Bewick might be following the red car. She then watched like a hawk and was soon convinced. She felt childishly excited, but she felt no nerves. Deliberately not thinking about it, she decided to follow.

Well before Lynn, the red Sierra turned left out of a small shoal of traffic into lonely fenland. Bewick didn't follow. He kept on, slowing, crawling, until the shoal had passed him. The Sierra's lights disappeared behind trees. Bewick did a handbrake turn on the now empty road and pursued. The Merc was fitted with road-hugging fogs so he switched them on to alter his lights' pattern.

Nothing moved on the road ahead. It was possible they'd clocked him earlier and had driven this stretch like lunatics. Bewick accelerated. The road was narrow, ditched on either side. The Merc was too old to have air-bags or a side-impact system.

Suddenly he was slowing. A dismal village slipped past. Duntney; one pub – The Eelman. A speckle of rain now, greasing the road. The brightly lit forecourts of a couple of small industrial units, then suddenly the blackness of the empty country, which stretched from here to the edge of the Wash. In Bewick's rear-view mirror the floodlights of Duntney shrank, but still shone like a frozen lightship in the encircling dark.

The grass verges raced towards him like a perspective diagram.

No tail lights, nothing. Was his quarry waiting up in the darkness ahead? He gave the Merc one very fast mile. He slowed, looked around. He was still alone in the flat arable with the drifting rain. He drove slowly until he found a field entrance, backed into it and opened a window. The rain had paused. He stepped out of the car and listened. Nothing. Silence. The air movement made no sounds. On the horizon, the loom of Duntney's lights. He might well have been in a boat, a featureless sea dividing him from the illuminated speck of the village. He now heard a ripple of water sound from the ditch beside him, completing the illusion. He stood stock-still, as if in a trance.

Bewick's waking dream broke: the alarm call of a bird a hundred metres or so ahead in the ditch. He even heard a bird, or a pair, take flight, but still saw nothing. The ripple of water he'd heard had been a hunting mink, maybe. The sound of wing beats diffused into the soft, wet air. He turned his back on Duntney. The low horizon, the towering clouds, he knew, were his imagination. His eyes searched and found nothing. It was true darkness.

At first it was a low drone, which stopped as suddenly as it had begun, like an insect which had settled. Then another note, a different note, from the opposite direction. Bewick looked over towards the glow at Duntney. It might have been illusory but he thought he saw a movement of lights there. He remembered the double bend and the bridge at the approach to the village. It was probably a headlight beam.

Sally's car came to a halt outside an unappealing pub called The Eelman. It rolled to a stop without her volition, it seemed. She stared at the pub without seeing it.

What on earth was Bewick up to? Had he noticed that she was tailing him? She had managed to glimpse his last manoeuvre in her mirror. This made her doubt that he'd noticed her at all. Surely, if he'd thought her car was hostile, he'd have waited until it was out of sight.

What was *she* doing, come to that? Her curiosity about him was compulsive. It was as if she were being powered along by forces she didn't understand, taken to a place not of her choosing.

The drone began again. Out in the fen darkness Bewick could see no hint of light. The drone jumped in volume. It was a car engine, that much was certain now. It sounded as if it had just been driven out from behind a building. It was close, maybe four hundred metres, moving slowly, no lights. He was within spitting distance of the Merc but he could hardly see it. The other car's driver had to be using some sort of night-scope. Bewick moved quickly towards the Merc.

As if to confirm his theory, the lights of the oncoming car now blazed into life. No time now to start the Merc and get on to the road. Behind him stretched a field as flat as a table. The ditches were dead straight. No cover. No escape. Two seconds?

The car crunched to a stop across the field entrance, blocking him in. It was the red Sierra. Bewick dived forward, as if he expected shooting. The Ford's doors sprang open. Bewick's dive became a shoulder roll. He was upright again, kicking out. The door slammed into the emerging figure. Jarred, the man stayed in the seat a split second. His head was at waist level. Bewick's second kick caught his jaw. The baseball bat the man was holding dropped and rolled. The balaclava'd head slumped and shook and stretched back. He fell out of the car, hands ineffectively clawing at the wool round his face. He stayed on his knees, moaning.

Bewick reached for the bat. The other guy was very quick. Before his hands closed on it, Bewick was rolling away to avoid the first blow of an iron bar. The weight of the bar slowed the man's swing. Bewick jumped, bouncing off the car's bonnet. The man was at him almost before Bewick touched down. But again the iron slowed him. Bewick caught the heavy bar above the man's head. He completed its downswing using its own weight. He seemed not to move quickly or to move much at all. But it was a continuous flow. The man lost grip as Bewick twisted and bore down. The man quickly straightened and kicked. Bewick was already turning as the kick came in. It hit him hard, but glanced. It knocked air from him; a disgruntled sigh.

Bewick continued what he was doing. Very fast came the second kick. Bewick anticipated, dropping further into his crouch. Another glance, a bloody welt across the temple. The third kick was on the way. Bewick opened up from his crouch. The iron bar moved like a lightweight racket in his hands. The man's kick turned into a leap. The bar whistled. A flicker of impact: fingers and the man's jacket, jerking him round. The man pirouetted and ran, grunting in pain. Bewick lifted the bar. Suddenly the man was stark against the lights of another car which slowed as he ran towards it.

She was blinded by the lights coming towards her. Bewick was unmistakable, even in silhouette. Beyond him, a man was running. Behind him, someone crawled on all fours towards another, stationary car, also with its lights on. She saw Bewick throw something. The bar made slow circles in the air. She realized how heavy it must be. The oncoming car stopped. The bar fell, bounced, hit the man and the car. It smashed a light and knocked the man over. Then he was on his feet and opening a door. By the time she was stopped herself and out of her own car, the car which had been blinding her had completed a tyre-burning turn and gone. A shape rose up behind Bewick. She heard herself shout a warning. Unnecessary. Whoever it was was trying to escape in the red car. It was racing towards her. She jumped for the verge. A foot slid. She heard the snap of her wing mirror above the gunned engine. She was slipping, losing balance, then righting herself. Bewick was moving towards her, his face streaming blood. She gestured that she was all right but he kept coming. He side-stepped, then an arm was round her, lifting, hurling, unbelievably strong. They both thumped down together, one of Bewick's hands under her. Shadow, the stink of grass and car fumes.

Irresistibly, Bewick handled her over the edge of the verge until they were lying side by side, flat, on the slope down to the big drainage channel.

Above, the steady drumming of her car's engine.

'Stay here.'

Bewick lifted his head, lowered it. He struggled out of his sweater. He bundled it into a ball and raised it. He left it above the parapet of the grass verge for some seconds. Then he was on his feet and into her car. He cut the lights and the engine. He stepped out of the car and crouched beside it, listening.

Sally tried to understand what he was doing. She too listened. A breeze was finding nooks and crannies in her car's bodywork: a barely audible fluting. Her engine creaked as it cooled. Far distant engines came to her out of the moist air, melting into the whisper of ruffled vegetation.

'Let's go. Follow me.'

Bewick went quickly to his car. The orders were firm; he was utterly confident that she would obey. Something inside her rebelled, but only briefly. Reason told her that this was a world she didn't understand: get on with it.

They drove fifteen miles at speed. Bewick made no allowances for her following. He expected her to drive as well as he did. Generally she managed.

There was a car between her and Bewick's Mercedes

when she saw him pull off the main road. He'd braked hard to do so and the other car overtook impatiently. Sally slowed and was overtaken herself. She braked to a crawl, and turned into the side road. It was narrow, dark, anonymous. Yet again, she asked herself what she was doing. She'd just seen how dangerous he could be.

Nevertheless, her steering wheel began turning. Far ahead up the lane she could see his tail lights, stationary. As soon as she spotted them they began moving away. They soon disappeared. A track opened up on the right. He'd turned off his headlights and was creeping down it towards a group of farm buildings. Sally followed, very slowly. As she drove into the yard, Bewick was already out of his car, sliding back an enormous metal door. He waved her forward. She drove into a high barn; dim in her sidelights she could see tractors and combines. She pulled over to leave room, and Bewick drove in moments later. The door was slid shut.

Suddenly the place was lit. Bewick stood by the big switch he'd thrown. He looked terrible. She went to him to see the extent of the cut across his forehead. The blood was barely coagulated.

'I've got a kit,' she said and returned to her car. She found the unused first-aid kit and a bottle of Evian she'd bought earlier that day; in another life.

Before she could attend to him, he'd turned the light out again and stepped outside. The main road was about a mile distant, she reckoned, but the drift of wind was away from them, so it couldn't be heard.

She stood beside him. The loudest noise was the drip of a tap across the yard. There was a smell of diesel from the big tank beside them. After listening for some time, he said, 'What the hell are you doing here?'

'I saw you drive past, that's all. I found myself following you.' She laughed, embarrassed.

He said nothing. He returned inside the barn. The door rumbled shut.

'You'll have to sit down,' she said. She'd always thought of herself as tall but she was dwarfed by him. Obediently he sat on a front wing of the Merc. She began pushing aside blood-caked hair to gauge the extent of his injuries.

'You could've been badly hurt,' he said.

'I wasn't though, was I?' She worked in silence for a while, uncovering a long split in the skin. 'I'm going to pull these edges together when I've cleaned them. Someone ought to look at this soon.'

He grunted something non-committal. She caught his benign body smell that she remembered so well. She could feel the warmth coming off him. 'Did you really think those people were going to shoot at us?'

'They had a night-scope. They could've seen us if they'd wanted to.'

'That doesn't answer my question.'

'I don't know. Wasn't worth the risk.'

'Who were they?'

'I don't know. Maybe something to do with Simmonds.'

'Who?'

Bewick explained briefly about the second murder and where he'd first seen the Sierra: when he'd been looking for Simmonds.

'So what were they after? Did they kill Simmonds, do you think?'

'Or they may have been looking for Simmonds, just as I was. They may not have known he was already dead.'

'I don't understand.'

'Whear and Simmonds were in the army together. One of them gets murdered. Maybe these guys tonight were army buddies of Whear. His murder scares the shit out of them for some reason. They go looking for Simmonds. They see me in his garden. They trail me. Then Simmonds is found dead. This makes it worse. They think I know too much, or I'm maybe responsible.' Bewick shrugged. 'One way or another, they want to stop me doing what I'm doing.'

'I see.'

'Might be something from my own past, but I doubt it.'

'How did you know to come here?'

'Belongs to a friend. I rang to clear it on my mobile.'

She was still cleaning up his face. She was forgetting how bruised and shaken she'd been feeling. There was some dirt in the corner of the gash. 'This could hurt.'

He shrugged again. She delved into the cut with the antiseptic wipe. She felt it must have caused pain. He seemed indifferent throughout. She pinched the edges of the cut and applied the medi-strips. Then

236

she continued wiping the blood away from the rest of his face.

She realized as soon as she began that this could turn into caresses. For a moment she was deliberately firmer than she needed to be. Don't be bloody stupid. He's a friend. Do it as for a friend. She became gentler. It was one of the most erotic things she'd ever done. Heat flooded through her. He wasn't looking at her until she bent her face close to try to see whether a particular speck was blood or dirt . . . then the grey eyes opened on her like a dawn breaking, slow and irresistible.

His hands were holding her face, but so lightly it was more a knowledge that they were there than a sensation of touch. Knowing what those hands were capable of, their strength, made the delicacy so poignant she might have cried. The kiss when it came, the sweet breath, the withheld power, sent a jolt through her she hadn't experienced ever before. Her eyes were shut and she was bathed in light.

Footsteps approached outside. They broke apart. Hurriedly Sally put the kit away and returned to her car. She was able to glimpse him in the mirrors. He sat where she'd left him for a moment. Then he went to the door. It rolled open a couple of feet before he was able to help.

'Victoria.'

'Hello, John. All well?'

A woman in her mid-forties stepped into the barn. A lean, brown, outdoor-weathered face, hair scraped back for practicality . . . intelligent, quick eyes sought out Sally immediately. Bewick introduced them. The woman gave Sally a friendly smile. Her handshake was as strong as most men's.

'Victoria Canning. Hello. I run this place.' There were many unspoken queries in the look she gave Sally, but Victoria at once turned back to Bewick. 'Want anything? Meal? Drink?'

'Best not.'

'No. Been in the wars again, I see.'

'Yes.'

'Still, you seem to have survived.'

'How's Jessie?'

'Graduated from pony to horse this winter.'

'Good for her.'

As they continued to talk about her daughter, Sally thought how extraordinary it was that she knew with complete certainty that this woman had been sexually involved with Bewick, perhaps still was.

Victoria's friendliness towards her didn't do anything to stop Sally feeling alienated, excluded from the landscape of his past. She asked herself what she knew of him. She knew one big thing: the tragedy of his first wife and daughter. Apart from that, nothing much. This exile from his history hurt. She hadn't anticipated hurt, despite Karen's warning. She felt stupid, once a cardinal sin in her world. Now . . . she wondered if feeling stupid only meant feeling out of control. Maybe out of control wasn't so bad. Maybe out of control could teach.

'Sally . . .'

'Sorry?'

'I said we'd better get going.'

'Of course.' She hadn't heard him.

'You all right?' Victoria Canning asked.

'Yes.' Sally smiled at her. 'It's been an unusual evening.'

11

Bewick asked her back for a drink. She accepted without thinking. Thinking, it seemed, had deserted her hours ago. He took an unusual route which brought them into Cambridge via Hills Road. He then took Long Road towards Homerton. Baccata Lane was a plain street of modest Edwardian terraced houses. Bewick left the parking space nearest his house for her and went further on to find one for himself.

Once again, Sally had the sense that she was being swept along on a tide. If she had questioned herself, she might have realized that the idea that she was being transported by some instrument of Fate conveniently shelved the matter of Anthony. But she didn't question herself.

She walked into Bewick's house and was calmer than she'd feared. The place had barely changed. It was as unrevealing of him as she remembered. Neutral colours, bland furniture; it reflected as little as possible, it seemed. There were two exceptions: a fruitwood corner cupboard and a bow-fronted chest of drawers, on which stood an ebony Georgian tea caddy.

'I'll light a fire, then I'll get you a drink.'

'Thank you.'

There were also the paintings, one over each of the fireplaces in the double room. They were a pair, abstracts that could perhaps have been visionary landscapes: blazing, hot primary colours and their complementaries.

She watched him as he briskly laid the fire. He had a light touch and was practical. He applied a single match to it. The flames began to spread. He squatted on the thick, soft hearthrug and said nothing. He watched the fire, a picture of contentment. A piece of his hair stuck up, stiff with antiseptic and blood. It modified his roughness, made him look absurdly young.

'It's like a meditation, watching flames, don't you think? Like watching water, I suppose.'

She was charmed by this brief speech. In a moment, the atmosphere in the room had become intimate. She was delighted at how natural and easy that intimacy was.

She knew nothing about him, she warned herself again. She wasn't sure she liked this stark habitat he had created for himself. The circumstances which had brought her here were so bizarre . . . Nevertheless, at that moment she felt, for once in her life, that she was in the right place at the right time. Even if she were never to see him again, she knew she would not forget this moment, watching him sitting on his haunches at the fire like an Indian villager.

Bewick went to the kitchen and returned with a bottle of wine and two glasses. The fire was now crackling and popping, making a soft roar in the chimney. Bewick sat on the coffee table and poured some wine.

'I know so little about you,' she said.

'And I you. Here's to us, and to knowledge of us,' he said and drank.

At that moment, Sally remembered that she hadn't contacted her parents. 'Oh!'

'What?'

'I was on my way to my parents when I started to follow you.'

'Ring them now,' Bewick said, holding up his grubby hands. 'I'll go and clean up, while you phone.' He was on his feet and gone.

Sally rang her parents.

'Your father was about to ring the police,' her mother said, and then proceeded to relate a potted history of the scrapes Sally had got herself into. Her mother's talkativeness, Sally knew, was to do with her relief. She was briefly touched. Nevertheless, it was a stream of criticism. She wanted her mother off her case.

'I'm sorry, Mummy.' She hadn't called her that for years. It stopped her mother immediately. Sally made arrangements to visit them soon and ended the conversation by telling her mother that she was on a friend's phone. To Mrs Vernon, phones were a luxury, long-distance calls an extravagance, and using a friend's phone was a serious favour. She quickly rang off.

Bewick came downstairs in a T-shirt and jeans, drying the back of his hair with a towel. 'I've left a clean towel for you in the bathroom if you want to do the same. It's a good shower.'

'I'd like to. Thanks.'

The jetting hot water on her aching body was the perfect refreshment. Under its pleasant assault, she closed her eyes. She was immediately removed from the world of sofas and rugs and fires; the domestic world downstairs. She was back in the darkness, pierced by glaring lights and sudden violent action: an unreal dreamscape where things happened in false time. She felt light-headed. She knew that she was going to make love to him.

He was sitting on the rug in front of the hearth. He turned to her, his face flushed from the fire, as if he hadn't moved for some time. She walked slowly towards him, in a trance. It was the intelligence and strength in his hands as much as anything else. The memory of the way that they had touched yet barely touched when he kissed her came flooding back. She felt a shiver of pleasure. He was leaning towards her. That brown hand was reaching out to her so slowly she wanted to scream.

They kissed.

She was overwhelmed with relief. The past entanglements, the continuing guilt loosened and slipped free. It was as if she had never known James, never suffered his arrogance, his casual cruelties. It was as if she had never tried, and succeeded, to make herself valued and loved in Anthony's life, for so little reward.

She wasn't inexperienced, but she felt the illusion of it. She felt childlike and nonsensically fragile in the face of his strength.

'You're bruised . . .'

She was naked from the waist down. Along her left hip was a cloud of blue bruising against her milky, immaculate skin. He kissed it carefully, allowing his tongue to linger in small explorations. She thought she would explode. She was wet, weeping her welcome. He stood and stripped and knelt. Then, with one hand underneath, he lifted her hips and entered her.

After the second time, after she had experienced every cliché of pleasure in the book, he lay on his side, still firm inside her. She lay mirroring him, feeling the heat coming off him, in a dream.

'You feel troubled . . .'

'Yes,' she said.

'Because of Anthony?'

'Yes.'

'It's got to be faced.'

She felt a shout of joy that he was taking what had just happened between them so seriously. 'Yes.'

'I've been waiting for you for a long time.'

She drove home in the dawn. She was too consumed with pleasure and tiredness, too flattered by the beauty and power of the body she'd been enjoying, to consider guilt.

The answerphone was winking like a nagging conscience when she got in. She knew guilt would come.

There was a knock at Jones's office door. It was opened by Baynes, who ushered in a smartly turned-out young Asian woman, who had a tight, apologetic smile.

'PC Desai, Sir,' Baynes said, and left.

Jones had assigned Baynes to supervising the watch he wanted kept on Smew's daughter, Julie. He'd told Baynes to try to find an officer who had a child at the same primary school as Julie's little boy. Baynes had come up with this lass, who now sat in front of him, neat knees together, her case notebook in her lap.

'All right, PC Desai, tell me what you know.'

'Yes, Sir.' She opened the notebook and began: date and time of trip to school, how she'd made her first contact with her target, the dialogue between them, date and time of next visit . . .

When Jones could stand it no longer, he interrupted. 'Very conscientious, very commendable.'

'Thank you, Sir.'

'So what d'you reckon? Is her bloke having a go at her?'

'Sir?'

'Is her bloke having a go at her?'

She glanced at him warily. Jones tried to look benign. He watched her adapt. She was quick, no mistake.

'I think he might be.'

'Might be as in likely? Or as in possibly?'

'Likely, Sir.'

'Why?'

'Well, Sir, she's got a figure, you know. She works out. And she likes to strut her stuff. When it's warm, she wears one of them little tops which shows off her stomach muscles. Well, we had a couple of days this week when we might've been in California. But she stayed covered up all through it. And there was a bruise on her leg she'd plastered with make-up. Wouldn't've seen it if I hadn't been looking for it.'

'Might be, as in *very* likely?'

'I think so, Sir.'

'What d'you talk about?'

'I haven't got around yet to complaining to her about my bloke.'

'To give her the opening?'

'Yeah, that's it.' She laughed. 'I've cleared it with Johnny. He doesn't mind being slandered in a good cause.'

Jones stretched in his chair. A few papers slipped on to the floor. He glanced down but didn't bother to pick them up. 'I met him, didn't I, at the Christmas Party? Nurse, isn't he?'

'That's it, Sir.'

'Well, thank him from me. I don't need much more. Tell me when you're convinced. You're OK to go on with this?'

'It's great being able to take Bobby to school.'

Baynes put his head round the door. 'CRSI, Sir? At eleven?'

'OK.' He turned to PC Desai. 'There may be a lot at stake in this.'

'Prison?' Jones's level of interest shot up with his eyebrows. 'Sir Michael Bleeding Dowling?'

'That's what this bloke Coleridge reckons.' Karen glanced at Bewick, who was watching her with the guarded neutrality she knew so well. She wanted to know where he had got the cut on his head. Was it any of her business any more? She hated how at ease he looked, despite the wound. She hated the fact that he'd got himself hurt and she knew nothing about it. She answered her own question: none of her business.

'Prison would be interesting,' Bewick said, stirring the tea he was making for her.

Karen had, in fact, gone to report to Peter Schrager at CRSI. He'd just left, but Frasier, the operations officer, had told her that Bewick was in. She'd gone to the office Bewick shared with Frasier. She was conscious of how much of a test this would be of her decision to join CRSI. Seeing Jones there too was a huge relief to her.

Bewick handed her the tea, which was much stronger than she liked. Had he forgotten, she thought, so soon? Then she realized he was taking it back. 'Bit strong . . .' he murmured, an apology. He returned it to her with more milk in it. She amazed herself by feeling grateful.

'Do you think this Coleridge guy has got it right?' Bewick asked.

'I don't see why not. There was an old press photo of Dowling lying around in the annexe, by the way, so I nicked it.'

She showed it to them. Dowling looked much the same as he did now, but had longer hair.

'Well done,' Bewick said.

'Prison?' Jones repeated to himself.

'Coleridge reckons Dowling is a bit of a fantasy

merchant. He's going to resign from writing the book about him. Coleridge keeps checking facts, as I said, and finds they're only half true, most of them.'

'But . . .' Jones was frowning. 'What's the connection? With prison, I mean – where does it take us?'

No one answered this for a moment and then Bewick said, 'He was in the army, not prison.'

'What?' Jones stared. Where the hell had he got that from?

'That's the only thing that makes sense, isn't it? Surely? You only go bail for someone to whom you feel loyalty or some obligation. Whear and Simmonds had never been to prison up to that point, so Dowling couldn't have met them there. Dowling's work has been trading in the City. Financial institutions aren't noted employers of ex-squaddies or ex-cons – so where does this sense of obligation come from? Whear, Simmonds and Dowling come from different parts of the country, so it wasn't school. The only melting pot where he might have met them, and bonded with them, is the army.'

'I'll buy that.' Jones turned to Karen. 'What about you?'

'Yeah, makes sense.'

'Which might also explain why two blokes – who could fight, by the way – tried to jump me out in the fens last night,' Bewick said.

'Serves you bloody right. I offered you back-up. You refused it. Anyway, what d'you mean, "tried"? Looks as if they made a half-decent job of it.'

'I think they wanted a bit more than that. I think they wanted me in a coma.'

Jones gave it the full Swansea sarcasm. 'Now why would anyone want that?'

'You reckon they were army, these guys?' Karen asked.

'They first picked up on me when I was at Simmonds's house. That's the only real connection. But since two ex-AOR soldiers are dead and one of them was Simmonds – and we think another, Dowling, is looking for protection . . .'

'These charmers could have been AOR as well?' Jones asked.

'That's my guess.'

'So what are they so frightened of, that they want you out of the way?'

'If we knew that, you could start making out arrest warrants.'

'Their HQ is out at Lotheny. AOR's is, I mean,' Karen said.

'I've put in a request to speak to them,' said Jones.

'So have I,' Bewick said. 'I've got Peter Schrager on the case. You'd better speak to Dowling. Grill the bastard.'

'Oh yeah? That'll be *so* easy,' Jones replied. 'You scare the living daylights out of most people, so why don't you come along? I could use a bit of flesh-and-blood threat.'

Bewick smiled. Then he turned to Karen. 'What're you doing here, by the way? Why aren't you monitoring your client's every move?'

'Dowling's gone to London. He's at his club until the weekend. Then he's invited the funding committee from St Anne's and one or two business chums down to his house, Ealand Priory.'

Bewick frowned. 'Who's vetting these people?'

'Just what me and Schrager asked. Coleridge reckons that Dowling's really inconsistent and has suddenly decided he doesn't care.'

'Well, well, well,' Jones said, very perky. 'Things are looking up.'

'What do you mean?'

'When your client gets assassinated, CRSI's reputation'll stink like a fishmonger's freezer in a power cut.'

Bewick sat beside Sir Terence Griffiths at the end of the long table, bright with reflections, in the gallery of the Master's Lodge.

There were eight fellows present – all the members of the committee that Sir Terence had formed as soon as it was realized that the murder of one of St Anne's porters might be an issue that could be manipulated by press enemies of the Oxbridge system.

Bewick had written a report, but wasn't reading from it. Beside him sat Jones, whom Bewick had insisted on bringing along. Feeling uncomfortable in the presence of Miller and Cranesmith, amongst others, Jones sat slumped, doing his best to imitate a hibernating animal of peaceable character. He was, as he'd hoped, ignored. Bewick, without any apparent effort, held the stage.

Bewick told them about the murder of Simmonds. He expounded the probability that the two killings were linked. He inferred the fatal link between Whear and Simmonds probably lay in the past – well before Whear began to work at St Anne's, back in the time when he and Simmonds were in the Air Operations Regiment together.

At the end of the gallery which led to the Master's accommodation, the door was open a crack. Beyond it, Miranda Griffiths stood, listening to Bewick's steady, deep-voiced delivery.

Bewick completed his report. The meeting was told that the date of the royal visit couldn't be altered to any time in the near future. Bewick and Jones were asked if there was any likelihood of their solving the case in the next week or so. Jones said it was very unlikely. Bewick advised the committee for the second time to compose a press release in cooperation with the royal visitor's office. They could now quote 'police sources' as being satisfied that the cause of the murders was completely unrelated to the college.

It was agreed that they should do this, but that the press release would be delayed until a week before the royal visit, in the perhaps vain hope that it would be unnecessary.

'We may have the whole thing sorted by then,' Bewick said, which produced a ripple of optimism.

The committee broke up. Bewick stayed behind to talk to Sir Terence. He told Griffiths he needed his help.

'Of course. Anything I can do.' Griffiths's reply

was prompt, smooth, with a hint that this was an assumption Bewick might have made for himself.

'I need to talk to somebody senior in the AOR. My boss, Peter Schrager, will possibly manage a contact, but they're a very secretive lot. I was hoping he might be able to co-opt your influence in Whitehall.'

'Such as it is, of course. Secretive organizations are one of my *bêtes noires*.'

'Thank you.'

'So, you're convinced, are you, that poor Whear's connections with the college are an irrelevance as far as his murder is concerned.'

'I didn't quite say that, Sir Terence . . .'

'You said that the reasons for his and Simmonds's murders lay elsewhere.'

'Yes, indeed,' said Bewick, mild and reassuring.

Griffiths picked up on his tone. 'You mean the motive for his murder was engendered elsewhere, but that the instrument of it . . .?'

'I can't yet discount the possibility.'

'Bloody right, you can't,' Jones said, when the conversation was related to him ten minutes later. 'Did you see Miller when you said the focus was moving away from the college?'

'Did *you*? I thought you were asleep.'

'He looked like a man who's just been told he hasn't got cancer.'

'I thought that, too. Did you ever get anyone to check his mother-in-Ely alibi?'

Jones hadn't. He felt found out. 'And what the

bleedin' hell're you on about, telling the best brains in the known universe that you're going to have the whole thing sorted by Tuesday? What the fuck's that about?'

'Shall we go to Ely tomorrow, Gio? They say it's going to be a nice afternoon.'

Sally Vernon waited for Bewick in the café by Great St Mary's. The broad walkway outside was busy: brisk undergraduates moving past slower tourists. A wino she'd often seen around sat on one of the benches outside the church. He was clutching his carrier bags, talking to himself. He was wearing two overcoats, despite the sunshine.

Sally was nervous. The guilt she was feeling over Anthony and his children wouldn't let her go. She knew it was a guilt that could be argued with. Anthony's fierce defence of his time, his work being the holy grail of his life, meant that she and even his own children would always come second.

Lip service was paid to her work, but Anthony's was blue-sky research and, subtly, he made her feel that her more practical work was less important. So she could easily enough find reasons for justifying what she had done. All very well; but she still felt guilty, even as she resented feeling guilty. Especially as she knew she wasn't committed yet to Bewick. Nor had he made any commitment either. He'd implied it, but what did that mean?

The memory of their night together was like a half-remembered dream now. He had been so tender that she had almost wished for rougher handling. And the pleasure . . .

She noticed a stir of attention around her. She glanced up to see Bewick. He made his way carefully across the room, as if aware of how his size could cause havoc amongst all the tablecloths and china. As soon as he sat down she realized that he wasn't staying. He looked at her gravely. She looked down at his hands and felt a pang of desire. Before he spoke she said, 'You have to go.'

It was gratifying to see the brief moment of surprise and then the pleasure he took in her quickness. 'How careful I'll have to be,' he murmured.

She smiled and said nothing. She was aware that they were becoming the focus of surreptitious attention.

'Gio Jones is waiting for me outside. Can you come over tomorrow evening?'

'I think so. I'll leave a message if not.'

He leaned forward, caressed her face and kissed her. Then he was gone. It was as if the room was suddenly emptied of life.

She knew now. She knew why she hadn't committed herself, why she couldn't. It wasn't sexual nerves, although she supposed that came into it. It was what she'd seen reflected in the faces of the women in the café: the widened eyes, the moistened lips, the sudden gravity. It was his power of attraction which made her fearful. With a man like Bewick, she was scared that she would feel herself to be constantly out-manoeuvred by other women, would believe herself dull. She could see herself raging with jealousy; permanently nervous, on the look-out for the woman who might take him away.

It was a failure of courage, it was cowardice, but she couldn't help it. She despised herself. Without waiting for the bill, she left too much money on the table and walked out.

They were in Jones's car. The fens were at their best. Under skies of sunlit cumulus, gigantic drifting shadows mottled the flat land.

The cathedral appeared on its ridge of rising ground, its island once, dominating the landscape as it had dominated the waterscape for more than half a millennium. They drove towards the massive embodiment of faith and power stamped on the horizon ahead.

'Like a bloody grain silo on the prairie, innit?' Jones flicked a glance at Bewick. They drove for another minute and then Jones said, 'I thought we'd agreed that Whear's and Simmonds's deaths were nothing to do with the college.'

'You've said that already, Gio.'

'You didn't give me a proper reply.'

'The obvious link between Simmonds and Whear is the army. Yes?'

'Agreed.'

'Well, I just think we shouldn't be blinded by the obvious, that's all. There may be another link.'

'Well, there is. The robbery that never went right.'

'Apart from that, obviously.'

'What, though?'

'I don't know. I just don't feel comfortable writing off the college, not yet. All that suppressed violence swilling around; all that hard-core religious faith. Look at that.' Bewick nodded at the vast stone ark ahead. The cathedral's detail was coming into focus: the Gatling-gun towers, the strange octagonal lantern in its nest of finials.

'What about it?'

'Think of what it cost to build that. There's no stone around here. Every inch of the thing had to be brought here by water or manhandled by block and tackle. Think what it cost. I don't mean money – I mean in terms of blind gut belief.'

'I'm thinking about it.'

'Turn that around.'

'How do you mean?'

'Into hatred.'

'For who?'

'For those who want to destroy your way of life.'

'But this isn't hundreds of years ago. People don't have that sort of faith nowadays. So they wouldn't hate that much either, would they?'

'Are you saying human nature's changed? Where do you think suicide bombers come from? Or Bobby Sands, come to that? He starved himself to death for his cause.'

'No. But –'

'The same thing's here now. Some people have that sort of faith. You saw that yourself at St Anne's.'

'Did I? I suppose I did. I still don't see how it can connect Whear and Simmonds.'

'Nor do I.'

Jones knew that whatever it was that had brought Bewick here, it was worth following along to see if he made anything of it. Jones thought about Brian Miller. There was a harsh quality to the man, a huge repression. He could imagine Miller labouring over love poetry long and hard and then offering it anonymously to Miranda Griffiths, as Bewick said he had.

What would Miller hope to gain? What was the fantasy? Was it nothing more than teenage fear of sexuality, carried on into adulthood? Or was it a dream of power and control?

Sally's phone rang. It was Miranda Griffiths.

'Miranda! This is a surprise. How nice to hear you.'

'Are you all right?'

'I'm fine,' Sally replied. She must have sounded strained. She remembered how intuitively quick Miranda could be. 'It's just the usual stuff,' she lied. 'Anyway, you're the one who should sound stressed. But you don't.'

'How do you mean?'

'The killing at St Anne's. It must have been a nightmare for you.'

'The focus of the inquiry has moved away from the college now.'

'Good. That's good news. Well, what can I do for you, Miranda?'

'Just be your usual sensible and intelligent self, the woman of judgement I know you to be. There's something I want to discuss with you.'

Sally laughed. 'What an irresistible invitation!'
They agreed to meet.

Jones had reached the first roundabout on the outskirts of Ely. He asked Bewick for directions, before
asking himself why on earth Bewick should know
better than him where Mrs Miller's house was. Nevertheless, Bewick did know. Of course he did. He always
bloody did.

Her house was in one of the older streets near the
cathedral. A fresh-faced, dark-haired woman answered the door; late twenties, Jones estimated.

'Yes?'

'Can we speak to Mrs Miller?' Jones asked.

She looked at him with deep suspicion. 'Who're
you, then? What d'you want?' She spoke with an odd
fen cockney, sloppy and stroppy. She kept an eye on
Bewick's massive presence.

'We're friends.'

'No you're not. 'Cos if you was you'd know she
was called Miss Quiggan.'

'I'm talking about Dr Miller's mother.'

'So am I. She always kept her maiden name. So
who the hell are you?'

'Police,' Bewick rumbled from behind, an edge of
menace. 'We're investigating a murder.'

You had to admit the bastard had his uses, Jones
thought. The woman had frozen, her eyes jumping
around as she tried to make a decision.

'A double murder,' Bewick added. 'So we'd like to

talk to Dr Miller's mother. Miss Quiggan, if that's who she is.'

'Well you can't. She's not here.'

'Where is she, then?'

'She's dead.'

Jones glanced at Bewick, who was doing his North Face of the Eiger impression.

'When did she die?'

'Year or so back.'

'I *see*,' said Jones, loading his voice with meaning, as if he really did see. 'Well, I think we should talk to you and have a glance around the house.'

'You can't. He wouldn't want it.'

'You're the housekeeper, are you?' Jones asked as if he didn't believe it.

'Sort of. He lets me stay here. You can't come in.'

'We'll come in if we have to. We have to verify Dr Miller's description of his movements.'

The woman looked uncertain. Bewick rumbled again. 'He's been lying to us.'

'But why d'you want to look?'

'He's been lying to us,' Bewick said again. He was beginning to frighten Jones, never mind the woman. Time for nice cop.

'Listen, love, I'll tell you how it goes. You don't let us in, we post a uniformed copper on your doorstep until we can get a warrant. Now, I don't know what your neighbours are like, but I know mine. Tongues'd be wagging like a pack of beagles. Here, look . . .'

Jones handed her his ID. 'All we need to do is have

a look round. Usual routine. Nothing dramatic. We want to try to see why he bothered to lie to us.'

'It's because of me. That's why it is.' She shoved Jones's ID back at him.

Jones went avuncular. 'Look, love, hadn't we better come in? Just while you tell us what's going on?'

The house was decently furnished in the style of someone making their modest choices thirty or forty years before. Bits and pieces of more modern living lay around the rooms like a more recent archaeological layer. No attempt had been made to harmonize these with the dead woman's belongings. The effect was strange and bleak.

'Him and me – we're together. We're an item.'

'How did that come about?' Jones asked.

'I started looking after his mum. I mean, that started about five years ago. She'd lost it and was very ill . . . Anyway, I was living here. When she had one of her turns, he'd be over for a night or two. So . . . He was very devoted. I liked that. He used to call her beloved. So . . .' She looked at her feet, perhaps remembering the first time. 'He was ever so nice in the beginning.'

'Yeah? And now? What's your name, by the way?'

'Fran. Fran Thoday.'

'So what's it like now, Fran?' He could see the temptation to disloyalty in her, but thought she'd probably pull back. Bewick seemed to sense it too.

'Is there a lavatory I could use?'

'Yeah, top of the stairs.'

Bewick left the room, quiet as a ghost. Jones watched Fran, her face settling into a truculent frown of stubbornness. He'd have to be careful with this one, or he could waste a lot of time. He wasn't interested in the fact that the Senior Tutor was screwing a woman twenty years younger. All he wanted to know was if he'd been here on the nights when Whear and Simmonds were shot.

It wasn't as if he was convinced that Miller was involved. Not yet, by any means. He could be, course he could. Jones wasn't discounting him as a suspect. What got to Jones was being lied to. It was another form of condescension. Also, although it constantly surprised him, in some ways Jones was tidy-minded. So he wanted to know.

Jones looked around the unappealing room. It wasn't a home. There were odd touches, though, which he guessed might be hers. There was an Escher print of an impossible staircase in a clip-glass frame, a vase of dried flowers and a couple of bright cushions.

'You've made it nice,' he said. He saw a look of relief for a moment. 'Nice touches.'

Fran shrugged. Jones wondered what Bewick was up to. Elsewhere in the house a washing-machine clicked into a new phase of its cycle and began its rhythmic sloshing.

'Tea?' Fran stood up. It was the first decisive thing she'd done.

'Great, ta.'

She left the room for the kitchen. Jones could hear nothing from upstairs.

Bewick was in the smallest of the three bedrooms. He had, with considerable care and in virtual silence, searched all the drawers in a chest which stood close by the window. He was now holding a sheaf of photos and looking down into the drawer from which he had taken them. In it was a photograph of an elderly woman propped up in bed. On the reverse was an inscription: 'The Beloved. 20.3'.

From overhead, Jones heard the cistern flushing. Fran came in with three mugs of weak-looking tea, just as Bewick came downstairs.

It took Jones and Bewick another ten minutes to establish that Miller hadn't been in Ely on the night of Whear's killing or, for that matter, Simmonds's.

Jones tried to get Fran to talk about her relationship with Miller. He saw that she thought she'd already said too much. He didn't doubt that with patience, he'd get a result. He also knew that wanting to know about her and Miller was probably idle curiosity, so he let it go.

On the way out, Bewick asked her if she knew when Miss Quiggan had died.

'About March time. Near the end of March.'

'Can't you remember exactly?'

'Why do you want to know?'

'Never mind. We'll go to the Register.'

'It was the twentieth, if you must know. Twentieth of March three years ago.'

'Thank you.'

They were standing under the octagon in the cathedral. Its columns and vaulting soared, lifting the eyes to the lantern: four hundred tons of lead and oak and glass floating high above them as delicately as a flower on water.

Bewick stared upwards. Jones consulted the guidebook.

'Bloke called Alan of Walsingham. Norman tower fell down, boom! Wrecked the middle of the cathedral. Our Alan had a vision of this amazing object: I mean, NASA eat your heart out. Found someone who was able to engineer the thing. Unique in medieval building. Well, well . . .'

Jones stared upwards, silenced by the majestically imagined structure.

'Faith,' said Bewick.

'That was then,' Jones replied.

'Our brains ain't changed.'

On the way out, they discussed Miller lying about where he had been on the night of Whear's murder. Jones thought that on its own it meant little. Most likely a nervous individual's panic. But . . .

'So what's all this about the day she died?'

Bewick told him about finding the photographs. 'They were inscribed "The Beloved. 20.3". Twentieth of March, presumably.'

'The day she died.'

'Yes. And I think she was dead when they were taken. That's why I asked.'

'Yeah?' Jones was silent for a while. They arrived at the car, parked next to a mossy stone wall. 'Does that help us?' he asked as he unlocked the car.

'Probably not.'

'What – I mean, what does it tell us about him? The Beloved. That meant to be ironic? Was he gloating? Reckon he loathed his mother?'

'Or the opposite. He looked after her.'

'Oh yeah, true.'

'Perhaps he couldn't bear to let her go.'

'So you take the final pic. Yuk. That's bonkers, isn't it? That's all about yourself. That's all about pitying yourself, isn't it? That's mourning porno, isn't it? What d'you reckon?'

'I'm not sure.'

'Who was it who kept his victims' corpses in his flat because he couldn't bear to let them go? Dahmer, was it? Nilsen? But this wasn't his victim, was it? Or *was* it?'

'I don't know. The only other example I know of someone drawing and photographing their mother after she'd died of natural causes isn't too promising.'

'Who was that?'

Bewick looked back at the massive age-stained towers of the cathedral. 'Adolf Hitler. He had faith.'

Sally had tried ringing him. She'd left messages, only to miss him each time he rang back. He apologized for being so taken up with the Whear–Simmonds case, sent his love, said he couldn't wait to see her again. Clearly he could wait. She found herself determined to put the worst possible construction on everything to do with him. She convinced herself, over the days of not seeing him, that she could do without this colossal upheaval in her life. She knew how to live by herself. She was her own woman.

She now decided to ring him to say that she thought it would be better if they didn't see each other for a while. After all, she'd told Bewick about Anthony the first time she'd met him again. Bewick had behaved as if Anthony didn't exist. And you showed him the way, a voice said. She ignored it. She knew how to live by herself, she told herself again.

When she got his answerphone, she realized she had to say this to his face. She didn't question why she was angry as she put the phone down. She glanced at the clock. She was supposed to be meeting Miranda Griffiths in half an hour.

Jones was perched on a table in front of the gothic window. He was in the college room which had been assigned to them by the Bursar. It had hardly been used since they'd found Simmonds. The police equipment was being cleared; the investigation was moving on. Jones was going over the visit of the day before to Ely. Interesting, but not a lot of use. Only odd thing was what Miller saw in Fran Thoday. Was her twenty-years-younger flesh that important to him? Poor Fran.

'Was this ours or theirs?' Baynes was holding a dog-eared plastic kettle.

'It's ours, Baynesie. Only servants of the Crown can afford anything so crap.'

'Right-o.'

The room emptied. He was alone. For a moment, he could see the appeal of a place like this. Idly he looked out of the window. There was that loopy papist, O'Keefe, lumbering over the grass: fierce eyes, bog-brush hair.

His mobile rang. It was PC Desai.

'She admitted it, Sir.'

'Julie?'

'Yes, Sir. We had a coffee. I was slandering my bloke something awful until she got fed up and asked if he hit me. It was me listening to her after that. Couldn't stop her, poor bitch. He hits her and she's frightened of him. She won't get out of it 'cos she thinks he'll kill her.'

'Well done.'

'Thank you, Sir, very much.'

Jones looked up. O'Keefe stood in the doorway. He looked at Jones as if he barely knew him.

'Do you know how long you'll be?'

'No,' said Jones, uncooperative.

'Roughly.'

'No idea. The policeman is an unpredictable creature.' Jones stared at him. Was he going to get an
apology from O'Keefe for knocking him over? Not,
it seemed. 'Why?' he asked, without charm.

'This is going to be my room. I asked to be moved
from a ground-floor set.'

Not surprised, Jones thought, remembering what
Bewick had witnessed. Or did the mad bastard fancy
an audience for his masochistic practices?

'And Professor Lucas says he would prefer not to
have stairs. His hip is a problem to him.'

'Well, I'm glad you're here, as a matter of fact,'
Jones said. 'I'd like to ask you what you were doing
having an argument with a tramp on the night of
Whear's murder. You said you came directly back to
St Anne's after the theatre. You didn't mention the
tramp.'

O'Keefe looked at him, apparently mystified. 'I
realize, Chief Inspector,' he said in cold, measured
tones, 'that your investigation is frustrating you, that
it's now a double murder, and that you must leave no
stone unturned, but inventing incidents for no serious
reason is beneath contempt.'

O'Keefe walked out. Jones was pissed off. Ever
since he'd come to this bloody college he'd been put
in his place. He glanced at his watch. At least there was
Miller. Dr Brian bloody Miller, purveyor of porkies.

*

'What do you want? I'm not sure I have the time. I've got a lot to do.' Miller looked at Gio Jones down his ascetic nose, his precise voice very clipped.

Jones had just climbed the dingy stone staircase of the Longhi tower and was breathing heavily, but was able to disguise it.

'Yes, well, of course my time is merely a matter of fun and frolics and farting about,' he said wearily. 'So I hardly dare mention it to a man with so much to do, but I want to know what you were up to on the night of the murder of Alan Whear.'

'You're very offensive. I've a good mind to report you to your superiors.' Miller's hollow-cheeked face was hot and blotchy, angry.

Jones sighed. 'Don't be silly,' he said.

'Silly?' Miller's voice cracked momentarily before he seemed to realize what a fool he could make of himself. He swallowed, then said again, 'What do you want, Chief Inspector?' and turned away, lifting his face to view his beautifully organized shelves.

It was suddenly clear to Jones how vulnerable to pressure Miller might be. Jones had taken a lot of shit, spoken and unspoken, from Miller and O'Keefe that morning. Well, maybe here was a chance . . . He looked around. Miller's room was that of an obsessive. Hours every week must be spent in here lining up all these files and books and CD-Roms and mini-discs: divisions of information, armies ready to attack.

'How would you describe your relationship with the Master's wife?'

Had Miller expected this question? Or had he told

himself to cool it completely? Jones had meant it to throw him, but it didn't.

'Cordial. I think Miranda quite likes me. She was a student when I was a postgraduate supervisor. We got to know each other then. I must confess I was a great admirer – along with hundreds of others. She's consistently friendly. Why do you ask?'

Jones changed tack. 'You told me that on the night of Whear's death you were at your mother's. You could hear her snoring, you said.'

'I think you must be mistaken.'

'That's what you told me.'

'I have absolutely no recollection of telling you such a thing.' Miller tried to chuckle, self-deprecating. It sounded hysterical. 'I must have been upset. My mother is no longer with us.'

'I know. She's dead.'

Miller winced at this bluntness. Then he said, 'I was at my mother's house, I should have said. She left it to me. I'm still –'

'No you weren't.'

'What?'

'You weren't there. Not according to your mistress, you weren't.'

Again Miller switched. His face tightened. His skin seemed to be sucked back into the harsh crevices around his mouth. His voice was dry, rough. 'What? What did you say?'

'You heard,' Jones said.

Miller turned away, as if from a nasty smell.

'You were here in college, weren't you?'

'No. Absolutely not. I resent this. I resent it.'

'Of course you do. Nobody likes being proved a liar.'

Miller said nothing.

'So what were you doing here?'

'I wasn't here.'

'Where were you, then?'

'Are you accusing me of something? If you are, you'd better tell me what it is.'

'I'm accusing you of telling porkies, that's what. My job is difficult enough without highly intelligent people like you messing me about. Look, I want to know and you'd better tell. Sooner or later I'll know, unless –'

'Unless what?'

'Unless we can do a bit of barter. You could tell me all about your jolly companions. All the dirt. Then you could keep your grubby little secrets, if that's what you want. Unless, of course, we find out it was you who shot Alan Whear.'

'This is disgusting!'

'Sure. Think about it.' Jones slapped down his card. 'There's my mobile number. Don't think royalty would be able to take a sex scandal on top of the murder, do you?'

Jones left and trotted down the dark, curving staircase of the Longhi tower, feeling more cheerful than he had done for a week or more.

They were sitting side by side on a low stone wall, near the place where Sally had first seen Whear's body in the punt. Just as then, the sun shone. A haze of green was blurring the outline of branches now and the grove across the river was loud with birdsong.

'I'm surprised you chose me to talk to about it, whatever it is,' Sally said. 'You must have friends who are closer than me.'

Sally had been flattered by Miranda's request, but was mystified by it.

'Not really. I feel comfortable with you. Most women I meet seem to dislike me.'

'I find that difficult to believe.'

'It's true. It's true of academe, at least. You seem to stand outside all that.'

'In what way? Outside what?'

'You're sexy, for a start . . . Outside all the gaucheness and envy.'

Sally was pleased for a moment. Then she thought of Karen and was brought back to earth.

'I was brought up with ponies and dogs, you see, and nice girls who had a bit of a struggle even with O-level cooking.'

'Same for me. I was a freak,' said Sally.

'Because you read books?'

'Exactly. They treated you with such a lot of kindness.'

'Yes, as if one had a terminal illness.'

They both laughed.

Across the river in the grove of trees, Jones heard the laughter and leaned forward to look. The two women were slightly turned away and were unaware of him. Jones had wandered into the grove to think. He'd been standing still, lost in a quagmire of disparate facts about the Whear–Simmonds case, when he'd heard the laughter. Jones eased back behind a tree, leaning his shoulders against it.

The two women were such a contrast. The sturdy brown-eyed blonde and the taller, blue-eyed, darker-haired woman. He'd once thought Bewick might settle down with Sally Vernon, but perhaps her cool, competent manner was too close to Bewick's own. He wondered what had split them up before they'd even really got together. He'd always assumed that the split had come from her. He wondered if she regretted it.

As for Miranda Griffiths – he knew how much she'd confessed to Bewick. It then occurred to Jones that he'd never seriously entertained the idea of this Lady Griffiths as a suspect. Maybe he should have done. She'd successfully deflected him from interviewing her, after all. But why? What could connect her to Simmonds? He glanced over at the two women again. Something had changed between them. Sally Vernon looked hunched, miserable.

It had taken Sally several minutes to realize that Miranda might be talking about John Bewick. Eyes shining, Miranda had sung the praises of this unnamed man, his intuitions, his curious power when listening, his ability to command attention when talking. Then she'd said, 'And the power is physical, too. He's built like a weight-lifter or something; a blacksmith.'

'What's his name?'

'Why?' asked Miranda, smiling. She was surprised

by the humourlessness that had overtaken Sally, until she realized its probable cause and felt awful.

'Not that I need to ask. You're talking about John Bewick, aren't you?'

Miranda saw, or thought she saw, the situation in a flash. 'My God, he's not your lover, is he?'

'No. Not at all. Of course he isn't,' Sally heard herself snap. Why was she denying it? 'I just know him, that's all.' She felt physically sick.

There was a silence. Both women's innate courtesy told them there was nothing to be said which could redeem the moment. Miranda assumed Sally's irritability was a measure of her emotional involvement and jealousy. She considered apologizing, but thought it would be crass to do so.

Eventually it was Sally who spoke. 'I was very fond of him once . . .' How could she tell her?

'Tell me about him.' Miranda's voice, warm with intelligent sympathy, tempted her to confide everything. Her private refusal to do so made her feel crabbed and sour.

'I saw him kill a man. Well, cause his death, I should say. It put me off.'

Miranda looked stunned; as intended. Sally didn't moderate what she'd said. It was only the truth, after all, if partial.

'Aren't you going to elaborate?'

'It was self-defence. He knocked the man over on to his own gun. It was the gun that killed him. It was an accident. The man died from gunshot wounds.'

'I see.'

'Yes, I expect you do. Would it have put you off?'

'I don't know. Thank you for telling me.'

'That's all right.' Sally stood. 'I think I'll go now. I'm sorry. I'm finding all this very difficult.'

'Yes.'

Sally nodded. Then she left. She walked away and soon found herself on the edge of the plain, grand lawn in front of the chapel. It was, she decided, what she needed. The strange, exalted space of her college chapel: she'd felt happier and more desolate there than in any other place in the world; never ordinary.

'Well,' Miranda said to herself, watching Sally disappear, 'another woman who dislikes me.'

The columns, slender as bundled saplings, drew the eye upward. Sally was looking along an avenue of delicate stone trees. Their branches, fantailing outwards, kissed the curve of their opposites to form a canopy high above. A choir practice was in progress. A motet was begun, faultless to her ear, but it was interrupted by the choirmaster with instructions she couldn't hear. It began again, a tide of gorgeous sound flooding the building.

Sally sat down to listen. She knew some of the male choristers: as ordinary and odd a bunch as any other. Listen, though, to what they were making here! At the edge of consciousness, her black anger smouldered. She knew she must address it, but not now, not yet, not while this brilliance filled the air.

The motet finished. The final echo faded. The choirmaster said something and there was laughter.

That faded too. Then there was a shuffling of feet and conversation, muffled and reverberating, as the choristers moved off. She realized that they were going to come past her. She wanted communication with no one. She bent forward and pretended to pray. She waited a minute, until she was sure everyone had passed her, then straightened up.

Why had she denied Bewick was her lover? Did she disbelieve in it so much? She thought perhaps she did. It seemed like a confirmation of her terrible uncertainty: that she wouldn't be able to deal with his attractiveness to others. It griped at her. It depressed her utterly. Into her darkness came the thought of Anthony's children, their vulnerability, their appeal. What on earth did she think she was doing? Was their betrayal the price of her pleasure? And Anthony: what had he done to deserve abandonment? She found herself in tears. Tears of self-pity, she decided. Again. She blew her nose, stood up and left.

Jones, who had just been for a pre-lunch jog, was in the bath. His mobile rang. It was Baynes.

'Hallo, Baynesie. What's up?'

Downstairs, the front doorbell rang.

'They identified the sole print of that boot ... Simmonds's workshop?'

'Oh yeah? What is it, then?'

'Yachting boot, they reckon.'

The doorbell rang again. Jones nearly dropped his mobile in the bath. He juggled with it, caught it and said goodbye to Baynes. Moments later, he charged out of the bathroom, a towel around his waist. He knew the house was full of his children – he listened to the radio gabble, the TV gabble, the pumping music from various parts of the house. 'Aaaargh!' he roared from the top of the stairs. A door opened, then another.

'Bloody hell, Dad, what was that? You really scared me.' It was Joanna.

'I'm having a bath! There are three of you! The bell's rung twice! Go and open the damn door!'

Pausing only to give him the full-on teenage sulk-stare, Joanna started down the hallway. Then the door was opened from the outside by Eilean, who'd been to the corner shop for the *Guardian*.

'See?' said Joanna, as if this was an entirely predict-able outcome. With the skill of a concert percussionist, she shut the sitting-room door behind her with just enough force to annoy but not enough to warrant a protest.

'She'll be out again as soon as she hears his voice,' thought Jones. The visitor was Bewick. Jones found himself standing up a bit straighter, pulling his stomach in, and told himself to stop it.

'Come on in, John,' Eilean said. 'Gio's having a bath. Oh, there you are!'

'Hello, John!' Megan appeared beside her father, giggling.

As predicted, the sitting-room door opened and Joanna emerged, calm, pretty and welcoming. Megan bounded down the stairs to spoil the moment her sister was hoping for. From the fifth step up, Megan launched herself at Bewick, who caught her easily. She glanced to see if her ploy had succeeded.

If Joanna was seething, she gave no sign of it. 'Let me take your bag, John, then you can give the brat a proper cuddle.'

My God, thought Jones, she's learning. She's going to be lethal. He exchanged a surprised glance with Eilean and went to get dressed.

The house had magically calmed a few minutes later when Jones, now dressed, came out of the bedroom. Barry's door was open and he could hear Bewick's voice from within.

'I need him to look like a squaddie, a bit skinhead,' Bewick was saying, 'so all that hair goes and then you need to shadow in up to his original hairline – and slim the face. Anyway, you know what I mean. Have a go. See how you get on.'

On the computer screen was the photograph of Sir Michael Dowling that Karen had given them, the epitome of a successful suit; the jawline beginning to fill in, the hair touching his ears and his collar.

Bewick turned to Jones. 'That's the Adobe software I gave him for Christmas. He'll have a pic of Dowling as a squaddie in next to no time.'

'What's all this about, anyway?'

'I've got an invite to the AOR base.'

'Bloody hell!'

Hours of phone calls made over three days by Peter Schrager, as well as mention of Bewick's acquaintance with Sir Terence Griffiths, had finally achieved the invitation. It had involved two MPs, a Permanent

Secretary, a General at the MOD (once Schrager's CO) and, finally, a member of the Cabinet. All this to scale the wall of non-cooperation surrounding the Air Operations Regiment, and even then they had needed luck.

'Colonel somebody,' Bewick went on. 'Second in command of the training base at Lotheny.'

'Well, who did you have to sleep with to get that then?' Jones was furious with resentment. Without telling Bewick, he'd been trying for days to get the same result.

'You're invited too.'

'Oh, thanks a bunch.'

'You don't have to come.'

'Oh, just get on with it, will you?' Jones closed the door on them, jealous of Bewick on every level, not least because of his ability to tame everyone he met, even Jones's beloved barbarian son.

Built as a reserve airfield for the US airforce in 1943, Lotheny had never been out of commission since it was used during the Berlin airlift, and shortly afterwards the Americans handed it over to the AOR.

Strategically planted blocks of forestry meant that Lotheny was invisible except from the air. The only indication of its presence was the occasional noise of mortar and small arms fire from its woods, and the infrequent view of Hercules transport aircraft falling out of sight behind the dark horizon of trees.

Lotheny's perimeter stood within a broad firebreak, between an eighty-metre outer curtain of conifers and the deeper, mixed-woodland block inside it. The perimeter was electronically surveyed twenty-four hours a day by various sensors, CCTV, and standing patrols of AOR soldiers with dogs. For any member of the AOR, breaching the perimeter unchallenged and penetrating to the inner edge of the woodland meant automatic promotion. Despite frequent attempts, this feat was last achieved in 1986.

Armed with Barry's doctored photograph, Bewick drove himself and Jones the twenty miles north-east from Cambridge. Turning off on to what would normally be small country lanes, he found himself on a broad and well-maintained road. It led into a dark belt of forestry.

For the first time, they saw signs of MOD activity: the red-on-white notices: 'This is a restricted area . . . within the meaning of the Act . . .'

A short chicane and they were at the entrance complex. They sat in the car, waiting.

'I suppose the buggers are checking us on the computer,' Jones said. 'We're probably being photographed as well.'

While they waited, they noted the potential defences: the huge, rising bollards, the steel-shuttered tank traps across the entrance, the steel double gates which would stop anything on wheels. There was no regimental insignia, no flag, no identification of the unit whose HQ it was.

A soldier in a flak jacket and helmet came out to

them. Jones produced his police ID and Bewick his passport. Then Bewick was asked to drive beyond the barrier and wait for the Colonel's ADC.

Captain Paton was extraordinarily polite, using old-fashioned phrases – 'I wonder if you'd be good enough to . . . I'd be obliged if . . .'. He led Bewick and Jones across a moderately sized parade ground.

'This is the main block, Officers' Mess and so forth. The AOR is unique in that all ranks eat in the Officers' Mess. The thinking is that if you're going to die together it's a nonsense not to eat together.'

'Sounds reasonable,' Jones said.

'Unique, though. Doesn't chime with the military mind. Which, by the way, considers us a bunch of renegades, unprofessional and impractical. Probably would've been combined with the paras or something years ago, except nobody'll put up with us.'

The main block was typical of mid-century military building: red-brick-classical, with half-moon swimming-pool steps up to a pillared entrance, utility detailing.

The Colonel took his time assessing Bewick and Jones when they entered; a long, slow look before he shook them both by the hand.

'Welcome to Lotheny, gentlemen,' he said unsmilingly.

Colonel Rucker-Whitman, MC, CB had military connections stretching back to the Peninsular Wars against Napoleon. He was an arresting figure. A slim, quick-moving man, he had tight, curly hair and facial features which might have placed his origins in the

Horn of Africa, except that his colouring was entirely European: straw blond, pale-skinned.

'Thank you.' Bewick offered nothing more.

Rucker-Whitman retreated behind his desk. 'What is all this about, gentlemen?' He glanced up to find Bewick looking at him now with a benign, unapologetic expression, like a man emerging from meditation. Jones, on the other hand, was shifting around in the chair he'd been offered, the picture of discomfort. 'How can I help you?'

'It's about two ex-members of your regiment.' Bewick paused to allow Rucker-Whitman to acknowledge what he knew about them. The Colonel's face didn't change. Bewick glanced at Captain Paton: a blank there as well.

'What about them?'

'They've been shot and killed.'

Now there was a reaction, a frown. 'Were they on security duties? A lot of our men move into the security industry.'

'They were murdered, separately; while they were alone,' Bewick rumbled.

'I see.'

Either Rucker-Whitman was being disingenuous or he was out of touch with his men. There must be someone in the regiment who remembered Whear and Simmonds. If so, then the camp would have been seething with rumours.

Rucker-Whitman looked up at Paton. 'You heard anything about this, Mike?'

'Nothing concrete, Sir.' Paton addressed Bewick.

'We're somewhat isolated out here. Rumours abound. One tends to discourage them.'

'So you heard a rumour?' asked Rucker-Whitman.

'Yes, Sir. About a soldier Whear, Sir. The local radio reported him shot and killed. Sergeant Atkinson thought he might be the same Whear who was with the regiment on the Ulster tour ten years ago.'

'I see. This the man you're talking about?' Rucker-Whitman asked Bewick.

'Yes. The other man was called Simmonds.'

Rucker-Whitman thought for a moment and then shook his head. 'Rings a bell. Doesn't bring a face to mind, I'm afraid. You said these men were ex-members. What do you think we might be able to tell you?'

'The circumstances of the men's deaths were very particular. We have various theories as to motive, but we need to verify them – or call them into question . . .'

The two men watched Bewick stonily, as if acknowledging the authority of an unloved superior officer.

'So if you could look out their service records for me, that would be a help. Even more helpful might be to be allowed to speak to this man Atkinson.'

The silence that now followed was electric with suspicion.

Rucker-Whitman took a deep breath. 'That would be possible,' he said. 'Of course. In fact, all army-service records are housed in Glasgow. Some of them may be classified – a number of our men go on to work for MOD intelligence outfits.'

'Understood.'

'Many of *our* operations, too, are secret, I'm afraid, and for them we are answerable only to the MOD and the Secretary of State. We are all subject to the Official Secrets Act. Access to our records is not a matter of course.'

'Understood.'

'Also, I would like to make it clear that I have an obligation to protect my men.'

'From what?' Jones was now sounding belligerent.

Rucker-Whitman leaned forward. He looked down at the desk a few feet in front of Bewick. He lowered his voice, as if he didn't want to be overheard. 'We have a lot of trouble with journalists. They can be very aggressive; very. I have to protect my men and their families from that sort of thing. We have a job to do.'

'The journalists too, I suppose,' said Bewick mildly.

'Come again?'

'Have a job to do.'

Rucker-Whitman seemed baffled for a moment. 'What sort of job do you call that?' he said. His mouth turned down. 'These people have no idea of the damage they do.'

Bewick smiled, and it could have meant anything. 'Would it be possible to have a word with this Sergeant Atkinson?'

'It would.' Rucker-Whitman raised his eyebrows at Paton, who quietly left the room.

'May I rely on your complete discretion, Colonel?' Bewick asked.

'Yes, you may.'

'Thank you. The first thing to tell you is that a number of years ago, after they left the regiment, Whear and Simmonds were involved in an incompetent burglary, for which they were prosecuted. Now, when Simmonds and Whear were arrested, someone posted bail for them, although, in fact, it was refused. There is a third man involved in all this.' Bewick slid the doctored photo of Dowling across the Colonel's desk. 'Do you recognize him?'

Rucker-Whitman looked hard at the photo, poker-faced. 'I don't think so. Vaguely familiar, maybe. These men left the regiment a long time ago. Why should I remember him?'

'Because he's now a public figure.'

Rucker-Whitman shrugged, but he looked uncomfortable. Neither Bewick nor Jones said anything, as if to prolong his discomfort. Rucker-Whitman looked down at the photo again. 'I suppose I vaguely do recognize him. Have I seen him on television?'

There was a knock at the door. Paton entered, with a man in his late thirties, wiry, very fit. His left hand and wrist were encased in first-aid strapping. The Colonel explained, in outline, Bewick's visit.

'We're talking nearly ten years ago, Sergeant Atkinson. Eighty to eighty-six.' Rucker-Whitman turned to Bewick. 'May I show him this?' he asked, indicating the photograph.

'Of course.'

'Do you recognize this man?'

'No, Sir.'

Atkinson answered so immediately that Jones

glanced over to catch Paton's reaction. Paton looked, or pretended to look, surprised. Atkinson's extra-prompt answer suggested that he'd made up his mind before seeing the photograph. Rucker-Whitman seemed aware of this, but not embarrassed.

'Are you sure?'

'Sure, Sir!'

'Take another look.'

Atkinson gave the photograph a brief glance and repeated that he'd never seen him before.

'Very well. Now, this officer here,' Rucker-Whitman indicated Bewick, 'is interested in asking you about a soldier you may have served with.'

'Yessir!'

'Do you remember a soldier called Whear?' asked Bewick.

'No, Sir.'

'Simmonds?'

'Don't remember them, Sir.'

'Not at all? This is a very serious matter, Sergeant. Look at this photograph again. Are you certain you don't recognize this man?'

'Sir.'

Paton intervened. 'I heard that you were wondering if the Whear who has been shot was the same soldier you served with long ago.'

'Not me, Sir.'

'Or a soldier called Simmonds?'

'No, Sir. No idea, Sir.'

'Do you know what this might have been all about?'

'No, Sir. No idea, Sir.'

Paton turned to Rucker-Whitman and made a face of mock despair.

'Sergeant Atkinson, I am ordering you to tell me all you know about these men,' said the Colonel.

'I know nothing about them, Sir.'

'Very well. You may go, Atkinson.'

'Sah!' Atkinson saluted and marched out.

'So,' Rucker-Whitman said, 'we don't seem to be able to help you. I suspect Atkinson knows a lot more than he's prepared to admit to, but –' He spread his hands in a classic gesture of resignation.

'If you think that, can't you get him to tell you what he knows?' Jones was getting more and more irritable. This lot were worse than the Plato spouters at St Anne's.

'Of course I could continue to try, but these are men trained to resist interrogation under torture. If there was something Atkinson wished to conceal from you, you wouldn't get it.'

'Doesn't say much for the discipline in this place,' Jones said.

Rucker-Whitman smiled. 'We're not a conventional force. And this isn't a battle situation.'

Jones felt put down. He wished Bewick would have a go.

As if prompted, Bewick said, 'Two men are dead. A third – or more – may be at risk. How many corpses would you require to call it a battle situation?'

'Point taken. I still don't see how we can help.'

'Do you know of any event that all these soldiers might have been involved in? On the battlefield, perhaps? In Ulster? What I'm really asking is, if I go to Glasgow and look up Whear's and Simmonds's service records, am I going to find anything unusual?'

'You might, but even if I knew what it was I'm not at liberty to tell you.'

'Why not?' Bewick said this with no emotional pressure; he was almost friendly.

'Because I don't know to what extent the records are classified. If I knew anything about this soldier and told you about it, I might be breaking the Official Secrets Act.' Rucker-Whitman smiled.

Both men were experts at remaining calm. The only difference, as far as Jones could see, was that the Colonel didn't expect Bewick to remain calm. There was a silence. Bewick gazed steadily at Rucker-Whitman and then he looked around the room. The silence stretched. Jones felt more and more awkward. Paton shifted from foot to foot. From having been bolt upright, Rucker-Whitman leaned over in his seat.

As he did so, Jones found himself staring, trans-fixed. On the shelves behind Rucker-Whitman's chair, various pieces of regimental silver were displayed. Amongst them, invisible until now, was a small, wooden shield with the arms of the regiment painted on it: a crescent of oak leaves with AOR in gold arranged around it, the whole enclosing a camel in silhouette; black.

So that was it! '*1 toy camel, black.*' And then the boot, Camel, inked in. Jones thought for a moment that something had been revealed to him. Something important, vital. But what? Second thoughts made him realize that these sick little games the killer had played told him nothing that he didn't know already.

'Perhaps, if I might make a suggestion, Sir,' he heard Paton say.

'What you must understand,' said Rucker-Whitman, ignoring Paton, 'is that I was not commanding officer at the time of these events.'

'What events?' Bewick asked.

'At the time you're describing,' Rucker-Whitman corrected himself.

'What events?'

'At the time you're describing.'

'Were you in the regiment at the time I'm describing?'

'Of course, but I was away on secondment.'

'When was that?'

'Oh, a few years ago.'

'Well,' Bewick said, turning to Jones, 'at least we now know that these events didn't take place a few years ago.'

'Perhaps if I might make a suggestion, Sir,' Paton repeated.

'Yes?'

'Perhaps if I were to talk to Atkinson, to try to find out anything he might know. On a persuasive basis, rather than – if he knows anything at all, that is.

'What do you think of that, gentlemen? Would that be a step forward?'

Neither Bewick nor Jones said anything. Eventually

Bewick stood. 'We won't waste any more of your time. I'll only say, Colonel, that the truth has an inconvenient habit, like cream or scum, of coming to the surface.'

He walked out; Jones followed.

On the way back to the car, Jones asked Paton about the black camel. 'Oh, we had our origins in the desert,' he said breezily.

'Yes?'

'Do you know why camels look so self-satisfied?' Paton asked.

'No.'

'The Arabs say that God has a thousand names. Man knows nine hundred and ninety-nine of them. Only the camel knows the thousandth.'

'What the bleeding hell are that lot playing at?' Jones grumbled, as Bewick's old Volvo cleared the forestry surrounding Lotheny. He felt threatened. The whole camp, its defences, its armaments, its dedication to violence, unnerved him. He felt as if he and Bewick had challenged its latent power and might have to pay for it.

He told Bewick about the black camel he'd found at each crime scene. 'What d'you reckon?'

'It possibly means that the killer wants to communicate why these men died.'

'I'm glad somebody does. Those bloody soldiers sure as hell don't.'

Bewick told Jones about Simmonds's cap badge being missing. 'I guess that would have had a black camel on it, too. Torn out recently. Presumably

Simmonds wanted to destroy any visible connection with his old regiment.'

'Yeah?'

'I wonder if Simmonds was frightened of the killer or of Atkinson.'

'*Atkinson?*'

'I think it was him I tangled with the other night. He's clearly got a lot he wants to keep under wraps, Sergeant Atkinson. Doesn't like anyone trespassing on his patch. What's he nervous of, I wonder? Or who, rather.'

'Would he know himself? Doubt if he does much listening. Or thinking, come to that. Why think when you can enjoy a good punch-up?'

Bewick was quiet for some time, then he said, 'I'm amazed we ever got into that place.'

'Bloody right,' Jones said, glad to voice his anxiety. 'I'm amazed we ever got *out*. So what now? Where from here? Tell you what, I'd rather have Plato than Nato. That snotty college is beginning to seem quite friendly after all.'

'At least we established that Whear and Simmonds were involved in something. Other than a bit of breaking and entering.'

'Yeah, suppose we did. *These events*, eh? He got fairly knickertwisted over that, didn't he?'

'I think we can assume something happened which makes them uncomfortable. Whatever it is, they're gambling we can't get at it, not via anything that's in the public domain. Rucker-Whitman is hoping the relevant part of the records will still be classified. I'll look at them, anyway. But if they give us nothing, I'm not sure where we go.'

It was one of the rare times that Jones had known Bewick to sound defeated.

13

Karen made her way to Piccadilly from King's Cross by bus. She didn't know London well. She was excited by it, as usual: the variety of the people, the churning restlessness of the streets. It also made her edgy, a place without any real connections for her. To compound her unease, she was suspicious of the summons which had brought her there.

'I asked him about the party at Ealand Priory. He said I should send someone up to discuss it. He meant you.' Schrager had been sympathetic, but she recognized a velvet glove when she saw one.

'Bloody hell.'

'He's paying.'

'Why the hell can't he do it by phone? We've given him a scrambler.'

'He's probably feeling insecure. He wants someone to hold his hand.'

'Holding hands is part of the contract, is it, Sir?'

'You know what I'm talking about. You only need to schmooze the bugger a bit. You never know, you might even get lunch out of it.'

'That's what worries me.'

'Find out what you can. He may unload a bit to you. That's why I want you to go.'

Karen got off at Leicester Square, and turned into

a narrow side street. Small ancient houses, tarts and pungent Chinese restaurants. Rows of bright-red dead ducks, wind drying; car-exhaust drying, more like. Gaudy fabrics, overbright neon. Sweet and sour, woks and steam. She'd chosen this route because a third of the way along was a tiny restaurant where she'd come with Bewick in the early days.

Huddled together with him in a corner above the noisy street, she'd felt an intimacy which had been as acute as sex. By taking her there, she thought, he'd shown her an unusual side of himself, something private; as if he'd said, Meet the real me. It implied that he liked the scruffy plainness, the smallness, the being thrown together with strangers to share brilliant speed-cooking.

She stopped. What the hell was she doing, indulging in this? People brushed past her. Ahead was the restaurant. She retraced her steps and walked quickly back to Leicester Square.

Five minutes later, she turned into the alleyway off Piccadilly beside the red-brick Wren church, as she'd been told to. She crossed a narrow street, turned right and left and found herself in St James's.

The building was huge. As she walked up the wide steps of the I and C, the Imperial and Commonwealth Club, she saw above the doorway a stone shield: '1911'. Then she was inside a huge marble cave, lit by dim bronze lamps.

She'd seen nothing to tell her that it was the I and C, but it fitted the description she'd been given. She liked that, cool.

The door was opened for her by a man in a morning suit, wedding kit. Behind the desk was a cheerful-looking bloke, similarly dressed, who was watching her like a hawk. Karen said who she was and told him who she was there to meet. It was no more than a ghost of amusement that passed across the man's face, but it annoyed her.

'*Detective Inspector* Quinney,' she added, staring at him.

'Yes, Madam.' The next glance he flicked at her was one of curiosity, maybe wondering what Dowling had got himself into. 'I'll page him right away.'

'Shall we have lunch?' Dowling steered Karen into the back of the Jaguar. The door was held open by his Indian chauffeur, a heavyweight minder.

'I'm all right, thanks.'

'Do you mind if I eat something?'

'Course not.'

'Right. We'll go to La Cucina.'

Bewick sat in Jones's office while Jones filled him in about his not-very-subtle blackmailing of Miller.

'Mind you,' Jones went on, 'doubt if there's anything useful Miller can tell us. Juicy maybe, not useful.'

'I don't know: ask him about Cranesmith. He's the only one of that lot who actually knew Whear.'

'And what about Miranda, Lady Griffiths?' Jones asked with heavy irony. 'Shall I ask him about her? Or have you seen her more recently?'

'Yes, you could ask him about her; by all means. Gio, what was that supposed to mean?'

The atmosphere was prickly. Bloody hell, Jones thought. Why do I do this? Why? Jones couldn't even work out who he was having a go at. Bewick? Karen? Sally? Himself?

'Nothing . . . Really. Sorry.'

'I reckon I'll go up to Glasgow, by the way. See what Whear's and Simmonds's service records will actually tell us, as I said.'

'If anything.'

'If anything. Have you told Smew what's happening to his daughter?'

'No. I'll have to, I suppose.' Jones sounded miserable.

'He may have something for us.'

'Sure.'

'Do you think this still has anything to do with the college, Gio?'

'If you mean, do I *want* the answer to lie in a world that I understand: then yes. I want it to be about villains and bad human relations, normal police work. Trouble is, I don't think it is.'

'You've got the best nose in the business. Just wanted to know where it might be leading you, that's all.'

'Oh . . . Well, at the moment I'd say I've got no further than smelling my own bum.'

Bewick laughed. 'Oh, by the way,' he said, 'there was a message on my answerphone from Niki Whear.

She's found something that Whear's written. I'll check it out.'

'What's the betting it's another bloody blind alley?'

The restaurant was white, light and high-ceilinged. The floor was pale marble. The tables were uncrowded, the chairs deeply upholstered. On the walls were black and white photographs of early Ferraris. The menus were as big as a broadsheet newspaper.

'Why are you so uncomfortable?'

Karen didn't reply at first, annoyed that he'd even noticed. She looked around. 'It's not my world,' she said eventually, 'and I'm not sure I want it to be.'

'Why not?'

'It's the sort of place where heavy deals are done.'

'Life is a series of deals though, don't you think?'

'Dodgy deals, then.'

'Same thing. Just that some deals in life are dodgier than others. I did a deal with a female recently. She was in the Olympics last time around, equestrian. I thought the deal was to do with love, friendship, the real thing already. Turned out that there was a lot of small print. Love me, love my horses, from the smell of their shite to the whites of their eyes when they're about to inflict GBH on you. Some deal.'

Karen wondered why he'd told her this. Was it to tell her that he was free? Or to identify himself as a victim?

'I meant cooked-up deals,' she replied, 'exploitative stuff.'

'What d'you think the horsewoman was up to? She

knew that all she really wanted was a relationship with Desert Orchid. She thought I'd do as a temporary stop-gap. Thousands of guineas later . . . How dodgy do you call that?'

'Surely you saw what she was up to?'

Dowling thought about this for a moment, then he nodded. 'If something's wrong between two people at the beginning, it sure as hell won't be any better further down the line. What you see at the beginning is what you get.'

'Maybe.'

'I mean, there's no point in trying to change people –'

'I thought we were the most adaptive species ever known.'

''Cos life's too short. What're you going to drink?'

'Fizzy water. So who is it's going to have a go at knocking you off, then?'

'You're quite a stroppy bird, aren't you?'

'Or is it some sort of fantasy you get off on?'

He looked at her hard. 'No, it isn't.'

For the first time, she believed him. She saw, like a glimpse through a closing door, a frightened man, troubled, hoping.

It was three and a half pages of lined paper, hand-written by someone who wasn't used to writing any-thing, apart from perhaps signing his name.

'I found it in Alan's bits and pieces. Thought I'd keep one or two things for William to know who his father was. There's hardly anything apart from some stupid photos. A lot of soccer programmes, fitness mags, that sort of thing, and this.'

Niki Whear watched Bewick closely as he glanced at the pages.

'Must've meant something to him. I mean, whatever it was he was going to write about. He never got around to actually finishing it, though.'

The three pages began with two or three lines of painfully neat letter-by-letter writing, saying very formally who he was, his age, where he was born, his rank and regiment. Then it began to detail how and why he had joined the army. By the second page, Whear seemed to have become bored by his own history. The statements became more and more generalized. As if he knew he was wasting his concentration on the introductory stuff and wanted to get on to the core of what he had to say. Up to this point, the tone of the writing was legalistic, as of a last testament. Page two was never completed. Whear perhaps wanted the new page, a clean sheet, to start what he wanted to say:

The fifteenth was an awful day. Rain, rain, rain. The heath was turning into a bog. That night was as black as a witch's arse. We thought thank God, back to the billet, might even make the pub, but some sadist had other ideas. The CO (C-R) would never had dreamt this one up. Transport – what we thought was to take us back to camp – just took us a couple of miles and booted us out near a farm ruins (North Farm) which was on the artillery range. 2 coy was already there. This was an assembly point for a live firing assault on another position. Intelligence (which was Lt Davies) said our enemy was a bunch of wankers from 8 Para. We was meant to occupy Hill 3 and get camouflaged. We wasn't to fortify it or dig ourselves in properly as we was only being held as support for the main attack, 2 coy, who was having a go on valley stronghold. 2 coy was to attack at dawn. Freezing fucking cold. Thirty kilo Bergen plus weapon (HMG), wet feet. So we get under the gorse bushes on Hill 3 and brew up. We talk about what happened night before. Pixie Kelly all dumb as per. Fuck him. Then we're ordered to split. Fire to transverse VS 3. Channel 80 (!) Christ.

There it broke off.

'What d'you think of it?' Niki asked.

'I wonder why he never finished it.'

'He never finished nothing.'

'I wonder if he thought it might put him in danger if he told the whole story. What do you think? Do you think it was setting the record straight in his own defence, or do you think it was going to be a confession?'

She shrugged. 'Like I say, he hated writing things. It humiliated him. I filled in all the forms. So it must have been serious, even to make him start . . . Confession, I should think.'

'Did he ever talk to you about army operations?'

'He said it was hell.'

'He was in the Falklands, wasn't he?'

'Yes. But that stuff he's written was from much

later. That was about his training afterwards. Something went wrong.'

'Did he tell you what?'

'No. He never did. It used to piss me off. I don't know what happened. Probably it *was* hell. But, Christ, did he play on it. It was his great excuse. He'd behave like a complete dick, then say it was because of his bad experiences. So I'd mother the bastard, no questions asked. But, as time went on, I did ask questions. He wouldn't tell me nothing. Just got moodier. In the end I told him to go back there and find a fucking mine to tread on.'

They were in the Jag as before, being driven by the chauffeur.

'Take us up the Mall again, Ashok, I like going up the Mall.'

The car had just driven down the Mall from Admiralty Arch. Now they circled the giant statue of Queen Victoria in front of Buckingham Palace and set off up it again. This seemed to be routine with Ashok. He nodded, patient, amiable: 'And then Horseguards, Sir Michael?'

'Please.'

Dowling's mobile rang. He glanced at the screen and switched it off.

'Haven't you got a business to run?' Karen asked.

'Sure. But everyone I employ is cleverer than me. Let 'em get on with it. No, I have to go to the office, course I do. Come and have a coffee, while I sort them out.'

'I ought to get back.'

'I ought not to be driving round in circles because I like the view.'

In fact, Karen was tempted. Two hours of relentless charm from a man whom everybody seemed to know and defer to – four tables of diners at La Cucina had greeted him on their way out – all this had affected Karen as Dowling had meant it to. She was aware of it. She knew what Dowling was working towards. She also suspected he knew that he wasn't going to get it. Never mind; she was flattered. Just the quality of the cloth he was wearing, for Christ's sake. The fineness of the shirt, the softness of the jacket, the way the creases fell out when he straightened his arm, that was enough for her to drift into luxuriating in her surroundings. It wasn't until two-thirds of the way through the meal that she'd allowed him to pour her a glass of wine. To Karen, it was a test. If she'd seen a flicker of self-satisfaction from Dowling when she accepted it, then, she'd decided, she wouldn't touch it. She saw none. So she'd taken a couple of sips, but still left the glass half full. Dowling didn't encourage her to drink any more.

That omission was maybe the sexiest thing he'd done. He was negotiating the rules of the game they were playing together very fairly. Most men tried to write their own. With John Bewick, it had almost seemed that he'd accepted hers, until she recognized her continuing powerlessness, her ignorance of him.

'A coffee would be good.'

*

'What d'you make of it?' Jones asked. He'd just read the two and a half pages of Alan Whear's unfinished statement. Bewick had asked Niki Whear to run off a copy from her fax machine. She'd told him to take the original. She was glad to be rid of it.

'Two things: the reference to the "night before", and Channel 80 with the exclamation mark. I need to ask Peter Schrager about the channel thing. The "night before" reference might just be extraneous detail. We both know the irrelevant crap that ends up in statements. But it might be important.'

'Got to be pursued, either way.'

'Where do these AOR people and the paras do their training exercises?' Bewick asked.

'Burgh Forest, probably. It's the nearest area to Lotheny.'

'Is it?' Bewick sounded surprised.

'Yeah, I suppose it must be about forty miles away. But next nearest is up in Lincolnshire.'

Jones thought of the forest, which wasn't a forest at all, but a heath of sandy hills with occasional clumps of Scots pine. A single public road crossed a corner of the heath. At both ends were notices warning all drivers not to get out of their cars. If they did they were quickly approached and then put under escort until clear of the forest. The place was littered with ordnance, both spent and unexploded.

Jones had driven across it twice. Once in driving rain, which somehow made more menacing the thud of artillery that he could hear even through closed windows. The second crossing was in sunshine and in silence, rewarding him at the forest's highest point with a glimpse of the distant North Sea, bright blue beyond golden gravels.

Jones remembered the caginess of the AOR officers at Lotheny. Bewick was right: whatever it was they were concealing was going to stay that way. This thing of Whear's gave them bugger all.

'Tell you what,' Jones said, depressed, 'I'm pissed off. All Whear had to do was keep writing for another half an hour. Could he do it?'

'Whatever happened was serious or he wouldn't have tried to write about it at all. There might be some veiled reference to it in the records. He's given us enough to be getting on with, Gio.'

'Has he hell.'

'I'm off to Glasgow tomorrow, to see what I can find. I'll give you a ring.'

'OK.'

'Go and talk to Smew, Gio. Cheer yourself up.'

It was completely unexpected when it happened.

The office was the penthouse floor of a converted warehouse off Fleet Street, with views up and down the river. Thick cream carpet, white furniture, glass desk with a small silver laptop on it, small cordless phone, no paper anywhere. On one wall was an enormous painting of a Spitfire, high above a patchwork of fields. Facing it was a big, bright, cheerful canvas, a road winding through a canyon with palm trees, dazzling scarlet and orange fields, blue crops, and a turquoise swimming pool by a terracotta house. Karen was looking at it while Dowling talked through a deal, a conversation which consisted almost entirely of percentages. One detail in the painting made her smile. After its passage through the impossibly coloured landscape, the grey snake of road joined a bigger one. Written on it at the junction she could see, upside down, that it said 'stop'. She didn't know why it amused her.

Suddenly he was sitting beside her, kissing her hand. It was a complete surprise. 'No,' she said, but he didn't stop. He reached out to caress her breast or her cheek. For a moment she was frozen. Then she hit him. She twisted away and to her feet. 'What the fuck do you think you're doing?'

He said nothing, but stood holding his face. 'Christ, you pack a punch.'

'Who the fuck do you think you are?'

'I'm sorry.'

Karen walked out. It had happened again. Hot with anger she stood alone in the lift and tried to cool down. Her image in the smoky glass was unruffled. What signals did she give off so that she got all this shit?

Jones's second visit to Harnton modified his views on it. It was still a lot better than most Cat. Bs, but with the element of surprise gone, his feeling about the place was much less upbeat. He caught for the first time the stale-air, nervous-sweat and disinfectant stink of an ordinary prison. He was aware this time of entering a place of wrecked lives, where faces were written over with disappointment and fantasy.

Smew, on the other hand, was livelier than pre-viously. It was almost as if the bastard was looking forward to seeing him.

'Mr Smew,' Jones said deferentially, marvelling at Smew's ability to elicit this deference; annoyed with himself for giving it.

'So what's the situation with my Julie?'

'Not so good, matter of fact.'

'You sure?'

'Well I am, yes, you see. Seems to be hitting her on a fairly regular basis.'

'Right. Remember this, will you? Eamonn King. He lives in Cherry Hinton. He's in the book. Call him –'

'Hang on, hang on . . . You could organize this. You asked me what was going on. I told you.'

'Would I ask you to do anything out of order? Be serious, Mr Jones. Just ring Eamonn and tell him to give my Julie's bloke his birthday present and to put my name on the card. You can do that, can't you?'

Smew made it clear that Jones's participation was part of the deal. Jones didn't reply. Would the informa-tion be worth it?

'You come up with anything yet?'

'I'm getting there.' Smew's self-confidence was rock-solid. 'Well?'

Jones sighed. 'I'll talk to Eamonn.'

'Nothing wrong, is there? A birthday card?'

'I'd rather bang the bastard up for assault.'

'Yeah. And suppose Julie don't give evidence? 'Cos

she won't, y'know. You waste time and money and it'll be Eamonn's job in the end, anyway.'

'OK.'

'Right, you do it or ask someone else to do it. When I hear from Eamonn, I'll tell you what you want.'

'Christ, can't I just warn the fucker off?'

'He's been warned. He's no good. He's an evil man, Mr Jones.'

Jones drove away from Harnton thoroughly humiliated. He spent the entire journey back to Cambridge asking himself what on earth he was doing. Accessory to an assault? It was serious. This was what he loathed about dealing with Smew. There was always some handle he wanted to have, even if it was illusory. He decided he'd contrive to have his call to Eamonn King recorded. He would talk to him as if completely naïve, entirely innocent of what his message might mean: Dai plod, Dai notebook-and-pencil.

Whisky again. A good triple, he reckoned. Another hired room. He knew the girls were supposed to think of their clients as sad bastards. He could live with that since he had killed. He still only went with the polite ones, however. The poor, friendly, damaged creatures. Sad bastard to sad bastard. His hand shook, although he wasn't nervous at all. He knew 'Lucy', who had a slight country burr to her London voice. She was a regular. He only needed to mention his room number. She knew the hotel.

Stop this worrying. Two have been dealt with.

Entering a battle of your own making has been an

understandable shock. The prize has been worth it. Always before, the story of your life has been shaped by outside forces, by the power of others. Now, for the first time, you're writing it yourself.

Calm yourself.

He lifted the whisky glass and saw with amazement that it was empty. He wondered if he'd have the strength to get up to refill it. Four soft steps outside the door. A discreet knock. Lucy. He stood.

14

'Honey, I've been let down by Mrs Carter . . .'

Sally hated this apologetic pleading that Anthony used sometimes. 'Yes? What d'you want me to do?' She regretted the tone of her voice as soon as she heard it.

'Are you all right?'

'I'm fine.'

'What is it? Something's the matter.'

'I've been asleep, just woken up. Tell me what you want.'

'The kids'll be alone after school.'

'When will you be back?'

'Six.'

'I'll be there. I'll leave now.'

She allowed him to thank her once, then put the phone down on him. She knew it wasn't fair, that he would be mildly troubled by it all evening, but she was at war with herself. Deep within, a bruised child was in open rebellion at what the adult was doing. Sally stomped around, collecting the bagful of work that she knew she wouldn't have time to glance at.

She was living with the decision she had convinced herself was the right one. She might be attracted to Bewick, in fact she knew she was, but . . . Her uncertainties about him, her inability to deal with them, her overriding guilt, had all come together in the conviction that she must stay with Anthony. He was the one who needed her. She must. That was where her duty lay.

Passing a mirror, she saw an angry stranger; a harridan. Sitting in the car, running a mental checklist before she set off, she felt sick. That stranger in the mirror was the future. That was who she was going to have to live with.

Sally couldn't bear it. She breathed deeply, and closed her eyes. She imagined her neck and shoulder muscles liquefying. She relaxed her face. She reminded herself that she'd lived with herself for so long now, feeling herself to be alone, to be self-sufficient, that nothing would really change. No man would stand up to too much scrutiny, she told herself.

Her hand was clumsy as she adjusted the driving mirror to look at herself. The angry stranger had faded. The woman who looked out at her now was wary, alert, something more like the acceptable self.

As she drove, for the tenth time that day Karen went over the episode in Dowling's office. What had she done? She wasn't dressed provocatively: just the opposite. She wasn't a flirt. She was direct, not a game player. She didn't wear make-up. All she did was keep her hair clean. Sometimes she wore perfume. This time she deliberately hadn't. Where the hell did men get it from?

At the traffic lights, she looked idly at the pedestrians moving over the crossing: the sad and the fat, the lumpy, the plain, the old and the ordinary. Even in this city of youth, student mecca, she stood out, it seemed.

Behind her, someone hooted. The lights were green. She moved off, realizing as she did so that she was only a couple of streets away from where Sally lived.

Sally sat with the wine she'd opened. She was in a trance of pain. She'd left Anthony's almost as soon as he'd returned. She had claimed pressure of work. Uniquely, she hadn't explained further, hadn't tried to lessen his obvious concern. She didn't want his sympathy. Her energy for negotiations had been exhausted, used up on making things pleasant for the children. She'd taken them out to the shop, indulged them; mild bribery: bubblegum, gobstoppers. She'd kept things cheerful and easygoing. When Anthony asked them, as he would, what was the matter with Sally, they'd reply that they didn't know what he meant.

She questioned even this small triumph now. How helpful was this disguise of her real feelings? Did people appreciate these efforts or did they rather despise them? She knew she admired directness in people. Debate and discussion underlay all civilized proceedings. How could people deal with you if you weren't prepared to make your position clear? She began to feel insane. She knew she had behaved badly and hated herself for it.

Sally had heard a car stop outside, but noticed she

hadn't heard its door slam. She half stood to look out of the window. She saw Karen. A moment's irritation was quickly overtaken by a sense of relief, which she couldn't immediately explain. The company of a fellow sufferer was welcome, perhaps.

She went to the door, her smile of welcome unforced, her warmth meant.

'Hello Prof, it's the Blonde.'

Sally led the way into the living-room.

'Is this OK?' Karen asked.

'Listen, you're always welcome, always.'

'Just an impulse . . . a lousy day . . .'

'Wine?'

'Not half.'

Sally poured some. 'So tell me about it.'

Karen heard the warmth in Sally's voice, the sympathy. From most people she'd have resented it, told them to mind their own. But here she was, having invited it. Sally was different. She made you want to confess. You knew she wouldn't let you down because she was kind of innocent, never mind her cleverness. 'This bloke made a pass at me. Grabbed me. So I clouted him good and hard.'

'Anyone I know?'

'Sir Michael Dowling. Who the hell does he think he is? Fuck him! He behaved himself at lunch. I was beginning to think he was OK. What really annoys me —'

'Yes?'

'What *really* annoys me is that you start thinking there's something wrong with you, that you're doing some sort of subconscious come-on all the time. Am I?'

'No, not at all. But I'm afraid you have a problem: you happen to embody what almost every man wants, and quite a few women, I'd guess. Which is a fair curse, I imagine.'

'Why?'

'Because – I may be wrong, but I'd have thought you'd always find it difficult finding out what people are attracted to. You'd have to tread so carefully.'

'Yes. I see. And you reckon people's looks are, like, a commodity? Like money? Yeah?'

'They're part of the bargain, aren't they?'

Karen looked thoughtful. 'Maybe . . . So, tell me about John Bewick. That's working out, is it?'

'Not really.' In her clear-headed way, Sally told Karen about her struggle with herself that evening and what she saw as her meanness of spirit. 'At least I know one thing,' she concluded.

'What's that?'

'At least I know that I really have got to stop fantasizing about John Bewick. At least I know that door must be closed.'

'Pardon my French, Prof, but what the fuck are you on about?'

Karen reminded herself that this woman was a top scientist, someone who ran her own lab, someone whose work some multinational thought worth funding to the tune of half a million a year. She was going on like a teenager with a dear Marge problem; looked like one too.

'I don't want Bewick pissed around,' Karen went on. 'He's an extraordinary bloke and there's something in him which could cut him off from people. It's . . . sort of dark. He doesn't get off on it, you know, he lives with it. Am I talking crap? I suppose it's pain. Like living with pain all the time. It quietens him. It also cuts him off. I couldn't get through to it and I knew I never would. That's why I left. He's so clever about people but I still feel he could get pissed around by the wrong female . . . Look, what I'm saying here is that Bewick probably needs you just as much as this Anthony bloke . . .'

'I don't know. There's duty, responsibility. A stack of guilt.'

'Forget it. Guilt, duty, responsibility. You're not *married*! No one has claims like that on you. Forget guilt, for Christ's sake. Go for life, not guilt. This Anthony fellow looks like a ruthless-angel type. He'll have women swarming after him. Are the children pretty too?'

'Yes.'

'No problem, then!'

'You make it sound so simple.'

'It is.'

Baynes knocked and entered Jones's office. Jones was leaning back in his chair, his hands clasped over his stomach. Baynes's knock had woken him up. He wasn't at his best. Why was it dark outside? Was it that late?

'What the hell do you want?'

Baynes looked around, observing the rubbish-tip

untidiness as if for the first time. He knew this would irritate Jones, but he'd had a hard day too. The office was like the aftermath of a surreal disaster where the desk had been cut off from the outside world by a paper blizzard, inches of paper falling in a matter of hours, communication only just re-established.

'Well?' Jones barked.

'That fellow who lives with Charlie Smew's daughter – the one we had down for the northern-villages job, not sufficient evidence?'

'What about him?'

'In hospital. They broke all the bones in his right hand and one of his legs.'

Jones felt sick. He tried to sound nonchalant. 'Yeah? Well, he was a nasty piece of work. Those that live by the sword, etcetera . . .'

'Never mind what they did to his face.'

'Why're you telling me this?'

'Incident concerning a known criminal who has crossed our path, Sir,' Baynes replied, getting very formal. 'But that wasn't it.'

'What wasn't what?'

'What I come in about. It's that wino, Old Foley. Some story about getting his coat back. He wants to thank you in person. Insists. I could chuck him out, but he'd probably come back and, frankly, he's stinking the place out.'

As soon as Jones entered the reception area, he smelt Foley's strange fruit-and-manure odour.

'I need a breath of fresh air, Foley, shall we go outside? Been stuck indoors all day.'

'That's no good. No good at all. Come outside, old man.' Foley patted Jones on the back and ushered him out of the reception area, like a stately-home owner might a social inferior whom he was mildly fond of.

They walked slowly downhill, past the Regency town houses on Maid's Causeway.

'Very grateful to you, very. Moral pressure must have been exerted, d'you see? Returned to me, nicely folded. My favourite. Simpsons of Piccadilly.'

'Really?' Jones hadn't intended to sound disbelieving.

'You want to see? I'll show you. Christ!' Foley struggled out of the larger, outer of the two overcoats he was wearing. Jones took a step back. It was like opening a slurry pit. He held his breath. Holding the coat, Foley marched a few paces to stand under a streetlight. He stabbed, with a very dirty finger: 'There! By appointment! Simpsons of Piccadilly!'

'A fine garment, Foley,' Jones said, making a token lean as if to read the label.

'Can't get quality like this nowadays. Can't be found. Like all quality, though, it attracts the light-fingered, the envious. Take this fellow . . .' Foley struggled back into his coat. In the distance, the still-flooded margins of Midsummer Common reflected a perfect half-circle moon.

'Which fellow?'

'The fellow who borrowed my coat.'

'Envious of your coat, you think?'

'Masquerading as me. He was seen to do it. Over there . . .' Foley waved his hand in a grand theatrical gesture, roughly towards Jesus Green. 'Poncing around, except that he was wearing a hat. One doesn't like one's name to be taken in vain. Anything you can do about that? Gives a chap a reputation.'

'Not really, Foley. That would be a civil action. You'd have to have access to a lawyer.'

'Ah . . .' Foley was silent a moment. He sighed. A sweet, corrosive smell filled the immediate air. 'My son's a lawyer. Teaches it.' Because of his National Trust accent, it was rumoured that Foley was the father of a Cambridge don who'd had to change his name to disassociate himself from him. Foley drew himself up to his full height. Jones realized that he must have been quite an impressive figure once, broad and tall. It was bloody sad.

'Who is your son, Foley?'

'Confidential, man. A confidence . . .' Foley had shrunk again to the bowed-over hobo. 'A confidence I'm obliged to keep.'

Karen was dreaming, and at first the bell was incorporated into the dream. Her father was fighting. He'd been hurt and the bell was saving him. As he came back to his corner he winked at her. The next ring woke her. Glance at clock. Press the light button. 02: 10. Bloody hell.

She slid out of bed, and on all fours crossed the floor to the bathroom. The top half of the window was clear glass. Keeping well back, she looked out. At the end of the street was the Jag in which she'd been chauffeured all day. Ashok was at the wheel. It must be bloody Dowling.

The doorbell rang again. Karen pulled on some jeans. Was he drunk? What the hell did he want?

She put the door on the chain before opening it. 'What?'

'I've come to say sorry.'

She didn't reply.

'I got you some flowers.'

'I don't want them.'

'I'm leaving them anyway. I'm sorry. It was the stupidest thing I've done since I was a teenager. I'm sorry.'

Still are a teenager, she thought.

'Go on, let me in. I was pissed, over-excited. I think you're fucking brilliant.'

'Thank you for apologizing,' she said in her best schoolmistressy manner. Then she shut the door, turned out the light and set off back up the stairs.

'Oh, don't be a cow, Karen. I mean this. I never done nothing like this in my life.'

She went into her bedroom and opened the window. 'Keep your voice down. I have to live with my neighbours.'

'When I say I think you're fabulous,' he whispered up at her, 'I get a shiver telling me it's true.'

'Goodnight.' Karen shut the window. She got into bed but didn't try to sleep. She hadn't heard him move away. Would she hear the Jag start? Of course she would. So he hadn't left, then. He was either on her doorstep or in his bloody car. Well this was bloody pointless. She wondered how she could make use of the fact that he was there.

Karen reached over for her mobile and looked in the number directory. It was late, but it was worth making the call. The worst he could do would be to tell her to piss off. She dialled.

When she heard the Jag start up and move off, she was disappointed. It had been a nice idea and would have put the bugger in his place. She went downstairs to see if he'd left the flowers, as he'd said he would. When she opened the door, he was standing there with about four dozen red roses in his arms.

'Oh, for God's sake!' she complained.

'I didn't reckon you'd pick 'em up till you heard the Jag clear off, so I told Ashok to wait round the corner.' He held out the roses to her. 'For you.'

'I told you, I don't want them,' Karen said.

'Take them to the hospital.'

'You take them.'

'OK.'

He sounded as if he meant it. She was surprised. She thought of the man who had effortlessly dominated La Cucina. This fellow seemed so childishly young in his submission to her . . . if it was that.

'I'm going to make some tea.' She went into the house. He followed. 'You don't really want me to take these to the hospital, do you?'

'Yes, I do.'

'You're a hard woman.'

'What'll you call me next?' she asked, remembering the insults of other disppointed men.

It wasn't until she was making tea that he calmed down and stopped trying so hard. She filled the teapot and wrapped a towel round it.

'What's that extra stuff you put in – after the tea bags?'

'Darjeeling. My Dad was in India when he was a kid. It was a habit of his – pinch of Darjeeling to give it an edge.'

'Part of the Raj, was he?' he asked, drawling Raj into posh.

'Not the way you think. My grandfather was a squaddie. Dad got to be an RSM.'

'What's with all those silver cups next door?' Dowling asked.

'He was army boxing champion; middleweight.'

'I used to do a bit of that.'

'When you were in the army?' She didn't need to be looking at him to get the impact this had. It was only a moment, a split-second freeze, but she caught it.

'No, no,' he said, 'when I was doing the wholesale stuff for my Mum's barrow in the market; when I was a teenage ruffian. I wasn't much good. I got a proper slapping a couple of times so I gave it up.'

'You changed the subject,' she said. They were drinking tea now.

'What's that?'

'Just now. I asked if you were in the army and you slid off like a piece of soap.'

'*What?*'

She could practically see his brain fizzing. 'You were in the army, weren't you?'

He stared at her, silenced.

'You went bail for a couple of lads a few years ago. Whear and Simmonds. They were in the army with you. They're both dead. That's what all this protection lark is about, isn't it?'

He still stared, silent.

'Whoever was after them is probably after you – for some reason. Be a help if you could tell me the reason.'

'I'd better go now.' He stood up, and picked up the roses from the sink. He extracted one, pricking his finger as he did so. He put it on the table. 'I'll take these to the hospital,' he said.

'You'll have to tell someone some day.'

'I'm not talking to you about it.'

'You don't talk to me about this, you don't talk to me about anything!' She was surprised at her own sharpness. 'I've had it up to here with men who don't talk to me. I'm telling you. This thing that happened, whatever it is, is too big a part of you. If I don't get told about that, I don't want to know about you. Right?'

The doorbell rang. Dowling looked at his watch. 'Who the hell's that?'

'The police.'

'What?'

'I told them I had a stalker.'

'You *what?*' Dowling burst out laughing. 'You had

me going there for a moment . . . So who do you reckon it is?'

'A friend.'

She went to the front door and opened it. Gio Jones stood there.

'Bloody hell, you look rough, Boss.'

'Ta. I feel like one of those teddy bears on the front of a truck. You all right?'

'Sure.'

'Still here, is he?'

'He is, Boss.'

'Was rather hoping he wouldn't be. More I think about it, the more I realize how little I'm suited to this job.'

She took him through to the kitchen.

'Sir Michael Dowling, this is Chief Inspector Giovanni Jones.'

Both men looked awkward. Dowling spoke first. 'A friend who just happens to be a policeman?'

'Yeah,' Karen said.

Dowling looked hurt. 'You distrust me that much?'

'No, no.' Jones shook his head. 'She knew I wanted to talk to you. Seemed like an opportunity, what with you being away in London for the foreseeable.' He yawned. Dowling said nothing.

'Tea?' Karen asked. 'Or Scotch?'

'Tea, ta. So, Sir Michael, it's late and I'm sure we all want our beds, so would you mind telling me what you were doing in the vicinity of Robert Simmonds's workshop the evening after he was murdered? Apart from getting your boots muddy?'

The skin of Dowling's face went matt as the blood drained from it.

'We have a witness who saw you in good light from ten metres away,' Jones added. 'You were there.'

'Many people get mistaken for me, y'know. I've got one of those faces.'

'Fair point, fair point. But how many of those who get mistaken for you would be intimately connected with the murder victim whose body was sitting a few yards further up the lane?'

'What the hell're you talking about, intimately connected?'

'You went bail for him and the other victim, Alan Whear, about six or seven years ago. Now, I don't know about you, but I'd want to be reasonably well acquainted with a potential criminal before I risked my money on him. What d'you think?'

Dowling stared, said nothing.

'Or is it a charity you run? Helping out ex-servicemen down on their luck? Even though you were never in the army? Were you?'

Dowling didn't move. Karen watched him, fascinated. He took a long breath. 'Yeah, I knew them.'

'So you were in the army with them?' Karen asked.

'I didn't say that. I said I knew them.'

'So why did you help out if you weren't all muckers together?' said Jones.

'That's none of your business. I'm telling you that I knew them to explain why I was in the lane that evening. I'd read about Alan Whear being shot. I was going to ask Bob Simmonds what he knew about it – if it was the same Alan Whear we both knew. That's why I was there.'

'And you went and asked him?'

'No, I didn't. I gave up. The place was surrounded by water after these floods we've been having. I even put my boots on, but the water got too deep.'

'Boots?'

'Sailing boots. I keep them in the car because they're lighter than wellies, more comfortable.'

'You own a boat, do you?'

'No. Friend of mine does. I sail with him very occasionally. I get sea sick, so it isn't often.'

'So can we see them? Your car's around the corner. At least I assume it's yours.' Jones gave Dowling a small smile, a bit smug.

Dowling looked at Jones hard. Then he settled himself down and took control. It was the public person, the man who ran meetings, who got his way, who kept his head.

'No, Chief Inspector, you can't look at them, unless you tell me why they're of any interest to you. Also, I'm not answering any more of your questions without being told what they're leading to. Probably with my solicitor present.'

Jones shrugged. Dowling appealed to Karen.

'I'm not part of the investigation,' she said. 'I don't know what he's on about.'

She was looking at Dowling with the kind of resentment which, in Jones's book, meant some shared history, an intimacy.

'You're going to have to tell me sooner or later,' she said. 'It's the only way forward.'

This was stripped-down, heart-to-heart stuff, this was. Jones immediately felt jealous.

'Maybe,' Dowling replied. 'Perhaps I will. Perhaps. Are you coming down to Ealand Priory with the others at the weekend?'

Karen imitated his intonation exactly. 'Maybe. Perhaps I will. Perhaps.'

Dowling nodded, as if acknowledging the justice of her reply. Then he turned to Jones. 'If you really are a friend of Karen's –' he began. Then, 'Here! What're you doing?'

Jones was on his mobile. He ignored Dowling and went out into the hall. 'DCI Jones here. I want four officers and a couple of cars ASAP. Fourteen Birchwood Road . . . OK . . . Yes, emergency.'

'What the hell's this?' Dowling had appeared in the doorway behind Jones.

'You're refusing to let me examine vital evidence. You're lying to me fit to bust. What do you expect me to do?'

Dowling turned to Karen, furious. 'This is your friend?'

'He must know something I don't,' she said. Jones came back into the kitchen.

'All right, Chief Inspector, what game are you playing?' The small room was thick with tension.

'It isn't a game, Sir.' Jones was deeply angry and he couldn't account for it. 'We find out that Whear had a record. His partner in crime, Simmonds, was in the army with him. When they were arrested, someone called Michael Dowling put up bail for them. Then this Dowling gets recognized at the scene of Simmonds's murder. Also, Dowling is looking for protection from a private security firm. Something's going on, for Christ's sake, and I want to know what it is. Also . . .' Jones checked himself. Should he tell Dowling about the sailing-boot print found inside Simmonds's workshop? Would those uniformed bastards turn up in time to secure the boot in question?

'Also . . .?' Dowling asked.

'Also, you were in that workshop.' Dowling stared at him, stony faced. 'I've got the proof of it,' Jones added.

'Crap! What proof?'

'Ring your solicitor!' Jones spat it out on another surge of unexplainable anger.

'Bloody right I will!'

'For God's sake,' Karen said, 'the both of you!'

It didn't break the tension, but it produced silence.

'You remember when we met?' Karen asked Dowling.

'What about it?'

'You were kicking straw and effing and blinding. On your own. By yourself. That a habit of yours?'

Dowling stared at her. She met his look square on. 'You'd seen the body, hadn't you? You'd seen your mate with half his head blown off. Probably saw it half the night. It was getting to you.'

Dowling breathed out a long sigh and stared at the

floor. Eventually he spoke. 'The problem –' he said and stopped.

'Did you go in?' Jones asked, knowing that they'd finally got there.

'Yes, I did,' Dowling replied, hardly audible.

'Why're you so reluctant to tell us all this?'

'How would it look? I didn't want to be involved.'

'Well, you are involved, Sir, so you'd better tell us.'

'There I am. I wade through all this water. Door's open. In I go. There he is, dead at his desk. Brains all over the wall. I damn nearly puke. Then I go. I check I haven't touched nothing. A few wet boot prints, which I rub off. That's it. I go. Slam the door. Then I begin to think. How the hell did anyone else get in here? He hadn't been dead long; a few hours. A few hours before, you'd have had to swim to have got into that place. How did the bastard get there to kill him? That got me really paranoid, let me tell you. It was like the scarlet fucking pimpernel . . . That's why I rang CRSI.'

'He got there by boat.'

Dowling looked stupefied at first. Then he hit himself in frustration. 'Christ, how dumb can you get? I only thought of the road . . .'

Was all this a performance, Jones wondered. Surely he must have thought of the river? Mind you, it was Bewick who thought of it first, not himself. If it was a performance, it was very convincing. He was a clever man, but was he that smart?

'You can take the boots, if that's what you want,' Dowling said. 'You can call off your reinforcements.'

Jones took out his mobile again and did so. Together he and Dowling went out to the car and transferred the boots from the Jaguar to Jones's Astra.

'Perhaps you should come down to Ealand Priory at the weekend as well.'

'What would that do for me, apart from annoy my children?'

'You might learn something to your advantage.'

'Oh, might I just? What sort of thing?'

'What's the point of a magical mystery tour if you hand out the itinerary before you start?'

'What's this bollocks?'

'Anyway, you're welcome to come. It'll be interesting, whatever. I'm going now.'

'Were you in the army?'

'Hope to see you at the weekend.'

'You were. I know you were.'

Dowling was driven away down the glistening road. The city was as silent as it ever was. Three o'clock. Jones wondered what he'd achieved. A thin rain began. He turned towards his car. Karen was standing in the lit doorway of her house. She gestured for him to come in. He hesitated. Did he really want to torture himself? Before he'd made the decision, his feet were moving towards her.

15

'So what's with this weekend he's organizing?'

'Search me, Boss.'

'He hasn't talked to you about it?'

'Eh?'

'What's going on between you and Dowling?'

It was ten minutes after Dowling had gone. By now, Jones was nursing the tail end of the Scotch Karen had given him.

'He fancies me, that's all.'

'And?'

'And what?'

'Come *on* . . .'

'And I said no. I'm fed up with men who've got secrets. Dowling is into secrecy big-time. That's all.'

'That's all?'

'Yeah, sure,' she said, very dry. 'By the way, I don't think he's your man. He's been mixed up in something, but –'

'But he's not been knocking off his comrades in arms? No, I didn't have him down as a killer myself, not at first. Now I'm not so sure, seeing him in action.'

'What does that mean?'

'He's in the frame. You heard him. Course he is. He's implicated. At the scene . . .'

'Begging your pardon, but that's crap, Sir, and you

know it,' Karen interrupted. 'That's just procedural crap. Where's the motive?'

Jones's blood was up. He realized now why he'd been so angry. He was jealous. He was ragged with desire for her. He was tired, too, with just enough Scotch to make him reckless. He wanted to do some damage.

'You want motive? I could give you half a dozen, and all of them plausible.'

'Well try *one*,' she said.

'They were blackmailing him. They were in something together. Dowling wants the past behind him. Those two –'

'Keep your voice down.'

'Those two,' Jones hissed at her, 'stood between him and a golden future. He's a volatile bastard but some of him is steel. Hundred per cent Sheffield.'

'So why's he looking for protection?'

'A blind. He pretends he's on someone's list, just like the other two. Oldest trick in the handbook.'

Seeing his anger and understanding it for the first time calmed Karen down. 'OK, Boss,' she said. 'You're probably right. So ... I promise not to socialize with the bugger before you've cleared him. Fair enough?' She smiled at him and then gave him an affectionate quick hug. 'Let's talk tomorrow.'

Outside, as he walked to his car through the damp air, Jones felt black misery; sour, sick jealousy. Patronized by Dowling, patted on the head by Karen ... and what the hell was Dowling up to with this weekend of his? What was he, Jones, likely to find out? Ah, sod it. He was too tired even to relish the condescending little embrace Karen had given him.

He rang Bewick next morning.

'This weekend at Dowling's. What d'you reckon? Any point in being there? You think we ought to go?'

'Of course we've got to go.' Bewick spoke quietly, but Jones knew there'd be no contradicting him. Told off again.

'Everything OK?' It was Peter Schrager. Karen, just stepped out of the shower, was dripping on to the carpet, annoyed with herself for not having left the answerphone on. She'd been looking forward to an uninterrupted evening by herself for a change.

'Why shouldn't it be?'

'What's the matter?'

'Nothing. Why?'

'Look, I rang to see if – Did you manage to get what Dowling was expecting at the weekend? This lunch he's giving? Does he expect us to be making his place watertight?'

'I don't know. Tell you the truth, he's a bit of a lunatic. He knows the threat is there. Half of him wants to be tucked up safe with a favourite toy, but half of him wants to be toughing it out, wants to show them he doesn't scare easy. He's a gambler too, which doesn't help.'

'And we're no closer to finding where the threat is coming from?'

'I think he doesn't know. He's got a good idea what it's about, I reckon, but he's not telling us that either.'

'I don't see how we can protect him then.'

'Nor do I, unless he talks to me. I'm working on it.'

'Good. Does he still want CRSI to cover this party, though?'

'Yes.'

'OK. I'll ring him. I'll tell him we'll turn up as a gesture of goodwill, but that our presence will form no part of the contract.'

'Fine.'

'Do you get on with him?'

'Yeah. He's harmless, really. Just a bit of a dick.'

'I'll suggest he adds that to his obituary.'

'Yeah. Just as long as everyone knows I'm not about to become his favourite toy.'

She put down the phone and returned to her shower. She felt quite as indifferent to Dowling as she'd said. She didn't feel threatened by him at all. She felt sorry for him, but didn't know why.

Later that evening, she was channel hopping and there he was on *Newsnight*. Paxman was trying to work up some enthusiasm for being confrontational but it was obvious that he liked Dowling too much.

Dowling was transformed. He was in his element. He was relaxed, playful even. His answers were commonsensical, amused. He was a master. Paxman was asking him how the dot-com companies could be pushing big-league players off the FTSE 100 when they had never been in profit and in some cases barely had a product. Dowling's answer was succinct. 'They're not. It's an illusion, like flared trousers. No one ever *really* wore those, did they? It's a fashion.'

'Do you own any dot-com shares yourself?'

'If I do, I've just convinced myself to take them down the charity shop before the season's over.'

Paxman gave him one of his looks, studio-grade irony. He turned to another camera to go through the next morning's headlines and wind up the show.

Karen switched off. She felt flattered again by Dowling's attention. She even felt a nudge of guilt. What an odd bloke he was. She was washing up when the phone rang.

'Did you see me on the box?'

'What're you talking about?'

'I was on the box. *Newsnight*. Thought you might have seen it. I like to know how I come over.'

'You were very good, I'm sure.'

'You saw it?'

'I just know you would be. You're a show-off. You'd do it well.'

'So you didn't see it?'

Karen thought for a moment and got nowhere. Does he really need this reassurance? She sensed, but didn't know why, that if she admitted she'd seen him, she would be taking a significant step closer to him.

'Sorry?'

'*Newsnight*. You didn't catch it then?' He sounded childishly disappointed.

It wasn't as if *Newsnight* was something she'd normally watch, anyway. 'Yeah, I saw it. You were very good. Very good. I was impressed.'

'Come out to dinner.'

'No.' She didn't trust him. She wouldn't until he told her the whole truth.

'Why not?'

'Because you won't tell me what happened to you. Why you want CRSI to protect you.'

'Would you if I did?'

'That's the basic minimum. Then we start negotiating.'

'You're a bolshie bint, that's for certain.'

'Sure. So . . .?'

'I'll think about it. See you at the weekend.'

Karen put down the phone. She felt a prickle of pleasure, a whiff of power.

Jones was on his way to bed when the call came through. Eilean was ahead of him on the stairs, her arms full of children's sports kit.

'Only if it's my sister,' she said and continued on up.

'See you in a minute.' Jones hurried into the livingroom to pick up before the answerphone cut in.

It was Bewick.

'Apologies, Gio. I was having a meal with one of the women from army records. I know it's late.'

Jones remembered Bewick was in Glasgow. 'Any luck with AOR?'

'It's been a day of it. This woman was really helpful. Least I could do.'

'Sure.' Jones could imagine. 'So did you get anywhere?'

'I think so. I'm just about to get on the plane.'

'Stansted. You want me to pick you up, don't you? You've got a nerve. It's my bedtime.'

'OK. See you tomorrow, then.'

Jones put the phone down. The bastard! He knew Jones would do it. Well, he felt like proving the bugger wrong this time. He really did. Anyway, he'd probably drunk too much. He went to the kitchen and breathalysed himself. He wasn't even near the limit. Oh, hell. He hauled himself up the stairs and said goodnight to Eilean.

Jones sat on a surprisingly comfortable metal seat and stared up at the canopy of the flight hall at Stansted. Four white steel struts opened up from each anchoring base. These in turn were linked to each other by cables. The effect was extraordinarily delicate. Above, the modular roof stretched away, like cells in a butterfly's wing . . .

Where the hell was Bewick?

The place was very quiet, more cleaners than punters. He'd checked the arrivals screen. Apart from the Glasgow flight, which had landed late, fog at Prestwick, there was only one more arrival listed. Why did it take this long?

He glanced up again. He noticed for the first time that the upper surfaces of the white struts were grey with dust. He felt like complaining to someone about it. Mad. He must be bloody tired. He yawned. Could he sleep on this thing? No support for your head, mate. Willing to bet it was deliberate. He tried dropping his head, but he didn't fancy a rotten stiff neck. Better to walk up and down. He could cover miles in this place . . .

'Hello, Gio.' Bewick was towering above him.

They walked out to Jones's car together.

'Very good of you, Gio, to do this.'

'What d'you mean? You bloody asked me! Good as. So what did you find out?'

'Whear's statement is beginning to make sense.'

'What was it about?'

'A live firing exercise. A young soldier was killed. There was a cock-up and he got hit.'

'How the hell did you find that out?'

'The inquiry was quite open. It's in the public domain. Probably be able to read about it in the *Guardian*.'

'So what was that bloody Rucker-Whitman git on about?'

'Self-important paranoia? I don't know.'

'Was that Channel 80 Whear mentioned to do with that?'

'That's right. That was the radio channel they were all supposed to be on to hear the live firing instructions – the area of fire, elevation and so on. The men doing the firing were switched on to the wrong channel. The instructor was screaming at empty radio space for them to stop. It wasn't until the men who were being fired on got on to the emergency channel that the men with the live ammo realized what they'd done. By then, one of the company they were firing at was dead. Official conclusion was that it was an accident.'

'So Whear was one of the guys firing at his mates, was he?'

'No. Whear and Simmonds were in the squad being fired on. There were five of them who actually came under fire. The lad who died, Simmonds, Whear, someone called Cobden and Atkinson.'

'The same Atkinson who was giving us all that shit out at Lotheny?'

'Probably.'

'Well then, let's get out there and grill the bastard. Let's nail him. Obstructing the police. Let's arrest the arsehole. Now! Christ!'

'Calm down, Gio. We need to talk this through. Let's suppose that the shooting of this soldier – he was called Kelly, by the way – wasn't an accident,' Bewick said. 'Suppose it was a fragging.'

'A what?' They were driving out of the car park now.

'That's what it's called, according to Peter Schrager. When you shoot someone on your own side deliberately during combat.'

'That's a fragging?'

'Yes.'

Bewick was silent. Jones glanced across at him and nearly crashed into the exit barrier. He lowered the window and inserted the programmed ticket. The screen wished him a safe journey. He told it to piss off and drove on through.

'But of course,' Bewick said, 'there are one or two difficulties with that idea. As I'm sure you'll realize.'

'Will I?'

'Think about it.'

Jones did, for as long as it took to get to the first

roundabout on the landscaped exit route. 'You mean if anyone wanted to kill Kelly, they couldn't have known that the buggers using the live ammo would foul up on the VHF.'

'Exactly. Far too risky for it to have been pre-arranged. Too many involved for it to have been a conspiracy.'

'So it was something that happened on the spur of the moment, you reckon? One of them realized there was live ammo flying about and thought now's my chance. If it happened at all.'

'Exactly. If it happened at all.'

Jones blew a lungful of air at the windscreen, momentarily misting it up. 'It's the only bloody game in town, innit?'

They joined the M11 heading north to Cambridge.

'Suppose we're right,' Jones said. 'What do you think we're investigating? Is it Kelly's murder that's being avenged? Or is it witnesses to his murder who are being knocked off? How do we decide that?'

'One of the reasons I was so late was that I wanted to find out if Kelly had any family we could trace.'

'Well?'

'His father lives in Fulbourn.'

'Well, clever old you.'

'Don't get bitter, Gio. Heard anything from Smew?'

'His daughter's boyfriend is in hospital. I'm an accessory to GBH. And I got a message to speak to one of Smew's ex-enforcers, Danny Hart, little shiteburger, which I'm looking forward to like having my teeth drilled.'

*

Karen was on her bike. There was an eight-mile circuit she did quite regularly, trying to keep the speedo at an average 20 mph. She was pushing up the long slope into Grantchester, enjoying it. She knew she was being wind assisted, but it was a good feeling mastering a slight uphill at a full 18 mph. Her mobile rang. She halted her lap timer and watched her heart-pulse monitor settle back. She unclipped her mobile and answered it.

'Michael Dowling.' He sounded different.

'Might've known it was you. The king of bad timing.'

'You win. I'll tell you what this is about.'

She felt a whizz of excitement. Did he mean what she thought he meant? 'About why you've been looking for protection?'

'Yes. That and the rest.'

'Well . . . good.'

'Come over to the Priory tomorrow?'

'Yes. That'd be fine.'

'I'll collect you.'

'No. It's OK. I'll drive myself, thanks.'

'Will you come with me? I need chaperoning.'

'*You?*' Sally gasped and then began laughing. '*You* do?' She looked at this svelte, strong woman in helmet and cycling gloves and thought that there was nothing left to surprise her. She laughed again in disbelief.

'I mean it,' Karen said.

'You'd better come in.'

Karen wheeled her bike into the hall and hung her helmet on it.

'What on earth is this about?'

Karen explained Dowling's offer. 'I just don't know the set-up. It's like the haunted house out there in the fens. And I'm not sure, you know, about *him*. He's already made one grab at me: well, you know that. He's apologized since, but –'

'*Has* he?'

Karen told Sally about Dowling turning up in the middle of the night and his confrontation with Gio Jones. Sally laughed during the telling. She was sombre by the end.

'You don't think he's implicated in any way in these shootings, do you?'

'He's implicated in something. When Gio Jones tried to put him in the frame, mind you, I found myself defending him.'

'Do you like him?'

'He's worked very hard at trying to make me like him. Full marks for effort. But he's a bit of a dick.'

Sally looked at her quizzically. 'I think you like him quite well enough for your own good.'

Karen looked back, defiant. 'And what about you? What about the one you like well enough for your own good?'

'Oh, I do, do I?' Sally replied, defiant in her turn.

'Yes, you do.'

Faced with Karen's certainty, Sally's resolve faltered again. She didn't answer.

'So, are you going to come and hold my hand?' she heard Karen say. 'He's invited the St Anne's funding committee to lunch there on Saturday – and John Bewick will be coming.'

The house, the sole survivor of a row of cottages that had been knocked down forty years before and hemmed in by their more modern successors, lay at the end of a cul de sac off a small lane on the outskirts of the village. The cottage had held on to a small, overgrown garden, where Bewick now sat on a grubby plastic chair, which would have disgraced a skip. He held a small china cup, saucerless, which was being filled with strong tea by Mr Kelly, whose bony hands shook as he poured. He was, in contrast to his garden, neat and spotlessly clean. He was small, wiry, late-fifties, but carried himself like a man who was well into his retirement, hunted, haunted.

'There,' Kelly said, pleased that he hadn't spilled a drop. 'Where was I?'

'David had just gone into the army,' Bewick reminded him.

Kelly seemed awed by Bewick, treating him with a deference which Bewick ignored.

'That's right. And he did just fine. Fine. They had some good times. After a few years, he applied to get into the special forces, you know, and he got accepted by the AOR. That surprised us. He soon fell in with a lot of Scouse lads . . .'

It began to spot with rain.

'Shall we be going indoors?' Kelly asked.

The mantelpiece was crowded with family photographs. The room itself was crowded with too much furniture. The statutory three-piece suite alone filled most of it. Small tables and cabinets filled up the rest. Here and there were pictures of soulful young women. It took Bewick a moment or two to realize who they represented. On top of a glass cabinet stood a plaster statuette of the Virgin as the Queen of Heaven, crowned, with stars on her blue cloak. The pictures were all of Mary, too.

'Young David rang up, you may as well know, the night before he was taken. Late.' Kelly said 'late' as if it was a sin. 'He never rang up late. Most unusual, it was, for him to ring up late. He wanted to speak to his mother, but she was very ill by then. I wasn't going to wake her. I regret that, to this day . . . No matter. She's with him now. Once she knew David had gone she was happy to go herself. She just let go and it wasn't long.'

Kelly looked sideways at the floor and was silent. Bewick was the next to speak. 'When your son rang that night . . . Can you remember what he talked about?'

'Nothing, nothing at all. He said there was something he wanted to chew over with his mother and I said I didn't want to wake her, her with her drugs she had to take, and he said OK, he'd ring the next day. I regret it, I do.'

'You may not have been able to wake her, even if you'd tried,' Bewick said, very quiet, barely audible.

Kelly looked grateful. 'That's right. That's what I thought.'

'So your son didn't mention what he wanted to say to his mother?'

'No. No, he didn't. They were very close. They'd talk about things, they would. David and me . . . we didn't discuss things much. We could spend a whole day together fishing, dawn to dusk, and hardly speak three sentences.'

'So he gave no hint of what it might have been about?'

'No, not really. He was upset, I could tell that.'

'How could you tell?'

'Oh, I could tell.'

'He didn't say anything that made you think he might be upset? You just knew?'

'He said something had happened that evening and that was why he wanted to talk to his mother.'

'Something bad?'

Kelly looked at Bewick, surprised. 'Bad – of course bad. Why would he want to talk to her otherwise? And so late, into the bargain? And why was he upset? David was having a lot of trouble.'

'Was he? What sort of trouble?'

'He was the only one with the faith.'

Bewick nodded at this, as if it was something he'd already thought. Kelly seemed reassured. 'David wasn't the fellow to wave it in your face, but it's something that gets known.'

'Of course. And the others in his company?'

'Whatever they were, they weren't Catholic. It's enough to alienate a man; to set you apart.'

'Sure. Even if the others weren't exactly Protestants,' Bewick murmured.

'That's right. *Difference*,' Kelly said, sitting up in his

chair, 'we're talking about difference. Difference can mean more than it should. All it needs is some thick bastard with a grudge.' Kelly sounded as if he'd come across a few himself.

'You think that might have had something to do with his death?' Bewick asked.

'No, I'm not saying that exactly. They wrote to me. After the inquiry, they sent some fellows round to explain. I . . . well, I have to say, I didn't really get it. It was all about VHF channels. Orders getting to be misunderstood. Arcs of fire; that sort of thing. I didn't see how any of it could've been deliberate, if you know what I mean. He was all right, the fellow that came. He was troubled by it himself; Lieutenant Colonel – had a son David's age himself and, well, it sounded to me like he was taking a lot of the guilt for it. Even though he wasn't there, you know.'

'He felt guilty himself about your son's death?' Bewick asked.

'On behalf of the regiment, like. He was . . . he talked about honour. You don't hear much about that nowadays.'

'Did he ever mention the difference between David and the others?'

'No, he didn't do that exactly. All I'll say about that is there's a squad of five or six men, you know, in a bad situation and the only one who doesn't come out of it is the man who's a Catholic. Something's going on. The outsider gets it. That's all I'm saying.'

'Yes, I understand. Thank you very much for talking to me about David.'

'I doubt we'll ever know the truth,' Kelly said.

Bewick smiled. 'Possibly not. But we might get close.'

It wasn't until they were leaving the cottage that Bewick asked Kelly about his other children. Kelly's daughter and the eldest of his sons were both teachers. His daughter was close, but Kelly hardly saw Brendan, who had spent a number of years in the USA. Another son, Sean, was in the Church, and was presently in Norfolk. A third son was an accountant who lived in Purley. All this was elicited effortlessly by Bewick, who had completely won the man's confidence.

The road ran straight as a ruler along the big fen drain, until it merged into the veil of moisture about a kilometre ahead, too light to be called mist, just a haze. The object which caught his eye was opposite a T-junction: a car, its tail in the air, its nose in a ditch. It was barely light. Probably been there half the night. He was the only one who left Lotheny at this time of the morning, while they were working the current roster. Whoever was in the ditch was lucky: after five weeks the roster was due to change on Friday. He slowed and stopped near the up-ended car. There was no one in the driving seat. As he approached it, he calculated how difficult it'd be to get the thing back on the road. He frowned. As far as he could tell, there wouldn't be a problem. Probably some bloody woman. It occurred to him that he'd seen this car before. Hadn't he seen it parked out this way of a morning?

He was only a few metres away when the man stood up.

'Sergeant Atkinson?'

'Yeah?' Atkinson didn't like the look of him. He was off his face on something or other. Eyes glazed, couldn't look at you. How the hell did he know his name? That stuck-up voice . . .

'Gavin Paul Atkinson?'

'Yeah . . . what is this?'

The man reached into his pocket. If the bloke hadn't looked and sounded such a snot-nosed nonce, Atkinson might have reacted, but he was off guard. He saw the gun appear. Even then his speed might have saved him, but he disbelieved his own eyes. Half a second later, he was dead.

16

It was raining again, heavy, relentless. Atkinson had been shot, like the other two, in the middle of the forehead. He lay in a mess of black blood and mud. Photographers were at work. Further up the road was his red Sierra.

'So, what do you think?' Jones turned away. On the horizon, under a ridge of dark cloud, bright skies: a relief to the spirit. 'Was that the motor which was following you?'

'Yes. So Atkinson *was* one of the guys I tangled with that night.'

'You said.'

'Three members of the squad now,' Bewick said.

'Who were all present when Kelly was killed. This is about the fragging, isn't it? It's got to be.'

'Possibly.' Bewick sounded sufficiently doubtful to irritate Jones.

'Listen, what else could it be?'

Bewick didn't answer, but stepped forward. He was looking down at the service beret which lay in the mud beyond Atkinson's head.

'What's that?'

'His AOR beret. Wouldn't have thought he'd be wearing it.'

Jones too had leaned over. 'Black camel again.

Present at every killing. Still telling us nothing much.'

They walked back to the car. Bewick didn't reply.

'Well, all right. I guess it's telling us . . . well, this joker is telling us that they were all killed because they were members of the AOR squad. Isn't he? It's got to be the Kelly fragging.'

'OK, let's suppose that this is about Kelly's death. Why has the killer waited nearly ten years to take his revenge?'

'Search me, sweetheart.'

'And if this is about the elimination of witnesses, then we should be looking very closely at Dowling.'

'I've looked, haven't I?' Jones said.

'Have you spoken to Danny Hart?'

'Not that it's your concern, but you may have noticed that I've got quite a lot on my plate,' Jones said sniffily as another two cars pulled up. The police surgeon and, oh God, that was all he needed, his Chief Super.

'Want me to talk to Hart?' Bewick asked.

Jones looked at him to make sure he meant it. 'That tune you're playing, have you any idea how beautiful it really is?'

There was mist rising from the half-drowned fields, just enough to define the edges of the headlight beams as night came on. All around was partial flooding. They had several times driven through axle-deep water. Twice Karen had thought of not continuing. It was Sally who persuaded her to go on.

At the gates, all the usual security was in place. It was

Dowling himself who responded to the answerphone and told Karen to drive through.

'With all that in place, you'd think he'd be reasonably confident, wouldn't you? Why is he still frightened?' Sally said. The question expected no answer and Karen gave none.

They were at the belt of woodland now. The road rose slightly on to its low causeway. As they emerged from the woods, the river course was invisible, its flood waters extending to the garden walls. All that was evident was the causeway, carrying the road. Ealand Priory itself was well placed on its rise of ground, all its buildings and courtyards on dry land. The moon spread a pale brilliance over the waters, which made the lights of the house seem warmer.

They drove over the river bridge and on to the forecourt. Dowling was waiting on the steps. He frowned when he saw that there were two people in the car.

Karen pulled up. 'Leave this to me.' She got out and went over to Dowling.

Sally watched them. Karen was doing most of the talking, and looked as if she were laying down the law. She was gesturing towards the oriel window to her right. The house looked pleasant, a bit ecclesiastical, like a minor bishop's palace . . .

Karen was striding back to the car, furious. She flung open the door. Dowling had disappeared. 'Look, I'm sorry about this, Sal, but we're going back. Stupid prick.'

Karen started the engine. In the dashboard tidy,

Karen's mobile started ringing. Sally extracted it for her. Karen was putting on her seatbelt.

'Answer that, will you? Unless it's CRSI, I'll ring them back.'

'Hello?'

'Listen,' said a warm, cockney voice, 'try to persuade her to come back, will you? She's got the wrong end of the stick. I was kidding. She flew off the handle before she let me explain. You're very welcome . . . whoever you are.'

'I'll try.'

Karen squealed tyres as she moved off.

'Karen, calm down. He wants us both to stay. He wants to explain –'

For an answer, Karen did a violent handbrake turn, wrenching the car in a tight circle to end up beside the oriel window.

'You can't see it from here, but in there is a fucking candlelit dinner for two. What does he think I'm here for, for Christ's sake?'

'To hear his life story. He's probably nervous. He wants it to be as normal as possible – I mean, that's when you usually pour your heart out, isn't it, with wine in the candlelight?'

Karen blew a huge sigh. 'Oh Christ, I suppose you're right.' She put a hand on Sally's arm. 'Yeah, you're right. Good girl, Prof.'

Ahead of them, Dowling came out on to the steps again. Karen drove slowly up to him and lowered the window. He looked uncertain.

'Right,' Karen said. 'No fucking candles. Right?'

'Right.' He was smiling.

The meal had been ordinary – heated-up ready-made dishes, fruit and under-ripe cheese. The wine, on the other hand, had been bought by price and was very good.

They'd eaten by electric light, as promised. The table could have seated twenty. Sally, Karen and Dowling occupied the end nearest to the log fire which slumbered in an enormous hearth.

Sally liked Dowling. After he'd told her, with a lot of pride, about the chair in paediatrics that he was going to fund, and had gone on at some length about the glories of Ealand Priory, she did most of the talking.

Dowling and Karen both became preoccupied, nervous: he of what he had to say, she of what she might hear. Sally ate a sliver of the boring cheese and then excused herself. She'd already been shown the room she was to stay in.

She stood at the door to her room and listened: she could hear a murmur of conversation, the voices calm. She reckoned she'd fulfilled her role as chaperone. The room was comfortable and too warm, like a hotel room. Sally turned the radiator off and opened the window. The smell of the wet land and wood smoke came in. In the moonlight, she could see a spreading cedar of Lebanon and a modest informal garden. The only sounds were distant engines.

*

'Why didn't you want to tell me?' Karen asked.

He thought before replying. 'Because I'm afraid of what you might think of me . . . or what I was then.'

'*Then* being when you were in the army?'

'Yeah. When I was in the army.' He said it with a sigh of impatience, as if he could barely believe his own foolishness.

'So what happened?'

'I ended up in a squad of Scousers. Me and this other fellow Kelly were the outsiders. Kelly had no idea. I was better with people than him and they treated me fair enough. But Kelly – the way he was treated – different story.

'We had a stupid CO at the time. Used to get off on thinking up really stupid exercises. And you could never please the bastard, either. The only men who had any time for him were masochists. Morale was low. Any unit depends on morale. There was a lot of drinking. I was one of the worst. I used to pretend to drink more than I did, too, to wind up the others. There was a place we used to go to, near the forest . . . the forest – Burgh forest – was where we did the exercises. Lamb and Flag, I think it was. It was very yokel, a rustic sort of place, out of the way. But it served good Adnams and we thought it was all right.

'There was this girl who was always there. I mean, there were girls around who came along in twos and threes, who came for a laugh once in a while, but this one, she was always on her own. And she was a bit odd. She could drink, for a start. She was educated, very clever. You know, she had those sort of eyes –

in-your-face eyes, and she was always talking out of the side of her mouth. She was good company, Liz. We'd tell her the filthiest fucking jokes and she'd laugh like a horse. Used to call us the licentious soldiery.

'But sometimes she'd go dark. I mean, as if someone'd turned the lights out. And she'd blank you. Could go on all evening. You wondered why she'd come there. You wondered why she'd bothered.

'I suppose, if I'd thought about it, I'd've realized that on the evenings when she just sat there with the same bloody awful look on her face, she was most likely praying for someone to go over and get her out of it. But we thought, fuck her, why doesn't she go home? Kelly tried once or twice, but he wasn't clever enough.' Dowling paused.

Was this unknown girl at the heart of the mystery, Karen wondered? What had happened to her?

Sally had dozed off. Suddenly she was awake again, her heartbeat quickened. A dream had woken her. Something to do with Karen's outline of the case, the murdered ex-soldiers, the connection to Dowling. But the dream hadn't featured Dowling.

Who?

What she remembered eventually was an image of someone's foot, spotlit as if in the beam of a small torch. It was pushing a piece of gravel backwards and forwards as a man was talking in a loud, mellow voice. O'Keefe – Brendan O'Keefe.

His voice in the dream had been like a commercial voice-over, portentous and seductive. Unlike a commercial, however, it was uttering a truth as uncomfortable as it was inescapable. What that truth was would not be dredged up. She was disturbed, thinking that perhaps this would haunt her, remaining ungrasped until – until what? She shivered.

She flung herself out of bed and dressed. Outside, the moon was high above the house. In its shadows, the cedars were stark black, but now were gathering skirts of mist. In the distance, electricity pylons made their inelegant strides across the drowned fields. Their perspective lines, diminishing to nothing, seemed to fix the house's isolation.

'What happened to her?'

'She was raped . . . by Atkinson and the others.'

Karen was trying to calculate how carefully she had to tread. She was so near now. She didn't want him to falter now. She couldn't think what to say. She tried to be friendly, but the words seemed to stick in her mouth.

'And you joined in, did you?' She couldn't believe how bitter she sounded.

Dowling shook his head, but she could see that the denial was more complicated than a single 'No'.

'What happened?'

'I didn't stop them, is what happened.'

The relief was only partial. She believed him. She was on the look-out for any hint of a game. At least he hadn't been fully part of it.

'So what happened?'

'I just told you.'

'No, you haven't. I want to know what happened.'

He looked at her and she returned the look, deadly serious. 'I want to know.'

He nodded. He took a big breath and continued. 'Everyone was completely pissed; rat-arsed. We'd just been through some stupid fucking exercise and knew we had another one the next day. We come into the pub and there's Liz, well on her way.'

'Tell me about Liz.'

'Oh, university student age, y'know. She was some sort of student doing a thesis or something. Anyway, one of the things about this pub is the landlord, who hadn't a clue. He'd been running the place for about fifty years and he still knew nothing. Liz was sitting there smoking a spliff and rolling another one right in front of him, sitting at the bar.

'So Whear, Simmonds, Atkinson, Kelly and me all come in – with a couple of others, who cleared off before it got too riotous.'

'Go on.'

'Well, I can't remember details. We practically drained the pub. We made a lot of noise. That's why we went there, to keep the wildlife awake, 'cos it was miles from fuck-all.'

He took a slug of the cognac he was drinking. His expression was that of a man entering a place he didn't want to go.

Sally stepped out of her room and listened. She heard the murmur of voices as before. She walked to where the landing looked down into the double stairwell. Opposite her was a big painting of a horse, life size, she estimated. Below, Dowling was speaking, a low, intense focus to his voice, unlike his normal jaunty manner. She found herself wishing Karen luck.

She remembered Karen's extraordinary generosity towards her. It made her think of John Bewick. To distract herself, she decided to look at some of the other rooms on the corridor.

The second room she glanced into she identified as Dowling's. Like the other, it seemed to be unlived in. It was smart and melancholy. She recognized it from the flamboyantly carved four-poster which he'd described to them at dinner. She saw a designer's hand at work here, as everywhere: the tiger rug, the display of antique weapons on the wall. As Karen had explained to her, it was a movie set: so Dowling could star in the story of a life he'd never lived.

'Well, next thing I knew, Whear said, "'Ere, come'n look at this!" and out there in the garden was Simmonds snogging Liz in the moonlight. He was the good-looking one, Simmonds. He was the one the girls were always grabbing to show them how to hold a snooker cue. So I thought, here we go again. Then she pushed him off and I saw how completely off her face she was. Talk about the lights being out – there was a bloody power cut an' all. But then she grabs him again and sticks her tongue in his mouth. It didn't look like she was enjoying it much, far as I could tell, through being totally blittered. But, what the hell, we were all pissed and I was thinking, maybe that's what she needs, a good seeing-to from Simmonds.

'Then I hear her shouting round the back. And there's Simmonds shagging her up against this tree, right? Now, it crossed my mind she could've been telling him to lay off, but it could've been her grind grunting. Frankly, I was too pissed to tell the difference. Good luck to them both, I thought.

'Next thing I knew was Simmonds puking in the flower bed and Whear and Atkinson were discussing who should shag her next. I told 'em to grow up. I made some crack about not wanting to put my straw in Simmonds's Guinness. I think I knew they were serious. I think I wandered outside and told 'em not to be stupid, or maybe that happened inside. There was no shouting until Kelly started up.

'Kelly'd been quiet all evening, sitting in the corner, just joining in enough to join in and not get any shit from the lads. I don't reckon he'd realized what was going on. Then he did realize. He went outside and started on Atkinson. Screaming at him. Next thing, he come back in with a bleeding face, holding his gut. He said something like, "Do you know what they're doing?" And I said something like, "Have you asked her what she thinks of it so far?" I kept remembering the way she'd been snogging Simmonds and I thought she was maybe having a good time. That's what I tried to tell myself. Don't know if I really believed it. That's what made me clear off. The whole thing was beginning to get to me.

'So why didn't I stop it? Don't know, do I? Part of

it was because I didn't want a working-over from Atkinson. He was a fit bastard. He liked fighting. He went looking for it. Any excuse. And I'd just seen what he'd done to Kelly.

'So I cleared off. And I got Kelly to come with me. Next day, the poor little sod was dead.'

'Kelly was?'

Dowling told her about the live firing exercise, during which Kelly was hit.

'The report called it "a tragic mistake". I'm not so sure about that. Getting thumped by Atkinson was like the last straw for Kelly. He went totally silent. Usually, there was some sort of comeback when Atkinson was having a go at him. All through the exercise he kept his trap shut. That began to get to Atkinson. Like he was – like Kelly'd made a decision. I think Atkinson thought Kelly was going to report him and Whear for the rape. When it happened, none of us saw it: it was a filthy night and the noise was unbelievable because there was artillery involved, but I reckon I heard one shot closer than I should have done.'

'You think Atkinson could have shot Kelly?'

'Over the years I've got myself convinced.'

Karen's head was whirling. 'And the girl? Liz?'

'I never saw her again.'

'No, I see. But she knew she'd been raped? Couldn't have been that drunk, could she?'

'No. She went into the local cop-shop and complained the next day. They assigned her a woman police officer, who talked her through it, I guess . . .

We were all interviewed by the Adjutant later on and told there was no case to answer because she didn't bring charges. We got a total bollocking and all that, but it was all overshadowed by what had happened to poor fucking Kelly the next day.'

'So . . . what a nightmare . . .'

'My nightmares came later. I knew I wasn't cut out for the AOR. The nightmares convinced me.'

He looked drawn, empty, depressed. He shrugged, as if he were a man who'd hoped for better in life but never expected it: a man who was now facing the crisis he had long dreaded and was finding himself armed – with indifference.

'It's all right,' Karen said. For a moment she put a hand on his arm. 'So who is this all about? Is it Kelly? Or do you think it could be Liz? Could we be looking for a woman?'

Sally had managed to find Radio Three. It was the last programme of the night. Someone was announcing a repeat of something that had been aired that afternoon. She'd hardly taken it in.

She'd been thinking about these rooms of Dowling's, with their interior decorator's chic and cliché. They made her realize how individual, despite its hiddenness, Bewick's house actually was: his spare rooms with their splashes of colour. The few fine pieces she'd noticed there – a cupboard, a chest, boxes – were all objects that contained other objects. It was as if he'd learnt to live with little, had learnt to be wary of pleasure. The fine things he allowed himself tidied life up. They kept other things out of sight, to be only occasionally relished. And yet ... What about the paintings? The hot primary brilliance of them was like an involuntary outburst of what he was repressing. Perhaps that was the same process ...

What was she doing, her thoughts endlessly returning to him? She felt tears come. What was this? Then she connected: on the radio, they were singing the motet she'd listened to in the chapel.

She stood at the window, where the chilled air was whitening to thick fog in the moonlight. Behind her the ethereal music rose and fell, and soared. Her tears were streaming. She'd known it at the time, she realized now, but hadn't dared admit it to herself. It was a strange, elated pain which flooded through her, bitter-sweet. She yearned to be touched by him again. She wanted to feel the heat coming off him, to catch his smell ...

Despite every difficulty she had placed in the way, despite every argument she had thrown into the battle, she was lost. She loved him, hopelessly and certainly. She knew it. It was as simple and as wretchedly complicated as that.

Bewick had been asleep for a couple of hours when Karen's call woke him. She didn't apologize, but immediately briefed him on her conversation with Dowling.

'Michael reckons it's more likely to be to do with the woman. He reckons Kelly's family would have been able to come by the names of the soldiers involved quite easily. The woman may have found that difficult. It might have taken her a long time.'

'Ten years?' Bewick objected.

'I know. But then she would have to've located them after they'd left the army. That might have been even more difficult.'

'True. Well done. I'd like to be able to tell Gio Jones all this. That OK?'

'Yeah, Michael understands that.'

'Where are you now?'

Someone was knocking. Still barely conscious, she dragged her dressing-gown around her and stomped to the door.

'Who is it?'

'Me, Karen. Got something for you.'

The door wasn't locked. She opened it. Standing behind Karen was Bewick.

'Just been briefing him on what Michael Dowling was telling me. There's champagne in the fridge, in case you didn't know. Michael said to help yourselves.'

Karen looked tired, drained. Sally couldn't meet Bewick's eye. She felt as if she was being eaten alive by his attention.

'Are you all right?' she asked Karen.

'I'm great. Michael told me everything. It's not a good story . . . I mean, he could've done better. Wasn't what my Dad would've called heinous. He didn't stop some drunken yobs from doing bad things. He was scared. Well, Christ, it wasn't heroic, but what the fuck. And it cost him to tell me. You know?'

'Sure.'

'Perhaps I should shag him. Reward for good behaviour. Whadya reckon?' Karen laughed and sashayed away down the corridor to her room.

Bewick stepped in and shut the door. It was now or never. Sally had to trust him with it, or what was the point? No more games, not now.

'I love you,' she said, looking at the floor. Her pulse was thumping. Her throat was dry. She looked up. He was transformed. His eyes were alive with delight.

'I wasn't sure you did. Thank God for that.'

'Come to bed.'

The edge of the bed was behind her knees now. She was on her elbows watching him kiss her from her knees to her clitoris. He was lost in his own pleasure. She moved her foot to rock it against his penis. She watched the ridged muscle on his shoulders shining as his tongue massaged. Then she fell back. She was becoming weightless. She was on fire. She wanted him inside her now. Whether she said it or not, he knew. He was there. She was consumed by sweetness, crying out.

After a couple of hours of deep sleep, she woke to feel him hard, pressed against her. She was glued together with his semen. She prised herself open and snuggled herself backwards on to him. He hardly woke. He breathed out a long sigh of pleasure then moved his hips to push himself deep into her and went back to sleep. Her own sleep was longer in coming. Wave after wave of contentment flowed through her. Everything now was going to have to defer to this.

17

Danny Hart was an ex-jockey who'd been thrown out of the sport for rigging races, but not before he'd made a considerable amount of money and had won an enviable reputation amongst the local fraternity as a reliable psychopath.

He was in his dressing-gown when he met Bewick at the front door of his hanging-basket-festooned villa near Newmarket. He looked nervous when he saw Bewick, keeping the door ajar only.

'What do you want Mr Bewick?' Hart said, looking at his watch with a pained expression. It was quarter to seven.

'I'm here on behalf of Chief Inspector Jones. You have something to tell him – from Charlie Smew.'

Hart didn't exactly relax, but he looked less nervous. 'Oh, that. Well, it isn't much really.'

'It'd better be something,' Bewick said. 'Chief Inspector Jones went the extra mile for this one.'

'Yes, well . . .' Hart gripped the door even more tightly. 'Mr Smew had a long trawl. All he come up with, on these two jokers as has been shot, was something about a rape. One of them was talking about it when they was in the Scrubs . . .'

'We know about the rape.'

'Oh, really? Well, the reason it come up was that

363

one of these clowns read about this female topping herself.'

'The woman who was raped?'

'As far as we know, yes. Her. Hung herself. It was in the papers and this fellow said something about it, like he always knew she was out to lunch, some'ing like that.'

'And that's all?'

'That's it, Mr Smew said. He said Mr Jones was looking for why someone might want to take these clowns out of the picture. He said there wasn't nothing else. Nothing financial – which Mr Jones was also asking about, he said. Nothing else – that's what Mr Smew'd heard. If there's anything else turns up he'll let you know.'

Rucker-Whitman had lost none of his poise. He wasn't going to apologize.

'I've been ordered to cooperate with you. In the light of what you've told me, I think that's the right decision.'

Bewick had driven to Lotheny immediately after leaving Danny Hart. It was still only eight-fifteen.

'Thank you, Colonel. I have very few questions.'

'I shall do my best to answer them.'

Sally opened her curtains and the world had vanished. Outside, the fog she'd watched forming had reduced visibility to about twenty metres.

She went downstairs. In the dining-room she met

Dowling's housekeeper, who had served the meal the previous evening.

'Hello, Mrs Pearson.'

'Hello, dear. Isn't this terrible? Took me nearly an hour to get here. Glad you're not an early riser. What can I get you?'

Sally ordered tea, toast and a boiled egg. It really was like a superior B&B. She took her second cup of tea back to her room.

A moment or two later, there was a knock at the door. Karen came in.

'Well?'

'What?'

'Have you sorted yourself out?'

'Yes. I think I have.'

'Glad to hear it. Where's John?'

'He left at crack of dawn this morning.'

Bewick's mobile rang. He pulled over and answered it.

'Where the hell are you?' Jones demanded.

'Suffolk. Near Burgh forest.'

'Oh yes?'

'Rucker-Whitman told me where The Lamb and Flag is. The Suffolk lads told me the nearest likely station. They're looking through their records even as we speak. At least they said they would.'

'Hang on. Hang on. This is gibberish.'

Bewick related what Karen and Danny Hart had told him. Jones began to understand.

'So you get the identity of the girl who committed

suicide, yes? Then we start tracing her nearest and dearest?'

'Something like that.'

'You do know how many women use false names when they make a complaint?'

'We have to start somewhere. I'll keep you up to date. See you at Ealand Priory.'

He didn't care any more. Life now could only be lived in his head. In the familiar room, dedicated to books, he sat at the table in the window, elegant Regency, scarred with use. The sunlight of many decades had bleached its red mahogany to a brown gold. Against the porcelain of the coffee pot which stood on the table, a letter was propped: as if its imminent opening was a pleasure to be savoured. In fact, he had read it a thousand times. He knew it by heart, but it had become a talisman, a spur to action. The pain it breathed . . .

His car had been overheating that day ten years before. It was nearly an hour later than promised that he'd arrived at the farmhouse. His journey hadn't been helped by the brief, explosive storm which broke about an hour from Cambridge, leaving a chill in the air.

At the farmhouse, his sister was nowhere to be seen. He searched and called. The place wasn't that big, so he quickly assumed that she'd taken her Jack Russell for a walk along the saltings: something he should have thought of immediately, as the terrier was a vociferous little tyke.

He went upstairs to the spare room to look out at the distant sea, as he always did, hoping perhaps to catch a glimpse of her out on the salt marshes. The window was open and he closed it against the cold. As he did so, he felt the first wave of unease. Not only had the dog not barked but he hadn't heard the old pet gander either – who usually made more noise than the dog.

He went downstairs in a trance. He found them together in the old stable, laid out on the straw, side by side, as cold as stone, the small white dog and the big white goose. Now he was numb with apprehension. Stepping out into the yard and seeing the barn door ajar, he knew with ugly certainty what she had done.

He had no memory of the next few hours. He had been led away like a sleepwalker by the ambulance men. The police surgeon had sedated him into unconsciousness at a neighbour's house.

No suicide note had been found at the time. For years it had tortured him. The punishment was doubled by her leaving her reasons to his guesswork. After seven years, he had decided to sell the farm. During its refurbishment, the note had been found. Finally, she'd told him . . .

He glanced again at the note in its stained envelope. He remembered his first reading of it: how, half blind with tears, words had leapt from the page, confirming all his worst fears. The blackness had hissed towards him. He was back in the nightmare, one of the living dead, where the only sustenance was grief; the only luxury, despair.

The relief from this pain, he knew, would be further pain; self-flagellating oblivion. He knew it with the certainty of a convert. A convert; ha! There was irony!

And now? Now, he didn't care what happened. Very soon he would have fulfilled his mission in its entirety. His drama of revenge was almost over. He felt empty. Planning this last act had loomed vast in his thinking. Now it was done. He doubted if it could be completed this time without discovery. He didn't care.

Elizabeth . . . Elizabeth . . .

In the dreamworld of his desire, the improper kisses they once – and only once – shared opened gates to a paradise neither of them had dared enter: except in imagination. All else was dross. Faith, ambition, achievement: for all he cared, they could now be sacrificed on the altar of his fantasies, in the great temple of might-have-been.

At the police station in Iken St Mary, Bewick had been told that when 'Liz' had made her complaint, she had called herself Elizabeth Anne Smith. After the complaint had been dropped, nobody bothered to check anything about her. The address she gave had been recorded by the WPC who interviewed her. Fictitious or not, Bewick knew he had to try to find it.

He drove along narrow lanes. It was the Suffolk of stock farming: hedges above ditched banks, shade-giving hedgerow oaks, rubbed smooth and greasy by the wool of generations of sheep.

The property existed. It stood on the last edge of high ground before the sea marshes began, still used for summer grazing by neighbouring farms. The road must have once traversed the yard. Now it took an awkward bend around it. There was just room for the old Volvo outside the five-bar gate.

He stood at the gate. The neat farmhouse to his right was pink-washed render under a pantile roof, no more than a cottage, really. To his left was a black timber barn, with a big fig tree at its gable end.

'Can I help?'

A weatherbeaten woman in her sixties came out of the barn.

'John Bewick: police.'

The woman laughed. 'Am I in trouble?'

'I'm here to ask about a previous owner. Who killed herself.'

'Ah . . . that.' Her face darkened. 'Come into the studio.'

She led the way into the barn. She flung a wet cloth over the plaster of Paris that she was working on, and went to the sink to wash her hands.

'What do you want to know?'

'Anything you can tell me.' Bewick's attention was caught by a figure standing on a beam high above the threshing floor in the middle of the barn. It was a bronze angel, looking down and spreading its wings protectively.

The woman followed his glance. 'Ah, yes. Elizabeth's angel . . . I nearly didn't buy the place, you know, when I heard what had happened here. But I loved it. So I tried to appease her spirit. The first work I did in here was for her.'

'Do you know Elizabeth's second name? Was it Smith?'

'No, it wasn't Smith. I forget what it was, though. I could look it up, I dare say.' She stood silent for a moment. 'I'm trying to remember if I *ever* knew it. Not sure I can say I do. It'd be on the deeds, of course. She was a co-owner, with her brother. That I do remember. Trouble is, the deeds are at the bank. Come to think of it, her brother was a fellow at one of the Cambridge colleges. I forget which. St Anne's, I think. He used this place at weekends and during the vacations. I never met him.'

'You can't tell me his academic subject, can you?'

'No.'

'Anything about him?'

'Is all this very important?'

'It might be very important indeed.'

She looked at Bewick, as if to assess his reliability.

'Yes. So what would you like me to do?'

'I need to be in Cambridgeshire as soon as possible. Will you look this up for me? Perhaps ring neighbours who might have known her brother? Who might have met him? Any form of identification or description would be helpful.'

'I'll try.'

Bewick wrote down his mobile number for her, also Gio Jones's.

*

'Gio, we could be looking for someone from St Anne's. Run the members of that committee past me.'

'Griffiths, Miller, Cranesmith, O'Keefe, the Svenson woman. Those are the ones who are coming here. How long are you going to be?'

'I'm on my way. Gio, I'm not being alarmist, but it could be any one of them.'

'The committee?'

'The committee; any one of them.'

Schrager's BMW drove slowly over the bridge and on to the forecourt of Ealand Priory, where Jones was waiting for him.

'I've tried to get you a couple of times,' Jones said. Why, he asked himself, did he make it sound as if it was *his* fault that Schrager hadn't answered?

'I don't use the mobile when I'm driving.'

'Quite right.'

'What's the beef?'

Jones told him about Bewick's concerns.

'I told the bloody client I couldn't guarantee his safety under these circumstances. What the hell's he playing at? Can't we put them off?'

'They're on their way. None of their mobiles are switched on. The Master, Griffiths, is giving a lift to the woman, Svenson, and to O'Keefe. Miller and Cranesmith are driving themselves.'

Schrager looked around at the fog. 'With a bit of luck, none of them'll get here. It was supposed to clear by lunchtime. I don't see that happening, do you?'

'No, indeed. So you agree with John Bewick's assessment, do you?'

'Don't you? Let's go and sort this idiot's security, shall we?'

'Sure.'

They set off across the gravel towards the house. 'Nothing I like better than a council of war and a cuppa,' Jones said. 'Organic biscuits, you get here, too.'

It was taken for granted that Sally would join them. They gathered in the sitting-room: Sally, Karen, Schrager and Jones. After a few minutes, Dowling appeared. He looked pale and depressed.

'OK. Tell me what I do,' he said to Schrager.

'First thing, this meeting with the St Anne's committee doesn't happen. You're ill.'

'All right.' Dowling nodded after a moment's thought. 'What am I ill with?'

'Gastroenteritis. You've been vomiting all night. You're now asleep.' Schrager looked at his watch. 'Who's your doctor, by the way?'

'Don't have one. Don't believe in 'em.'

'Probably irrelevant,' Schrager said. 'Nobody's going to ask, are they? So: doctor came at 08:30, left fifteen minutes later. You're in your bedroom and you're asleep. The doctor said you weren't to be disturbed and he's coming back this evening. How many doors to your room?'

'One.'

'Good. OK, that's the story. We're clear on that?

All we tell the staff is that you're ill and that you're asleep.' Schrager turned to Sally. 'Could you speak to them?'

'Sure.'

'What about Robin Coleridge? Do we tell him anything more?' Karen asked.

Dowling barely hesitated. 'No. He's about as discreet as a bleeding tabloid.'

'Right.'

'Listen, Schrager,' Dowling said. 'These people from St Anne's – you sure about one of them being, you know, the one we're after? Sounds crazy to me.'

'If Bewick thinks it's a possibility, then it's a probability,' Jones said. His conviction was such that Dowling seemed to accept it at once.

'Still, I don't want to offend them,' he said.

'Understood. How about your housekeeper giving them coffee, something like that?'

'Yeah, that's good. Somebody can do a tactful apology, can they?'

Karen nodded at Sally. 'There's your woman.'

Schrager looked at her. Sally nodded.

'Let's take a look at your room, Sir Michael.'

Returning from the kitchen, Sally met a pleasant-looking man in the hallway.

'Hello, I'm Robin Coleridge, the great man's biographer and general sycophant. Do you know what's going on?'

Sally introduced herself. As instructed, she told him as little as possible. Dowling was unwell. The doctor had seen him. He was now asleep and not to be disturbed.

'So what do we do about the St Anne's lot?'

'He's asked that we give them coffee and apologies.'

'Does Mrs Pearson know about this?'

'Yes. I've just come from the kitchen.'

'I see. Oh, well ... I was going to hand in my resignation today. I suppose I'll have to postpone it. Well, this will have to be my last service to my meretricious master, then, won't it? Last commission for the mad gambler. Will you be helping out?'

'I'll be there.'

'Jolly good. You look very fetching, I must say. Do you have a lover?'

'Yes.'

'Shame. Never mind, I shall nevertheless be delightfully entertaining purely for your sake.'

Sally knocked at the door and entered Dowling's bedroom. Schrager acknowledged her and turned back to Dowling. 'Stay away from the window,' he told him. He pointed to the lines he'd marked on the carpet with gaffer tape. 'No closer than that.'

'OK.'

'I know visibility is restricted, but we don't know what we're dealing with.'

Jones was kneeling on the seat in the window embrasure. 'Looks to me as if it might be getting better.' He could see the cars below much more clearly.

'Everything OK?' Schrager asked Sally.

'Mrs Pearson is disappointed not to be cooking lunch, I think, but apart from that . . .'

'Good. I'll be bodyguarding Sir Michael. This door remains locked for the duration.'

Jones was looking out over the terraced lawns. Twenty minutes earlier, the brightness in the sky had briefly haloed the position of the invisible sun. Now it had closed in again. It was gloomier than before. The shadows under the cedars were deepening. He could no longer see the tops of the trees. He saw lights go on in the kitchen.

He heard cars approaching, and walked round to the front of the house. The contingent from St Anne's were arriving. He calculated that Bewick wouldn't get there for a good forty minutes. Never mind, they were only there to avoid an attack on Dowling. Easy enough: just give the Plato-spouters coffee and biccies, then turf them out . . . He had a bleak premonition it wasn't going to be that simple.

They were all in the big dining-room. Sally had addressed them, telling them the version of events that had been agreed. The committee had accepted it with reasonably good grace, but it nevertheless remained an awkward gathering. The members of the committee knew each other too well to enjoy conversing, especially when all felt they had wasted a lot of time and were to waste a lot more.

Robin Coleridge had persuaded Mrs Pearson to let him mull some wine, which he now handed round.

Sally was talking to O'Keefe when Coleridge came over. 'Mulled wine, Sir? To warm the cockles, fog-stranded as you are?' Coleridge winked at Sally. O'Keefe accepted some wine, and Coleridge danced off to exercise his charm elsewhere.

O'Keefe was looking very odd. By wearing a white buttoned-up shirt under a purple top, he'd made himself look like an off-duty bishop. Sally doubted if this was an accident.

'Why aren't you having any wine?' O'Keefe asked her belligerently.

'I go to sleep if I drink during the day.'

'I hear this place has got a chapel with some work by Pugin in it,' he said.

'I didn't know that, but –' Sally looked round for Coleridge and called him back again.

'Yes, you're quite right,' Coleridge agreed. 'It's not original, of course. It came from a church in Cromer which was bombed by a zeppelin in the First World War. Do you want to see it?'

Karen had just been approached by Dowling's snotty secretary and asked if she'd like to hand round some cheese straws. Karen nearly told her to fuck off, but managed to decline the offer so graciously that even the secretary realized that Karen might have better things to do.

The most nervous of the committee members was Cranesmith, Karen reckoned. He was doing nothing overt, but he wasn't socializing and he was looking around as if he was trying to escape.

*

Bewick drove through the belt of woodland, the trees melting into a white gloom. He'd been longer than he'd calculated. He'd hit dense fog about twenty miles away and it hadn't opened up since. As he emerged from the half-visible woods on to the shallow causeway, he was able to see – where he could see anything – how little the flood water had fallen. It reflected the fog, making it seem thicker. It wasn't until he was on the bridge that the number of cars parked on the forecourt immediately beyond became visible.

Jones was waiting for him.

'Hello, Gio.'

'Got a name for us yet?'

'No.'

'Schrager is guarding Dowling. The St Anne's lot have been told he's unwell. So they've been given coffee in the dining-room, and they're being entertained by your Sally Vernon and –'

Jones saw Bewick's attention switch. Karen was coming out of the house.

''lo John.'

'What is it?'

'That Coleridge bloke is pissed. He's showing the buggers round the house and slagging off his boss at the same time. What a jerk.'

'Where are they at the moment?'

'In the hall, I think. He's showing them the chapel. Sally's with them.'

*

In more normal circumstances, Sally would have delighted in the chapel: its rich colours, its mordant glitter. As it was, she acknowledged that it might well appeal to O'Keefe, but otherwise hardly gave it a glance.

She knew that she was meant to keep an eye on the group, but didn't know what she was supposed to do if anything happened. One of them might be armed, she'd been told, which felt insane. But each of these murders, she reminded herself, had been a shooting. She wished Jones and Bewick would get there.

'Isn't it gorgeous?' Coleridge was saying. 'It's the only real quality in the entire building. I know it's gothic revival, but it makes the rest of the house look like Edwardian amateur theatricals.'

This was greeted with a mumbled embarrassment, at the rudeness and disloyalty of what he was saying. The St Anne's committee began to emerge from the chapel just as Karen, Bewick and Jones entered the great hall.

Jones scanned the group. He felt a jolt of nerves. 'Where's Cranesmith?'

'I'll check the dining-room,' Bewick said.

Jones turned to Karen. 'Keep an eye?' Then he followed Bewick.

The dining-room was empty.

In the office, the CCTV was picking up intermittently on the ghostly image of Cranesmith's car as it made its way slowly along the driveway towards the exit.

'He said he thought he'd slip away, as the meeting was cancelled,' Dowling's secretary explained. 'He told me he'd be leaving and asked what he was supposed to do.'

'Well, we've got him, haven't we? We just don't open the gates,' said Jones.

'We're not here to make arrests, Gio, are we? Let him go.'

'Don't you think it's him?'

In the great hall, Sir Terence Griffiths came up to Sally. 'We think we'll be off now, Dr Vernon. It was nice to see you here. I didn't know you were connected at all to Sir Michael.'

'Oh, I'm not. Just a friend of a friend, you know. Only joining in because he's unwell.'

Griffiths lowered his voice. 'He really is unwell, is he? It's not his way of saying he wants nothing more to do with us, is it?'

'Not at all. He's very enthusiastic about the project. We were discussing it last night at dinner.'

Griffiths looked relieved. 'Because our royal visitor is coming very soon. That is good to hear.'

They had only just left the office when Bewick's mobile rang. Jones realized almost at once that it must be the woman from the farm. Bewick said little. Finally he closed the call.

'Well?'

'Miller. She thinks it was Miller.'

When Bewick and Jones reached the great hall,

however, the only members of the committee present were O'Keefe, Griffiths and Svenson.

'Where's Miller?' he asked Sally.

'I don't know. He was here a minute ago.'

'Did he go into the chapel?'

'We all did.'

Bewick went to the door of the chapel. There was nowhere you could hide in it that would be unseen from the doorway.

'Will somebody tell us what the hell's going on?' Coleridge was red in the face with irritability.

'Later.' Bewick turned to Karen. 'Keep an eye. Don't try anything. No heroics.'

Bewick ran, Jones following.

In the bedroom, Dowling stared at Schrager and Bewick in disbelief. Jones was on watch outside the door.

'That wanker?! Miller? I don't get it.'

'It was his sister who killed herself. After she was raped by your squad,' Bewick said. 'I don't know how he found that out, or when. All I know is that he began making inquiries at about the time he sold the farmhouse he'd shared with her. That was shortly after his mother died. His feelings for his mother were weird enough, so God knows what was going on between him and his sister.'

'Where was he making inquiries?'

'At AOR. I saw their CO today. He told me that a couple of years ago someone had been asking how to trace some ex-members of the regiment. He was sent away with a flea in his ear. But a determined researcher would have been able to find them, from information in the public domain. Miller is a historian. That sort of research would come easily to him.'

'Miller . . . So, what do we do?'

'Having misplaced our prime suspect, you mean? Well, we've got to find him. Do you mind if I bring Gio Jones in on this?'

Something was racketing around Jones's head: a half memory. It was one of those moments, familiar enough to him, when he wished he'd paid more attention at the time. It wasn't until the door opened and Bewick asked him to join the others that he remembered what it was.

'Alfred "Gothic" Warrington,' Jones announced as he entered the room. He slumped on to the window seat. He was glad to sit down.

'Come again?'

'Miller. He was interested in Ealand Priory, its design. He said something about this Warrington bloke designing the house, and how keen the fellow was on secret passages, that sort of thing.'

'Coleridge was saying something about that. Do you know anything, Sir Michael?'

Dowling didn't answer. He was on the phone to his secretary. 'Find Coleridge. Tell him to come up here.'

There was silence. Outside, the light level was like early evening. In the room there was an unusually depressing gloom.

At first, Jones couldn't explain his own unease. It took him some time even to realize that he was beginning to feel frightened. His frown caught the attention of Bewick, who looked a question at him.

'Gio?'

Then he got it. Miller was here, actually in the room, perhaps. Very close. He could smell him. Lavender. Where? He bent forward. That was it –

Jones put his finger to his lips. He pointed to Dowling and then pointed to the bathroom. Bewick was on his feet in a moment and ushering Dowling silently towards the bathroom. Dowling complied without hesitation. Jones gestured to Schrager, and they both headed for the bathroom as well. Jones shut the door.

'Lavender,' he whispered. 'I smelt the bugger. There must be some sort of cavity under that window seat. He's in there. When was this bathroom put in?'

'Last year.'

'Safe enough, then.'

Bewick opened the door. He glanced out and then shut the door again. 'Lock yourselves in. And not a sound,' he said to Schrager. 'Come on, Gio.'

They stepped out of the bathroom. They heard the chink of the lock, then nothing. Bewick gestured to the curtain to the left of the seat. Jones obediently positioned himself there. Bewick moved slowly, making no audible sound, to the far side of the seat, and from there to the display of antique weapons. With infinite care he began to remove a sword from the wall, untwisting wire, checking the support of the other pieces as he went.

It was a full minute or more before Jones heard anything. A scratching: Miller too was trying not to make a noise. A faint creak betrayed him from below. Jones glanced at Bewick, who nodded his acknowledgement that he had heard it too. He went on untwisting the wires, steadily, silently.

Jones had forgotten about Coleridge. He heard him now: quick, resentful footsteps up the staircase. Bewick's mute command was urgent. Jones understood. Stop the bastard; but quietly. Jones moved. He made no noise across the boards. He calculated he'd reach the door well before Coleridge.

Then, turmoil.

The last board before the door squealed like a wounded animal. Jones checked. Bewick's warning 'Gio!' snapped out. Jones dropped. The slam of a gun. Coleridge in the doorway, screaming. Swish and metal clang behind him.

'Schrager!'

Coleridge went on screaming. The bathroom opened. Bewick was tugging at the window seat but couldn't overcome whatever lock had been thrown. He threw the sword aside. Dowling and Schrager were on their knees beside Coleridge. Bewick was heaving Jones to his feet. 'C'mon.'

Along the landing, down the stairs. 'I didn't think he'd shoot. Then I realized in that sort of light he could mistake you for Dowling.'

They reached the front door. A moment of

hesitation from Bewick. 'Leave this to me, Gio. Get Schrager and tell him. I'll do a sweep through the orchard and up to the wall.'

Relying on Jones's obedience, Bewick moved off at once. He was soon swallowed up in the fog. Some sense told Jones that Bewick was moving off in the wrong direction. Impossible to explain to someone like Schrager. Anyway, he'd seen the dislike on Schrager's face at taking orders from his employee, Bewick. And Bewick at least had natural charisma. Jones credited himself with all the innate authority of a sticky bun.

Do it yourself. Be careful, but do it yourself.

A building loomed out of the greyness; Jones wondered what it was. Then he heard the creak of the rope in a fairlead and the slap-slop of water. It was the boathouse. He went to the door and pushed it open very slowly. No one. There were spaces for two dinghies. Only one was moored there. Jones walked to the open end of the boathouse. He stood and listened.

There was a movement of air now. The moisture passing his face felt colder. Then he heard something: the distant squeak of oars and the plip of water under a boat's stern. It faded. Then a few seconds later he heard it again. He looked back at the other dinghy riding high on the flood water. Its oars were in it. Shit, no! He had a terrifying vision of how he'd be, rowing after the bastard, lost in an enclosed white world. Time for some honest cowardice. He went back.

After the third call, Bewick came running out of the grey gloom.

'He's taken a dinghy. There's another. We could follow –'

'Possibly.'

As if to answer them, they heard a dull, deadly thud from the water beyond the boathouse.

They were all gathered by the pierced stone parapet as the two boats appeared out of the thinning fog, at first a mere darkening of the grey, then shape and movement, then finally an out-of-focus image, steadily advancing.

The first boat grounded some ten feet away. As the second became visible, there was a murmur of pity and disgust. Sprawled in the sternsheets, his half-destroyed head hanging over the stern, lay Miller. His hand still gripped the gun with which he'd shot himself.

Epilogue

The royal visit to St Anne's had, in the end, been postponed by royal request. This was a convenient decision, as the contractors building the Sir Michael Dowling wing at the City Hospital were behind schedule. But now, on a sunny day in late October, it was finally going ahead.

Gio Jones walked away from the guarded gateway of St Anne's. He was feeling cheerful. While he had been tangling with St Anne's, he'd felt continually oppressed, he realized. His own fault. The truth was that most of the fellowship had been civil enough. Now that the case was over, they'd gone out of their way to be friendly. In fact, he'd been invited to join the royal visit celebrations, but it would have meant being just about the only one there without a gown and hood, denoting massive brain power, and he didn't fancy it. So he'd watched from the sidelines. Even Bewick had been wearing a gown. When they'd gone inside for the ceremonial bit, he'd come away.

Since the case had ended, his family had returned to him as well. There was a new energy in the house, less fractiousness. He was even sleeping most of the night again.

His mobile went just as he got to his car.

*

'Come down off of there, Sir.'

Baynes, accompanied by PC Desai, was staring into the darkness – up at the top of an eighteen-foot-high construction of lumber, old doors and brushwood which was the municipal bonfire for November the Fifth. It stood on Midsummer Common, halfway between the road and the river. There were few lights nearby, but the moonlight was bright enough to reveal the figure sitting in a broken chair perched on top of the bonfire.

'Come on, Sir.'

The figure didn't reply. Baynes turned to Desai, made a face and shrugged.

'Yeah, I know,' she muttered in sympathy. 'What would you call the offence? Wearing a dodgy costume?'

The man wore a tall hat, embroidered jerkin and lace collar, in the style of the early seventeenth century. A cloak flowed down over the sides of the chair. Still he said nothing.

'I suppose we could get the Fire Brigade. They get cats out of trees.'

'Only when there's a press photographer in the vicinity.'

'I didn't have you down for a cynic.'

'You did talk to Gio direct, did you?'

'Yeah, he was on his way back anyway, said he'd be down soonest.'

'Back from where?'

'The royal visit at St Anne's. He was helping out.'

*

Jones looked across at the municipal bonfire. At this distance, there wasn't enough light to see the silly sod who was supposed to be perched on top of the thing. Jones knew from the drug boys that there was some hash around which was spiked with something hallucinogenic. Perhaps the bloke was tripping out.

A familiar figure was approaching. 'Helloah!' said a large, syrupy voice.

Was it his imagination, or could Jones smell the bugger from here? Old Foley stopped several yards short of the stack of wood, gazing upwards. The figure at the top was exactly how Jones imagined Guy Fawkes to have been – or was the costume modelled on an illustration he could vaguely remember? The hat kept the face in deep shadow, so Jones had no idea what the man looked like, but the clothes were spot on. He thought the bloke might be mumbling something, but very quietly, to himself. He sat rigid in the broken chair, gripping the ends of the arms. A nutter. This was going to take half the bleeding night. What sort of stunt was the daft bastard trying to pull? Jones sighed and wished he hadn't. That smell. Old Foley was at his elbow, gesturing to the bonfire.

'My son, the lawyer,' he confided. 'Complete fruit-cake, may I say.'

At that moment, the man on the bonfire raised his face to the moonlight. Jones recognized him straight away. It was Brendan O'Keefe. The mumbling rose in volume. Somewhere across the city, Jones heard the wha-wha of a patrol car. As if in response, O'Keefe's rich voice boomed across the darkened common: 'O insupportable, O heavy hour . . .' Then the lush voice hardened into something plain, unornamented. 'The soul of man did ne'er conceive, nor the malice of hellish or earthly devil ever practise, such a deed . . .'

O'Keefe reached below his cloak. Jones heard water. Sounded as if O'Keefe was thoroughly wetting himself. As O'Keefe raised himself out of the chair, Jones smelt the high-octane stench and understood; too late. O'Keefe opened his mouth as if to cry out, but no sound came.

None of them saw the match or the lighter or whatever he used. They were twisting away. Thrown to the ground by the roaring explosions of flame as hidden canisters went up all over the bonfire. Above the storm of flame they briefly heard snatches of Latin prayer, but nothing then except the crackle of the pyre.

refresh yourself at penguin.co.uk

Visit penguin.co.uk for exclusive information and interviews with
bestselling authors, fantastic give-aways and the
inside track on all our books, from the Penguin Classics
to the latest bestsellers.

BE FIRST ▼

first chapters, first editions, first novels

EXCLUSIVES ▼

author chats, video interviews, biographies, special
features

EVERYONE'S A WINNER ▼

give-aways, competitions, quizzes, ecards

READERS GROUPS ▼

exciting features to support existing groups and
create new ones

NEWS ▼

author events, bestsellers, awards, what's new

EBOOKS ▼

books that click – download an ePenguin today

BROWSE AND BUY ▼

thousands of books to investigate – search, try
and buy the perfect gift online – or treat yourself!

ABOUT US ▼

job vacancies, advice for writers and company
history

Get Closer To Penguin . . . www.penguin.co.uk